THE CORBACCIO

o chiamar dueij alieo rigua
ma tua fara dichinata/ ad ch
i ad una uecchia ratolosa uirza
piu dactu elt da huomini/ piu da
colare omaij che da apparir tra
. de lasciamo staréjllo che tu p
rio agstuto q uegniamo adijl
stuto cóceduto. q hsto ueduto se
rimostrj nellalere cose no dehe
rhiutuato praguneraj q lamiete
rodo cun nibtro lasciato adestui
c./Atij lanatura tata digiu
oue coles e femina p cuij simusa
ito luomo piu degnia cosa q
uia ipte dauatij lano le ntre pa
e ella eij dipsona grade q bene
nata q neluu so fosse ad tuo
nicolo qptutto se cosi ben con
fettuoso tu eggio ipte alaina
minij me di bellezza che abbia
tto chella studij ilsuo co mille
j unguétij doue tu iltuo rate
i cu chiara illauij· angi tidur
llo quatug tu poco tene curj/.
olle atudie soma mete adgluo
à lasuua piisino adg lasua
e se no mugania ilmio giudicio
nolt fiozita/ q dinete cadre
q ella pur nel mio stuta molij

the
CORBACCIO

Giovanni
BOCCACCIO

Translated and edited by

Anthony K. Cassell

University of Illinois Press

URBANA CHICAGO LONDON

Frontispiece: The Widow as Luxuria, a marginal illustration from Codex Pluteo XLII, 34 in the Biblioteca Laurenziana, Florence. Photo: Pineider.

Quotation from Macloed edition of Lucian (p. 125) courtesy of the Loeb Classical Library, Harvard University Press, and the translator. © 1967 by the President and Fellows of Harvard College.

Publication of this work was supported in part by a grant from the Andrew W. Mellon Foundation

LIBRARY OF CONGRESS CATALOGING IN PUBLICATION DATA

Boccaccio, Giovanni, 1313–1375.
  The corbaccio.

  Bibliography: p.
  I. Title.
PQ4272.E5C6 1975   853'.1   75–9844
ISBN 0–252–00479–5

To
N. N. T.

Contents

Translator's Preface

FOR six hundred years *Il Corbaccio* has suffered nearly total neglect in the Anglo-Saxon world because of the language barrier. I hope that this first English version may rescue it from such unmerited obscurity. The translation, based on the fine recent edition by Tauno Nurmela (*Suomalaisen Tiedakatemian Toimituksia: Annales Academiae Scientiarim Fennicae,* ser. B, 146 [Helsinki, 1968]), is intended not only for the use of scholars of literature and history, but also for the amusement and delight of the general reader. My one goal was to make the reading of the work in English as pleasurable as it is in Italian, but as I began I was faced with the difficult choice of style and language. To translate this complex fourteenth-century work with an exaggeratedly modern diction or with artificial Shakespearean or Victorian archaisms would have constituted a distortion of the author's style, for Giovanni Boccaccio used the contemporary language of his city, with all its popular expressions and proverbs. I chose, therefore, to adhere as closely as possible to the original while using a neutral and natural English without affectations or Italianisms. Medieval rhetoric presented a further difficulty. Boccaccio's sentences, measured to the canons of *ars dictaminis,* form poetic units in prose as firm and solid as the metrical units of poetry. I thus attempted to keep his periodic style as intact as possible within the limits of modern English syntax. Like poetry, however, this careful prose cannot be rendered inviolate; practice by necessity fell below the ideal. Boccaccio's prodigal inversions and changes of tense forced me to make many displacements and changes; compromise was necessary for the sake of sense and readability. Since the medieval system of punctuation is arbitrary and alien to our own usage, the punctuation and paragraph divisions are my own, although they often follow modern editions.

To avoid swelling this volume beyond a reasonable length, I have cited books and articles in the "Notes to the Translation" solely under the author's name, date of publication, volume, and page number. The reader can find full bibliographical data in the "Bibliography of Works Consulted" (p. 165).

This translation would have been neither begun nor completed without the advice and encouragement of Dr. Charles S. Singleton of the Johns Hopkins University. I am grateful to Dr. Robert D. Cottrell, who read the original draft and made comments and suggestions, and to my colleague, Dr. Curtis Blaylock, who was so helpful at the end of this project. As I came to final touches, Dr. Paul F. Watson and Dr. Richard C. Trexler were most generous in sharing their knowledge of Florentine sumptuary laws with me. I wish to express my thanks to the Medieval and Renaissance Center of the Ohio State University for permitting me to reproduce materials necessary for the completion of my work, and to the Research Board of the University of Illinois for its generosity in defraying the costs of preparing and reproducing the final manuscript. I acknowledge the kindness of the editors of *Modern Language Notes* in permitting me to reprint here some material which appeared in volume 89 (1974, pp. 60–70) of that journal. An especial word of gratitude must be made to Dr. Tauno Nurmela of the University of Turku, Finland, who sent me a copy of his fine edition when it appeared and who permitted me to use his work as a basis for my own. Finally, my deepest thanks go to my wife, Janet, not only for her aid and advice in language and editing but also for her unflagging encouragement.

Introduction

The *Corbaccio* by Giovanni Boccaccio (1313–75) recounts the story of a dream: a rejected lover falls asleep and, by the visitation of a spirit from Purgatory, is supposedly cured of his senseless passion for a certain widow. The plot is simple, but thematically and structurally it is a puzzling and intriguing book. Its vehement antifeminist tirades, its bewildering inconsistencies in moral outlook, and its unevenness of tone and style defy the critic to treat it as an organic unity. These qualities have led historically to two divergent opinions: one holds that it is an abstract and edifying moral tale, while the other treats it as the author's own confession of an unhappy love affair. In other areas of Boccaccio studies, most recent critics have abandoned the purely autobiographical approach and have begun a more productive re-examination of his works as literary inventions founded in medieval tradition. Unfortunately, this fresh evaluation has not yet been fully extended to the *Corbaccio*. Vincenzo Crescini's view that Boccaccio's works constitute a diary persists despite the lack of historical proof. His most influential follower in this regard was Henri Hauvette,[1] who, while recognizing the bizarre, contradictory qualities of this treatise, brushed aside the critical problems presented by the author's use of the first person and dismissed doubts which might have undermined an empirical interpretation of the narrative: "Let us consider the *Corbaccio* as one of the sources of Boccac-

---

1. Vincenzo Crescini, ed., *Contributo agli studi sul Boccaccio* (Turin, 1887); Henri Hauvette, "Une Confession de Boccace 'Il Corbaccio,' " *Bulletin Italien,* 1 (1901), 3–21; *Boccace, étude biographique et littéraire* (Paris, 1914), pp. 329–43. Michael Leone in "Autobiografismo reale e ideale in *Decameron* VIII, 7," *Italica* 50 (1973), 242–65, repeats Hauvette's opinion.

cio's biography" (p. 5). The work was thus reduced to a querulous confession of a decrepit Boccaccio, too old for love and embittered by rejection. Considering the progress made in Boccaccio studies since 1901, the genesis of this work requires radical reappraisal.

Certain superficial details could indeed lead us to believe that the pitiful narrator is in some way to be identified with the writer himself. The narrator is reputed to be "a great connoisseur of the feminine figure," a middle-aged man who is insultingly told to go home and weed his onions. The Spirit reveals that he excells in the art of literature in spite of early paternal dissuasion. The possible parallels of this persona to Boccaccio are worthy of attention: from the *Decameron* and elsewhere we are well aware of the author's appreciative eye for the ladies; we know that the onion appeared on the coat of arms of Certaldo, the town where Boccaccio's family originated; and we know of his contemporary reputation as "Dominus Johannes Boccaccius poeta" from many official documents. However, it would be difficult indeed to make any positive identification of personal elements in the *Corbaccio*. The author is never named within its pages, and his high social position makes such an embarrassing public confession highly improbable, for in 1354 and 1355 he had reached the zenith of his participation in civic affairs and was serving as Florentine ambassador to the most powerful men of his time (among them Pope Innocent VI, the Emperor Charles IV, and Niccolò Acciaiuoli, a boyhood friend who had become Grand Seneschal of the Kingdom of Naples). It could be argued that the work's strictures against the widow's showy dress appear to reflect the tenor of contemporary Florentine sumptuary legislation regulating women's finery. These ordinances, first promulgated by the city in 1330, were abrogated in 1354, and jurisdiction over the curtailment of luxury was given over to the episcopal court. However, civic statutes were reissued in stronger form not only in 1355 but also in 1356 (see Appendix). Since the writer held such distinguished appointments at this time, the *Corbaccio*'s denunciations might represent a public demonstration of support for these laws by a respected official. The prevalent extravagance in feminine fashions and the city's regulations made as strong an impression on the author as earlier abuses had made on Dante.[2]

2. Pier Giorgio Ricci, "Notizie e documenti per la biografia del Boccaccio," *Studi sul Boccaccio*, 6 (1971), 1–10, speculates that Boccaccio may have been a judge. For Boccaccio's embassies see Natalino Sapegno, *Il Trecento* (Milan, 1934), pp. 282–83,

Boccaccio's use of the first-person narrator, similarly, cannot be considered as evidence that the work is confessional, for it directly follows the convention of medieval didactic literature[3] in which the "I" was meant to invite identification with the reader rather than the author. Since both the literary protagonists in the *Corbaccio,* the narrator and the Spirit, use the first person even in those passages assimilated verbatim from the writer's predecessors, autobiographic interpretation is doubly uncertain. Indeed many astute critics have observed that Boccaccio often ignored his own empirical experience or that of his contemporaries in favor of evidence taken from classical authors or from some medieval writer who he believed had been raised to their status of authority. For example, Bernhard König has shown that the meeting in church and other love sequences in Boccaccio are formulated on established topoi; Manlio Pastore Stocchi has noted Boccaccio's refusal to include recent firsthand information or maps in the *De montibus* (begun 1355–57), preferring to rely instead upon ancient and sanctioned narrative accounts; and Vittore Branca has proven that even the famous description of the Black Death in the *Decameron,* often cited as an eyewitness account, is to a great extent based on a passage in Paolo Diacono's *History of the Lombards.*[4]

Boccaccio's literary procedure was different from ours. For him, as for his predecessors, the first task of writing was "inventio," and the word retained its Latin connotation of "discovery." It was not the creation of

---

and Vittore Branca, "Profilo biografico," in *Tutte le opere di Giovanni Boccaccio* (Milan, 1967), I, 83–127, 147–50, 161. The abrogation of the sumptuary laws can be found in the Archivio di Stato di Firenze, *Provvisioni,* 41, ff. 14^{rv} (25 April 1354). See Richard C. Trexler, *Synodal Law in Florence and Fiesole, 1306–1318* (Città del Vaticano, 1971), pp. 26, 113. Sumptuary laws were enacted in Florence many times during the fourteenth century; important restrictions against women's finery appeared also in 1364 and 1365 (*Provvisioni,* 52, ff. 79^r–80^v, 106^r–107^r). The synodal laws on women's clothing of 1310 had inspired Dante's famous misogynistic invective and "prediction" ("sarà in pergamo interdetto," *Purgatorio* XXIII, 98–108).

3. See E. Philip Goldschmidt, *Medieval Texts and Their First Appearance in Print* (London, 1943), esp. pp. 89ff.; Leo Spitzer, "A Note on the Poetic and Empirical 'I' in Medieval Authors," *Traditio,* 4 (1946), 414–22.

4. Bernhard König, *Die Begegnung im Tempel, Abwandlungen eines literarischen Motivs in den Werken Boccaccios,* Hamburger romanistische Studien, Reihe A, Band 45 (Hamburg, 1960); Manlio Pastore Stocchi, *Tradizione medievale e gusto umanistico nel "De montibus" del Boccaccio* (Padua, 1963), p. 50; Vittore Branca, *Boccaccio medievale* (Florence, 1956), esp. pp. 209–13.

new subject matter or the reporting of personal experience that was important to him, but the arrangement of literary material into an ordered structure and its expression in a new poetic form. On the authority of Isidore of Seville, Boccaccio states that the origin of the Greek word "poesis" is not the verb "poio" ("I make"), but the substantive "poetes," a very ancient word, he says, meaning "exquisita locutio" ("careful expression") in Latin.[5] In the *Genealogia* XIV, ix, Boccaccio stressed the three most commonly used divisions of rhetoric involved in the art of literature: compilation of material (inventio), arrangement (dispositio), and expression (elecutio):[6]

> Poetry is indeed ... a certain passion for carefully discovering and stating, or writing, that which one finds. It proceeds from the bosom of God, and I believe this passion is given only to a few minds at creation; for this reason, since it is so marvelous, poets have always been the rarest of men. The sublime effects of this passion are such that, for example, it compels the mind to desire speech and to devise strange and unheard-of inventions, to arrange these meditations in a certain order, to adorn the composition with an unusual weaving of words and meaning, and to conceal truth under a fabulous yet seemly veil.[7]

The technique Boccaccio outlines is purely traditional. The literal level of poetry was false; it was a mere veil ("velamento"), or rough "cortex" ("bark"), beneath which was hidden a nucleus of truth.[8] The "corteccia" or "integumentum" ("covering"), as it was often called, was the fictional surface formed by an artificial juxtaposition of poetic elements, which both concealed and revealed an allegorical or moral lesson. This veil, in theory at least, hid the truth from the profane eyes of the

5. Giovanni Boccaccio, *Genealogie deorum gentilium libri,* ed. Vincenzo Romano, Scrittori d'Italia (Bari, 1951), II, 700–703; *Boccaccio on Poetry: Being the Preface and the Fourteenth and Fifteenth Books of Boccaccio's Genealogia Deorum Gentilium,* ed. and trans. Charles G. Osgood (Princeton, 1930; reprint, New York, 1956), p. 40.

6. Compare Cicero, *De inventione* I, vii, and *Ad C. Herennium de ratione dicendi* I, ii; Boccaccio relies heavily on Cicero throughout the discussion of poetry in the fourteenth and fifteenth books of his *De genealogia.*

7. *Genealogie,* II, 699. Osgood's otherwise excellent translation in *Boccaccio on Poetry* I find too free at this point; the rendering is therefore my own.

8. An explanation of literary terms is found in D. W. Robertson, Jr., "Some Medieval Literary Terminology, with Special Reference to Chrétien de Troyes," *Studies in Philology,* 48 (1951), 669–92.

vulgar herd, yet allowed it to appear to the man of intellect who could penetrate within.

In an original composition, whether a play, an epic, a satire, or a dream vision, just as in the compilation of encyclopedic volumes, writers of the Middle Ages paid close attention to the models of each genre and to the conventional list of commonplaces surrounding them. They imitated their predecessors closely and assiduously. This process of literary assimilation continued into the Renaissance, but with a different intention: for Boccaccio, the custom of formulating one's writings on the texts of others was no longer simply a publishing of truth, and thus a Christian work of mercy, but also a process of self-aggrandizement. The texts of writers of authority were incorporated so that the writer might in some way take on their greatness. Boccaccio was fully aware of the power of his pen not only to establish his own fame, but also to change and form a new reality through art. In the pages of the *Corbaccio*, his characters reveal the force of literature: poets can render whom they please "so famous and so glorious to the ears of men that whoever hears anything of that person considers him to have the soles of his feet above the heavens ..." (p. 72).

Poetry was distinguished from history and literal truth by reason of its being an artistic combination of events and facts not joined in nature. It is significant for our understanding of the *Corbaccio* that Boccaccio identifies the work not with history but with the artifice of poetry and traditional medieval poetics (pp. 72–73). In this way, we are to see the *Corbaccio* as a "fabula" or a fiction, and not as a diary.[9]

The formal elements of the treatise are part of a wide artistic tradition and contest autobiographical intention and interpretation. The narrator refers to his work as a "trattato," a technical term meaning a "philosophical treatment."[10] The oneiric revelation he undergoes follows the

9. Boccaccio defines "fabula" in the *Genealogie,* XIV, ix (II, 706); Osgood, *Boccaccio on Poetry,* pp. 48–49. See also Edmond Faral, *Les arts poétiques du XIIe et du XIIIe siècle; recherches et documents sur la technique littéraire du moyen âge* (Paris, 1924); Antonio Viscardi and Gianluigi Barni, *L'Italia nell'età comunale,* Società e costume, panorama di storia sociale e tecnologica, 4 (Turin, 1966), 120; and Gioacchino Paparelli, "Fictio. La definizione dantesca della poesia," *Filologia romanza,* 7 (1960), 1–83.

10. Ernst Robert Curtius, *European Literature in the Latin Middle Ages,* trans. Willard R. Trask (New York, 1953; reprint, 1963), p. 222; Nurmela, ed., *Il Corbaccio,* pp. 8, 145.

ambitious and challenging structure of the medieval dream or vision form, with its usual bewildered first-person narrator (the counterpart of Everyman in medieval drama), and its almost standard number of conventions, topographical and narrative, symbolizing the dreamer's confused state of sin. Dreams and visions had always been one of the ways to describe supernatural realities while permitting the narrator to escape the opprobrium of claiming superior prophetic powers and wisdom. The literary tradition is long and illustrious. Among the classics, the dream of Er of Pamphilia (Plato's *Republic*, X, 13–14), Cicero's *Somnium Scipionis,* and Macrobius' *Commentary on the Dream of Scipio* helped provide a set theoretical and literary model for later times. Judeo-Christian writers had found dreams an ideal means for diffusing their own teachings. The biblical rapture of St. Paul, St. John's Apocalypse, and the apochryphal Book of Enoch were followed by such works as the *Dialogues* of St. Gregory the Great and a myriad of revelations of saints and mystics, among which the visions of Alberic, Fursey, Drycthelm, and Tundale are some of the most famous and influential. The convention governed the structure of many late medieval works: Alain de Lille's *De planctu Naturae,* Guillaume de Lorris' and Jean de Meung's *Roman de la Rose,* and the Middle English *Pearl* all bear its shape. Even Petrarch's *Secretum* represents a distinguished example.[11]

Boccaccio himself had used dreams often throughout his literary career: the *Filocolo* contains the dream of Florio; the *Teseida,* the vision of Arcita's soul, reminiscent in many aspects of Cicero's *Somnium Scipionis* and Boethius' *Consolatio Philosophiae;* the *Commedia delle ninfe fiorentine,* the dream of Caleone; the *Ninfale fiesolano,* the dream of Africo; and the *Fiammetta,* the vision of Venus. Nor is the *Corbaccio*

11. For a history of the dream-vision, see Howard Rollin Patch, *The Other World According to Descriptions in Medieval Literature* (Cambridge, Mass., 1950); Francis Xavier Newman, "Somnium: Medieval Theories of Dreaming and the Form of Vision Poetry," (Ph.D. dissertation, Princeton, 1962); E. J. Becker, *A Contribution to the Comparative Study of Medieval Visions of Heaven and Hell* (Baltimore, 1899); J. A. MacCulloch, *Early Christian Visions of the Other World* (Edinburgh, 1912); August Rüegg, *Die Jenseits Vorstellungen vor Dante and die übrigen literarischen Voraussetzungen der "Divina Commedia"* (Cologne, 1945); Adolfo Mussafia, "Sulla visione di Tundalo," *Sitzungsberichte der philos.-historischen Classe der kaiserlichen Akademie der Wissenschaften,* 67 (Vienna, 1871), 157–206; *La Visione di Tugdalo,* ed. Francesco Corazzini (Bologna, 1872). See also Vittore Branca, *"L'Amorosa visione* (tradizione, significati, fortuna)," *Studi di filologia italiana,* 7 (1950), 20–47 for the tradition as Boccaccio knew it.

alone in having its framework totally couched as a dream-vision: the *Amorosa visione* parodied and burlesqued the tradition, while the *De casibus illustrium virorum* returned to its conventional solemn and serious tone.[12]

It should be noted in passing that critics have mistakenly viewed the *Corbaccio* as a strict imitation of Dante's *Divina Commedia;* however, the similarity exists merely in verbal reminiscences natural to a writer imbued with the language of the *sommo poeta*. The *Corbaccio* belongs to a far wider tradition than that represented by the fortune of the *Commedia* and follows the purely formal schema of conventional intellectual dreams far more closely than the features of Dante's great theological poem.[13]

Typically, the dream-vision depicted the progress of ethical education and spiritual enlightenment of a person lost and morally bewildered, who, having strayed from the norms of his society and religion, sorrowed over his confusion and past misfortunes. Abandoning his companions for solitude, he made his way to his own chamber, or to an open place by a stream, where he fell asleep and experienced rapture in a dream or trance. The experience generally took place in early spring in an allegorical setting having a conventionalized topography. Following his appetites instead of reason and immersed in a state of self-indulgent lethargy, the visionary found himself in a beautiful meadow dotted with herbs and flowers, and he continued down his symbolic path of dalliance until he became lost in a trackless waste, or, perhaps, a dark forest. Often he was swept along above the ground, only later to have extraordinary events or circumstances impede his progress in a desert valley surrounded by high mountains filled with thorns, rocks, and nettles, and inhabited by wild beasts. The despairing dreamer then met a guide whose appearance (described sometimes briefly, sometimes in minute detail) struck the narrator dumb with fright. There followed a dialogue or debate—the usual pedagogical method of medieval schools—between the protagonist and his teacher, in which the dreamer would show the greatest ignorance

12. See the *Amorosa visione,* ed. Vittore Branca (Florence, 1944), p. 385.

13. Attilio Levi indicated many formal analogies and echoes in *Il Corbaccio e la Divinia Commedia* (Turin, 1889). Nicola Bruscoli (*L'Ameto, Lettere, Il Corbaccio;* Scrittori d'Italia [Bari, 1940], p. 302) stated that the "introduction and the epilogue are a tortuous paraphrase of Dante." Julien Luchaire (*Boccace* [Paris, 1951]) believed the work to be both an imitation and a parody of Dante's poem. Henri Hauvette (*Boccace* [Paris, 1914], p. 333) saw the comparison as exaggerated.

or stupidity toward his guide's instruction. The protagonist of the *Corbaccio,* for example, a learned man of letters, does not find it amiss to accept the teaching of a mere merchant. Lastly, even the dreamer's waking followed convention. Christian visions typically relied upon St. Paul's description of rapture in II Corinthians XII: 2–4, and it is only to be expected that the dreamer here would return to the world in a state of doubt whether he had been rapt in the flesh or not.

On the merely structural level of the dream, then, we can firmly state that the work follows tradition very closely and that it is clearly free of any autobiographical suspicion. Boccaccio probably chose the form not only because of its perennial popularity but also because he believed it would offer an excellent vehicle for expressing his own message against lechery.

Some critics have considered the *Corbaccio* exceptional among Boccaccio's works, especially in its negative attitude toward love and women. They see it as an anomaly which marks a sudden break between the writings leading up to and including the *Decameron* and those of the poet's later life. Yet the *Corbaccio*'s satirical antifeminist bias certainly is unique neither in Western tradition nor among Boccaccio's own productions. The writer revealed the same oscillation between diatribe and blandishment throughout his career, and in doing so he fully exhibited the medieval inheritance of a dialectical attitude toward women: first, the sublimated earthly lady of troubadour poetry, or the "donna angelicata" of the *dolce stil novo,* exalted with epithets ascribed to the Deity; second, woman abased, the snare of Satan, daughter of the temptress, Eve, who lays her traps for men. The opposition between the chivalrous exaltation of love in the *Decameron* and the bitterness of the characters in the *Corbaccio* is traditional, for palinode and reprobation belong as much to the conventions of courtly love as do the rules of service and devotion. The phenomenology and psychology of love in the work follow the canons codified approximately two centuries before in Andreas Capellanus' *De amore.* Certainly nowhere would one find a clearer embodiment of Capellanus' definition of love as a "passio," a "suffering," "something undergone," than in the *Corbaccio.*

As Torraca pointed out, Boccaccio wrote equally vehement antifeminist passages in the early *Filocolo* and *Filostrato.*[14] Even the *Decameron* itself was not always kind to the ladies. The Introduction to Day

14. Francesco Torraca, *Per la biografia di Giovanni Boccaccio* (Rome, 1912), pp. 307–9.

I, for example (I, 21–22), places deprecatory remarks in the mouths of the women themselves, and in Day I, 10, Pampinea, the Queen, inveighs firmly against feminine witlessness and senseless loquacity (I, 64).[15] Boccaccio was to give free rein to a fervently misogynistic satire in the *Trattatello in laude di Dante,* as his description of the *sommo poeta*'s marital woes ends in a Theophrastian crescendo against all womankind. Within the *Corbaccio* itself this ambivalence is obvious. A curious, secret esteem for the widow accompanies the bitter love-passion of both protagonists; the characters experience such contradictory emotions that they seem unable either to conceal or to reconcile them. The lover's description of his first glimpse of the widow totally contradicts the bedroom-eye view given by her late husband. Yet even this Spirit lapses as he attacks the alleged hideousness of the woman's body: between the lines we detect his continuing delight in and nostalgia for her lost youth and charm. He will use her comeliness later as a touchstone to compare the good looks of the protagonist, and his repeated contradictory protestations of her ugliness will be belied by his final order to hate her beauty.

Particularly in its antifeminist satire the *Corbaccio* shows a close dependence upon a literary convention, and indeed, upon one lacking originality. Even in classical times, misogynistic treatises had become reduced to compilations and variations of established commonplaces. Medieval charges against women to convince men of their undesirability —loquacity, pride, vanity, destructiveness, avarice, lust, prostitution, murder, infanticide, ambition, venality, faithlessness, ficklessness—were as predictable as they were tiresome. Each treatise seems a faithful imitation of the last, yet the relation between particular works is hard and often impossible to establish, for the similarity is often due not only to a well-divulged written source or to a powerful oral tradition[16] but also to the constancy of human nature.

15. Giovanni Boccaccio, *Il Decameron,* ed. Charles S. Singleton, Scrittori d'Italia (Bari, 1955), 2 vols. All quotations are from this edition.

16. There have been many studies of this convention. Carlo Pascal, "Antifemminismo medievale," *Poesia latina medievale, saggi e note critiche* (Catania, 1907), pp. 151–84, and "Misoginia medievale," *Studi medievali,* 2 (1906–7), 242–48; Theodore Lee Neff, *La Satire des femmes dans la poésie lyrique française du Moyen Âge,* Romance Monographs, 53 (Paris, 1900); August Wulff, *Die frauenfeindlichen Dichtungen in den romanischen Literaturen des Mittelalters bis zum Ende des XIII^en Jahrhunderts* (Halle a. S., 1914); Arthur Keister Moore, "Studies in a Medieval Prejudice: Antifeminism" (Ph.D. dissertation, Vanderbilt University, 1943—a summary of this dissertation was published by the Joint University Libraries [Nashville, Tenn., 1945]); Francis Lee Utley, *The Crooked Rib* (Columbus, Ohio, 1944);

Misogynistic treatises exhibited a very loose structure, with the charges and invectives juxtaposed in an order defying logic.[17] The *Corbaccio*'s antifeminist tirades are no exception to this, in spite of the relatively strict discipline and order of the dream-vision. For both major elements Boccaccio follows tradition. Theophrastus, Hildebert of Tours, Marbod of Rennes, Bernard of Morlaix, Alexander Neckam, Walter Mapes, and the ribald Goliard of the *De conjuge non ducenda* ("On Not Taking a Wife"), to name but a few, certainly exhibit this haphazard quality fully in their antifeminist works.[18] The defrocked priest, Matheolus, rambles on in a most flaccid and prolix style in his *Lamentations;* and Jean de Meung's "Jaloux" and "Vieille" exhibit no discipline at all in their famous digressions in the *Roman de la Rose.* Despite its striking originality of expression, the *Corbaccio* is faithful to the norms established by its predecessors, and is clearly a bravura performance to outdo them. Hauvette's opinion that it was written "under the impetus of extreme emotion in one of those moments when the writer allowed himself to be carried away unreasonably in an emotional outburst"[19] is a view which must be tempered severely. The work required many years of collection and preparation and reflects the writer's study not only of the dream-vision tradition but of many treatises on the subject of lechery as well. In the last century, Pinelli noted how indebted the work was to Juvenal's *Satire VI.*[20] We possess Boccaccio's *florilegium* of antifeminist excerpts in the *Zibaldone laurenziano,* which he had begun to assemble sometime before 1350; many passages of the *Corbaccio* are direct imitations of Boccaccio's own copy of Theophrastus' *De nuptiis* (*On Marriage*) and Walter Mapes' *Valerius Rufino ne ducat uxorem* (*Valerius*

Katharine M. Rogers, *The Troublesome Helpmate* (Seattle and London, 1966); Vern L. Bullough and Bonnie Bullough, *The Subordinate Sex: A History of Attitudes toward Women* (Urbana, Ill., 1973).

17. Gilbert Highet, *Juvenal the Satirist: A Study* (New York, 1954; reprint, 1961), p. 93; Wulff, *Frauenfeindliche Dichtungen,* pp. 42, 98–100.

18. For Theophrastus, see *Patrologiae cursus completus: Series Latina* (hereafter cited as *PL*), ed. Jacques-Paul Migne (Paris), XXIII, 288–91; Hildebert, *PL,* CLXXI, 1418; Marbod, *PL,* CLXXI, 1698; Mapes, *De nugis curialium,* ed. M. R. James (Oxford, 1914), pp. 142ff., and *PL,* XXX, 262–69; the Goliardic *De conjuge non ducenda* is found in *The Latin Poems Commonly Attributed to Walter Mapes,* ed. Thomas Wright, Camden Society, 16 (London, 1841).

19. Hauvette, "Une confession," p. 4.

20. Giovanni Pinelli, "Appunti sul 'Corbaccio,'" *Il Propugnatore,* 16 (1883), 169–92.

to Rufinus That He Not Take a Wife) transcribed into that notebook.[21] The "Notes to the Translation" indicate many further commonplaces and parallels in preceding works.

We must be careful, on the other hand, not to exaggerate the opposite view: the work is no mere sterile, mechanical combination of passages from earlier authors. The writer's own casting of images and commonplaces sets his production apart. Without the scholarly footnote we would often be unaware of the author's vast debt to his predecessors, for his care in selecting and arranging his material gives the effect of spontaneity, though not always of consistency.

In writing this "curious little book," Boccaccio quite obviously did not display the artistic equilibrium achieved in the *Decameron*. The uneven treatment accorded to basic Christian themes is the most perplexing: the charity, mercy, gratitude, and humility opening the treatise play little part in the body of the narrative. The final outcome of vengeance and wrath, unconvincingly allied to righteous anger, belies the devoutly religious attitude with which the narrator began. Jolted from this to passages of vivid comedy and biting satire, the reader feels the moral and artistic disequilibrium of a work left unpolished. Whereas in his masterpiece the author's tone was smooth and his intent clearly hedonistic, here he was torn between the serious moral didacticisms of a *remedia amoris,* and the psychological intricacies of love, hatred, and revenge required by the plot. Though his narrator sets out in humility and, toward the end, reaffirms his purpose to teach, the moral preoccupation clearly does not prevail. The resultant puzzle constitutes a major problem.

Disturbed and often scandalized evaluations have persisted throughout the history of criticism on the *Corbaccio*. Indeed, we learn from Ser Lodovico Bartoli (the Florentine notary who rendered the treatise into *ottava rima,* probably ca. 1387) that Boccaccio himself despised the work.[22] In Spain the Church placed it on the Index in 1631,[23] but only

21. Giovanni Boccaccio, *Zibaldone boccaccesco mediceo-laurenziano, Pluteo XXIX–8,* ed. La Biblioteca Medicea-Laurenziana (Florence, 1915).

22. Guido Mazzoni published the text of this rhymed version in an article, *"Il Corbaccino di Ser Ludovico Bartoli,"* in *Il Propugnatore,* n.s. 1 (1888), 240–301; see p. 301, st. CCLXXIV. See also Pio Rajna, *"Il Corbaccio ridotto in ottava rima da Lodovico Bartoli,"* in *Studi su Giovanni Boccaccio* (Castelfiorentino, 1913), pp. 72–85.

23. *Indice expurgatorio del año de 1631* (issued under the authority of Cardinal

after it had passed as a moral tract for some three hundred years. The Victorian strictures, however, make the most entertaining reading. The work offended the sensibilities of John Addington Symonds, who deplored it not only as a "profoundly disgusting composition," but as "odious and profligate"; Pio Rajna found it *"profondamente immorale"*; and Marcus Landau, with Attilio Levi and Henri Hauvette, censured the language and regretted the author's excesses, but admitted the book's value as a document on cosmetics.[24]

Boccaccio's words still seem far from timid, though we, now used to the stronger stuff of the present day, feel no outrage at them. Criticisms overemphasizing the immorality of the *Corbaccio* merely cloud our ability to examine the work as a literary artifact lacking the usual delicate artistry of its author.

There is clearly a tension between Boccaccio's desire to entertain us with a ribald depiction of earthly love in its roughest and most carnal aspects and his intent to give the work a universal allegorical significance and moral purpose. Boccaccio's portrayal of his characters' human qualities is often strangely at odds with his loftier aim. The result is a work which flows in incongruous patterns with a rapid succession of moralizing, ribaldry, sincerity, comedy, earnestness, satire, sermonizing, folly, and even near hysteria. The author fails to harmonize or reconcile the various paradigmatic schemata into a balanced work of art, and the ultimate message of the work, intentionally or not, parodies the solemnity which the tradition of otherwordly visions usually displays. The *Corbaccio* presents no view of an afterlife at all but merely the fouler, earthly aspects of the "Court of Love" (p. 14). The setting symbolizes earthly desire: the visionary attains no transcendence, nor is his dream, as the reader will see, ultimately a truly salutary experience.

As we begin, the work purports to be a revelation granted by the grace of God through the mercy of the Blessed Virgin. But how strange is this unveiling of the *invisibilia Dei*! The Spirit-guide, that traditional "em-

Antonio Zapata), p. 703, col. b; Caroline Brown Bourland, *Boccaccio and the Decameron in Castilian and Catalan Literature* (New York, 1905), p. 13.

24. John Addington Symonds, *Giovanni Boccaccio as Man and Author* (New York, 1895), pp. 67–70. Rajna, *"Il Corbaccio,"* p. 73; Marcus Landau, *Giovanni Boccaccio, sein Leben und seine Werke* (Stuttgart, 1877), p. 179; cf. Gustav Koerting, *Boccaccios Leben und Werke* (Leipzig, 1880), pp. 241–42, who echoes Landau's sentiments; Levi, *Il Corbaccio e la Divina Commedia*, p. 24; Hauvette, *Boccace*, p. 336.

bodiment of manifestly genuine wisdom,"[25] differs considerably from his predecessors in the convention: no symbol he, no personification of Lady Philosophy, no saint, no honored shade of some illustrious ancestor, no Virgil, historical and figurative of natural wisdom, but merely the pathetic shade of the widow's husband, cuckolded and ridiculous, who has observed his wife's foibles and tells all. The dream really gives no new mode of vision, for the guide's teaching grants no point of view superior to that of the morally floundering protagonist. The Spirit's privileged position is nothing more than that of some mundane voyeur spying on milady's boudoir as she revels with her lover. The "invisible things" revealed are ultimately those arcane wonders hidden by the widow's weeds—"the secret parts covered by her clothes" (p. 52). The incongruity is striking, yet in this way the actual content of the work betrays the philosophical and sacramental terms which frame it.

The problem becomes even more involved and puzzling as we reach the conclusion. In the proemium the narrator-protagonist, in a mood of gratitude for a recent favor granted by divine intervention, vows to acquit himself of a task at once useful and merciful. This, he insists with the humility of any medieval scribe, is his sole purpose, "e altro no." At the termination of the debate between the Spirit and dreamer, we are assured that the effects of divine intervention are complete: "I firmly decided to abandon the evil love of that wicked woman. Divine grace was so favorable to this resolve that within a few days I regained my lost liberty" (p. 77). The tone suggests that some relief and a return to a nobler religiosity might be experienced here. We, as readers, have now finished the text and expect to be led through a catharsis to a quiet denouement. However, we are doomed to disappointment. The protagonist does not escape the erotomania into which he has fallen; he takes up the note of betrayal, outrage, and revenge again in the closing lines: "She is to be stung by the sharpest goad you bear with you" (p. 77). Having experienced the dream as a warning, and written the treatise in supposed gratitude, the narrator still attains no real conversion. The same profound emotional and moral disequilibrium of the beginning, the same insurmountable power of earthly love, familiar to us from the *Decameron,* replaces what should be a pious and joyful thanksgiving imparting true Christian charity. Instead, we have a continuation of the

25. Newman, "Somnium," p. 319.

sinful duality of carnal attraction and hate which are recognizable as the properties of lust. The Spirit, oddly for a shade who burns with charity (p. 9), had sanctioned and abetted the normal development of earthly anger, counselling not Christian love, but hate and enmity: "What you have loved you must hate; and whatever you were ready to do to earn someone's love, you must be ready to do the contrary so that you gain hatred" (p. 72).

The naive Spirit of the *Corbaccio* was apparently incapable of seeing beyond the emotional duality of love and hatred to the third saner and more righteous possibility expressed by Dante's rational, syllogistic mind in the *De monarchia* III, 2: ". . . ad non odire necessario sequitur aut amare aut non amare; non enim non amare est odire . . . ut de se patet" (". . . 'not hating' implies either 'loving' or 'absence of loving,' for 'not loving' does not mean 'hating'. . . . This is clear.").[26] In the *Corbaccio,* anger and revenge for personal affronts, censured in the *Decameron* as being cruel, become the very basis of a supposedly ethical action.[27] One can therefore see the cause, in part, for the ambiguity of the ending. Boccaccio's depiction of love and hate as mutually exclusive opposites, one curative of the other, is a betrayal of both classical and medieval tradition. In the *Remedia amoris* (vv. 655–69), Ovid himself cautioned against this very misconception: "To hate a woman once loved is a crime: that is an end fitting to savage minds. It is enough to be indifferent: he who ends love by hating, either loves still, or will find it hard to end his misery. Shameful is it that a man and woman lately at one should be foes forthwith; the Appian [Venus] herself approves not such strife as that. . . . It is safer and more fitting to separate in peace." When the author has the Spirit exhort the protagonist to hatred, he depicts him as ingenuously encouraging the same base and morbid interest in the widow that the pro-

26. *Opere di Dante Alighieri,* ed. Fredi Chiappelli (Milan, 1965), p. 371. Translation adapted from *On World Government* (*De monarchia*), trans. Herbert W. Schneider (New York, 1949; reprint, 1957), p. 53.

27. See the beginning of *Decameron* VIII, 8 (ed. Singleton, II, 154). The Spirit of the *Corbaccio* himself had contrasted divine wrath with sinful human revenge earlier: "Truly you speak like a man who does not yet show he knows the ways of Divine Goodness; for you believe that the Most Perfect acts like you mortals . . . whose minds never rest until each tiny offense received is fully revenged" (p. 13). It is odd that this heaven-sent messenger will himself recommend personal vengeance.

tagonist had felt since first falling in love with her. Evident in the ending of the *Corbaccio* are the same oscillations that Alain de Lille uses to seize the contradictory qualities of carnal love following the familiar "quid est amor" topos: "Love is peace joined with hatred, faith with fraud, hope with fear, and fury mixed with reason. . . ."[28] But even more than merely showing that his protagonist continues in his lustful attraction, Boccaccio has reversed a major scholastic position: the precedence of *caritas* over *vindicatio*, of charity, the greatest theological virtue, over retributive justice. Thus, despite the conventional philosophical and religious elements which the author tries to incorporate into the treatise, the result is a fundamentally anti-ascetic work. The combination of various components produces strange juxtapositions which create an impression of conflict and contradiction rather than a complete and artistic homogeneity.

The *Corbaccio*, either by design or accident, forms in the history of Italian letters a kind of anti-*Vita Nuova* in which the structures and the spirit of the *stil novo* see their dialectical rejection and antithesis. The author's intention is not to say "that which had never been said of any woman," but to collect all the antifeminist sayings with which one had always slandered every woman.[29] The many echoes of the *Divina Commedia* taken outside their original context throw the *Corbaccio*'s lack of truly profound spirituality into sharp relief. Vituperation colored with obscenity and clothed with the worst of classical and medieval antifeminist abuse replaces the exaltation of delicate womanliness and its purifying role as a diffuser of virtue and a guide toward heavenly bliss. The author begins on a religious tone, but does not maintain it until the end, for his psychological bent was not upward toward the profoundly spiritual and philosophical but downward toward the immanent, the natural, and the comic.

By portraying the narrator's visionary experiences as fruitless, Boccaccio reveals his own artistic conflict (and, perhaps, a besetting religious and moral one). This lively "realistic" account of the sinful development

28. *PL*, CCX, 210; Thomas Wright's edition in *Anglo-Latin Satirical Poets and Epigrammists of the Twelfth Century*, II (London, 1872), p. 472, contains the complete text. Migne shows a lacuna at this point.

29. See Nicola Bruscoli's interesting yet neglected comments in the end notes to his edition of the *Corbaccio*, pp. 303–4.

of lust and hatred overwhelms the process of spiritual enlightenment. Surely those who have seen the *Corbaccio* as evidence of the author's own religious conversion are mistaken.[30] In the *Corbaccio*, as in the earlier *Amorosa visione*, "Johannes tranquillitatum" inverts the outcome of the traditional dream vision, "the secular form most closely analogous to the mode of prophecy,"[31] and betrays once again his inveterate penchant for playing literary and moral truant, and his desire to cling to a world of human sensations and sensibilities rather than to a transcendent ethic.

Two problems remain: the date of the work and the meaning of the title. The *Corbaccio* is the last fictional work that Boccaccio was to write; yet, despite its significance, we have no contemporary accounts, personal references, chronicles, manuscripts, or biographies to indicate exactly when the author wrote it. Until recently critics thought it was dated internally ca. 1355: that is, immediately after the composition of the *Decameron*, which Boccaccio completed ca. 1351–52. However, the latest scholar to approach the problem, Giorgio Padoan, concluded that it came from the succeeding decade, 1365 or 1366. His opinion, though based on the historical interpretation of various allusions within the text, has not met with universal acceptance. The two most recent editors, Ricci and Nurmela, have rejected his proposal, and my own reservations are fully stated in the Notes to the Translation.[32] The traditional dating of ca. 1355 still seems most plausible.

The meaning of the title has also caused much debate. Abandoning the many subtle explanations of their nineteenth- and early twentieth-century predecessors, recent critics agree on the literal meaning "evil crow" or "wicked raven." The description of the widow's efforts to appear beautiful bears verbal parallels to a well-known fable from

30. This traditional view has reappeared. In a recent article Marga Cottino-Jones states that the *Corbaccio* is "the work which announces the author's moral and intellectual crisis and the consequent dramatic change in his way of thinking and writing" ("The *Corbaccio:* Notes for a Mythical Perspective of Moral Alternatives," *Forum Italicum*, 4 [1970], 490). Compare the text for note 2 above; a contemporary witness claims Boccaccio despised this work.

31. Newman, "Somnium," p. 326.

32. Giorgio Padoan, "Sulla datazione del *Corbaccio*," *Lettere italiane*, 15 (1963), 1–27; "Ancora sulla datazione e sul titolo del *Corbaccio*," ibid., 199–201; Nurmela, ed., *Il Corbaccio*, pp. 18–21, 156; *Opere in versi, Corbaccio, Trattatello in laude di Dante, Prose latine, Epistole*, ed. Pier Giorgio Ricci (Milan-Naples, 1965), pp. 492–93, 1271, note 2. See my Notes to the Translation, 86, 87, 96, 231, 286, and 299.

Phaedrus (*Liber fabularum* I, 3) and Babrius (LXXII) telling of the presumptuous crow who bedecks itself in peacock's feathers in an attempt to conceal its own drabness with their splendor. This tale was widely used in the sermons, homilies, and literary works of the Middle Ages as an exemplum to reprove feminine vanity, and it is only natural that it came to Boccaccio's mind as he wrote his treatise on the same subject.[33]

ANTHONY K. CASSELL

Champaign, 1975

33. For a full discussion of this see Anthony K. Cassell, "The Crow of the Fable and the *Corbaccio:* A Suggestion for the Title," *Modern Language Notes,* 85 (1970), 83–91.

The Corbaccio

[PROEMIUM]

Whoever without good reason hides benefits he has received by being silent, in my opinion, most clearly shows himself thankless and ungrateful for them. Oh, what wickedness, displeasing to God, distressing to men of judgment, whose evil fire dries up the fount of pity! In order that no one may justly reprove me for this, I intend to set forth in the following humble treatise, a special grace which was recently granted to me, not because of my own merit, but solely by the beneficence of Her, Who implored it from the One, Who wills that which She wills Herself. In so doing, I not only shall repay part of my debt, but shall also, without doubt, render service to many who will read about it. Thus, in order that this may come of it, I pray devoutly to Him, from Whom both that which I must say, and every other good, has always proceeded and proceeds, Who is the generous Giver of all (as is seen by His works) that His light will so enlighten my intellect and direct my hand as it sets forth the present work, that I may write that which will be to the honor and glory of His most Holy Name, and that this work may be of use and consolation to the souls of those who may chance to read it and this is my sole purpose.

* * *

[NARRATIO]

Finding myself alone not long ago in my chamber (which truly is the only witness of my tears, sighs, and lamentations), I happened, as I had often done before, to begin thinking very hard about the vicissitudes of carnal love; and pondering over many past occurrences and musing to myself about every word and deed, I concluded that through no fault of mine I had been cruelly ill-treated by her whom I had chosen in my madness as my special lady and whom I honored and revered above all others and loved far more than life itself. Since it seemed to me that I had received abuse and insult in this affair without deserving it, after many sighs and lamentations, driven by resentment, I began not merely to weep bitterly but to cry out loud. I suffered so much, first bemoaning my stupidity, then the insolent cruelty of that woman, that by adding one grief to another in my thoughts, I decided that Death must be far easier to bear than such a life; and I began to cry out to him with the greatest longing. After calling upon him many times and realizing that, cruelest of all things, he flees most the one who most desires to die, I tried to think of a way to force him to take me from this world. Yet upon deciding how I might do this, a cold sweat and self-pity came over me, mixed with a fear of passing from one baneful life to a worse one if I carried it out. This fear came to me with such force that it almost entirely crushed the resolve which I had previously thought so firm. Thus, going back to my tears and former lamentations, I so prolonged them that the desire for death, chased out by the fear of it, returned again; but when it had been taken away, as in the first instance, and my tears had returned, a thought came to me in the midst of this battle, sent, I believe, by Heavenly Light, and it began to speak quite compassionately in my troubled mind:

"Oh, poor fool! Where is the meager power of your reason (no, rather, the explusion of your reason) leading you? Now, are you so dazed that you do not realize that while you believe that someone else is treating you cruelly, you alone are the one who is being cruel

2

to yourself? Is that lady to whom, without seeing how, you chained and entrusted your liberty, the wretched and painful cause of your burdened thoughts, as you declare? You are deceived; you, not she, are the cause of your torment. Show me where she came and forced you to love her; show me with what weapons, authority, or force she led you here and holds you weeping and grieving! You cannot show me, for it is not so. Perhaps you wish to say, 'She should love me, knowing that I love her; and by not doing so, she is the cause of this grief of mine; with this she leads me here and with this she holds me'? This is not a valid reason at all. Perhaps she finds you unpleasing. How do you expect anyone to love a person whom she does not find attractive? Therefore, if you have begun to love someone who does not like you, it is not the fault of your beloved if harm comes of it, but rather your own fault for not knowing how to choose properly; you alone, therefore, if you are grieving over not being loved, are the cause of it. Why do you blame others for what you have done and are doing to yourself? Surely for having harmed yourself, you would deserve the gravest punishment before any just judge; but insofar as it is not punishment that you require for consolation (since, on the contrary, it would be adding pain to pain), it is not now the time to go in search of this justice. But let us see, since you are being cruel to yourself, what you perhaps have done.

"Whatever a man does, he does solely for his own pleasure or for someone else's, or to please both himself and others, or else he does it for the opposite reason. But let us see if your blindness leads you to pleasure or displeasure. That it is not your pleasure is quite obvious; because if you found pleasure in it, you would not grieve and weep over it as you are doing. It remains to be seen if this displeasure of yours is the pleasure or displeasure of anyone else. But this is not the time to inquire whether it is the pleasure of anyone other than the lady for whom you bring yourself to this, she who surely either loves you or hates you or else does neither. If she loves you, without any doubt, your affliction displeases and distresses her. Now, are you unaware that by troubling and harming others one neither acquires nor maintains love, but merely hate and enmity? Apparently you do not value the love of this woman as much as you would have it believed, since you do that which displeases her with such animosity and desire to do worse.

"If she hates you, and if you have not completely taken leave of your senses, you must clearly realize that you can do nothing better to please her than hang yourself by the neck as quickly as possible. Do you not see people every day who, out of hatred for someone, risk life and property to expel and banish that person from the earth, acting against human and divine law? The more sadness and wretchedness they sense in those whom they hate, the more pleasure and happiness they feel themselves. You then, by being sad, by weeping and lamenting, give great pleasure to this enemy of yours. Who but the stupid delight in giving pleasure to their enemies? If she neither loves you nor hates you nor cares for you at all, what use are these tears, these sighs, this suffering which so consumes you? It is the same for you to do this for her as to do it for one of the beams in your room. Why then are you grieving? Why do you yearn for death, something which she herself, whom you believe to be your enemy, did not seek to give to you? It does not appear that you have yet felt how much sweetness there is in life, since you so capriciously yearn to take yourself from it, nor that you have well considered how much more bitterness there is in eternal torment than in those of your foolish love affair, whose torments come to you in the same manner and proportion as you pursue them. If you will only be a man, you can chase them away—something which would not happen with eternal woes.

"Therefore, dismiss, or rather banish, this foolish desire completely and, at the same time, stop wishing to deprive yourself of something which you did not earn; stop wanting to gain eternal torment and to give such great pleasure to someone who wishes you ill; let life be dear to you, and try to prolong it as long as you can! Who knows whether by living you will yet be able to see something of her, by whom you consider yourself so gravely offended, which will make you exaltedly happy? No one. But everyone can be cer-

4

tain that all hope of revenge, or any other joy in things which remain here below, flees everyone at his death. Therefore, live; and just as she, by working against you in wicked ways, strives to make your life a misery and to give you cause to yearn for death, so you, by staying alive, will make her grieve at your living."

Divine consolation in the minds of mortals is a wondrous thing. This thought, sent, I believe, by the most holy Father of Lights, took away almost all the darkness from the eyes of my mind and at the same time sharpened and cleared their vision; so that finding my error so obvious, not only did I feel ashamed as I looked upon it, but, moved by due repentance, I wept about it bitterly, reproved myself, and felt less self-esteem than before. But drying my face of its wretched and pitiful tears, and convincing myself that I had to leave my solitary dwelling—certainly very harmful to anyone whose mind is less than healthy—I left the room trying to appear as composed as my earlier sinful mood allowed. After a search, I discovered companions who were helpful in my sufferings; once I was among them and when we had gathered, as usual, in a pleasant spot, we began at first to speak in careful order about the fickle operations of Fortune, the stupidity of those who embraced her without restraint, and the madness of those same people who tied their hopes to her as to a stable object. We turned from this to the everlasting things of nature and to their wondrous and praiseworthy order, all the less admired by all of us, the more heedlessly we see them used among us. From these, we passed on to divine things, though even their most peripheral details can scarcely be understood by the loftiest intellects, so far does their excellence surpass the intelligence of mortals. Discussing such lofty, sublime, and noble subjects we spent the rest of that day. The coming of night forced us to adjourn for then; and, having feasted upon food almost divine, I arose and retired, consoled, to my regular chamber with all my former distress chased away and nearly forgotten.

When I had eaten sparingly of my usual food, I was unable to forget the sweetness of the past discussions; I spent much of that night repeating them all to myself with matchless pleasure. But

5

after continuing for a long time, natural necessity overcame my delight, and I gently fell asleep. Sleep overcame my senses with all the greater force because of the time which my earlier sweet thoughts had taken from it.

While I was wrapped in the deepest slumber, my enemy Fortune, believing that she had not done me sufficient injuries during my waking hours, contrived to harm me even as I slept. As various forms presented themselves to my imaginative faculty, which is not bound by sleep, it happened suddenly that I seemed to enter upon a delightful and beautiful path, more pleasing to my eyes and all my other senses than anything I had seen before. I did not seem to recognize the place, wherever it was; and I did not seem to care about recognizing it once I felt its delight. Indeed, the further I went down the path, the more pleasure it seemed to offer me, because it excited the hope that if I arrived at the end of the path, a boundless joy, such as I had never before experienced, awaited me. Hence, a desire to reach it seemed to burn so fervently within me that not merely did my feet hasten to attain it, but it seemed to me that by some strange course of events I had been lent the swiftest wings; while I flew more rapidly with them, the nature of the path changed; and where I had seemed to see green grass and various flowers at the entrance, I now found such plants as nettles, brambles, thistles, and yews. Moreover, turning around, I saw myself pursued by a fog thicker and darker than any ever seen before. This immediately enveloped me and not only impeded my flight, but also caused me to abandon almost all hope of the good promised at the entrance of the path.

Finding myself thus motionless and suspended here, it seemed ages before I could discover where I was, no matter how much I looked around me. Yet when after a long while the fog thinned (though the sky was dark because night had fallen), I knew that my flight had left me in a desolate wilderness, rough and harsh, rankly overgrown with trees, thorns, and brambles, without any track or path, and surrounded by rugged mountains—so high that their summits seemed to touch the heavens. Neither by my physical

6

sight, nor by my mental judgment could I in any way seem to recognize or comprehend from what direction I had entered it; nor (what frightened me more) could I, furthermore, discern a way by which I could escape from there and return to tamer regions. Besides this, everywhere I turned, I heard the roars, howls, and shrieks of many ferocious animals, which, judging from appearances, seemed surely to infest this wilderness. At this, both grief and fear came equally into my heart: grief brought continuous tears to my eyes, and sighs and lamentations to my mouth; fear hindered me from deciding which of those mountains I should approach to leave that valley, since many mortal dangers appeared on every side. Thus being hindered as I have described, bereft of all aid and counsel, and expecting almost nothing but death either from hunger or from some ferocious beast, I seemed to stand weeping among the prickly thornbushes and the stark trees, doing nothing but sorrowing in silence for having entered there without foreseeing where I was to end up, and calling upon God's help.

As I stood thus, quite drenched by my tears and already forsaken by almost every hope, behold, from that direction where the sun rose in the wretched valley, a solitary man was slowly making his way toward me. From what I could afterwards discern at closer range, he was of great stature, gaunt, muscular, and scarcely pleasant in appearance, with dark skin and hair (though partly white due to his age—which seemed to be sixty or perhaps more), and his robe was very long, wide, and vermilion in color, though, despite the darkness of the place where I was, it seemed far brighter to me than those which our craftsmen dye here. As has been said, while he came toward me with slow steps, he made me partly afraid and partly brought me hope. He frightened me and I began to dread that that place had perhaps been given to him as his own, and that, if he took offense at seeing someone else there, to avenge this affront he might set the beasts of the place upon me (since they were tame to him alone) and have me torn to pieces. He brought me some hope of salvation because he appeared full of gentleness as he approached me. The more I looked at him and the more I thought I had seen him not here, but at another time and place, I said to myself, "This man, as one who knows this region, perhaps will show me the way out of this place, and also if there is the least spirit of pity in him, he may even kindly lead me to it."

While I was thinking this, he, without yet saying anything, had come so close to me that I could make him out very clearly, and remembered who he was, and where I had seen him; and I was only struggling to remember his name—imagining that if I called him by it, asking for his pity and help (as if showing by this a closer familiarity), he would give me swifter and more friendly aid in my need.

But while I was searching for it in vain, he called me by my own name with a very gentle voice and said, "What evil fortune, what cruel destiny has led you to this desert? Where has your prudence, where has your discretion fled? If you have your usual perception, do you not understand that this is where the body dies, and, what is far worse, where the soul is damned? How have you come here? What arrogance led you?"

Upon hearing his words and seeing his compassionate looks, I began to shed torrents of tears in self-pity before I could find voice for an answer.

But when by my tears I had somewhat given vent to my renewed grief and had gathered the strength of my courage, not without shame I replied in a broken voice, "In my judgment, the false pleasure of fleeting things (which in the past has often led astray others far wiser than I, and perhaps to no less peril) led me to this place before I realized where I was going—here where, since I perceived my whereabouts, I have remained in unbearable misery and utter despair, for there has been darkness all the while. But since Divine Grace, as I believe, and not my own merit, has brought you before me, I beseech you, if you are he whom I have often seen elsewhere in the past, and if there is any humanity in you, take pity on me for that love which you owe our common native city and also for the love of God, to Whom all things are due; and, if you know, teach me how I can leave such a terrifying place as this, for

I already feel myself so overcome by the fear of it that I hardly know whether I am dead or alive."

At that moment, as I looked into his face, it seemed to me that he was laughing a little to himself at my words.

Then he said, "If I did not know it in any other way, indeed your presence here and your words clearly show me that you have taken leave of your senses and that you do not know whether you are dead or alive; if you had not taken leave of them and if you had remembered what eyes those were and who possessed them, whose light, as you put it, opened the path which led you here and made it appear so beautiful to you, and if you had known how much they once meant to me, you would not have dared to beg me for your salvation, but, seeing me, you would have striven to flee for fear of losing whatever hope there still remained to you. If I still were the man I once was, certainly I would not bring you help, but confusion and harm, since you have so thoroughly deserved them. But because my wrath has been changed to charity since I was banished from your mortal life, I shall not deny your request for aid."

Since I was paying the closest possible attention to his words, when I heard "since I was banished from your mortal life" and realized immediately that he was not the one I thought, but his shade, a sudden chill ran through my bones, and my hair began to bristle. I lost my voice and had the feeling that I would have fled him, had I been able. But as it often happens to a dreamer, that in the greatest need he is unable to move for anything in the world, so it happened to me as I dreamed: I had the feeling that my legs were taken from me entirely and that I could not move. This new fear was so strong that I cannot imagine what made my sleep so sound that it was not then broken; and because of this dread, I seemed to stay there without answering or speaking.

The Spirit saw this, smiled, and said to me, "Do not be afraid; you may speak to me in confidence and feel secure in my company; for I assure you that I have come not to do you harm, but to take you from this place if you will have complete faith in what I say."

I heard this, and remembering how much power spirits have

over men, I regained my lost confidence. As I raised my face to him, I humbly begged him to hurry and take me from there before some other peril came upon me.

He then said, "I am only waiting for the right time to do what you ask; for you must learn that although the entrance to this place is very wide for anyone who wants to enter it through madness and lust, it is not so easy to leave again, but, on the contrary, arduous; and one must act with both wisdom and fortitude—virtues which cannot be had without the help of Him at Whose will the journey here was made."

Then I seemed to say, "Since we cannot leave at once and we have time to talk, if you do not mind, I would like to ask you a few questions."

At this he gave a kindly reply, "You may confidently ask anything you like until such time as I come to ask you a few questions and comment briefly upon them."

Then I said in an eager voice, "Two questions are nagging me equally, each that I ask it before the other, so that I shall put them to you both together: I beg you please to tell me what this place is, whether it has been given to you as your home, and if anyone who enters it can ever leave by himself; afterwards, explain to me who it was who wanted you to come here and help me."

To these words he answered, "This place is given different names by various people, and each one is correct. Some call it the 'Labyrinth of Love,' and others the 'Enchanted Valley,' and a good number the 'Pigsty of Venus,' and many the 'Valley of Sighs and Woe'; and besides these, some name it in one way and some in another, as each one sees fit. It is not given to me as my home, because death prevented me from entering ever again such a prison as this, into which you are rushing. It is true that the place where I dwell is harsher than this, but less perilous: and you must know that whoever falls down here through lack of wisdom cannot leave unless Heavenly Light draws him forth, and then, as I have already told you, with wisdom and fortitude."

At this I then said, "Alas, as you hope that He Who can may

set at rest your most fervent desires, answer me about one thing before you proceed to anything else. You say that you have a harsher but less perilous place than this as your abode; and I already know from your own words and from my memory that you do not live in our world; where is your place then? Are you in that eternal prison where one enters and remains without hope of redemption? Or are you in the place where, sooner or later, true hope promises you salvation? If you are in the eternal prison, I certainly believe that it is a harsher dwelling place than here, but how can it be less perilous? And, if you are in that place which still promises you rest, how can it be harsher than this?"

"I am," answered the Spirit, "in the place which definitely promises me salvation; and it is less perilous than this because you cannot sin there and therefore fear to come to worse—something which one continually does here. Many persist in this so long that they fall into that blind dungeon where Divine Light is never seen shining with grace or pity, but always burning with severe and irrevocable justice to the great pain of anyone who experiences it.

"However, my dwelling place, as I said before, is certainly far harsher than this—so much so that if the certain, joyful hope for the better which we enjoy did not help both me and others who are there to bear its hardship patiently, you could almost say that the spirits, who are immortal, would die there. So that you may understand in part, learn that this garment of mine (at which you marveled when you saw me because you probably never saw me in anything like it when I was among you, since you mortals believe it is to be worn only by those elevated to some honor above others) is not cloth woven by hand but a fire fashioned by Divine Art, so fiercely burning that your fire is like the coldest ice in comparison; for it milks all the humors from my body with such force that no charcoal or stone turned to lime in your furnaces was ever so sapped by the fire, so that all your rivers joined together and turned flowing down my throat would be a small sip for my thirst. And two things bring this upon me: the first is the insatiable craving which I had for money while I was alive; and the second, the unseemly patience with which I bore the wicked and shameless ways of her upon whom you wish you had never set eyes. But, for the moment, enough of this talk about the hardship of my dwelling place to which, truly, the torment which is born here cannot be compared except insofar as it is as beneficial as this is harmful.

"But so that your frightened spirits may entirely regain their strength, your second question must have a satisfactory answer; know, therefore, that He with Whose permission I have come here (or rather, to put it better, by Whose command) is that infinite Good Who was Creator of all things and because of Whom and in Whom all things have their being; and to Whom your welfare, your repose, and your salvation are of much greater concern than to yourselves."

I declare that as I heard these words from the Spirit, knowing my peril and the beneficence of the Sender, I felt a great humility enter my heart which made me recognize the loftiness, the power, and the eternal immutability of my Lord and His continual benefits toward me; and in comparison, my baseness, my own frailty and ingratitude, and my countless offenses done in the past against Him, Who now in my need overlooked my sins and showed Himself merciful and generous toward me as He had always done. From this knowledge, such great contrition and repentance for my evil deeds came to me that not only did it seem that my eyes were wet with many real tears, but also that my heart melted into water, just as snow in sunshine. Therefore, both because of this, and because I felt myself too lacking in gratitude for such great and lofty works, I remained silent for a long time, and I was sure that the Spirit knew why.

But then, when I had stood like this for a while, I began to speak again, "O fortunate Spirit! Searching my conscience, I understand perfectly well that what you say is true. That is, that God has more care for us mortals than we have for ourselves, who continually go sinking in our wicked deeds, while He goes uplifting us always with His loving compassion, showing us His eternal beauties and calling us to them like a benign father. Yet nonetheless, since I measure

Divine Goodness according to the workings of terrestrial affairs, it makes me marvel that He should now move Himself to help me, because I feel I have greatly wronged Him."

At this the Spirit said, "Truly you speak like a man who does not yet show he knows the ways of Divine Goodness; for you believe that the Most Perfect acts like you mortals, who are changeable and imperfect, whose minds never rest until each tiny offense received is fully revenged.

"However, since contrition for the sins you have committed (which I sense has entered you) shows you that you must be obedient and attentive to future teachings, I would like to consider only one of the causes for which Divine Goodness was moved to send me to help in your afflictions. It is true, according to what I heard when this task of coming here to you was given to me, not by human, but by angelic voice (which, one must believe, never lies), that whatever life you have led, you have always held in especial reverence and devotion Her, within Whose womb our Salvation was enclosed and Who is the living fountain of mercy and Mother of grace and compassion, and that you always had complete hope in Her as in a fixed terminus. This was manifest to Her divine eyes, and when She saw you more than usually lost and trapped in this valley because you had taken leave of your senses, and saw the peril you were in, without awaiting your request, just as She often does, most generously, in the affairs of Her faithful, She moves of Her own will without awaiting prayers to help the needy with timely assistance, She asked grace on your behalf from Her Son and pleaded for your salvation. For this I was commissioned to come as Her messenger; and I did so, nor shall I leave you until I have brought you again to a place of complete liberty, should it please you to follow me there."

Whereupon, when he was silent, I declared, "You have answered my questions very well; and in truth, since the revenge of God is to make yourself fair again to please Him more, I have compassion also for you; and I greatly desire to facilitate that task if ever I can with any deed of mine; and on the other hand, I am very happy to hear that after your penitence you are destined not be to be damned in Hell but to ascend to the Kingdom of Glory. The beneficence and mercy of Her Who has sent you for my salvation in this affair by now is not new to me: She has made it known to me in the past in many other perils, although I have been ungrateful for so many benefits by achieving little in Her praise. But I devoutly pray Her Who has the power to do as She wills, that just as She has snatched me many times from everlasting death, She may direct my steps toward eternal life and sustain and preserve them until I, being Her most faithful servant, arrive at the goal.

"For Her sake, I pray you to satisfy me yet again by answering one question: does anyone dwell in this valley, which you call by various names without assigning it a definite one, other than those whom Love once chanced to have banished from his court and sent here in exile—as I think he has exiled me—or does it belong only to the beasts which I heard roaring round about the whole night through?"

At this he smiled and answered, "I know quite well that, as yet, the ray of true light has not reached your intellect; and just as many fools do, you consider that which is sordid misery to be supreme happiness, believing that there can be some good in your concupiscent and carnal love. Therefore, pay close attention to what I will now tell you. This wretched valley is what you call 'the Court of Love'; and these beasts, which you say you heard and hear growl-ing, are the wretches—of whom you are one—who have been caught in the net of false love; while they speak of such love, their voices have no other sound in the ears of well-disposed men of dis-cretion than that which apparently comes to yours; and because of this, I called it a 'labyrinth' before, because men become as trapped in it as they did in that of old, without ever knowing the way out. I marvel at your asking about it, inasmuch as I know that you have sojourned here already—not just once but many times—although perhaps not with the difficulty which you suffer at present."

I was almost overwhelmed by remorse for my sin when I recog-nized the truth he had touched on; after I had nearly recovered, I answered, "I have indeed been here many times before, but with better luck, according to the opinion of corrupt minds; and I remember having left here in various ways, more by the grace of Another than by my own wisdom; but grief had so gripped me and fear had so drawn me out of myself that I did not remember being here ever before. Now I know very well, without a clearer explanation, what makes men become beasts and what the wildness of the place and the valley's other names, that you indicated to me, signify, and why I see in it neither track nor path."

"Now then," said the Spirit, "since the shadows are beginning to leave your intellect somewhat and the fear you had when I found you is already abating, there is something I would like to speak to you about until the light appears to show you the way out of here; and because I see that you are tired, I would suggest for your benefit that we sit down if the nature of the place permitted it; but since we cannot do that here, we will speak standing up. I know (and if, on the other hand, I did not know it, a short while ago your words made it clear to me—and also the place where I found you makes it obvious) that you are cruelly entrapped in the grips of love. Nor is it more hidden from me than this, who the cause of it is; and you must have understood this from my speech, if you recall what I said before concerning her upon whom you wish you had never set eyes. However, before I go on, I tell you that because she was once more dear to me than was fitting, I do not wish you to feel ashamed before me, but to talk with me about it as openly and confidently as if I had always been a stranger to her. In reward for the pity which I have for your ills, I beg you to explain to me how you fell into her snares."

At this, I replied, putting aside all shame, "Your request forces me to tell you something which I have never told except to a trusted friend, and which I revealed to her alone by some of my letters. Nor should I be more ashamed of this before you than before any other, even if your liberality did not reassure me; nor should you be disturbed about it, since, when you departed from our life, as canon law shows us, she who was your wife was yours no longer, but became free unto herself; for this reason by no act could you reasonably say that I contrived to take possession of anything of yours.

"However, leaving aside this discussion, which has no place here, and proceeding to the explanation you request, I declare that, to my misfortune a few months past, it happened that I began talking about various things with someone who was formerly your neighbor and relative, whose name there is no need to mention now. While we were discussing in this way, it occurred—as it often happens that a man jumps from one subject to another—that upon leaving the first, we came to speak of worthy women; and having said many things of the ancients, praising some for their chastity, some for their magnanimity, and others for their bodily strength, we came down to the moderns, among whom we found a very small number to commend, although he who took up the discussion at this point did name some from our city, and among others named her who was formerly your wife, whom in truth I did not yet know. (Would that I had never known her later!) Moved by a certain affection for her, he began to say remarkable things, affirming that in generosity there had never been her equal; and he endeavored to show her (beyond the nature of womankind) an Alexander, recounting some of her acts of liberality, which, so as not to waste time in anecdotes, I do not care to relate. Afterwards, he said that she was endowed with more natural good sense than perhaps any woman who has ever been known, and moreover that she was also most eloquent, perhaps no less so than any expert and flowery orator had ever been; and beyond this (which pleased me very much, since I fully believed those words), he said that she was charming and gracious and possessed of all those manners which are commendable and praiseworthy in a great gentlewoman. As this certain person narrated these things, I confess that I said silently to myself, 'O happy the one to whom Fortune is kind enough to grant the love of such a lady!'

"Since I had nearly made up my mind already to try and be the one who became worthy of that love, I asked her name, her station, and the whereabouts of her home (which is not the one where you left her), and he explained everything to me fully. For this reason then, when I left him, I firmly resolved to see her, and, if I found my judgment of her confirmed, to put all my efforts into making her my lady, as I would become her servant. Without putting off the matter, I went at once to that place where I believed I could find and see her at that hour; and Fortune (she who was never indulgent except in things which were to turn out badly for me) was so favorable in this regard that it turned out just as I intended. I will tell you a wondrous thing: although I had no other indication about her except the black color of her clothes, and though I was looking among many women who were there in the same clothing as she, I understood immediately as I glimpsed her face there where I first saw her, that she must have been the one I was seeking. Since it was always my opinion, and still is, that a love revealed is either filled with a thousand troubles or else cannot reach any desired result, I did not dare ask if it was as I believed, because I had firmly decided not to confide any of this to anyone in any way except to him to whom I opened all my secrets after I became his friend. But again Fortune (who was to be helpful in a few matters concerning this desire of mine) favored my second intention as she had my first —inasmuch as I heard some woman behind me chattering with her companions saying: 'Alas! Look how the white wimple and black weeds suit such-and-such a lady.' One of her companions, who chanced not to know this lady, asked her (causing me, with ears intent upon their words, so much pleasure that I could not express it!), 'Which one is she of all those who are there?' To which the lady who had been asked, replied, 'The third one seated on that bench is the one I am talking about.'

"From this answer, I understood that I had guessed correctly; and, from that hour, I knew who she was. I will not lie: when I saw her stature and, a little later, watched her walk a while, and con- sidered her gestures a little, I presumed (but falsely) not only that he, whom I had heard talking about her, must have spoken the truth, but that there must have been far more good in her than he had said.

"Thus completely deceived, I at once felt a fire rushing to my heart as if moved by the things I had heard and by the sight of her, just as a flame does on oily things. So fiercely did it burn me that anyone who had looked at my face would have seen an unmistakable signal; and as the signs brought to my face by the strange fire faded, this flame, which at first went licking at the outer parts, in the same way afterwards passed inward and became more intense; from then on, I felt it growing only inside.

"In this way, then, as I have recounted, I was trapped by her whom I had seen to my misfortune, because her appearance, full of wickedness and artful guile, gave me hope of future mercy."

The Spirit, who, I believe, had heard these things not without some amusement, hearing me fall silent, began to speak in this way: "You have clearly shown me how and why you were first ensnared and how you put around your own throat the chain which still constrains you. But I hope it will still not trouble you to explain to me if and how you ever revealed this love of yours to her (for I seem to have heard before that you did) and, afterward, to tell me whether you had from her any hope which enflamed you more than your own desire had done beforehand."

To this I replied, "Since I clearly know that if I wanted to conceal it from you I could not (since it seems to me that you hear the truth about my affairs from whatever source you get it), I will hide nothing from you. It is true, as I told you before, that since I had fully believed what that person had said who had shown her to be of such great worth, I plucked up courage and wrote to her, reasoning as follows: 'If what he says about her is true, according to reason one of two things should ensue if I reveal my love to her honorably in a letter: either she will hold my love dear and take it as fully as I can give it, and will tell me so in reply, or, she will hold it dear, but not wishing to take it, will discreetly discourage me.'

"Since I anticipated one of these two results (although I desired the first more than the second) in a letter of mine full of those words that one may honorably say about such a matter, I informed her of my ardent desire. In reply to this letter there followed a short

note from her in which, although she answered nothing openly concerning my love, she still made it clear, in words quite lamely
thrown together and looking like poetry (but which were not
poetry, since some feet were too long and the others too short), that
she desired to know who I was. And I will tell you more: she endeavored to show in this letter that she had some notion of a philosophical opinion, however false it may be. That is, that a soul passes
on from one man to another, something which I am sure she learned
during sermons and not out of a book or at school. In this letter,
comparing me to a worthy man, she showed by flattery that she
wanted to content me, affirming afterwards that she liked best those
men who possessed wisdom, prowess, and courtesy together with
ancient nobility. By that letter, or rather by its style, I understood
quite easily that the man who had told me so many things about her
had either been very much deceived about her natural intelligence
and flowery eloquence, or else he had wanted to deceive me.

"However, I could not for that reason even reduce in the slightest
the ardor that I had conceived, let alone extinguish it; and I decided
that what she had written had, for the time being, no other intent
than to give me courage to write again, and to give me hope for a
more specific reply than that one. From that note, I could understand that in affairs of this sort both experience and convention
pleased her. Although I did not feel myself endowed with those
qualities, having neither wisdom, prowess, nor nobility (as to courtesy, since my intentions were good, I needed only to practice it),
nevertheless, I was fully prepared to do everything in my capacity
to deserve her favor. As best I could, I assured her in a second letter
of the pleasure I had taken in the first I had received; but I did not
hear afterwards, either by any letter of hers or by any message, her
opinion of what I wrote."

Then the Spirit said, "If there were no further developments in
this love affair, what induced you when the day was over to desire
death so fervently for this—with so many tears and so much grief?"

In reply to this, I answered, "Perhaps it would be more proper
not to speak of it, but because I cannot refuse you, since you ask,

I shall tell you about it just the same. There were two things which had nearly led me to utter despair: one was the recognition that, whereas I believed I had some understanding, I realized I was almost a beast without intellect (and certainly this is something to be more than a little distressed over, considering that I have spent the best part of my life trying to learn something, only to find then, when the need arises, that I know nothing); the other was the way in which she went about revealing to someone else that I was in love with her; and for this I called her several times a cruel and wicked woman.

"In the first instance, I found I had acted stupidly in several ways, and above all in believing too easily, without seeing more of her, such lofty things of a woman as that person had told me, and afterwards, without seeing either where or how, for having entangled myself in the snares of love because of these things, and for having shackled and given my liberty and subjected my reason to the hands of a woman; for my soul, which used to be mistress when accompanied by these, without them became a vile servant. Neither you nor anyone else will deny that these things are something to grieve about until death.

"In the second place, in my opinion, she had done wrong in many ways and had quite clearly shown that the one who had so abundantly dwelled on her excellent virtues when speaking with me, had told brazen lies. Because, as I think I understood, she is in love with a man who is called 'the second Absalom' by his neighbors (not because he is, but because he thinks he is), she showed him my letter to make herself dearer to him, and with him mocked me as a fool. Furthermore, he too has already talked about it with others, making up a story about me just as he liked; and moreover, as true as I am standing here, he, in order to draw out the tale, was the one who had the answer to my letter (about which I told you before) written to me. Besides this, according to what I saw with my own eyes, she pointed me out with a sneer to several other women saying, I believe, 'Do you see that dolt? He's in love with me; look how lucky I can count myself!'

20

"Certainly both I and others know how honest were and are those ladies to whom she pointed me out, because, as must be understood, just as her lover tells tales about me among the men, so does she among the women. Ah! How shameful and improper for a man— not to say a gentleman, for such I do not consider myself, although I have grown up and have always associated with worthy men and am quite properly informed of the ways of the world, although not fully—to be pointed out by a woman to other women like a madman, first with her snout, then with her finger! I will tell the truth: this induced such indignation in my mind that I was often very close to using words that would have dishonored her; but since some small spark of reason still showed me that I would bring far greater shame upon myself than upon her by doing so, despite my great agitation, I restrained myself and was driven to that anger and sinful desire which you are asking me about."

The Spirit then remained thoughtful for a while, his face showing that he had grasped my words and meaning very well, and mumbled to himself I know not what before saying anything which I understood; then, turning to me, he began to speak in a very gentle voice, saying, "I believe I have understood full well from your words how you became enamored, and of whom, and the reason and cause of your despair. Now I hope you do not mind if I speak somewhat at length for the good of your own salvation and perhaps that of someone else; we will begin first with you, because you yourself were the origin of your own error, and from this we will come to speak of her with whom you foolishly fell in love, although you scarcely knew her. And lastly, if we have enough time, we will say something about the causes that brought you to so much grief that you almost went out of your mind.

"Starting with that which we have promised, I declare that many reasons may justly cause me and anyone else to reproach you; but so as not to seek out all the causes, I would like to touch on only two of them to shorten the discussion: the first is your age; the second is your studies. Each one of them in itself, and both together, should have made you cautious and circumspect about the traps of love. And first your age: if your temples already white and your grizzled beard do not deceive me, you, now some forty years out of swaddling clothes, should know the ways of the world—it is now twenty-five years since you began to learn them. If your long experience in the toils of love did not chastise you enough in your youth, at least the cooled blood of your years, now near to old age, should have opened your eyes and made you recognize the fall to which the pursuit of this mad passion was to lead you; and, moreover, it should have shown you whether you had sufficient strength to raise yourself again. Had you considered this affair reasonably, you would have realized that in battles of love women require young men, not those who are fading into old age, and you would have seen that empty flattery, highly desired by women, is ill-fitting for youths, let alone for those of your equal. How are dancing, singing, jousting, and arms suitable or proper to you now that you are mature—things of no consequence, but greatly pleasing to women? You yourself not only will say that they are unfitting for you, but with unquestionable arguments will censure even the youths that indulge in them.

"How is it proper at your age to go about at night, to disguise yourself, to hide anytime that a woman pleases, and not only where, perhaps less unseemly, you choose, but even where, unfittingly and shamelessly, the woman chooses, perhaps to glory in having an elderly man acting like a simple delivery boy? How is it fitting at your age, if necessity should require it (for the vicissitudes of love are very often full of necessity), to take up arms and defend your safety or perhaps that of your lady? Certainly I believe that you would answer likewise that all of them are wrong, without my continuing to cite any more cases. If it did not appear so to you, it would surely appear so to me and to everyone else who sees you with a more discerning eye than you chance to, being so handicapped. Your age, therefore, is now ill-suited for love affairs. At your time of life, it is proper not to follow passions, or to permit yourself to be vanquished at their approach, but to overcome them. With virtuous works which may increase your fame, it is your duty to set an excellent example to many young men cheerfully and sincerely.

"But we must come to the second part, something which makes love unbecoming in young men, let alone in the elderly, unless I am mistaken: that is, your studies. If I understood correctly before, while I was alive (and now I know it plainly to be the truth), you never learned any manual trade and always hated commerce; of this you have boasted many times to yourself and others, crediting your intellect, which is hardly suited to those things in which many grow old in years and in sense each day become younger. The first proof of this is that they think they know more than anyone else when their earnings turn out fairly well according to their calculations, or turn out well by chance, as most usually occurs; whereas in fact they are quite ignorant and know nothing beyond how many steps there are from the warehouse or from the shop to their home. And they think they have vanquished and confused everyone who would set them right about this when they say, 'Tell him to come and cheat me!' or when they say, 'I have it figured out before I go inside!' as if there were nothing to knowledge except either cheating or making money!

"Far more than your father would have wished, then, right from your childhood you liked studies pertaining to sacred philosophy, and especially that part dealing with poetry, which perhaps you have pursued with more fervor of spirit than with heights of genius. This, not the least among the disciplines, must also have shown you what love is, what women are, and who you are yourself and what your duties are.

"You must, therefore, have seen that love is a blinding passion of the spirit, a seducer of the intellect, which dulls or rather deprives one of memory, a dissipator of earthly wealth, a waster of bodily strength, the enemy of youth, and the death of old age, the parent of vices, and the inhabiter of inane breasts, a thing without reason or order, without the least stability, the vice of unhealthy minds, and the stifler of human liberty. Oh, are these not such manifold things that they should frighten not only the wise but the foolish?

"Turn over in your own mind ancient history and modern events and look how much evil, how much fire, how much death, how much destruction, how much ruin and slaughter this damnable passion has caused! And a host of you wretched mortals, among them you yourself, throwing away your judgment, call it a 'god' and, in need, make devout prayers to it and sacrifice your minds to it as if to the Highest Helper! You recall how many times you have done this already, or are doing it, or will do it—unless, perhaps, since you have taken leave of your right senses, you do not see by yourself that you are outraging God, your studies, and yourself. If your philosophy did not show you that the things I have said are true, and if you did not remember the experience of them, which, for the most part, you have had yourself, the wall paintings of the ancients will show you; these consistently reveal Love as a young, naked archer, with wings and blindfold, clearly symbolizing his effects.

"Moreover, your studies should have shown you (and did show you, had you wished to see it) what women are. Of these a great many call themselves and have themselves called 'ladies,' although very few are found among them. A woman is an imperfect creature excited by a thousand foul passions, abominable even to remember, let alone to speak of. If men considered this as they should, they would go to them in the same way and with the same desire and delight with which they go to any other natural and inevitable necessity; just as they hastily flee those places when their superfluous burden is released, so they would flee women, after they have done their duty to restore deficient human progeny (as do all other creatures who are far wiser in this than men!). No other creature is less clean than woman: the pig, even when he is most wallowed in mud, is not as foul as they. If perhaps someone would deny this, let him consider their childbearing; let him search the secret places where they in shame hide the horrible instruments they employ to take away their superfluous humors. But let us pass over whatever has to do with this subject. Since they are very well aware of it, they secretly consider any man a fool who loves them, desires them, or follows them; and they also know how to hide it in such a way

24

that it is neither known nor believed by many stupid men who consider only the outer shell; moreover, there are those who, while well knowing it, dare to say that they like it, and that they would do, and indeed do, thus and such. These are certainly not to be numbered among men!

"Let us come to the other faults of women, or at least to some of them, since to say everything the year, soon to begin again, would not be long enough for us. After they have reflected on their low and base condition, they put all their efforts into aggrandizing themselves with their abundant malice (which never makes amends for their fault, but always increases it). And first they set traps for men's liberty by painting themselves with a thousand ointments and colors, adding to that which nature has lent them in beauty or looks; and most of them make their hair, produced black from their pates, like spun gold, sometimes with sulfur, sometimes with rinse-waters, and most often with the rays of the sun. They arrange it in tresses behind their backs, now loose upon their shoulders, or now twisted upon their heads, depending on the way they think they look most charming; and then first with dances, then with songs, and sometimes (but not always) exposing themselves, with the hook hidden in the bait, they catch the wretches who happen along, and will not let them go. Thus, this woman and that one and countless numbers become the wives of this man, of that man, and of many—and mistresses of a far greater number.

"Thinking they have climbed to a high station, though they know they were born to be servants, they at once take hope and whet their appetite for mastery; and while pretending to be meek, humble, and obedient, they beg from their wretched husbands the crowns, girdles, cloths of gold, ermines, the wealth of clothes, and the various other ornaments in which they are seen resplendent every day; the husband does not perceive that all these are weapons to combat his mastery and vanquish it. The women, no longer servants but suddenly equals, seeing their persons and rooms adorned like those of queens and their wretched husbands ensnared, contrive with all their might to seize control. Wanting to make a special test to prove that they are the mistress of the house, they brazenly set about doing wrong, arguing that if what is not permitted to a servant is permitted to them, clearly they can be sure they are the mistress and ruler.

"At first they give themselves over to new fashions, to unwonted, no, even wanton frivolities, and to unseemly pomp; and no woman thinks herself either beautiful or worthy of consideration except insofar as she resembles the public prostitutes in her manners, her mincing, and her behavior. The latter cannot bring into the city clothes in such a number, so odd, and so indecent that they are not taken up by those women who are believed chaste by their stupid husbands, who, having ill-spent their money, allow these things to be used in the ways we have said so that it may not seem wasted, heedless of the target that arrow is meant to strike. How fierce women become at home because of this, the wretches know because they experience it; like swift and starving she-wolves come to occupy the patrimonies, property, and wealth of their husbands, hurrying now here, now there, they are in continual quarrels with servants, maids, factors, with their own husbands' brothers and children. Of the latter they pretend to be the tender guardians, whereas they really only desire to ruin them—moreover, so that they may appear loving to those for whom they care little, no sleep is to be had in their beds: each one spends the night arguing and quarreling, saying to her husband: 'I certainly see how much you love me; surely I'd be blind if I didn't notice that someone else is dearer to you than I! Do you think I'm fooled and that I don't know whom you're chasing, whom you're in love with, and whom you talk with every day? Of course I do; I've better spies than you think! Poor me! For it's been so long since I came here, yet you've never again said to me even once when I come to bed, "Welcome, my love." But, by the cross of God, I'll do to you what you're doing to me. Am I now so skinny? Am I not as beautiful as so-and-so? But do you understand what I'm saying? For one who kisses two mouths, one mouth must stink. Get over there! So help me God, you'll not touch me! Chase after those whom you deserve, for certainly you didn't deserve me; go show yourself for what you are. You'll get what's coming to you. Remember, you didn't drag me out of the mud! God knows who and what class of men they were who would have considered themselves lucky to have taken me without a dowry! I would've been lord and master of all they owned! And to you I gave so many gold florins! I could never even command a glass of water without a thousand reproaches from your brothers and servants; one would think I were their lackey! I was surely unlucky to ever have set eyes on you; may he who said the first word about it break a leg.'

"With both these and many such words, and many others more searing, they torment the poor wretches every night without any legitimate or just reason. There are countless numbers of men who chase away their fathers, some their sons, some who are divided from their brothers, and others who do not wish to see either their mother or their sisters in their house, and so they leave the field open to the lady victor. When the women see their possession settled, they turn all their attention to pimps and lovers. And let it be clear to you that she who seems most chaste and virtuous in this cursed multitude would rather have one eye than be content with just one man. And if two or three men were enough, it would be something; and perhaps it would be tolerable if these two or three were better than their husbands, or were at least their equals. Women's lust is fiery and insatiable and for this reason knows no discrimination or bounds: the servant, the workman, the miller, even the black Ethiopian, each is good provided he is up to it. I am certain that there would be those among them who would dare to deny this—as if one were unaware that while their husbands were away or else left sleeping in their beds, many have already gone to the public brothels in disguise! And they were the last to leave these places, tired but unsatisfied. What will they not dare to satisfy this bestial appetite of theirs? They pretend to be timid and fearful; and when their husbands ask them, they refuse to climb to any high place, however worthy the cause might be, for they say that they become dizzy; they refuse to go to sea because they say their stomach does not permit it; they refuse to go out at night because they claim they fear ghosts, spirits, and phantoms. If they hear a mouse in the house, or the wind moving a window, or a tiny stone falling from above, all of them shudder and their blood and strength flee them as if they were threatened by a mortal peril.

"However, they lend great courage to the shameful things they want to do. How many in the past have gone and go up yet to the tops of houses, palaces, or towers, called and awaited by their lovers? How many in the past have dared and dare every day to hide their lovers from their husbands' eyes under either hampers or chests? How many have had them enter silently into the same bed with their husbands? How many are constantly found following the one who performs best, alone, at night and amidst armies, even across the sea, and through church cemeteries? And, what is a greater disgrace, there are countless numbers who dare to take their pleasure even though their husbands are looking. Oh, how many children perish before they are born in those women who are most afraid or most blush for their disgusting faults! Thus the wretched savin is always found more peeled than other trees, although women have numberless other remedies for this. For the same reason how many babes, born in spite of their mothers, are cast into the arms of Fortune! Just look at the foundling hospitals! How many children are killed even before they have tasted their mothers' milk! How many of them are abandoned to the woods, how many to the birds and beasts! So many die such awful deaths that when all things are well considered, woman's least sin is to have followed her lecherous appetite.

"This execrable feminine sex is suspicious and bad-tempered beyond all comparison. Unless they are informed of it, nothing can be discussed with a neighbor, relative, or friend, without women's immediate suspicion that you are working against them to do them harm—although men ought not to wonder greatly at that, since it is natural always to fear from others the wrongs we do to them; and for this reason, thieves usually know how to hide their belongings well. Women's every thought, design, and action aim at nothing else but to rob, lord over, and deceive men, thoughtlessly believing that everything they do not know about contains similar plots against them. Because of this, they visit, summon, and cherish astrologers, necromancers, witches, and diviners; and the latter, in all their necessities, though using nothing but fables, are abundantly aided and sustained, even enriched by the property of the wretched husbands; and if from these, women cannot fully learn their husbands' intent, they contrive to guard themselves fiercely against their spouses (whom they very rarely believe, however much they tell the truth) with haughty and poisonous words.

"As instinctively as animals, they immediately fly into such a burning temper that tigers, lions, and snakes have more humanity when enraged than do women; the latter, whatever the cause for which they have lost their temper, run instantly for poison, fire, and sword. From this, no friend, relative, brother, father, husband, or any of her lovers is spared. In her anger each one would like nothing more than to throw into chaos, lay waste, and turn the whole world, the sky, God, and everything in the universe above and below at once into nothingness, than to be able, when she regained her composure, to use a hundred paramours for her pleasure. If time allowed us to continue narrating how many atrocities their fits of anger have caused, I have no doubt that you would declare it the greatest miracle ever seen or heard that God puts up with them.

"Moreover, this wicked band is extremely greedy. And setting aside the continual thefts from their husbands, and the robberies from their child-wards, and the extortions from those lovers who do not overly please them—most obvious and common matters— let us consider to what degradation they subject themselves in order to increase their dowries a little. They will refuse as a husband no slobbering old man with rheumy eyes and trembling hands and head, as long as they hear that he is rich, since they are certain that they will be widows within a short time, and since he does not have to satisfy them in the nest. Nor are they ashamed to submit, offer, and allow their limbs, hair, and face (made up with so much care), their crowns, graceful garlands, velvets, cloths of gold, their many ornaments, necklaces, trifles, and such dainties to be fondled by the paralytic hands and toothless, slavering, fetid mouth—and this is far worse—of him whom they believe they can rob. If his already dwindling nature grants him children, he has them in this way. If not, he cannot for this reason die without heirs! Others come, who make her belly swell; and even if nature has made it sterile, spurious pregnancies give him children so that, as a widow, she may longer live in lecherous pleasures at the expense of her ward. Only fortune tellers, flatterers, quacks, and groping fondlers in whom they take delight make them not merely courteous but prodigal; for these, women never show the least caution, thrift, or avarice.

"They are all fickle and without constancy whatever. In one hour they want and refuse a single thing at least a thousand times—unless it involves those things which have to do with lechery, since these they always want. As a rule, they are all presumptuous and pretend that for them everything is seemly and that nothing is too good, that they are worthy of every honor and all greatness, and that men are worthless and cannot exist without them; and they are grudging and disobedient!

"Nothing is harder to bear than a rich woman; nothing is more unpleasant than to see a poor woman become testy. Of the tasks imposed on them they only do those which they think will earn either ornaments or embraces. If they are obedient in anything beyond this, they feel they have been reduced to slavery; and, therefore, they are never willing to do anything they are supposed to except when the spirit moves them. Moreover, as at home as are the black tails in ermine, they are not only loud-mouthed, but boring. Wretched students suffer cold, fasting, and vigils, and after many years they find that they have learned very little. Women, even if they remain in church one morning just long enough to hear Mass, know how the firmament turns; how many stars there are in the sky and how big they are; what the course of the sun and the planets is; how thunder, lightning, hail, rainbows, and other things are created in the air; how the sea ebbs and flows; and how the land produces fruit. They know what is going on in India and Spain; how the homes of the Ethiopians are made, and where the source of the Nile is found; and whether crystal is generated in the north from ice or from something else; with whom their neighbor slept; by whom that other woman is pregnant and in what month she is to give birth; and how many lovers that other has, and who sent her the ring and who the belt; and how many eggs their neighbor's hen lays a year; and how many spindles she uses to spin an ounce of linen; and, in brief, they return fully informed about all that the Trojans or the Greeks or the Romans ever did. If they cannot find anyone else to lend them an ear, they chatter incessantly with the maid, the baker's wife, the green-grocer's wife, or the washerwoman, and become greatly put out if they are reproved for talking to any of them.

"It is true that from this so sudden and divinely inspired knowledge of theirs springs an excellent doctrine for their daughters. They teach them all how to rob their husbands, how to receive love letters and how to answer them, how to bring their lovers into the house, how to feign illness so that their husbands will leave the bed free for them, and many other evils. He who believes that any mother delights in having a daughter more honest or virtuous than herself is a fool. It does not matter if they must go to their neighbors to ask for a lie, a perjured oath, an evil deed, a thousand feigned sighs, or a hundred thousand false tears, for when they are necessary, women lend them. God knows where they keep them so ready and swift as they do for their every whim (for, as far as I am concerned, I could never begin to guess)!

"It is true, of course, that they are willing to let one of their defects be proven, and especially those that others see with their very own eyes, and don't they have ready their 'It wasn't like that! You're lying in your teeth! You're seeing things! You've left your brain at the menders! Try drinking less! You don't know where you are! Are you all right in the head? Even without a fever you're raving and rambling on nonsensically,' and other such little barbed words of theirs? If they say they have seen an ass fly, after many arguments to the contrary you will have to give in entirely; if not, mortal enmity, treachery, and hatred will immediately take the field. So brazen are they that they say straight off to anyone who belittles their intellect one jot, 'And weren't the Sibyls wise?'—just as if every one of them should be the eleventh! It is a wondrous thing that in so many thousands of years that have passed since the world was made, amid so great a multitude as has been that of the feminine sex, only ten wise and celebrated women have been found among them; and each one thinks she is either one of them or worthy to be numbered among them. Among their other vanities, when they wish to exalt themselves far above men, they say that all good things are of the feminine gender: the stars, planets, Muses, virtues, and riches. If it weren't indecent, to this you would only want to reply, 'It's quite true they're all feminine, but they don't piss!'

"Furthermore, they very often boast far more thoughtlessly, saying that She, in Whose womb was enclosed the sole and general Salvation of the whole universe, a Virgin before giving birth and after the birth a Virgin still, was a woman like them, along with a few others—not many, however—of whose virtue the Church of God makes special mention and solemn observance. For this, women imagine they must be respected, arguing that nothing can be said against them about their baseness which cannot be said against those others who were most saintly beings, as if they want the shield of their defense to remain in the arms of the latter, who resembled them in nothing but one thing. This, however, must not be granted, since that only Bride of the Holy Spirit was such an undefiled, virtuous being, so pure and full of grace, and so completely remote from every corporeal and spiritual uncleanness, that in respect to the others, it is as if She were not composed of natural elements but were formed of a quintessence fit to be the dwelling place and hostelry for the Son of God, Who, wishing to become flesh for our salvation, prepared Her for Himself *ab eterno* as a worthy abode for such and so great a King, in order not to come

32

and inhabit the pigsty of modern womanhood. If nothing else showed Her to have been separate from this vile crowd, Her ways, all so different from theirs, would show it. Similarly, Her beauty was not artificial, colored, or painted, and is now so great that it makes the angels in the Blessed Kingdom joyful to look upon it, and (if one may say so) it adds glory and wondrous delight to the blessed spirits. While Her beauty was here below in mortal limbs, it was never looked upon by anyone without having the opposite effect of that beauty which vain women strive to improve by painting themselves; because, while this beauty of theirs arouses and awakens the lustful appetite and indecent desire, that of the Queen of Heaven banished every base thought and every shameless desire from those who gazed upon Hers and so marvelously kindled them with a burning and charitable ardor for Good and for virtuous deeds that, devoutly praising Him Who had created it, they decided to put this well-kindled desire into action. From this, no vainglory or pride came to Her, but Her humility so grew from it and chanced to have such great strength that the incommutable decree of God hastened to send to earth His Son of Whom She was the Mother. The other few who strove to resemble this most reverend and true Lady with all their might, not only did not follow worldly pomp but fled it with supreme effort; neither did they paint themselves to appear more beautiful in the eyes of strange men, but despised the beauty Nature lent to them, awaiting that of Heaven. Instead of wrath and pride, they possessed mildness and humility, and overcame and vanquished the rabid fury of carnal desire with admirable abstinence by showing wondrous patience in torment and temporal adversity. Preserving their souls immaculate from these things, they were worthy to become companions in eternal glory of Her Whom they had striven to resemble in mortal life. And, if Nature, mistress of all things, could be justly accused, I would say that she had cruelly sinned against such women, subjecting and hiding such great spirits, so virile, so constant and strong within such base limbs and within such a vile sex as the female; because, if you well consider who these ladies were and who those are who wish to mingle in their number and be honored and revered among them, you will see quite well that the first group ill-matches the second, or rather, that they are completely opposite to one another. Let this depraved and adulterous band be silent, then, and let them stop decorating their chests with the honors of others, for certainly women like those of whom we have spoken are rarer than phoenixes. If any of them truly leaves the crowd, she merits much more honor than any man insofar as her victory and the miracle are greater. However, I do not believe that there was any need for our forefathers, not to mention ourselves, to trouble with honoring any of them for her merits; and I hope that they find black swans and white crows before there is any need for our successors to take the trouble to honor any more of them, because the footprints of those who followed the Queen of Angels are covered up, and our women have willingly lost the path; nor, of course, would they want it to be shown them again; and, even if anyone takes the trouble while preaching, ears close against his words like those of the asp at the sound of the charmer.

"Now I have not told you yet how greedy, reluctant, ambitious, envious, slothful, and raving this perverse multitude is; nor how imperious, wearisome, affected, nauseating, and importunate they are in having themselves waited on; nor many other things which could be recounted, far more unpleasant than the ones I have narrated; nor do I intend at present to tell you, for the tale would be far too long. But from what has been said, you must surely be able to understand what each and every one of them is like and into what a blind and dismal prison he falls who stumbles beneath their sway, whatever the cause may be. It seems to me quite certain that if any of them ever comes to hear the truth of their malice and defects which I have shown, they will be in no hurry to recognize themselves at once, or to feel ashamed at being recognized by others, or to reform themselves with all their strength and intelligence as they should; but, as is their custom, they will go scurrying to something still worse and will say that I speak these things not as a man of truth but as a man who dislikes them because he likes

34

his own sex. But would to God that I had always disliked women in the same way which I disliked that other abominable sin, since I would have gained much of the time which I lost running after them; and in the world beyond, where I am, I would suffer far less torment than the one I am bearing!

"Let us, however, turn to something else. Your studies at least should have shown you who you are, even if natural wisdom had not revealed it to you; and they should have reminded you and explained that you are a man made in the image and semblance of God, a perfect creature, born to govern and not to be governed. He Who had created man a little beforehand showed this clearly in our first father by placing all the other creatures before him and having him name them, and subjecting them to his dominion and by doing the same thing later with the one and only woman in the world, whose gluttony, disobedience, and persuasions were the cause and origin of all our miseries. Antiquity excellently preserved this order; and the present world still preserves it in the papacies, empires, kingdoms, principalities, provinces, peoples, and generally in all magistratures and priesthoods and other high positions, divine as well as human, by preferring and entrusting the government of all men and women to men only, and not to women. Anyone with judgment can see quite easily how valid and cogent an argument this is to show how greatly the nobility of man exceeds that of woman and of all other creatures. Not only from this can one, or must one, grasp that this ample privilege of nobility is merely granted to a few excellent men. No, rather, it will be understood that it belongs also to some who are inferior in respect to women and the other creatures, for it will be quite clearly recognized that the basest or lowest man in the world, who is not deprived of the good of his intellect, is worth more than that woman who is temporally considered more excellent than any other, inasmuch as she is a woman.

"A most noble thing, therefore, is man, who was made by his Creator a little lower than the angels. And if the least man is of so great account, of what worth must he be whose virtue has raised him above the others to some excellence? Of what worth must he be whom sacred studies, philosophy, have removed from the vulgar herd? From their number you have taken yourself by your intellect and studies, and, aided by the grace of God (which, when requested, is denied to no one who is deserving), have become worthy to mingle among the greatest. Why do you not know yourself? Why do you debase yourself in this way? How can you consider yourself of so little worth that you go and subject yourself to a wicked woman, foolishly believing about her something which never pleased her? For your sake I cannot console myself about it; and the more I think it over, the more it disturbs me. Rather than visiting the multitudes gathered in churches and other public places, it is fitting for you, and I know you are aware of it, to frequent solitary places, and there, by studying, working, and versifying, to exercise your intellect and to make an effort to better yourself, and, as best you can, to increase your fame more with deeds than words; for after that, salvation and eternal repose, which everyone who desires aright must want, are the goal of your long diligence.

"While you are in the woods and remote places, the Castalian nymphs, with whom these wicked women would compare themselves, will never abandon you. Their beauty, as I have heard, is celestial. Such beautiful ladies as these will neither shun you nor mock you; rather, they will enjoy lingering and journeying in your company. As you yourself know, who are acquainted with them far better than I, they will not put you to discussing or disputing how many cinders are needed to boil a skein of coarse flax, or whether linen from Viterbo is finer than that of Romagna, or whether the baker's wife has the oven too hot, or if the servant girl has left the bread to rise too little, or to see whether there are brooms to be had to sweep the house. They will not tell you what madam so-and-so, and madam such-and-such did the night before, or how many paternosters they said at the sermon, or whether it is better to change the ornaments on some dress or other than to leave them as they are. They will not ask money for cosmetics, powder boxes, and ointments. With angelic voice, they will narrate to you the things which have been from the beginning of the world down to this day; and, sitting with you upon the grass and flowers in the delightful shadows beside that spring whose last ripples will never be seen, they will show you the causes of the variations of the weather, the toils of the sun and the moon, what hidden power nourishes the plants and also tames brute animals, and from what place rain down the souls into men. They will show you that Divine Goodness is eternal and infinite, by what steps one rises to it, and down what precipices one plunges to the opposite place. After they have sung with you the verses of Homer, Virgil, and other worthy ancients, they will sing your own, if you wish. Their beauty will not arouse indecent ardor in you, but will banish it; and their ways will be irreproachable teaching for virtuous works.

"Why then, being able to have such companionship whenever you wish, and as much as you wish, do you go searching beneath the mantles of widows, or rather, beneath those of devils, where you might easily find something which would disgust you? Ah, how just would it be for these most distinguished ladies to banish you as unworthy from their most beautiful chorus! How often do your desires turn to women! How often, on leaving them, fetid, corrupted, and unashamed of your bestiality do you go again to mingle with those who are most pure! Certainly, if you do not stop this, it seems to me that it will happen to you, and deservedly so. Indeed, they have their scorn just as do those others who are called 'ladies'—although they are not. And how shameful it would be for you, were this to occur, you can be quite sure.

"However, since I think that I have said enough about those things which you should have considered when you subjected yourself foolishly to the unbearable yoke of that woman who thinks herself a great savante, and so that you may not think her different from the others, I intend to show you in detail something besides that which I promised you, which you could not see well for yourself: who she is, and what are the habits of this woman over whom you are now in misery for having foolishly become her servant. You will

see where and into whose hands your sin and your overly rash gulli-
bility led you.

"Our marriage brought me the first news of this woman we are
talking about—whom more correctly I could call a dragon. Since I
was left alone by the death of my first wife (with whom I was far
less unhappy than with this one), it happened, I know not whether
caused by my sin or by heavenly influence, that I was married once
again to her whom I scarcely knew, this marriage being both the
will and pleasure of my friends and relatives. Just like all the rest
of her kind, she, who had already been the wife of another and
had learned the art of trickery very well, entered my home like
a tame and simple dove, but (so that I do not go into too much
detail) no sooner did she see her chance to reveal the secret treachery which she perhaps had kept long hidden, than she changed at
once from a dove into a serpent. From this I realized that my gentleness, which I had shown too meekly, was most certainly the
cause of all my ills. I must confess: for a while I tried to bridle this
unruly creature, but all my efforts were in vain because the evil was
already so deeply rooted that it was easier to bear it than to cure it.
Thus, realizing that everything I did about it was only adding wood
to the fire or oil to the flames, I bowed my shoulders, entrusting
myself and my affairs to Fortune and to God.

"Therefore threatening, clamoring, and sometimes beating my
family, she ran through my house as if it were her own, becoming
a fierce tyrant in it although she had contributed to it but a small
dowry. Whether I had or had not done something just the way she
wanted it, exaggerating lavishly and profusely, as if I were from
Capalle and she of the House of Swabia, she would begin to reproach me with the nobility and magnificence of her family—
just as if I did not know who her people once were and still are at
present—although I am quite certain that she knows nothing else
about them except for the fact that she, out of vanity, I believe,
often goes around counting the shields hung in churches, and
argues from their age and number that she is of the noblest blood
and more, since there were so many knights among her ancestors.

38

But if there had been hung a single shield for ten evil men of her clan (more fortunate in increasing their number than in any honor or worth), and one shield (as well fitting to her as a saddle on a pig!) removed for each of the chivalrous, I have not the slightest doubt that where hundreds of shields of the wicked would appear, not one of the knights' would be seen. Bestial fools (among whom she is an even greater beast than the elephant!) believe that knighthood consists of ermine-lined vestments, of a sword, of gilded spurs (things which every little artisan, every poor workman can easily obtain), of a scrap of cloth, and of a tiny shield to have hung in the church after death—whereas it actually consists of those who nowadays call themselves knights and not of anything else. But the man knowledgeable about matters concerning knighthood and about the reasons for which it was founded knows how far these fools (more hostile to all of these things than the devil to crosses) are from the truth.

"Starting out, then, with this stupid self-conceit and arrogance (though I still hoped—in spite of the fact that I had laid down my arms like a coward, considering it the lesser evil—that she might sometime repent and cease the tyranny she had assumed), she went so far that, whereas I believed I had brought peace and tranquility into my home, I realized too late that I had brought war, fire, and bad luck upon it, and began to wish that it would burn down. Anywhere in our city, however full it was of quarrels and disputes, began to seem quieter and more peaceful to me than my house; and so when I saw nightfall forcing me to return, I became dejected, as if some tiresomely strict and powerful warden had forced me into a dark and dismal prison.

"Therefore, having become complete mistress of both me and my property, she first imposed her own rule on how we lived and how extravagantly, not as reason would have had it, considering my position, but as her excessive appetite required. She acted likewise in what she wore—not wearing what I bought for her, but making dresses just as she pleased. Over whatever holdings of mine she had control, she had to check the accounts and take the produce and distribute it as she liked. Highly insulted because I did not make her my treasurer and guardian as soon as she wanted over a certain amount of money in my possession, until she got what she wanted, she reproached me a thousand times for being suspicious, especially of her, and praised herself, on the other hand, as having more loyalty than Fabricius or whatever other loyal men there have ever been.

"Since I do not want to narrate everything in fine detail—she challenged me over countless matters, and never laid down her arms after any of these battles except as victor. I, wretch that I am, not very shrewd in this, became meeker than usual and followed her will, believing that by suffering I was easing my anxiety and anguish. To my bitter pain, that lukewarm apathy is now warmed by the vermilion garment you see me wearing, as I have told you before.

"But we must proceed further. Since, in this way, I had become the servant and she the mistress, seeing no resistance against her, she began to show and put into practice more brazenly the lofty virtues that your friend told you about with such solemnity. But since he was not so closely familiar with them as I was, I would like to recount them to you in more orderly fashion.

"To begin from the beginning, I affirm by the sweet world which I await (and I hope that it may be granted to me soon) that in our city there is not, nor has there ever been, nor will there ever be a lady, or woman (as we intend to put it, and will do so more correctly) whose vanity was so great that the vanity of her about whom we are speaking would not greatly surpass it. Because of this, thinking she wanted her cheeks nicely puffed and red, her buttocks ample and protruding (having heard perhaps that these things were most highly prized in Alexandria and for that reason were a very great part of the beauty of a lady), above all else she strove to make these two features abundantly conspicuous in herself. This she did through efforts made at my expense, for sometimes I fasted in order to save.

"First, if there was a plump capon (many of which she had fattened up with great diligence), it had to be set before her cooked; and also *pappardelle* with Parmesan cheese, which she did not eat from a bowl but from a basin, like a pig, as ravenously as if she had just then escaped from a long fast in the Tower of Famine. About the milk-fed veal, the partridges, the pheasants, the fat thrushes, the turtledoves, the Lombard soups, the lasagne cooked in broth, the elderberry fritters, the white chestnut cakes, and the blanc-manges of which she had the same bellyfulls as peasants do of figs, cherries, or melons when they are placed before them, I do not care to tell you. Aspics, salt meat, or anything else vinegary and bitter were her mortal enemies because they are said to be drying. I am certain that if I told you what an impressive taster and bibber of fine mulled wine she was, of *vernaccia da Corniglio* and of *greco* and of whatsoever other fine, sweet, and palatable vintages, you would not believe it because you would think it was impossible to believe about Cinciglione. However, if you had seen her cheeks when I was alive, and if you had heard her chatter a while, perhaps you might easily believe me; in fact, you would think you had understood by her words alone, without my saying anything. And fully did she succeed in becoming plump-cheeked and big-bottomed. I do not know if she has slimmed them down because of the many fasts that she underwent for my salvation after my death; but even if she had done so before your eyes, and if I had to lay odds from what you saw, I would not believe it."

With all the grief and compunction that I felt for my sins which the truthful words of the Spirit had made clear to me, at these words I declare that I could not restrain my laughter.

But he continued without changing expression, "Nor was my dear lady, rather your dear lady—no, rather, the devil's—content merely to have a lot of flesh, but she wanted it shining and clear, as if she were a prize damsel about to be married, who had to bolster up a small dowry with beauty. To bring this about, after her cure of eating well, drinking well, and dressing well, she became extremely intent on distilling, making ointments, finding various animal fats, herbs, and other such things; and not only was my house full of stoves, retorts, pots, vials, shrubs, and powder boxes, but in addition there was no apothecary nearby in Florence, or any gardener in the countryside, who was not kept busy, the first making sublimated quicksilver, purifying verdigris, and producing a thousand lotions, and the others going to search and fetch wild roots and herbs, never heard of except by her; and what is more, even the bakers were troubled with cooking eggshells, wine dregs, pottery glaze, and a thousand other strange things. After she had smeared and painted herself with these concoctions as if she had to go and sell herself, often it would happen that, not being on my guard while I kissed her, my lips got all caught in the glue; and better sensing that greasy mess with the nose than with the eyes, not only did I have trouble keeping down the food in my stomach, but could scarcely retain the soul in my breast.

"Now, if I told you with how many kinds of lye she washed her golden locks and about the amount of ashes with which they were made, some fresher and some less so, you would marvel—and far more so if I sketched for you the various kinds of rituals she used in going to the steam baths, and how often she went to those places—from which I used to believe that she would come back clean, and from which she came back even greasier than before. Her utmost desire and favorite pastime were certain old biddies, of whom there are a great many around our city, who go about peeling other women, plucking their eyelashes and brows, shaving their cheeks with thin glass, smoothing the hide on their necks, and removing little whiskers; nor was there ever a time when two or three were not found in close consultation with her, for often they had other agreements, because, in addition to their profession (under whose title they boldly visit other people's wives and houses), they are excellent madams and go-betweens for enabling Master Shaft to re-enter the Obscure Valley from which he had been chased after many tears.

"It would require more than a week to tell everything that she did to this end, so much did she glory in that artificial loveliness, nay, repulsiveness of hers, to whose preservation she devoted far too much industry, for if the sun, air, day, night, fair weather and foul did not turn out fully to her liking, they offended her terribly; dust, wind, and smoke she hated with a vengeance. If, when she had finished washing, by some misfortune a fly were to land on her face, there was such uproar and pandemonium that in comparison the loss of Acre was a delight for the Christians.

"I will tell you about one of her lunacies, the like of which has perhaps never been heard. It happened (among other times that a fly landed on her glazed face) that one landed there after she had used a new type of make-up; outraged, she strove several times to strike it with her hand, but it took off swiftly—you know how they do—and kept coming back, so that, unable to catch it and completely enraged, she took a broom and went chasing it, rushing first here, then there, all over the house to kill it. It is my firm opinion that if at last she had not killed either that one or another which she thought was that one, she would have exploded with anger and venom. What do you think she would have done if one of the shields and gilded swords from one of those ancient knights of hers had come into her hands? Certainly she would have set about the fray with that! And what else? This used to happen during the day when you could bear it with less irritation; but if by a great misfortune a mosquito were heard around the house at whatever hour of night it might have been, the footman, the maid, and all the rest of the household had to get out of bed, and with lights in hand, begin the search for the wicked and perfidious mosquito, the disturber of the repose, peace and quiet of the lady-in-make-up; and before they went back to sleep, they had to present it dead or alive to her who said that it was humming to spite her and lying in wait to ruin her fine, lovable face.

"What more? Above all else, to anyone who was not concerned in these matters, it was a laughable thing to have seen her when she adorned her head—with what art, diligence, and care it was done; on that verily hung the law and the prophets. In her younger years (perhaps she does not add very well, since she admitted to twenty-eight, although she was closer to forty than thirty-six), she would arise very early and summon her maid. Let us omit April and May —but in December and January, she would first ready six species of green plants or as many flowers from wherever she procured them, and out of them make some of those little garlands of hers. Then when she had rubbed her face, throat, and neck thoroughly with various preparations and had put on those clothes which were closest to her heart, sitting herself down in some part of our room, she first placed before her a mirror and sometimes two so that she could clearly see herself in them from every side and know which of them reflected her appearance less accurately. Here, on one side, she would have the maid stand, and, on the other, she would have perhaps six little vials, some thin glass, resin, and other such nonsense. After she had had herself diligently combed and had twisted her hair upon her head, she placed on top of it a certain tangle of silk which she called her 'tresses,' and attached it with a net of the finest silk; having been handed the appropriate garlands and flowers, placing these first on her head and distributing little blossoms everywhere, she would deck out her head just as she had sometimes seen a peacock's tail painted with eyes; nor did she fasten any of them without consulting her mirror.

"But when her age became too obvious, and her hair which had begun to turn white (although she constantly had many plucked out) required veils, then, just as she used to take the herbs and flowers, she filled her lap with those and filled her bosom with small pins and with the help of her maid began to veil herself.

"Each time she would say to the girl, with, I think, a thousand rebukes, 'This veil was a bit yellowed; this other hangs too much to this side; make this other come further down! Make that one covering my forehead tighter! Take away that little pin which you have put over my ear and place it a little more over there; and make a narrower pleat in that one which is to go under my chin; take that piece of glass and remove that little hair on my cheek under my left eye!'

"If her maid carried out a single one of these commands and many others not quite in the way she wanted, chasing her off, she would curse the girl a hundred times saying: 'Off with you! You are only fit to wash dishes. Go! Call madam so-and-so for me.' At the latter's arrival, she tidied herself all over again; and after all this, wetting her fingers with her tongue, she preened herself like a cat, now here, now there, returning first this hair, then that one to its place; and from then on, she looked at herself in the mirror perhaps fifty times, sometimes from the front, sometimes from the side, and, as if positively delighted with herself, she could hardly tear herself away. But nevertheless, she had the good woman look at her several times, and would question her with care, asking if she were tidy and whether anything were amiss, just as if her reputation or life depended upon it. When she had heard many times that everything was all right, she joined her friends who were waiting for her, again asking advice about it even from them. Of course, I know that one could say that this is nothing strange, either in her or in other women; and I am certainly not telling it as something strange, but rather as something disgusting, corrupt, and evil, in order to show that her habits are no different from those of the others, and so that you may more readily believe the results of these habits when I tell you them as I shall soon.

"To anyone who might have asked why she fussed so much over her make-up, even more sinful than other women, she would quickly reply that she did it to be more attractive to me—adding that with all this she could not do enough to please me and prevent me from leaving her and chasing after the servant girls, scullery maids, and low, evil women. But of course she was lying brazenly about this, for I did not chase after the scullery maids; and she cared very little whether she pleased me or not. Rather, as I noticed several times, when any youth or any other man even slightly good looking passed in front of the house, or wherever she was, just as when a falcon's hood is removed, it preens and turns its gaze upon itself, so did she, so eager was she to be looked at. If anyone passed by without looking at her, she became as deeply disturbed as if she had been greatly insulted. And if, having looked at her, someone chanced to praise her beauty and she heard him, there was such great reveling and such great joy that nothing could ever equal it; nor was there anything that fellow could have asked which she would have done more than quickly and willingly if she could. But if, on the contrary, he criticized her, she would gladly have killed him with her own hands. She would listen more eagerly than any of her sex to such things as songs, serenades, and *mattinate;* and she held the greatest grudge against any woman for whom, or for whose love, they were composed and sung, because she wanted all of them to be dedicated to herself, thinking she was far more worthy of that honor and everything else than any other woman.

"In order to say no more about this subject, I declare that these are the elegant and praiseworthy habits, and the great intelligence and marvelous eloquence of the woman about whom your friend told you, ill aware of the facts. This was her great constancy and her lofty strength of courage. This was the great diligence and continual care which she had for decency, as women of nobility (among whom she wished to be counted) must have, and for which she must be deservedly remembered among ancient worthy ladies when they are mentioned. After a few words, you will hear a little about her generosity, for which she was compared to Alexander. With this vanity and exquisite elegance of hers (if one should call 'elegance' dressing like a buffoon and adorning herself like those who have to please countless numbers in a short space of time, yielding themselves for any price, and being accommodating with her eyes, and more talkative than ladylike reserve requires), she had acquired herself many lovers, who did not find the race for her favors like the Palio, in which only one of the crowd wins; no, rather, of the crowd, many reached the desired end, as she arranged it. Not only could I not satisfy her burning lust, nor one lover, nor two besides me, but a multitude were not sufficient to quench a single tiny spark of it. I have not spoken to you about this, nor do I intend to speak about it at length, since it would be the wrong medicine for the illness which I have come to cure, for I know that men who desire women's affection take greater hope and, in consequence, add more fuel to their love, the more they hear of women's ardor.

46

"Touching briefly on this subject, then, I declare that just as I formerly suspected, I now know for a fact that she is in love with a certain nobleman of the world, in the past more courageous than fortunate, whose weight she has already felt many times, and whose intimacy she has enjoyed just as she did my marriage debt with no regard at all for her honor or for mine. Nor was it enough for her to give merely herself to him; but in order to show her generosity (as your friend said, she was generous), she helped him once, twice, then several times, not with her own property but with mine, first with a horse, then with a suit of clothes, and again with a good deal of money were he in very great straits; so that whereas I thought I had a treasurer, I had a waster, a squanderer, and a spendthrift. Since neither my rightful love was enough for her, nor that which she chose as she pleased, she added a certain neighbor of mine (for whom I bore more affection than he respect for me) to satisfy her fiery appetites. Although first I, then each of these in turn, poured cooling water upon her flames, she nevertheless tied herself in closer bonds with one of her relatives; and I think it is best not to mention several others now known to me whom she wanted to test in arms-bearing and in hitting the quintain, because it seems to me that I have said too much. By lending a helping hand to each one in these matters, by paying go-betweens, and by spending money on tasty morsels and make-up, did your bizarre lady show the distinguished generosity revealed to you by your friend. Since I want to go on to her other splendid and singular virtues in the manner I have adopted, I will perform two tasks at once while I tell you about them, for I will also show you how one must understand what she means by the words 'what she likes' which she used in her letter to you and which you perhaps did not understand very well.

"The sequence required that I deal with her courtesy, which she distinguishes from her generosity: the latter signifying the use of things by giving them or by throwing them away, and the former the use of oneself when saying 'yes' freely to anyone who asks for love. In this she was certainly not merely courteous, but most obliging—provided it was someone who had the daring to ask. Although her appearance was imperious, many of these were nevertheless undaunted; and things turned out well for them. By 'well' I mean in reference to their desires, for by virtue of their request, they immediately got what they wanted. Thus she rightly says that she likes courtesy (just as one who could never refuse courtesy when she was the one to be asked, would wish that no one else refuse it to her now that she is reaching the age when she will have to ask). I am really amazed that something which was never before denied to anyone, was denied to you; nor can I see anything behind it but, I believe, God's love, because He had denied to you something which you should have avoided as you would avoid Hell had it been asked of you! Therefore, if you had understood another type of courtesy from reading her letter, you have now understood what kind she means.

"A very wise lady, indeed, is this lady of yours; and since like attracts like, as a first principle you must believe that wise people please her, just as she says in her letter. But, as you know, the things for which men and every other person are generally called 'wise' are varied. Some are called wise because they understand God's Scripture thoroughly and can teach others; others because they can give excellent counsel concerning civil and ecclesiastical questions, being very learned in laws and decretals; others because they are experienced in the government of the republic, know how to avoid danger, and follow useful policies in time of need; some are considered wise because they can well manage their warehouses, their merchandise, their craft, and their household affairs, and know whether or not to delay according to the changes in the times. I do not mean you to understand that she is wise in any of these or many more praiseworthy ways that one could enumerate, because she does not care about Holy Scripture, philosophy, laws and statutes, public or private management, or anything like that; for if you had understood it in this way, you would not properly comprehend the wisdom in which, according to her letter, she delights. There is another class of wise people which you perhaps never heard recorded among the philosophical sects at school, and this is called the 'Cianghelline sect.' Just as those who followed the doctrine of Socrates were called 'Socratics' and those who followed that of Plato, 'Platonists,' the new sect has taken its name from a great and worthy lady, whom you may have heard mentioned many times, called Madam Cianghella. Her opinion was taken as conclusive after a long and serious debate in the Council of Ladies of Discretion: that all those women who have daring and courage, and can find the way to be with as many men as often as their lecherous appetites require, are to be called 'wise' and all the others 'stupid and silly.' This then is the wisdom which delights and pleases her; this is the wisdom which she has pursued many years with long vigil, and in which she has become wise and expert beyond any Sibyl. Meanwhile, since Madam Cianghella is no longer alive, nor Madam Diana who succeeded her, there have been many discussions between this woman and some of her associates concerning who most worthily should hold the chair of their school. This is that wisdom with which she would like to see every man and woman be wise, or learn to be so; therefore, be deceived no longer if you understood wrongly, and believe your friend, assured that she is wise!

"It seems to me to be certain that just as you misunderstood the two things spoken of above, so likewise you fell into error over the third thing, something about which she was always exceedingly delighted—that is, to see men full of prowess and vigor. I believe you thought she liked, wanted, or desired the sight of brave and vigorous men jousting with iron-tipped lances, or in bloody battle amid a thousand mortal perils, or besieging cities and castles, or, with sword in hand, killing each other. This is not the case. She is neither so cruel nor so treacherous as you seem to believe, that she loves men so that they kill each other. And what would she do with the blood which gushes forth red as a man dies? Her thirst is for the refinèd kind that living, healthy bodies can render without needing to have it back again. That prowess which she likes, then, no one knows better than I. It is not used in public squares, or in fields, or upon city walls, or breast plates on, or with basinet upon the head, or with any slashing sword; it is used in the boudoir,

49

in hidden places, beds, and similar locations suited to it, where without the coursing of horses, or the sound of brass trumpets, one goes to the joust at a slow pace. And she considers him to have the prowess of either Lancelot, Tristram, Roland, or Oliver, whose lance does not bend for six, eight, or ten jousts in one night in such a way that it is not then raised again. She loves such men as these above everything else, even if they have a face like the Saracen of the Piazza; she finds these exceedingly attractive and praises them beyond measure. Therefore, if the years have not sapped your usual strength, you should not, as you did, despair of pleasing her with your prowess, believing that she wished you to be, perhaps, Morold of Ireland.

"Her nobility, of which she says she likes the ancient kind, has already in part been spoken of; in this I assure you that, although according to what I have shown she may have indeed made clear what she likes about the preceeding things, about this she does not know what to say, because she has no idea of gentility—what it is, from where it proceeds, or who one should or should not call noble —except that she wishes to show herself noble and therefore, as a noble woman, desires and loves noble things. The vainglory and ostentation that she takes in this nobility of hers is so great that, in truth, it would be excessive for those of Bavaria, the royal house of France, or for any others, if any others are known to be more ancient or whose deeds to be more glorious.

"But of course if she wishes to show herself an ancient gentle-woman by demonstrating her liking for ancient nobility (the first of these she can show at once nowadays with her face alone, without any words—that is, that she is ancient—that she is either a lady or a noblewoman, I do not believe she could ever show) she had to write to you that she likes great speakers, inasmuch as she speaks more than anybody else; and I tell you that she chatters so much, that it alone would help the moon bear its toil far more than did all the cymbals of the ancients put together. Not to mention the great and lofty boasting that she indulges in when she gossips with the other women, saying, 'Those of my house, and my ancestors, and my relations. . . .' This seems to her a very fine thing to talk about; and she is totally overjoyed when she sees that they are listening to her and she hears herself say, 'Lady so-and-so of such-and-such,' and sees a circle forming around her. In a brief space of time she will tell you what they are doing in France, what the King of England is commanding, whether the Sicilians will have a good harvest or not, if the Genoese or the Venetians will bring back spices from the East and how much, whether Queen Giovanna slept last night with the King, and what the Florentines are arranging for the state of the city (although this could be quite easy for her to find out were she to dally with one of those in power, who keep secrets in their breasts as well as a basket or sieve holds water); and she will tell so many other things besides these, that it is a miraculous thing to imagine where she gets all that breath.

"Certainly if it is true what those physicians say, that that member, which the brute animals, birds, and fish exercise most, is most pleasing to the taste and most healthful to the stomach, no mouthful should ever be more tasty and better than her tongue, which never leaves off chattering, never slackens, and never stops: yak, yak, yak from dawn to dusk! Even at night, I declare, when she is sleeping it cannot cease. Anyone who might not know her, hearing her talk about her integrity, her devotion, her piety, and her family, would surely think her a saint and of royal lineage; and on the contrary, for anyone who does know her, hearing her the second time (and sometimes for the first) is enough to make him want to vomit his soul. To disapprove of her stories and lies, of which she has a greater store than any other woman, would be the same as wanting to fight with her—this she would do at the drop of a hat, because she thinks she excels Galehaut of the Distant Isles or Febus in bravery. Many times in the past she has boasted that, if she had been a man, she would have given her heart to surpass not only Marco Bello in strength but also Bel Gherardino who fought with the bear.

"Why am I dwelling on this? If I wanted to tell everything or even the most notable of her deeds, there would not be enough time for it. If you have as sharp an intellect as I believe, you can understand quite well, even from those things you have heard, exactly what her habits are like, and of what her great virtues, generosity, wisdom, and other qualities are comprised, and what those virtuous women might be in whom she takes delight. Therefore, without further talk of these, I shall return to something which you cannot have known—and to something of which you yourself happen to have great esteem: that is, the secret parts covered by her clothes, which, to your good fortune, you never saw. (Would that I had never seen them either!) I hope that listening to me will not upset you.

"However, before going on, I wish to dispel a thought, which perhaps you have had or could have in the future, by settling one objection which you could make. You perhaps have said to yourself, or might say, 'What is it this fellow is talking about? What way is that to talk? What words are these to use?' Or, 'Are they fitting to anyone, not to mention an honorable man, and one who has his steps directed toward eternal glory?' Since I do not want to keep on quibbling, there is but one response to this objection, which, I am certain you will readily agree yourself, is not only good but also appropriate. You must know, therefore, that a shrewd doctor cannot always heal every illness or every patient with sweet-smelling ointments, since there are many illnesses and many patients who do not respond to these and who require foul-smelling remedies if they wish to be led back to health; and if there is any sickness which one may wish to purge and cure with foul words, arguments, and demonstrations, ill-conceived love in man is one of them, because in a short time a foul word has more effect on the scornful intellect than a thousand decent and pleasant persuasions poured into the deaf heart through the ears over a great length of time. And if ever anyone was corrupted with this putrid, vile malignancy, certainly you are he. Therefore I, who have come here for your salvation as Another willed, have had recourse, and still do, to the quickest remedies, because I do not have much time; and thus to sweeten your disordered appetite, I have to dwell even more extensively on things such as you have heard because these words spoken thus are the pincers with which one must break and cut the hard chains which have dragged you here; and these words thus spoken are the reaping hooks and the hatchets with which one chops down the poisonous shrubs, the spiny thornbushes, and the twisted brushwood which have massed in a hedge before you to prevent your seeing the way out. These words thus spoken are the hammers, the picks, the battering rams which must break the lofty mountains, the hard rocks, and the precipitous cliffs to make a road for you by which you may leave unhindered so great an evil, so great an outrage and peril of so deadly a place as is this valley.

"Therefore, endure hearing them patiently; nor let it appear to bother your sense of decency; nor consider what is caused by your own pernicious sickness to be the sin, defect, or indecency of the physician. Imagine that these words of mine, so filthy, so sickening to hear, are that bitter draught which the shrewd doctor has given you in times past during your bodily illnesses because you had indulged too much in things which delighted and pleased your taste; and think that if to heal the corruptible body those bitter remedies not only are withstood, but are administered even against the will of the patient, what kind of bitter dose must one suffer to cure the soul, which is an eternal thing?

"I think that I must have satisfied you quite fully concerning something which might have made you doubtful, or could have in the future, about my style and about the words of my speech. Therefore, as I return to the subject, and since I want to tell in some detail about certain matters concerning this woman who recently became the possessor of your soul (those things, I mean, that could not be known to you by sight or that you could not even imagine, since you escaped them), I would like to begin first with that beauty. So well did her skills avail her that this dazzled and deceived not only you but also many others less smitten than you: that is, concerning the freshness of her facial complexion, which, being artificial yet looking like morning roses, was considered natural by many others along with you. But if it had been possible for you and for the other fools to have seen it, as it was possible for me, when she got out of bed in the morning before she put on her make-up, you would easily have realized your error. When she arose from her bed of a morning, she had (and today I believe has more than ever) a face green and yellow, discolored with the hue of swamp-fumes, knotted like molting birds, wrinkled and encrusted and all sagging, so different from the way it looked when she had time to preen herself that one could scarcely believe it had he not seen it as I did a thousand times in the past. Who is not aware that smoke-grimed walls, not to speak of women's faces, become white when white-wash is applied to them, and what is more, become colored according to whatever the painter chooses to put over the white? Who does not know that by kneading, dough, which is an insensible thing, not to speak of living flesh, swells up and rises whereas it had seemed musty? She rubbed herself and painted herself so much and made her skin, which had sagged during the stillness of the night, swell up enough that to me, who had seen her beforehand, it seemed an unnatural wonder. If you had seen her, as I saw her most mornings, with her nightcap pulled down over her head, with the little veil around her throat, so swamp-faced, as I have just said, sitting on her haunches in her lined mantle, brooding over the fire, with livid rings under her eyes, coughing and spitting great gobs of phlegm, I have not the least fear that all her virtues, of which your friend spoke, would have had as much power to make you fall in love with her once as seeing that would have made you fall out of love a hundred thousand times. What she must have been like when the Pisans rode with red on their lances with her head swathed up tight and alleging a headache, whereas the pain was at the other end, you may imagine. I am quite certain that if you had seen her like that or saw her when you said that the flames rushed from her face to your heart at the sight of her as they do on oily things, you would have thought you had met up with a load of dung, or a mountain of manure, from which you would have fled, as you do from something disgusting; and you would flee it still, and will flee it, if you reflect on the truth I am telling you.

"However, we must go on. You saw her big and sturdy; and it seems as certain to me as the beatitude which I await that, looking at her bosom, you judged it to be just as firm as you saw her face, without having seen the sagging wattles that her white wimple hides. But your judgment is far, far from the truth. And although as experts many could give true testimony to what I say, I hope that without further witnesses you will believe it from me who perhaps had longer experience of it, since I was unable to do anything else. Be assured that there is no tow or any other padding in that swelling which you see above her belt, but only the flesh of two puffed and blighted plums, which were once perhaps two unripe apples, delightful to both the touch and sight—although I do believe that she brought them thus misshapen from her mother's body; but let us pass over this. They—whatever the cause may be, either because they were pulled too much by others, or because their own excess weight stretched them—are so beyond measure lengthened and dislocated from their natural position that perhaps (or rather, without doubt) if she let them droop, they would reach her navel, empty and wrinkled like a deflated bladder; and certainly if things such as these, like the hoods they wear in Paris, were in vogue in Florence, to be fashionable she could toss them over her shoulders *à la française!* And what more? Her belly more or less corresponds to her cheeks, pulled taught by her white wimple; lined with thick, wide furrows like a young she-goat, it looks like an empty bag, sagging just like the empty skin that hangs from the chin to the chest of an ox; and perhaps no less than the other pieces of cloth, she must raise it aloft whenever she wishes to empty her bladder obeying natural necessity, or, following pleasure, when she wants to put the devil in the oven.

"The order of my discourse requires things strange and far different from those passed; the less you shun these things, or rather the more diligence with which you gather them into your intellect, the more health they will bring to your sick mind. Although truly I do not quite know where I should begin to speak of the Gulf of Setalia, hidden in the Valley of the Acheron beneath its dark woods, often russet in color and foaming with foul grime and full of creatures of unusual species, but yet I will tell of it. The mouth through which the port is entered is of such size that although my little bark sailed with quite a tall mast, never was there a time, even though the waters were narrower then, that I might not have made room for a companion sailing with a mast no less than mine without disturbing myself in the least. Ah, what am I saying? King Robert's armada all chained together at the time that he enlarged it could have entered there with the greatest of ease without lowering its sails or raising its rudders. A wondrous thing it is that never a boat entered it without perishing and without being hurled forth from there vanquished and exhausted, just as they say occurs with Scylla and Charybdis in Sicily: that the one swallows ships and the other casts them forth! That gulf, then, is certainly an infernal abyss which could be filled or sated as the sea with water or the fire with wood. I will be silent about the sanguine and yellow rivers that descend from it in turn, streaked with white mould, sometimes no less displeasing to the nose than to the eyes, because the style I have picked draws me to something else. What shall I say further to you therefore about the village of Evilhole? Placed between two lofty mountains, from here sometimes just as from Mongibello, first with great thunderclaps and then without, there issues forth a sulfurous smoke, so fetid and repulsive that it pollutes the whole countryside around. I do not know what to say to you about it except that, when I lived near it (for I remained there longer than I would have liked), I was offended many times by such blasts that I thought to die there something other than a Christian death. Nor can I otherwise tell of the goaty stench which her whole corporal bulk exudes when she groans excited sometimes by heat, and sometimes by exertion; this is so appalling that, combined with the other things I have already spoken of, it makes her bed smell like a lion's den, so that any squeamish person would stay with far less loathing in the Val di Chiana in midsummer than near that.

"For this reason if you and the others who go buying pigs in a poke are often cheated, no one should wonder at it. Because, like the others, you have your sight more directed to the appearance than to the substance; for this reason alone, perhaps, you are to be reproached less, although it is more fitting for you than for many others to follow the truth of things rather than impression. Had you seen this and not realized your mistake, you should be reproached more than any other beast who bears human form. Although I have spoken briefly, I believe, considering the great amount that one could say, I have so revealed to you the truth which perhaps was hidden from you, that if you did not abandon your error, you should be considered more bestial than any other foolish beast.

"I am leaving many things unsaid because I want to come to that grief to which your folly led you yesterday; and in order that I may truly show you how foolish you were, by adding new things to the old, I would like to begin from a somewhat earlier point. I have shown you in many ways exactly what the excellence of that woman's mind and manners was; and I would have told you many things about her great age, had I considered you so stupid as not to have realized it from her face. Nor have I hidden from you those parts which drew your carnal desire to love her as much as the false opinion of her virtues drew your mind. Now I would like to speak to you of her righteous perseverance both during and after my death, so that at the same time I may benefit both you and me: me, because while I am speaking of it to someone so that he may know about her, I will vent upon her somewhat the burning indignation which her habits have kindled in my mind; and you, since the more things you hear about her which are justly to be censured, the more base you will consider her and so hasten your recovery.

"Because this perverse woman became worse each day doing wrongs which she should not have committed and which I should not have had to bear, because my reproaches to her were to no avail, and because I did not know how to obtain any useful advice about how to suffer it any longer, my heart was placed in such pain and hidden affliction that the blood around it abscessed, being heated more than normally by burning anger. Just as the pain was concealed, so the sickness was also hidden and did not appear until the corrupted blood suddenly seized my heart and carried me from the world in scarcely an instant. No sooner was my soul unwrapped and released from my mortal body and earthly shadows, and led back to the pure air, than I, with an eye more discerning than before, saw and recognized the kind of mind this perverse and evil woman had, who without doubt never felt a joy like the one which she felt at my death, as if she thought when I had been taken from her, that she had won a glorious victory in one of her long battles— and she very soon afterwards showed this clearly to anyone who would pay attention, as you will hear.

"But all the same, since she had an abundance of cunning, she first secretly removed many of my belongings and some of that money which I had foolishly entrusted to her keeping and which was to be left to my children (I had not previously fully arranged my affairs and my last will and testament, because I had no time to settle it properly, due to my sudden, untimely death) and filched as much as she liked; then, with an almighty noise she gushed false tears—a trick that she can do better than any other woman— and, weeping ever more strongly, she began to curse with her tongue the misfortune of my death and to call herself wretched, abandoned, grieving, and disconsolate; whereas, with her heart, she cursed the life which had lasted in me so long and considered herself more fortunate than any other woman. In truth, there would have been neither man nor woman who, on seeing her, would have doubted that she truly felt in her heart what her lies proclaimed. Yet it must be quite enough for me that He Who as a just judge gives rewards according to merits knows both of these and of her other deeds.

"Well, then, after all the funeral services were completed, and my body, dust, returned to dust, this worthy lady desired to live more dissolutely in her old age than she thought she could in her youth, and, feeling herself warmed by that wealth which should not have been hers (for she could not have supported herself either with her dowry or with her patrimony in what she planned to do), she wished neither to remain in my house nor to return to that of her high-born family. With piteous words she said that she wanted to retire to some little cottage close to a church of holy people, so that there, a lonely widow, she might end the rest of her days in prayer and church-going. The force of these lies of hers was so great, and so artfully did she know how to tell them, that many people were simple enough to believe that all would turn out as she said, as firmly as they believe they must die.

"She got as close, then, as she could to the friars' church in which you first met her, not, of course, to say prayers—of which I believe she knows none, nor ever cared about knowing any—but so that she could satisfy her lecherous cravings more easily without having too many eyes upon her, especially those of people for whom her honor was of some concern, and, even though every other man might fall short, so that the friars, who are most holy, merciful men, and consolers of widows, might not fail her. Here, as you may have seen, she goes playing peek-a-boo with whomever she meets, with her black hood over her head and pulled down far in front of her eyes out of modesty, as she would have it believed. Yet if you have paid close attention, sometimes she opens it and sometimes she closes it, still having no idea how to put aside her habitual vanity. At almost every word she pulls down her wimple from her chin or thrusts her hands outside her cape, since she thinks them beautiful and especially in contrast to the black.

"Leaving the house cloaked in this way, then, she enters the church; however, I would not have you think that she enters it to hear divine service or to worship, but to lay her nets. Since she has long known that young men to her liking, brave, valiant, and wise from all parts of our city assemble here, she has made of this church a baited trap such as birdcatchers make to snare doves, and, because no one can see the snake that lies hidden in the grass, she often catches big ones. But since she delights in changing her food often, soon after, sated, she goes back to catch fresh game, and although she may still have two or three ready, she does not for this reason stop birdcatching. You (surely believing you had a thousand eyes), who fell into the birdlime without being able to avoid it, know whether I am lying or telling the truth.

"Arriving at the church then, looking carefully around with her eyes swiftly taking in whoever is there, she begins endlessly grinding out a sorry string of beads for her paternosters, changing them first from one hand to the other and then from the other to the first without really ever saying a single prayer, since she is busy enough just chattering with this woman and then with that one, and whispering now into someone's ear, and then into someone else's, and in the same way first listening to one and then to the other—although this last thing seems very irritating to her; that is, listening to any of them, because she thinks she speaks so well herself. And thus she spends all her time in church, never doing anything else. Perhaps someone might say, 'What she doesn't do in church, she makes up for in her cottage'—something which is totally untrue, for though anyone else might be deceived about it, and not believe the facts, I cannot be deceived, since I would feel it, were she to perform some good or to say either a prayer or paternoster; for just as cool water is sweet to heated bodies, so would I feel my burning refreshed by them.

"But what am I saying? Perhaps even I am deceived; perhaps she says them in another's name. Indeed, I now know that not long ago a man left your world whose death transfixed her with so great a grief that she remained almost a week without wanting to suck an egg or taste *pappardelle*. But I spoke so confidently because I believed and now know that her prayers and paternosters are French romances and Italian songs in which she reads of Lancelot and Guinevere, Tristram and Isolde, and of their great exploits, their loves, jousts, tournaments, and battles; and when she reads that Lancelot, Tristram, or someone else meets with his lady secretly, and alone, in her bedchamber, she goes all to pieces because she thinks she can see what they are doing and would willingly do as she imagines they do—although she manages to suffer her craving for it only a short time.

"She reads the *Song of the Riddle* and that of *Florio and Blanche-fleur* and many other such things; if, perhaps, she is not intent upon such reading, like a wanton young girl, she plays with certain little animals which she keeps at home until the hour in which her most desired plaything comes to join her. So that you may know something more of her present life than you do, I assure you that after my death, in addition to her other admirers, she took for her lover the 'second Absalom,' about whose pleasures I told you something which was very unseemly a short time ago. Although, for more legitimate motives, this man should have withdrawn from such an enterprise, he nevertheless set about it, ungrateful for the good that God has granted him. But the offense will not be un-avenged; for unless one tells lies in the world where I dwell (a thing which I neither think nor believe), he has by his wife a certain son whom he nourishes and raises as his own, who belongs to him less than Christ belonged to Joseph. This son, when grown up, will avenge every one of my grievances against him, if I should term them grievances; for this reason he is not, as he believes himself, exempt from the common proverb which you use which says, "As doth the ass unto the wall, to him in turn it doth befall!' If he tills another's lands, it is just that the other sow his in return.

"To such a good and saintly life near the friars, then, did that woman retire, who, while I lived, was not my lady but my torment —she who, before death separated me from her, was as honest and as praiseworthy as you have heard. She practiced and delighted in the ways and virtues which I have told you; and moreover, she is exactly as I have briefly sketched her to you. Therefore you can see the woman for whom your feeble sense, knowledge, and discretion blinded you, and for whom they put your soul, liberty, and heart in the chains of love and unbearable grief and led you here at last into this desert valley. On this account I can never reproach you enough.

"But we must come to the last part of our promise, so that by grieving more for what you have done, you may merit pardon and salvation more quickly. You, poor wretch, consider yourself scorned by her; and neither you nor I would deny that you were scorned, for should I do so you would believe it; but had you known who was responsible, as now you must, you ought not to have taken it so seriously as you did. In order that you may see that she acted in this matter just as she usually does in other things, and so that you may banish her from your mind completely, I would like to tell you what and how I heard of the note you sent her.

"It is true that people often come here from there who tell us in part what is happening; nevertheless, in some contingencies God occasionally allows us to come here, and especially either to make those who should be concerned about us remember us, or in such a case as this for which I have come to you. And it happened that I came here the night after the day you wrote the first letter to this lady of yours. After I had visited several places, I was drawn by a certain charitable affection, which makes us love not only our friends but also our enemies, to enter the home of that woman with whom you fell in love; and looking all around while I searched every part of her house, I happened to hear news of the letter about which you are so disturbed.

"Part of the night had already gone by when I entered her bed-chamber; and having thoroughly looked about, as I had in the rest of the house, I was about to leave when I saw a lamp alight inside before a figure of Our Lady, little troubled by her who keeps Her there. Gazing toward the bed where she lies, I saw her not alone, as I was hoping, but disporting merrily with that lover about whom I spoke a little while ago. For this reason I paused yet a while, wanting to see what their revelry meant. I had been there only a short while when, at the request of her companion, she arose and lit a taper, and taking that letter you had sent her from a small coffer, she returned to the bed with the letter and the light in her hand. Here, while in turns one held the light and looked on as the other read, I heard your name mentioned and mocked with amazing guffaws: calling you first 'driveler,' then 'nincompoop,' 'Sir Lout,' and sometimes 'filthy,' they embraced and kissed at almost every word. Mixing their words amid the kisses, they asked each other if you, when you wrote those things, were awake or dreaming. And at times they said:

—Do you think that fellow has a long shaft?

—Did you ever see anybody do anything so stupid?

—Certainly this fellow's got the wrong end of the stick!

—For sure, he's taken leave of his senses and wants people to think he's clever!

—God, curses upon him!

—Go home and weed your onions and leave gentlewomen alone!

—What will you say?

—Would you ever have believed it?

—Oh! Wouldn't you like to see his hide tanned with a stick?

—No! Rather, you'd want to smack him about his cheeks with catgut until one or the other had had enough!

"Oh, you poor wretch! How their words ripped you to shreds! And how much less they thought of you than slops tipped out after nine! Your Muses, so loved and praised by you, were then called madness, and everything to do with you was considered stupid insanity; and, besides this, there was something much worse: because of you, Aristotle, Cicero, Virgil, Titus Livy, and many other illustrious men, your friends and acquaintances, I believe, they trampled like mud, mocked and degraded, debased and despised more than rams from Maremma. On the other hand, exalting themselves with words enough to make the very stones leap from the walls and run away sickened, they said that they alone were the honor and glory of this world. I realized quite clearly that the food and drink with which they had gorged themselves, and the desire to gratify each other's whim by mocking you had drawn them out of their senses (though they perhaps had never been in them!). With these and many other such scornful words, they passed much of the night; and in order to make you speak and write again so that they could mock and deride you, they then and there fashioned between them the answer that you received. By responding to it, you gave them reason for saying as much again, or worse, about the second letter as they had said about the first. Were it not that her youthful paramour feared that writing too much could turn into something else, perhaps because he was suspicious of her vanity and fickleness, rest assured that you would have got as far as the fourth and the fifth. In this way, then, did you give your wise and worthy lady and her foolish lover cause for laughter; and whereas you thought you would acquire love and favor, you suffered as the butt of a practical joke.

"Because I was very unhappy to see and hear this (not out of any love for you, for as yet I did not know you well, but because I could not bear such an abomination), I left there scornful and grievously troubled, not on my account but on hers. This, as you say, you did not find out from anyone in particular who told you, but by inferences you drew from the words of a pernicious person of perhaps little wisdom; and yet from the little you understood, you began to despair. Now what would you have said if you had heard this story in such detail when your mind was still far from sound? I am certain, without giving it another thought, that you would have hanged yourself by the neck—and hopefully the noose would have been strong enough to hold you, and not snap so that you could fall and escape, because you surely deserved hanging and worse. But if your mind and intellect had been as healthy as they should have been, and if you had considered those things which I have been talking about (not, certainly, those things which you failed to learn from your studies, but those things which they could have shown you had you wished to look), you would have laughed over not seeing her differ from the general run of women. Perhaps you are laughing to yourself about this now, and are wise if you do.

"What I have said about this part I shall say again about the second: had you, yourself, wished to ponder how great is the vanity of women, you would have understood that your gaze was not disagreeable but very dear to her, and you would have remembered what you have said many times in the past: that is, since they pride themselves on being thought beautiful and do everything to be so, the more they see themselves looked at the more beautiful they believe they are, trusting more in the number of their oglers than in their very mirrors. Since they are unhappy if anything to do with their ostentation should remain hidden, she wanted it to be seen by the other women, and pointed you out with her finger to show them that she was still to be considered beautiful and admired, since she still found lovers, and especially you, who are reputed by all to be a great connoisseur of the feminine figure. Therefore, you would have seen that her pointing you out was done as an honor, not as a censure. Indeed, someone else could say the opposite: that to show that she had quite returned to God and had completely abandoned the reprehensible life she used to enjoy, she pointed you out with her finger saying, 'Do you see how the devil opposes my salvation; do you see whom he has now placed before me in order to make me return to something which I fully intended, and intend, not to continue any more?' Or perhaps she used those same words with which she had shown your letter to her lover. Others would say that she did it neither in one way nor in the other, nor for one reason nor the other, but only in her desire to babble and chatter— something of which she is very fond because she thinks herself so eloquent—and that since she had run out of material from which to tell some grand lie about herself, she pointed you out in order to have the means to tell it. But whatever the reason might have been, you should have had immediate recourse to this infallible truth: that is, that no woman is wise and thus none can act wisely. If the blame were justly to fall on anyone, it should be you, since you believed, because you had looked at her a few times or because you bore her some love, that you had caused her to be in her old age something which neither nature nor perhaps chastisement could have made her in her youth: that is, wise or capable of acting wisely. You, therefore, are responsible if you came to grief over it, since you did not think about those things which you should have, concerning either her or yourself.

"However, let us ignore the fact that women are as proud, horrible, spiteful, and worthless as my words have reminded you, and as her letter made so mockingly clear; and whether she pointed you out to those women for any of the aforementioned reasons or whatever else; and let us come to the burning love which you bore her and talk about how insane you were in that. I wish to presuppose that what your friend told you about her worth was true. If you had believed him, you will never make me believe that you bore a lecherous love for her, because you would have known that her virtues were opposed to your depraved desire, and, consequently, if she had these virtues, you never would have succeeded in doing what you wished in that affair; so that not her virtues, but surely her appearance drew you to love her; and something you either heard or saw of her gave you hope of being able to fulfill your lewd desires. But were the eyes of your head turned so awry that you did not see she was elderly and already disgusting and sickening to look at? And besides that, what blindness of spirit had so clouded the eyes of your mind, that when you came to despair over your foolish desire for her, it made you pine for death in bitter grief? What wretchedness, what lack of spirit, what arrogance had made you so forgetful that when she failed you, you thought that all the rest of the world would fail you and that therefore you wanted to die? Don't you see now what a trifling matter it is? Are you so cowardly, so dissipated, so mired down in slime, so newly sprung from the woods or caves, or so shunned by every man in the world that you chose her as your sole refuge and only good, so that if she failed you, you should yearn for death? What pleasure, what honor, what advantage did you ever have from her, or was ever promised to you, except by your own stupid and foolish hope which she later took away from you?

"What could your hope justly promise you from her? Certainly nothing except to hold in your arms those flabby, sagging, and stinking members which you certainly would have coveted less had you known, as you do now, the commerce she made and still makes of them. Since you have that prowess which delights her so much, perhaps you hoped to receive the same pay for being able to embrace her as was formerly given to the knight of whom I spoke earlier? You were deceived, because when that was so, she was spending my money; nowadays, since she believes she is spending her own, I do not doubt in the least that you would find her fist far tighter than you thought. That generosity, for which perhaps your friend praised her so highly, has gone. Yet if you did not hope for this, how else could she have helped you? Could she lessen the number of your years? Yes, perhaps those which are yet to come, since she has already lessened those of others; but I do not believe that you would have wanted this. And add to them she could not, since God alone can do that. Could she teach you many things which you do not know? Yes, evil ones perhaps, since she has already taught some of them to others; but I do not believe that you are looking for these; she could show you nothing else because she knows nothing but vice. Could she give you bliss, living or dead? Yes, perhaps, if that is bliss which she defined by mocking you with her lover, because she has given bliss to many in this way in the past; but since the light of your intellect has returned somewhat, I do not believe you consider this bliss but torment. True bliss she neither has nor ever will have, since she has already condemned herself to eternal torment by her carnal pleasures. What, therefore, could she do for you? I surely do not know, nor do I believe that even you knew, or could ever know. Perhaps she could have made you one of the Priors, nowadays something so much desired by your fellow citizens; but I cannot see how, remembering that in your Capitol the ears of your senators are not lent to those rapacious wolves of high and noble lineage from which she is descended. But you could well say, 'Yes, she could,' if she were as alluring to all those involved in the scrutiny as she was to you, and if she had consented. But this seems impossible to me; for in my opinion, scarcely could even one other be found, let alone so many, who could be so dazzled with her as you were. Oh, what a wretched life you lead! How many noble acquaintances would you boast about to your discredit if I named them to you now by their titles, whereas you did not want to remember them for your advantage? By how many great and noble men would you be esteemed if you wished! Yet because of that excessive and reprehensible scorn of yours, you approach no one; or even if you do approach someone, you can bear to be with him for only a very short time unless he deigns to do for you what you should do for him: that is, indulge your habits and humor you, whereas you should eagerly indulge his and second him. And when it seemed to you that you were not so well received as you desired after approaching her in your most humble way, you did not leave her as you would have done and would still do those who can advance you, whereas she would always degrade you. But you called upon death to take you, while you really should have called upon it after you had considered what your soul had debased itself for, to whom and to what disgrace it had subjected itself—to a wheezing, withered, and sickly old woman, a meal now more for dogs than men, more worthy now to watch the cinders in the hearth than to appear in public to be looked upon.

"Alas, let us leave aside what you have acquired by the grace of God from your studies, and let us come to that alone which has been granted you by nature. If you are as contemptuous as you appear to be concerning the other things, seeing this, you will weep and lament, not for having been scorned or perhaps rejected, but for having permitted yourself to be lured and caught in the nets like a kite. Nature has granted you the great favor of being a man, whereas the one you were weeping about so pitifully is a woman; and how much more worthy and noble a thing man is than woman our words have shown in part before. Moreover, if she is large in person, well-proportioned in her limbs, and, in your opinion, is perhaps fair of face, you are not small and are quite as well formed as she. Nor do I see you in any way defective, nor does your face have less beauty among men than hers among women, in spite of the fact that she tends hers with a thousand preparations and as many ointments, whereas you wash yours either rarely, or never, even with clear water. No, rather, I will tell you more: yours is much fairer, although you give little care to it; and you do well, since such a concern is most improper for men. Up to this point, nature has granted her one favor more than you, for unless my judgment deceives me, though your beard is very grizzled and your temples have turned from black to white, she has still been in the world many more years than you, although perhaps she has not put them to such good use. Thus, by counterbalancing the first thing in which you outdo her, with this last, in which it seems that she outdoes you, and since by the central issue you are equal, I declare that she should have met and fallen in love with you as readily as you did with her. Therefore, if she did not, do you want to pine away because of her perverseness? With good reason she has more to regret than you, inasmuch as she loses by her obstinacy, while you gain from it, if you consider everything carefully.

"Yet you still fix the eyes of your mind upon something which you think puts you at a great disadvantage compared to her and of which I made no mention when I was balancing off the others; and you believe that this may be the reason for which you were scorned. That is, it seems to you that she is noble, whereas you do not think you are yourself. Supposing that this were so, you would not have been rejected for it, if you consider who the 'second Absalom' is, who is so much in her favor, and if you carefully consider who some of the others are. But in this respect I believe you are wrong, and seriously so, first for this reason: that in leaving the truth, you follow the opinion of the vulgar crowd which always directs its eyes more to appearances than to the truth of things. Do you not know what is true nobility and what is false? Do you not know what it is that makes a man noble and what it is that prevents him from being so? Most surely I know you do; nor is there such a novice in the schools of philosophy who does not know that we all receive our bodies from one single father and mother, and that all our souls are equal and from one single Creator; nor did anything make one noble and the other base except that, since each one equally had free will to do whatever he preferred, he who followed virtue was called noble and the others, on the contrary, following vice, were considered base. Therefore, nobility first came into the world from virtue. Come and look now among her living relatives and also among her ancestors and you will see how many of those things which make men noble you will find in her family. The possession of strength, which first came to them because of their prolific offspring, which is a natural gift and not a virtue, once made them rich, for with this strength they robbed, usurped, and occupied the possessions of their less powerful neighbors—a vice abominable to God and creation. Waxing proud on their riches, they dared to do what formerly nobles were accustomed to, that is, to take knighthood; by this act they disgraced themselves, the ermine, and other military decorations at the same time. What glorious exploit, what imposing act, what deed worthy of fame did you ever hear any of them perform for the state or for private good? Certainly none at all; the beginning, then, of their nobility was force, plunder, and pride—very fine roots for such a praiseworthy tree! The life of those who are now living is such that to be dead is far better. But even if there had been any valorous man among them, what good is it to her? You or anyone else could just as well pride yourself on it as she. Nobility cannot be handed down except as are such things as virtue, knowledge, and holiness; everyone must seek it, and, whoever would have it, let him acquire it for himself.

"However, whatever this may have been in the others, direct your attention a while to the woman who is our subject, who seems such a noble thing to you, and consider who she is at present or was in the past. If I who have lived with her am not mistaken, and if you have well absorbed what I was saying about her a little while ago, she has so many vices in her that she would tarnish the imperial crown with them. What nobility, therefore, can she hurl in your face? Or for what lack of nobility can she rebuke you? In truth, were it not that it would appear flattery, I would show you quite easily and with true arguments that you are much more noble than she, although shields of your ancestors are not seen hanging in the churches. But I want to tell you this: if you had any speck of nobility in your spirit, or had you that which once the lineage of King Ban of Benwick possessed, you would have sullied and spoiled it by loving her. Besides that which has been said, I could now pass on to many other subjects; and with both longer discourse and harsher words I could rail against the infamy of the evil woman with whom you fell in love, your folly, and the sin which you committed; but since I hope what I have said will be enough, I shall await what you wish to say."

I had listened to the truth of the Spirit's long discourse with bowed head, because I realized my error. Hearing him finish and fall silent, I raised my head and said somewhat tearfully, "Blessed Spirit, you have shown me clearly the duties of one my age and learning, and, especially, the baseness of that woman whom my mistaken judgment revered as noble, and had chosen for the lady of my mind, and also her habits, her defects, her marvelous virtues, and many other things; and by reproving me with words far sweeter than my sin deserved, you have shown me how much men naturally surpass women in nobility, and who I am in particular. These things, one by one and all together, have so completely reversed my opinion and changed my mind, that without any doubt at all, I now think the opposite of what I thought before. But though She Whose prayers implored you to come to me is most merciful, I could scarcely ever hope for forgiveness or salvation even though you promise it to me, so grave and displeasing seems my sin. For this reason, though you came for my good, I fear that it may seriously redound to my harm, since, though previously my situation was harsh and I was bound by heavy chains, still, I did not recognize the peril in which I found myself or even my worthlessness, and I could bear those ills with less anguish than I will be able to bear them from now on. Each one of my tears will increase a thousandfold, and my fear will become so intense that it will kill me; so that, if I believed I was in a bad state before, I now believe I am in the very worst."

Then the Spirit gazed at me most compassionately and said, "Do not be afraid; be reassured and persevere in your present good will! If only the sinner has true and proper contrition, Divine Goodness is so mighty that it completely takes away any grievous sin, even though it may proceed from perfidy and iniquity of heart, washes it from the mind of the sinner, and pardons freely. You have sinned naturally and out of ignorance—something far less offensive in the eyes of God than a sin of malice. You must recall the magnitude and the enormity of the sins committed out of malice which He has washed with the waves of the fountain of His true pity, and, in addition, how He has placed in glory those who once sinned as enemies and rebels to His Kingdom, because they were properly contrite and had fully atoned. If I am not deceived, or rather, if your tears do not deceive me, I see you so remorseful that you have already deserved forgiveness for the offense; and I am quite certain that you desire to make amends as far as you are able for the sin you have committed; to this I urge you as strongly as possible, so that you might not fall into that abyss from which no one may raise himself again."

At this I then said, "God, who alone sees and knows the hearts of men, knows if I am grieving and repentant for the evil I have done, and whether I weep with my heart as I do with my eyes. But since you give me hope of salvation by contrition and atonement, and since I already have the first, I would greatly value your teaching me what I must do to fulfill the second."

To this he replied, "If you want to atone fully for the errors you have committed, you must act in the opposite way to what you have done; but this must be understood correctly. What you have loved you must hate; and whatever you were ready to do to earn someone's love, you must be ready to do the contrary so that you gain hatred. And hear how to do it so that you may not be deceived by misunderstanding the words I have said with good intent. You loved that woman because you found her beautiful and because you hoped she would grant you carnal pleasure. I wish you to hate her beauty, since it was the cause of your sin, or could be in the future. I wish you to hate everything about her which you judged sensually attractive. I want you to love and desire the salvation of her soul; and whereas you used to go eagerly to where you thought you would see her, in order to give delight to your eyes, I want you likewise to hate this and flee from it. I wish you to avenge the offense she has done to you, for it is something which will bring salvation to both of you at the same time.

"If I have heard the truth many times in the past, everyone who has delighted and delights in the study of something which you do so excellently, can render even by fiction whom he pleases so famous and so glorious to the ears of men, that whoever hears anything of that person, considers him to have the very soles of his feet above the heavens both because of his virtue and his merits; and so, on the contrary, however virtuous, however worthy and upstanding a person may be who enrages you, with words which seem believable, you cast and hide him in the depths of Hell. For this reason, prepare yourself to belittle and vilify this deceiving woman just as you were ready to exalt her; you will easily manage this because you will be telling the truth. As far as you are able, make her see herself and likewise expose her to others with your words. Whereas in exalting her you would have acted improperly, told brazen lies, laid traps for the minds of many who are as gullible as you were, and raised her to such arrogance that no one could have touched the soles of her feet, so by doing this you will tell the truth, disabuse others, and humble her, for it could still be the cause of her salvation. Do it then; begin as soon as you can and expose her. And let this expiation be sufficient as far as this sin is concerned."

To this I then replied, "Surely if God will grant me enough of His favor that I may ever find myself outside of this labyrinth, I will endeavor to atone as you instruct; and I will need no other goading or urging to clear my spirit of such a great offense. While there is some force or power in words used with skill, I will leave none of my successors to avenge the outrage I have received, if only I am granted enough time either to tune my rhymes or to draft my prose. In truth, the revenge which most men would judge should be taken with the sword, I will leave to my Lord God Who never let wickedness go unpunished. Truly, unless a premature death robs me of the time, in order to show her that not all men are to be mocked in the same way, I shall make her realize her stupidity, bringing such grief to her and so vituperating her baseness that she will wish she had never set eyes on me, just as I have wished and wish never to have set eyes on her. Now I do not know: unless I change my mind, our city shall have a little something to sing about besides its misfortunes and wretchedness for a while; moreover, I will strive to leave testimony about her wicked and indecent acts in more lasting verse to those yet to come."

After I had said this, I fell silent; but because he was silent as well, I began again, "While you are delayed, waiting for that which is to come, I beg you to satisfy one of my desires: I do not recall that I ever had any kinship, familiarity, or friendship with you at all while you lived in the mortal world; and it seems certain to me that there are many in the region where you now dwell who were my friends, relatives, and companions while they lived, so that if someone were to come from there for my salvation, why was this toil imposed upon you rather than upon any of those?"

To this question the Spirit answered, "In the world where I am, no regard is paid to friendship, kinship, or familiarity with anyone; if anyone can perform some good, he is quick to do it. Certainly it is true that for this service and for any other, many, or rather, all there beyond would have been more competent than I. We all burn with charity so equally that anyone would have been ready and willing to do it; but, nevertheless, it was my duty, because the thing for which I was to come and rebuke you for your salvation concerned me particularly as something that was once my affair. It appeared quite evident that you should be more ashamed of it before me than before any other, because it seemed that by indecently desiring my possessions you had done some harm to them. Besides this, anyone else would have been more ashamed than I to tell you what was to be told about my affairs. Nor could you trust anyone else about it as much as you can trust me; moreover, no one would have known how to recount everything as fully as I, although I have left out many things. And this, I believe, was the reason why I, above any other, was chosen to come here and cure you of that sickness for which medicines, as a rule, are rarely found."

To this I then said, "Whatever the reason might be, I believe what you would have me believe; and for this I recognize and shall always recognize my obligation to you. Therefore, since I am willing to show you my gratitude for such a great benefit, I beg you, by the peace which you await with such burning, that if I can perform any task to aid and alleviate the pain which you bear, that you impose it upon me before I take my leave of you, assured that as far as I am able I shall fulfill it without fail."

Then, at this, the Spirit declared, "The evil woman who was my wife is completely given over to cares other than honoring my memory, as you may have heard; my little children cannot, for they are not old enough, and I have no other relative who cares for me (if only they would concern themselves as little with seizing the property of the wards whom I left behind!). Therefore, I shall impose on your generous offer: may it please you, when you are freed of this entanglement (which with the help of God will be soon), to give alms for my consolation and for the alleviation of my pain, and have some Masses said in which there will be prayers on my behalf; this will be enough for me. If I am not mistaken, the hour of your freedom approaches; therefore, direct your eyes toward the east and look upon the new light which seems to be rising. If it is what I believe it to be, this is no longer the time for words, but for departure."

While the Spirit was saying these last words, I understood his wishes perfectly, and it seemed that I raised my head toward the Orient and saw a light rising very slowly over the mountains, just as the dawn rises in the east before the coming of the sun. After this had lit up a great part of the sky, it immediately grew to huge proportions; and stretching toward us just as we sometimes see the sun make a long strip of light upon the earth as it passes between two dark clouds, so, without approaching further except with its rays, it made a shining, luminous path which did not pass the place where we stood. No sooner did this come upon me than I recognized my error with far greater bitterness of conscience than I had done before. Then when I had savored it a while, it seemed to me that a certain very heavy and ponderous weight was raised from my back, and it made me, who before felt motionless and unable to move, immediately feel light and swift without knowing why; and it seemed that I had leave to go. Because of this, I said to the Spirit, "If you think it is time to depart, I implore you that we leave this place because my lost strength and good will have returned to me, and I think I see the way clear."

The Spirit replied to this quite happily, "I am pleased at that; come and let us go at once; but watch that you never stray from the path of light which you see before you and along which I shall go, because if you were caught in the thorn bushes which you see filling this place, it would take another effort beyond this, for which I have come, to drag you out of them. And God knows whether or not your prayers for help would be granted as they now have been."

In response I seemed to say quite happily, "Well, God willing, let us go at once, and do not fear to trust in my care and wisdom. For certainly if, instead of the mockery which I have already received, a hundred thousand prayers were to oppose me, they could not put me back into the chains from which I am freed by the mercy of Her (to Whom I have always acknowledged my obligation—and now more than ever) and, afterwards, by your kind teaching and generosity."

The Spirit then set out; and, going along the luminous path, he directed his steps toward the lofty mountains. Still speaking of pleasant things, he started up one of them which appeared to touch the sky, and labored hard as he drew me after him. When we had reached its peak, it seemed that here I saw the open sky shining over all, felt the soft, sweet, joyous air, and saw the green plants and flowers in the fields. These things completely comforted my breast, afflicted as it was by its past distress, and brought back its former joy. Thus, as it pleased the Spirit, I turned back to look at the place from which he had drawn me, and it seemed not a valley but a thing deep as Hell, gloomy, and filled with darkness and painful regrets. When he told me I was free and could act according to my own judgment, the joy I felt was so great that I wished to throw myself at his feet to thank him for such a great kindness, but he and my sleep disappeared at the same time.

Awakening, therefore, and finding myself completely bathed in sweat like a man who had labored, and as if I had climbed with my real body the mountain which it seemed to me I had climbed in my dream, I was filled with wonder and began to think about the things I had seen and heard. While I went on repeating them to myself one by one and considered whether it was possible for them to be true as I seemed to have heard, I admitted that many of them were perfectly true. As for those which I could not then know, upon being informed of them later by another, I found them to be no less true than the rest. For this reason, most surely inspired by God, I prepared for my successful departure from the wretched valley.

Seeing the sun already high above the earth, I arose and went to my friends with whom I usually consoled myself in my afflictions, and I recounted everything I had seen and heard just as it had happened. After they had explained every detail of my dream to me thoroughly, I found that they were all in agreement with my own interpretation, so that both because of their urging and because of my understanding which had returned to me partly improved, I firmly decided to abandon the evil love of that wicked woman.

Divine Grace was so favorable to this resolve that within a few days I regained my lost liberty, and I am my own again as I once was. Thanks and praise be to Him Who brought it about! Without fail, if time be granted to me, I hope with my words so to chastise that woman—who, though she is a contemptible thing, presumes to mock others with her lovers—that she will never show a letter sent to her without recalling mine and my name with grief and shame. And God be with you.

* * *

[CONCLUSIO]

O little work of mine, your end has arrived, and it is time to give my hand its rest. For this reason, strive to be useful to those—and especially to the young—who, with eyes closed, set out without a guide through unsafe places, trusting too much in themselves; you will give testimony of the beneficence I have received from the Mother of our Salvation. But above all, see that you do not come into the hands of evil women, especially into those of her who surpasses every demon in wickedness and who has been the cause of your present toil, since you would be ill received. She is to be stung by the sharpest goad you bear with you; swiftly and fearlessly this will attack and wound her, if the Giver of all Grace grants it.

EXPLICIT

List of Abbreviations

Aen.: Aeneid. (Virgil)

Am. vis.: Amorosa visione. (Boccaccio)

Anglo-Latin Sat.: Anglo-Latin Satirical Poets and Epigrammists of the Twelfth Century.

Antiche rime: Antiche rime volgari secondo la lezione del Codice Vaticano 3793.

Ars amat.: Ars amatoria. (Ovid)

Comm. in somn. Scip.: Commentariorum in somnium Scipionis. (Macrobius)

Conf.: Confessions. (Saint Augustine)

Conv.: Convivium. (Dante Alighieri)

Decam.: Decameron. (Boccaccio)

Epist.: Epistolae. (Dante Alighieri)

Exp. Eth. Nicom.: In decem libros Ethicorum ad Nicomachum expositio. (Saint Thomas Aquinas)

De civ. Dei.: Ad Marcellinum de civitate Dei contra paganos. (Saint Augustine)

De mon.: De monarchia. (Dante Alighieri)

Inf.: Inferno. (Dante Alighieri)

Latin Poems: The Latin Poems Commonly Attributed to Walter Mapes.

Metam.: Metamorphoses. (Ovid)

Par.: Paradiso. (Dante Alighieri)

PG: Patrologiae cursus completus: Series Graeca. Ed. J.-P. Migne.

PL: Patrologiae cursus completus: Series Latina. Ed. J.-P. Migne.

Purg.: Purgatorio. (Dante Alighieri)

Notes to the Translation

In these notes I have referred consistently to the following translations:

Alain de Lille. *De planctu Naturae: The Complaint of Nature*. Trans. Douglas M. Moffat. Yale Studies in English, 36. New York, 1908.

Andreas Capellanus. *De amore: The Art of Courtly Love*. Trans. John Jay Parry. Records of Civilization. New York, 1941; reprint, New York, 1959, 1969.

Giovanni Boccaccio. *De claris mulieribus: Concerning Famous Women*. Trans. Guido A. Guarino. New Brunswick, N.J., 1963.

———. *Genealogie deorum gentilium: Boccaccio on Poetry, Being the Preface and the Fourteenth and Fifteenth Books of Boccaccio's Genealogia Deorum Gentilium*. Trans. Charles G. Osgood. Princeton, 1930; reprint, New York, 1956.

———. *Trattatello in laude di Dante: The Earliest Lives of Dante*. Trans. James Robinson Smith. New York, 1901; reprint, New York, 1963.

Dante Alighieri. *De monarchia: On World Government*. Trans. Herbert W. Schneider. New York, 1949; reprint, New York, 1957.

For the translation of quotations from the *Divine Comedy* I have consulted the monumental version of Charles S. Singleton (Dante Alighieri, *The Divine Comedy*, Bollingen Series, 80 [Princeton, 1970–75]), and the three-volume rendering by John D. Sinclair (*The Divine Comedy of Dante Alighieri* [Oxford, 1946; reprint, Oxford, 1961]). I have often, however, adapted both these translations and those listed above, mainly to demonstrate verbal parallels in the *Corbaccio* which would not otherwise be evident in English.

Greek and Latin citations are given in the Loeb Classical Library version; biblical references are to the Vulgate and are cited in the Douay-Rheims text. All other translations are my own.

For conciseness books and articles are given in these notes under the author's name, date of publication, volume, and page number; full bibliographical data can be found in the Bibliography of Works Consulted (p. 165).

1. *ungrateful for them:* This "Proemio" to the *Corbaccio,* with its solemn and pious tone, bears an interesting contrast to that of the *Decameron* (I, 4), which expresses gratitude only to "the gracious ladies":

E per ciò che la gratitudine, secondo che io credo, tra l'altre vertù è sommamente da commendare ed il contrario da biasimare, per non parere ingrato, ho meco stesso proposto di volere, in quel poco che per me si può, in cambio di ciò che io ricevetti, ora che libero dirmi posso, e se non a coloro che me aiutarono, alli quali per avventura per lo lor senno o per la loro buona ventura non abbisogna, a quegli almeno a' quali fa luogo, alcuno alleggiamento prestare.

Since among the virtues, gratitude is in my opinion especially to be praised, and its contrary to be censured, therefore, so that I may not appear ungrateful, I have decided, now that I may call myself free, to try and give, as far as I am able, some solace in return for what I have received, if not to those who aided me, and who by reason of their good sense or good fortune may chance not to need it, at least to those to whom it may be useful.

The wording of the "Accessus" of the *Esposizioni* (pp. 1–2) resembles the "Proemio" of the *Corbaccio* in its wording and religious tone, although it contains no reference to the Virgin Mary.

For the rhetorical importance of the proemium in medieval works, see E. R. Curtius (1953), pp. 70, 179, 410; and B. Nardi (1961).

2. *fount of pity:* Cf. Dante's *De mon.* II, v, 5, and *Epist.* V, 3. The usage was based on a common proverb: "La'ngratitudine fa seccare la fonte de la misericordia" ("Ingratitude makes dry the fount of pity"). Cf. Paolo da Certaldo, *Libro di buoni costumi,* ed. A. Schiaffini (1945), p. 67.

3. *treatise:* "Trattato." In medieval philosophy, the term "tractare" had the specific sense of "treating philosophically"; Dante, for example, referred to the *De monarchia* as a *trattato* (E. R. Curtius [1953], p. 222).

4. *Herself:* The Virgin Mary. The enigmatic circumlocution is probably in imitation of *Inf.* III, 95–96, and V, 23–24: "Vuolsi così colà dove si puote/ciò che si vuole" ("Thus it is willed there where what is willed can be done"). Even more especially it echoes the phrase used by Bernard in reference to the Virgin (*Par.* XXXIII, 34–35): "Anchor ti priego, regina, che puoi/ciò che tu vuoli . . ." ("I pray you, Queen, who can perform what you will").

5. *this is my sole purpose:* "E altro no." These words stress the initial

moral intent of the work. Discussing the dream-vision form in general, H. R. Patch ([1950], p. 89) comments, "The purpose of teaching . . . often by symbolism, is fairly constant in all the literature of this type, early and late, inasmuch as the framework of these stories implies that the vision itself is granted primarily as an exhortation, a warning or an encouragement to others to whom it may be described."

6. *my special lady . . . whom I . . . loved far more than life itself:* A commonplace complaint in the tradition of courtly poetry. Boccaccio's contemporary, Chiaro Davanzati, for example, wrote the following lines in his misogynistic "Or tornate in usanza, buona giente" (*Antiche rime*, III, 83):

> Et intendete una gran falsitate,
> Che m'à fatto una donna, cui servente
> 'L mio core è stato in molta lealtate. . . .

> And hear a great fraud played on me by a woman toward
> whom my heart, as her servant, bore great loyalty.

7. *in the midst of this battle:* The traditional medieval "battle of thoughts." Compare, for example, Dante's *Vita nuova*, Ch. XIII, and also the episode in Boccaccio's *Fiammetta* (Ch. IV; pp. 59ff.), where the heroine is torn with doubts concerning Panfilo's fidelity.

8. *the expulsion of your reason:* A topos deriving, perhaps, from the tirade of Philosophy in Boethius' *Consolatio,* metric II; compare also the reproof of Natura in the *De planctu* (*PL*, CCX, 442; *Anglo-Latin Sat.* II, 449-50):

> Heu! inquit, quae ignorantiae caecitas, quae alienatio mentis, quae debilitas sensuum, quae infirmatio rationis, tuo intellectui nubem apposuit, animum exulare coegit, sensus hebetavit potentiam, mentem compulit aegrotare, ut non solum tuae nutricis familiari a cognitione tua intelligentia defraudetur, verum etiam tanquam monstruosae imaginis novitate percussa, in meae apparitionis ortu tua discretio patiatur occasum?

> "Ah!" said she, "what blindness of ignorance, what alienation of your mind, what feebleness of your senses, what infirmity of your reason has clouded your understanding, has forced your spirit into exile, has dulled the power of your feeling, has made your mind become ill, so that not only your intellect is cheated out of its quick recognition of your Nurse, but that even your power of discerning, as it were, smitten by a strange and monstrous sight, suffers a collapse at my very appearance?"

See R. H. Green (1956), 649-74, and n. 27 below.

9. *hope of revenge, or any other joy:* This surprising (to modern ideas) juxtaposition is quite traditional. In speaking of those sullen because of anger, Aristotle had described the effects of taking revenge: "The sullen are angry for a long time and are mollified with difficulty. . . . But they are

appeased when they have taken vengeance. The infliction of punishment [revenge] calms the surge of anger and brings delight in place of sadness." St. Thomas glossed, "Sadness is replaced by delight, inasmuch as a man takes pleasure in vengeance" (*Exp. Eth. Nicom.*, ed. C. I. Litzinger, 1964, I, pp. 347, 351; *Exp. Eth. Nicom.*, pp. 222, 223). Lactantius (*De ira Dei* I, 97) said that there was gratification in the revenge or judgment of God. Compare Boccaccio's tale of Rinieri and the widow Elena (*Decam.* VIII, 7; II, 139): "Lo scolare, tutto lieto seco medesimo disse: —Iddio, lodato sii tu; venuto è il tempo che io farò col tuo aiuto portar pena alla malvagia femina della 'ngiuria fattami in premio del grande amore che io le portava" ("The scholar, completely delighted said to himself: 'Praise be to Thee, O God! the time has come, when I, with Thy help, may punish this wicked woman for the wrong she did to me as a reward for the great love I bore her'").

10. *the most holy Father of Lights:* Cf. James I: 17.

11. *the eyes of my mind:* Cf. *Purg.* X, 122: "la vista de la mente" ("the sight of the mind"). An expression common in Boccaccio; cf. *Decam.* VIII, 7 (II, 145): "gli occhi dello 'ntelletto" ("the eyes of the intellect").

12. *mind is less than healthy:* Cf. Petrarch, *De vita solitaria* I, vii and Seneca, *Ad Lucilium epist.* 10, 1–2; p. 56.

13. *sufferings:* All the traditional stages of love present in the *Decameron* and outlined by V. Branca ([1956], p. 147) in his *Boccaccio medievale* are to be found in the *Corbaccio* as well. The Italian critic lists them as follows:

    I) *in eius (mulieris) apparitione stupor.*
    II) *amor terribilis et imperiosus.*
    III) *diutina lassitudo.*
    IV) *tempusculum in auge rote volubilis.*
    V) *in malorum profunditatem deiectio.*
    VI) *amici solatio.*

Not one step is absent in the events of this treatise: the flames of love cause wonderment in the protagonist; love overcomes him and he silently vows fidelity; he becomes disappointed upon the first revelation of woman's true worth as she betrays herself in her first letter; Fortune aids him, only to lure him further into her clutches; his being rejected hurls him into "utter despair," as he realizes that he has become "a beast without intellect"; the protagonist turns finally to a philosophical discussion among his friends in order to seek solace.

14. *fickle operations of Fortune:* Here Boccaccio lists the three main forces acting upon human life, Fortune, Nature, and Providence, which had played such a great part in the *Decameron*. Boccaccio never firmly stated the relationship of one to the other as had Dante in the *Conv.* IV, xvi and in the *Inf.* VII, 70–96. For discussions of Fortune in the Middle Ages and the early Renaissance, see A. Doren (1922–23), pp. 71–144; H. R. Patch

(1913–14), pp. 13–28; (1922); (1923); E. Panofsky (1962), p. 225; and V. Cioffari (1940a), pp. 129–37; (1940b); (1944); and (1947), pp. 1–13; T. Nurmela (1968), pp. 146–48, n. 49.

15. *I . . . retired . . . to my regular chamber:* F. X. Newman ([1962], p. 254) notes that this is a convention in dream-visions: "There are no communal dream poems; indeed, often enough we find, in the narrative preceding the dream itself, that the dreamer-to-be makes a specific gesture of separating himself from his normal community." In the *Somnium Scipionis* (Cicero, *De re publica* VI, x), we read: "Deinde, ut cubitum discessimus, me et de via fessum et qui ad multam noctem vigilassem, artior quam solebat, somnus complexus est" ("When we had separated to take our rest, I fell immediately into a deeper sleep than usual, as I was weary from my journey and the hour was late").

16. *much of that night:* Cf. Cicero's *Somnium Scipionis* (*De re publica* VI, x): "Post autem apparatu regio accepti sermonem in multam noctem produximus . . ." ("Later, after I had been entertained with royal hospitality, we continued our conversation far into the night . . .").

17. *imaginative faculty:* St. Augustine's idea that the dreams which we see in sleep are a type of spiritual vision was generally held in the Middle Ages and early Renaissance. They are caused by images or forms (intentions) received from the senses, held in the memory, and presented to the imagination. This latter faculty has the cogitative power to combine the images into phantasms which may or may not bear a relation to the reality we have experienced. The whole process takes place in the sensitive soul and not the intellect, but the fact that dreams have a corporeal cause does not prevent them from being also a divine revelation sent by God (*De Genesi ad litteram* XII; 4, 10, 11, 13, 21). Apparently Boccaccio meant to base his literary dream-vision on these widely accepted principles.

18. *swiftest wings:* Many traditional aspects of the dream-vision form are present in the *Corbaccio.* Flying is a common element in the introduction of such a work (cf. F. X. Newman [1962], pp. 293–95).

19. *I now found:* "Mi parea trovare." Boccaccio uses the word "parere" to stress the extraordinary "seeming" quality of dream experience. To avoid awkward repetition I have rendered it into English only when essential.

20. *a fog:* Boccaccio may have borrowed this idea from *Purg.* XV, 142–45. In the terrace of the wrathful, a dark, suffocating cloud of smoke rolls along the path and envelops the penitents; there, as here, it appears to symbolize the blinding effect of anger on reason.

21. *the entrance of the path:* Descriptions of otherworldly landscapes often contain the element of the thorny valley and path (H. R. Patch [1950], p. 131). However, the tradition of the path as a moral allegory can be roughly broken into two: first, the Classical and Renaissance tradition of Hercules at the *bivium,* where the fork in the road represents a moral choice; and the second, the medieval tradition of the single path, characteristic of Brunetto Latini's *Tesoretto* and Dante's *Commedia,* for exam-

ple. Petrarch's famous account of his ascent of Mont Ventoux, although not an "otherworldly" visit, belongs to the latter tradition (H. Baron [1968], pp. 17–20, 47–50). The present treatise of Boccaccio also follows this second, medieval form.

Another version of the story of the two roads is quoted in Daly's translation in B. E. Perry (1965), p. 490. See also E. Panofsky (1930); E. Tietze-Conrat (1951), pp. 305–9; T. E. Mommsen (1953), pp. 178–92; A. S. Bernardo (1962), pp. 57–61.

22. *brambles:* Compare the traditional "brambles of lust" (*vepres libidinum*) of St. Augustine, *Conf.* II, 3, ii.

The setting is reminiscent of Dante's "selva oscura" ("dark wood"), "esta selva selvaggia e aspra e forte" ("that wood savage, harsh, and dense," *Inf.* I, 2, 5), and the description of the Wood of the Suicides (*Inf.* XIII). In the *Esposizioni* (pp. 20–21), Boccaccio embroiders on Dante's conception in Canto I quite extensively:

> Dice prima che ell'era 'selvaggia,' quasi voglia dinotare non avere in questa alcuna umana abitazione e per conseguente essere orribile; dice appresso ch'ella era 'aspra,' a dimostrare la qualità degli alberi e de' virgulti di quella, li quali doveano essere antichi, con rami lunghi e ravolti, contessuti e intrecciati intra se stessi, e similemente piena di pruni, di tribuli e di stecchi, sanza alcuno ordine cresciuti e in qua e in là distesi: per le quali cose era aspra cosa e malagevole ad andare per quella; e in quanto dice 'forte' dichiara lo'mpedimento già premostrato, vogliendo, per l'asprezza di quella, essa esser forte, cioè difficile a potere per essa andare e fuori uscirne.

> He states first that it was "savage," as if wishing to indicate that it contained no human habitation, and was, in consequence, horrible; he then states that it was "harsh," to show the nature of its trees and shoots, which must have been ancient, with long twisted branches, tangled and snarled all together, and likewise filled with thorn-bushes, brambles, and sticks, growing disorderedly and jutting out here and there. Because of these things it was harsh and difficult to move about in. Insofar as he says "dense," he explains the impediment previously shown, meaning that it is dense because of its harshness: that is, difficult to walk in and get out of.

Such descriptions were commonplace, however; we may compare the following lines by Boccaccio's contemporary Eustache Deschamps (*Oeuvres* III, p. 374, st. 1122ff.):

> Verdeur n'y a, esbatement ne joye,
> Fors espines, ronses, tristesce, esmay,
> Langour, freour, dur penser qui m'anoye;
> Le chahuant ses chans de mort m'envoye . . .

> There is no greenery, happiness or joy;
> Nothing but thorns, brambles, sadness, worry,

weakness, fear, harsh thoughts which burden me;
the owl sends me his songs of death.

For this and other such parallels, see H. R. Patch (1919) and (1950), pp. 204–12 et passim. See also M. L. Brown (1917), pp. 411–15.

23. *rugged mountains:* Lofty mountains are a traditional feature of Christian visionary accounts. See E. J. Becker (1899), p. 13; H. R. Patch (1950), p. 128; and F. X. Newman (1962), p. 291. Later in the *Corbaccio,* the ascent of these mountains is supposed to signify a transcendence of the sinful state the dreamer now suffers, and he will look back on this valley in great awe (cf. n. 330 below). Compare the "altura" in the *Am. vis.* I, 50.

24. *surely to infest this wilderness:* "Che per tutto ne dovesse essere piena" (literally, "that it must have been completely full of them").

25. *forsaken by almost every hope:* In the *Secretum* II (esp. pp. 560, 592), Petrarch complained of Fortune's abuse; he felt like one "ab innumeris hostibus circumclusus, cui nullus pateat egressus, nulla sit misericordie spes nullumque solatium, sed infesta omnia . . ." ("surrounded by countless enemies, without any way of escape, as if he had no hope of pity or comfort, but as if threatened on every side . . ."). Boccaccio's Petrarchan echo is obvious, but the theme of the lost and bewildered narrator-protagonist is one of the conventional elements of the dream-vision form. See F. X. Newman (1962), pp. 256–57.

26. *our craftsmen dye here:* Fourteenth-century Florence was the leading cloth-finisher of Europe. Red silken garments ("vermiglio" or "scarlatto") were generally worn by doctors and lawyers. Cf. C. Merkel (1898), p. 107. Concerning the Spirit's garment, see nn. 44 and 45 below.

27. *spirit of pity:* Cf. *Inf.* XIII, 36: "Non hai tu spirto di pietade alcuno?" (Have you no spirit of pity?")

28. *self-pity:* Compare the situation in Dante's *Vita nuova* XXXV: "Quando li miseri veggiono di loro compassione altrui, più tosto si muovono a lagrimare, quasi come di se stessi avendo pietade . . ." ("When people in misery see compassion in others, they are more readily moved to tears, as if taking pity on themselves . . .").

29. *the false pleasure of fleeting things:* Cf. *Purg.* XXXI, 34–35: "Le presenti cose/ col falso lor piacer volser miei passi" ("Present things with their false pleasure turned aside my steps"). In *Am. vis.* XXXIX, 78, the guide (unidentified) ends with a Christian exhortation to leave the "ben transitorio e fallace" ("the false and transitory good"), but in the very next lines of Canto XL, 1–3, the protagonist pays no heed:

> La donna mi parlava, ed io mirando
> con l'occhio andava pure ove'l disio
> mi tenea fitto, non so che ascoltando.

The lady spoke to me, and I, gazing, yet moved with my eyes to the place where desire held me fixed, listening to I know not what.

It is noteworthy that the *Corbaccio* also ends with the protagonist returning to his libidinous earthly interests. See Introduction, p. xxiii, and n.
337 below.

30. *darkness all the while:* That sin, and particularly lust, brought the loss
of the light of reason was a commonplace. Compare, for example, St.
Augustine's *De civ. Dei*, Bk. XI, Ch. 10, and Alain de Lille in the *De
planctu Naturae* (*PL*, CCX, 443; *Anglo-Latin Sat.* II, p. 452): "Haec,
scilicet sensualitas, concupiscentiae nocte mentis lumen eliminat." ("Lust
extinguishes the radiance of the mind by the night of desire.")

31. *our common native city:* Florence. Boccaccio preferred generic or classical terms, names, and references in the *Corbaccio* (see n. 232 below,
"those in power" ["reggenti"], for example). This tendency toward
generality emphasizes the initial universal moral and didactic intent of
the treatise as opposed to that of the earthly, hedonistic *Decameron*, where
precise historical names and places abound, anchoring the tales in the
immanent and earthly. (Cf. G. Getto [1966], p. 10.)

32. *I beseech you . . . for the love of God:* Cf. *Inf.* I, 130–31: "Io ti richeggio/
per quello Dio . . ." ("I beseech you, by that God . . .").

33. *your words clearly show me:* Cf. *Inf.* X, 25: "La tua loquela ti fa mani-
festo . . ." ("Your words clearly show").

34. *what eyes those were:* The eyes of the Spirit's widow.

35. *my hair began to bristle:* Cf. *Aen.* XII, 868: "Arrectaeque horrore
comae et vox faucibus haesit" ("and his hair stood on end in terror, and
the voice stuck in his throat"). The fear of the dreamer is conventional in
the dream vision. Cf. F. X. Newman (1962), p. 257.

36. *do not be afraid:* In the *Somnium Scipionis* (*De re publica* VI, x), the
elder Scipio exhorts: "Ades, inquit, animo et omitte timorem. Scipio, et,
quae dicam, trade memoriae" ("He said, 'Courage, Scipio, do not be
afraid, but imprint my words upon your memory' ").

37. *the entrance . . . through madness and lust:* Compare the words of
Minos (*Inf.* V, 20). Boccaccio elaborated upon this biblical echo in the
Esposizioni (p. 288): *"Non t'inganni l'ampiezza dell'entrare,* la quale è
libera ed espedita a tutti quegli che dentro entrar ci vogliono: ma l'uscire
non è così" ("Let not the breadth of the entrance deceive you, for it is
free and unencumbered for all those who wish to enter it: but the way out
is not so").

38. *Pigsty of Venus:* Perhaps an allusion to the Circe episode of the *Odys-
sey*. In the *De mulieribus claris,* Boccaccio used the same image in the tale
of Iole (p. 104): when a man cedes to love, "tunc pudoris hostis et sce-
lerum suasor, rubore et honestate fugatis, parato volutabro porcis, gan-
nientes effundit in illecebres coitus" ("then the enemy of chastity and the
encourager of crimes casts shame and honor aside, makes ready the pigsty,
and, grunting, gives himself up to the allurements of copulation"). In
the *Esposizioni* (p. 69) he describes Dante's desert as follows: "Colui
che nel vizio della lussuria si lascia cadere, per ciò che la lussuria per la

sua bruttezza è simigliata al porco, esso diventa porco, quantunque effige umana gli rimanga . . . e così quello luogo è selvatico, sì come privato d'ogni umana stanza" ("Since lechery is compared to the pig because of its filth, whosoever allows himself to fall into the vice of lust becomes a pig, although he may still have human shape . . . and thus that place is savage, since it is completely without human habitation").

39. *Valley of Sighs and Woe:* The dark valley of the dream-vision tradition may find its source in "the valley of the shadow of death" of Psalm XXIII or Isaiah IX:2, but the "val des faux amants" ("the valley of false lovers") was a common theme in Arthurian romances. See L. A. Paton (1903), p. 81, and H. R. Patch (1950), pp. 130, 207.

40. *set at rest your most fervent desires:* Cf. *Par.* IV, 117: "Tal puose in pace uno e altro disio" ("It set at rest the one desire and the other").

41. *eternal prison:* Cf. *Purg.* I, 41: "Fuggita avete la pregione etterna?" ("Have you fled the eternal prison?") Compare also *Inf.* III, 1–9.

42. *the place . . . promises . . . salvation:* I.e., Purgatory, where souls are cleansed for Heaven.

43. *blind dungeon:* Cf. *Inf.* X, 58–59: "Se per questo cieco/carcere vai . . ." ("If you go through this blind prison . . .").

44. *honor above others:* Scarlet or vermilion silk robes were the distinctive garment of doctors. In the *Decam.* VIII, 9 (II, 159), Lauretta bemoans: "Tutto il dì, i nostri cittadini da Bologna ci tornano qual giudice e qual medico e qual notaio, co' panni lunghi e larghi e con gli scarlatti e co' vai e con altre assai apparenze grandissime" ("Every day our fellow citizens return to us from Bologna, some as judges, some as physicians and some as notaries, with long wide gowns and robes, of scarlet and ermine, and many other decorations of distinction"). See C. Merkel (1898), pp. 107–8; A. Viscardi and G. Barni (1966), p. 190.

45. *a fire fashioned by Divine Art:* A description of the guide's garment— often involved and lengthy—is conventional in the dream or vision tradition. Boethius, for example, took great pains in depicting the symbolic dress of Lady Philosophy in the *De consolatione;* Boccaccio, on the other hand, completed his description in a few short lines. J. Luchaire ([1951], p. 206) believed the costume here to be "a sort of Nessus' tunic." P. G. Ricci (*Opere in versi* [1965], p. 480, n. 11) proposed that Boccaccio took his idea from Dante's punishment of the hypocrites and the lustful in the *Divina Commedia*—the gilded lead hood of *Inf.* XXIII, 61–66, and the purging fire of the lustful in the *Purg.* XXV, 112–17. T. Nurmela ([1968], p. 15, n. 104) suggested that it was perhaps modeled on the punishment of the hypocrites and the heresiarchs, while M. Cottino-Jones ([1970], p. 498) indicated a resemblance to Medea's mythological robe of poisonous fire.

Many further interpretations could be given for this garment, however. The dead husband's position is similar to the marital situation described in the Goliardic *De conjuge non ducenda* (*Latin Poems,* p. 84):

Qui est cum conjuge semper affligitur,
et mori cupiens languere cogitur:
hic dolor maximus dolorum dicitur,
ut rubus ardeat qui non consumitur.

He who has a wife always has trouble,
and is constrained to languish in his desire for death;
This is said to be the greatest pain of all;
for he burns red who is not consumed.

The burning cloak also bears some relation, at least, to that of Natura in the *De planctu Naturae* of Alain de Lille (*PL,* CCX, 439; *Anglo-Latin Sat.* II, p. 444): "Haec vestium ornamenta, quamvis plenis suae splenditatis flammarent ardoribus . . ." ("Although these decorations of the garments flamed with the glow of their own full splendor . . ."). Note the Spirit's later statement that all shades in Purgatory burn with the flame of charity ("tutti di carità ardiamo") p. 74, and n. 324 below.

46. *all your rivers:* An echo of *Inf.* XXX, 64–69.

47. *never set eyes:* Cf. *Inf.* XXVIII, 87: "La terra che tale qui meco/ vorrebbe di vedere esser digiuno" ("the city upon which a person here with me would wish he had never set eyes").

48. *your second question:* I.e., concerning "Who wanted you to come here and help me." (Translation, p. 10).

49. *in Whom all things have their being:* The Latin formula "Regem cui omnia vivunt," taken from the *Officium defunctorum,* was added to the margin by the scribe of the Mannelli MS. Dante used it in the conclusion to the *Vita nuova* ("Colui a cui tutte le cose vivono"). Boccaccio himself repeated the same words in the Conclusion of *Decam.* I.

50. *O fortunate Spirit:* Cf. *Par.* III, 37.

51. *Her as in a fixed terminus:* The passage is reminiscent of *Par.* XXXIII, 1–21.

52. *answered my questions:* "M'hai soddisfatto alle mie domande." Cf. *Inf.* X, 126: "E io li sodisfeci al suo dimando" ("And I satisfied his question").

53. *make yourself fair again:* Cf. *Purg.* XVI, 31–32: "E io: 'O creatura che ti mondi/ per tornar bella a colui che ti fece' " ("And I: 'O creature who cleanest thyself to return fair to Him that made thee' ").

54. *damned in Hell:* "Ruinare allo'nferno." Boccaccio had used this Dantesque expression in *Am. vis.* III, 5–6: "Tu disii/ di rovinar con doglia al tristo centro" ("You wish to be damned in pain to the center of evil").

55. *She wills:* See n. 4.

56. *concupiscent and carnal love:* The passage appears reminiscent of Andreas Capellanus' *De amore* III (pp. 314–15):

Heu, quantus inest dolor, quantave nos cordis amaritudo detentat, quum dolentes assidue cernimus propter turpes et nefandos Veneris actus hominibus coelestia denegari! O miser et insanus ille ac plus quam bestia reputandus, qui pro momentanea carnis delectatione gaudia derelinquit aeterna et perpetuae gehennae flammis se mancipare laborat!

Alas what an affliction it is and what bitterness to our hearts when we grieve constantly to see men reject the things of heaven for the sake of the foul and shameful acts of Venus! O wretched and insane, to be looked upon as lower than beast, is that man who for the sake of a momentary delight of the flesh will reject eternal joys and strive to hand himself over to the flames of ever-burning Gehenna! Compare also *Am. vis.* II, 52–54: "Tu guardi là, e forse ti diletta/ il cantar che tu odi, il qual piuttosto/ pianto si dovrìa dire in lingua retta" ("You gaze there and perhaps the song you hear delights you—a song which rather should be called weeping in righteous speech"). In contrast to the words of the Spirit of the *Corbaccio,* the narrator of the *Filostrato* (Proemio, p. 17) confesses himself "quasi dalla mia puerizia infino a questo tempo ne' servigi d'Amore" ("in the service of Love almost from my childhood until this time"). See P. Rajna (1890).

57. *labyrinth:* Boccaccio gives an entirely different description of this labyrinth in Lezione XVIII (p. 283) of the *Esposizioni:* "Egli fu, e ancora è, un monte tutto dentro cavato e tutto fatto ad abituri quadri a modo che camere, e ciascuna di queste camere ha quatro usci, in ciascuna faccia uno, li quali vanno ciascuno in camere simiglianti a queste, e così poco si puote avanti andare, che l'uomo vi si smarrisce entro senza saperne fuori uscire" ("There was, and still is, a mountain entirely hollowed out and made into square dwellings like rooms, and each one of these rooms has four doors, one in each wall, which lead to rooms similar to these; hence, one can make little progress, for a man gets lost inside without knowing the way out").

58. *remorse for my sin:* Cf. *Inf.* X, 109: "Allor, come di mia colpa compunto ..." ("Then, feeling remorse for my sin"). See below, n. 312.

59. *grief had so gripped me:* "Sì m'avea il dolor sostenuto." "Sostenere" here is used in its sense of "to grip," "to hold," or "to apprehend." In an autograph letter recently discovered in the Archivio di Stato di Perugia, Boccaccio wrote: "Pochi dì fa messer Brasco duca di Spuleto sostenne in Ispuleto messer Anichino di Mongardo con da .XII. de' suoi compagni et ànnogli mandati presi in Montefalcho ..." ("A few days ago, messer Blasco, Duke of Spoleto, apprehended messer Anichino Baumgarden with twelve of his companions and sent them prisoner to Montefalco"). The full text of the letter is in R. Abbondanza (1963), pp. 6–7.

60. *the light:* See nn. 30, 323, 327.

61. *speak standing up:* A. Levi ([1889], p. 16) suggested that this echoes the Brunetto Latini episode in *Inf.* XV, esp. pp. 37–39.

62. *a trusted friend:* According to the rules of Andreas Capellanus' *De amore* II (p. 267), the lover may divulge his love only to a trusted confidant: "Nam permittitur amatori sui amoris secretarium invenire ido-

neum, cum quo secrete valeat de suo solitiari amore, et qui ei, si contigerit, in amoris compatiatur adversis" ("For the lover is allowed to find a suitable confidant from whom he may get secret comfort in his love affair and who will offer him sympathy if things turn out badly").

63. *as canon law shows us:* As a youth Boccaccio studied canon law, a lucrative profession at the time. See the *Genealogie* XV, 10 (II, 776); C. Osgood (1930), p. 132. P. G. Ricci ([1971], pp. 1–10) suggests that Boccaccio became a Florentine judge; hence his title "dominus," although he had never earned a university degree in law.

64. *a very small number to commend:* A similar comment is found in the "Conclusio" of *De mulieribus claris* (p. 448): "In nostras usque feminas, ut satis apparet, devenimus, quas inter adeo perrarus rutilantium numerus est, ut dare ceptis finem honestius credam quam, his ducentibus hodiernis, ad ulteriora progredi . . ." ("As can be clearly seen, I have reached the women of our time, in which the number of illustrious ones is so small that I think it more suitable to come to an end here rather than proceed further with the women of today . . .").

65. *I would become her servant:* Cf. *Am. vis.* XLIV, 52–63. It is in error, I believe, that G. Padoan ([1963a], p. 9) has stated that the aristocratic and courtly conception of love "here vanishes completely." The narrator-protagonist of the treatise follows the canons of Andreas Capellanus' first two books very closely in spite of the Spirit's ardent antifeminism.

Rinieri of *Decam.* VIII, 7 (II, 133) also made up his mind to serve his lady and win her in the same fashion.

66. *at that hour:* Here Boccaccio is again following Andreas Capellanus (*De amore* I, p. 6): "Incipit enim cogitare, qualiter eius gratiam valeat invenire, incipit etiam quaerere locum et tempus cum opportunitate loquendi . . ." ("He [the lover] begins to plan how he may find favor with her, and he begins to seek a place and a time opportune for talking . . ."). Compare Caleone's words in Boccaccio's *Comedia delle ninfe* XXXV, 102: "Mi levai, e con ferma speranza, più volte cercando in ogni luogo ove belle donne si ragunassero, per vedere questa andai" ("I arose and in firm hope went several times searching every place, where beautiful women might gather, in order to see her").

67. *black color of her clothes:* Compare the appearance of Elena in the tale of the scholar and the widow (*Decam.* VIII, 7; II, 133): "Davanti agli occhi si parò questa Elena, vestita di nero sì come le nostre vedove vanno, piena di tanta bellezza, al suo giudicio, e di tanta piacevolezza quanta alcuna altra ne gli fosse mai paruta vedere . . ." ("Before his eyes appeared this Elena, dressed in black as do our widows, filled with more beauty, in his opinion, and with more charm than any other woman he had ever seen . . ."). Troilo's first look at Criseida in the *Filostrato,* I, 26, bears close comparison:

Così adunque andandosi gabbando
or d'uno or d'altro Troilo, e sovente

or questa donna or quella rimirando,
per caso avvenne che in fra la gente
l' occhio suo vago giunse penetrando
colà dov'era Criseida piacente,
sotto candido velo in bruna vesta
tra l'altre donne in sì solenne festa.

While Troilus was thus going about, mocking first this man and then the other, and often gazing now upon this lady and now upon that, as he glanced among the crowd his wandering eyes chanced to penetrate there where stood the charming Criseida, beneath her white veil in her black gown, among the other ladies at this so solemn festival.

68. *as I glimpsed her face:* "Come il suo viso corse agli occhi miei." The conventional psychophysiology of love posited the eyes as the entrance through which the "intentio" or image of the beloved entered the heart, the seat of the sensitive soul and of the appetites. For Andreas Capellanus, love arose "ex visione alterius sexus" ("from the sight of the opposite sex"); in fact, blindness was a bar to love. (*De amore* I, 1, 5; pp. 3, 12.) This traditional theory was central to Italian poetry from the Sicilian School on.

69. *a love revealed:* Cf. *De amore* II (p. 310): "Amor raro consuevit durare vulgatus" ("When made public, love rarely endures"). Andreas Capellanus did allow the lover a confidant in his secrets, however.

70. *the white wimple:* "le bianche bende." This contemporary dress for widows consisted of strips of white cloth worn about the head and neck. Compare *Purg.* VIII, 73–75; XXIV, 43; and Cecco d'Ascoli, *L'Acerba*, Lib. IV, 4397–98.

71. *the third . . . on that bench:* For the traditional use of the number three, see G. Billanovich (1947), p. 158, n. 1, and V. Branca (1956), p. 11. B. König (1960) indicated Boccaccio's consistent use of medieval topoi in describing the meetings of his various lovers.

72. *just as a flame does on oily things:* Cf. *Inf.* XIX, 28: "Qual suole il fiammeggiar de le cose unte/muoversi pur su per la strema buccia . . ." ("As a flame on oily things is wont to move only on their outer surface . . ."). The common expression "vinto da falso parere" ("overcome by false appearance") appears also, for example, in the Proemio of the *Filostrato* (p. 17).

only inside: Here Boccaccio is following a convention of "courtly" love poetry, as he had before in previous works (see n. 68). Cf. *Fiammetta* (p. 11):

Non altramente il fuoco se stesso d'una parte in un'altra balestra, che una luce, per un raggio sottilissimo trascorrendo da' suoi partendosi, percosse negli occhi miei, nè in quelli contenta rimase, anzi, non so per quali occulte vie, subitamente al cuore penetrando ne gìo.

Il quale . . . rivocate a sè le forze esteriori, me pallida e quasi fred-dissima tutta lasciò . . . cacciata la pallidezza, me rossissima e calda rendè come fuoco. . . .

Just as fire shoots from one place to another, so a light running in a slender beam out from his eyes struck mine, nor did it find content-ment within them; rather, by certain secret ways, suddenly it went penetrating to my heart. Calling its exterior forces to itself, it left me pale and almost freezing . . . when the paleness was chased away, it made me very red and hot as fire. . . .

73. *I will hide nothing from you:* Macrobius (*Comm. in somn. Scip.* I, vii) had declared that the spirits of the dead were endowed with knowledge of the future. Boccaccio's immediate inspiration in this regard seems to have been Dante's *Inf.* X, 100–108, where it is explained that damned souls have knowledge of the past and future but not of the present.

74. *answered nothing openly concerning my love:* Ovid urged the lady in love as follows (*Ars amat.* III, 473–78):

Postque brevem rescribe moram: mora semper amantes
Incitat, exiguum si modo tempus habet.
Sed neque te facilem iuveni promitte roganti,
Nec tamen e duro quod petit ille nega.
Fac timeat speretque simul, quotiensque remittes,
Spesque magis veniat certa minorque metus.

After brief delay write back: delay ever spurs lovers on, if but its term be brief. But neither promise yourself too easily to him who entreats you, nor yet deny what he asks too stubbornly. Cause him to hope and fear together; and as often as you reply, see that hope becomes surer and fear diminishes.

In the *Roman de la Rose,* Jean de Meung also recommended that the lady's letters keep her lover in balance between hope and fear (IV, 30; vv. 13665–68). Compare the experiences of Rinieri in the *Decam.* VIII, 7 (II, 134): "Lo scolar lieto procedette a più caldi prieghi ed a scriver lettere ed a mandar doni, ed ogni cosa era ricevuta, ma indietro non venivan risposte se non generali" ("The scholar, overjoyed, continued with more ardent prayers to write letters and send presents, and every-thing was received, but no answers came in return except such as were couched in general terms").

75. *some feet . . . short:* The protagonist is referring to the erroneous meter of the woman's awkward poetry.

Compare the situation in Ovid (*Ars amat.* III, 481–82):

A! quotiens dubius scriptis exarsit amator,
Et nocuit formae barbara lingua bonae!

Ah! how often has a message inflamed a doubting lover, or some barbaric phrase done harm to beauteous shape!

76. *during sermons and not . . . at school:* T. Nurmela ([1968], p. 154, n. 160) has suggested that the preachers spoke of the transmigration of souls as a warning against false doctrine. However, it seems more likely that the protagonist is accusing the clergy of heresy, in view of the Spirit's later disparaging and sarcastic description of them as sinners and lechers: "most holy, merciful men and consolers of widows" (p. 59).

77. *flattery . . . to content me:* Cf. *Decam.* VIII, 7 (II, 144–45): "Le tue lusinghe non m'adombreranno ora gli occhi dello'ntelletto . . ." ("Your flatteries will not now cloud the eyes of my intellect"). In a similar manner, Elena sets her trap for Rinieri. Both the widow of the *Corbaccio* and Elena herself act contrary to the rules of Andreas Capellanus (*De amore* II, vi; p. 268): "Et firmiter credimus esse tenendum, ut, si mulier alicui spem sui largiatur amoris vel alia sibi amoris primitiva concesserit, et ipse tali non reperiatur indignus amore, magna mulieris iudicatur offensa, si diu sperata denegare contendat. Non enim probam decet feminam sua quaecunque sine causa retardare promissa . . ." ("We believe we must firmly hold that when a woman has granted any man the hope of her love or has given him any of the other preliminary gifts, and she finds him not unworthy of this love, it is very wrong for her to try to deprive him of the love he has so long hoped for. It is not proper for any honest woman to put off without good cause the fulfillment of any of her promises . . .").

78. *proper not to speak of it:* Cf. *Par.* XVI, 45: "Più è tacer che ragionare onesto" ("Silence is more proper than speech").

79. *a cruel and wicked woman:* Cf. *Decam.* VIII, 7 (II, 145): "una vile e cattiva e rea feminetta" ("a base, evil, wicked woman"). In that tale, the widow Elena likewise had divulged Rinieri's suit to her paramour.

80. *the second Absalom:* An ironical and conventional nickname ridiculing the paramour's conceit; cf. II Kings (II Samuel), XIV:25: "Sicut Absalom, non erat vir pulcher in omni Israel, et decorus nimis; a vestigio pedis usque ad verticem non erat in eo ulla macula" ("But in all Israel there was not a man so comely, and so exceedingly beautiful as Absalom: from the sole of his foot to the crown of his head there was no blemish in him"). See also *Inf.* XXVIII, 137; and *Am. vis.* VIII, 7–9:

> Nel riguardar più innanzi affigurai
> il viso d'Ansalon, che più bellezza
> ebbe che altro nel mondo giammai.

> By gazing further on I made out the face of Absalom, who had more beauty than anyone else in the world ever had.

The story from Samuel was commonly used in the Middle Ages as an *exemplum* of pride and vanity; cf. J. Ulrich (1884), p. 46.

81. *associated with worthy men:* In *De amore* II (p. 242), Andreas Capellanus stated: "Praeterea omni conatu curare debet amator cum bonis assidue conversari et malorum societatem penitus evitare. Vilium namque consortio amatoris iuncta persona sui ipsius contemptum parit

amanti" ("Furthermore, a lover should make every attempt to be constantly in the company of good men and to avoid completely the society of the wicked. For association with the vulgar makes a lover who joins them a thing of contempt to his beloved"). Rinieri in *Decam.* VIII, 7 (II, 133), lived in Florence "onorato molto sì per la sua nobiltà e sì per la sua scienza, cittadinescamente" ("as a citizen, greatly honored both by reason of his rank and for his learning").

82. *pointed out by a woman:* The paragraph's *non sequiturs* vividly portray the protagonist's agitated state of mind. Capellanus had warned that a poor man would fear that the woman would scorn his poverty (*De amore,* I, p. 4).

83. *by doing so:* "Ciò faccendo," "da tale impresa." A repetition in the text.

84. *sinful desire:* That is, his yearning for death.

85. *you almost went out of your mind:* "Che quasi te a te stesso fecero uscir di mente." Cf. *Purg.* VIII, 15, where Dante used the expression to the opposite effect: a soul sweetly singing *Te lucis ante* draws the Wayfarer out of himself ("che fece me a me uscir di mente"). Boccaccio often perverted such Dantesque echoes in the *Corbaccio.*

The Spirit here indicates that his speech will be divided into three sections: first, he will deal with the question of the protagonist's guilt, his age and his studies, which should have taught him what women are, what love is (pp. 23ff.), and who he, a man and poet, is himself (pp. 35–37); second, he will discuss the peculiar habits and ways of the widow (pp. 37–69); third, he will treat the causes of the protagonist's grief, in particular, the widow's social position, and the question of nobility (pp. 69–71).

86. *old age:* Traditional divisions of man's life vary in timing the onset of old age. St. Thomas Aquinas had placed it at fifty years of age, although the generally accepted year was forty-five, the view which Dante held (*Conv.* IV, xxiv, 3). Most discussions caution that the divisions vary according to the individual's constitution. However, one can suppose that the protagonist is in his early or middle forties. That this reference should be of help in dating the treatise is open to question, for we have no evidence to show that the protagonist's age should correspond to Boccaccio's own. For a treatment of the "seven ages of man" in literature, see J. W. Jones (1853), pp. 167–89; H. Green (1870), pp. 406–9; F. Novati (1886), p. 42, n. 2; A. Della Torre (1905), p. 69; *Conv.,* eds. Busnelli and Vandelli (1934), II, pp. 304–7; and n. 87, below.

Contrary to the Spirit's teaching, but in agreement with the lusty tendencies of the narrator-protagonist of the *Corbaccio,* the staged author of *Decam.* IV, Introduction (I, 273), had claimed that he would never abandon love: "Io mai a me vergogna non reputerò infino nello stremo della mia vita di dover compiacere a quelle cose alle quali Guido Cavalcanti e Dante Alighieri già vecchi e Messer Cino da Pistoia vecchissimo onor si tennero, e fu lor caro il piacer loro" ("Never to the end of my life shall I consider it shameful for me to take pleasure in those things in

which Guido Cavalcanti and Dante Alighieri in their old age, and Messer
Cino da Pistioa in extreme old age, took honor and delight").

87. *first is your age . . . mad passion was to lead you:* A textual night-
mare. The passage contains an anacoluthon in all extant texts and has
lent itself to many interpretations. For simplicity we quote Nurmela's
edition of the text:

> L'una è la tua età, la seconda sono gli tuoi studi; delle quali ciascuna
> per sè e amendune insieme ti doveano render cauto e guardingo
> dagli amorosi lacciuoli; e primieramente la tua età, la quale se
> le tempie già bianche e la canuta barba non m'ingannano, tu dov-
> resti avere li costumi del mondo; fuori delle fasce già sono degli anni
> quaranta e già sono venticinque cominciatoli a conoscere. E se la
> lunga esperienza delle fatiche d'amore nella tua giovanezza tanto
> non t'avea gastigato che bastasse, la tiepidezza degli anni, già alla
> vecchiezza appressatisi, almeno ti doveva aprire gli occhi a farti
> conoscere là dove questa matta passione, seguitando, ti doveva far
> cadere . . . (p. 68).

It will be noted that the pronoun "la quale" is left without a verb and
"cominciatoli" seemingly without a reference.

Many critics have seen in this Gordian paragraph an indication of the
work's date of composition, and, to explain away the difficulties, most
have simply added forty to Boccaccio's birthdate, 1313. This method,
with some ingenious sophistications, has been the basis of most con-
siderations on the subject (see G. Padoan [1963a, 1963b]; T. Nurmela
[1968], pp. 18–21 and p. 156, n. 179; and V. Zaccaria [1969], pp. 338–
40). Padoan, however, believed the numbers had nothing to do with
Boccaccio personally, but were to be added together to indicate the year
of composition, thus giving 1365 (Florentine style) or 1366 (new style).
The critic was persuaded that the repetitious phrase "fuor delle fasce già
sono degli anni quaranta, e già sono venticinque" was to be interpreted
as a cabalistic warning of the end of the world. However, nowhere in the
text is there the slightest indication that this is Boccaccio's intention. Such
an interpretation could only be ascribed if the passage were to be read out
of context.

Earlier, G. Billanovich ([1947], p. 163, n. 1) had questioned the
validity of using the sentence for dating the treatise at all since the numbers in question, he asserted, offered only an approximation; they were
"judiciously rounded by addition or subtraction" to match "the abstract
universality" of the treatise. His suggestion deserves better reception.
Previous critics who had used the sentence to date the work had based
their assumption on the strict identification of the protagonist with
Boccaccio himself, but it seems most probable that something more
general and less personal is intended. We have no external proof that the
work is autobiographical at all. Indeed, we have no more reason to apply

these schematic numbers to Boccaccio's life than we have for taking Dante's artistic clocking of his fictional otherworld journey as history.

The most obvious interpretation is that Boccaccio is referring to the protagonist's stages of life ("la tua età"; "your age"), and, by the numerals 40 minus 25, the transition from childhood to adolescence at roughly fourteen or fifteen years. A. Della Torre ([1905], pp. 69–101, esp. p. 97) notes that the writer often referred to the traditional schema of the "ages of man" in his works, and quotes abundant textual precedents which assume that adolescence begins at about fourteen years and ends at about twenty-five. As is well known, the chronological divisions of man's life were far from settled and precise in classical and medieval writings. The Romans understood *adolescentia* generally as the age between fifteen and thirty. In St. Albertus Magnus' *De aetatibus sive de iuventute et senectute* ("On Ages or on Youth and Old Age"; tr. 1, cap. 3) puberty (*aetas pubertatis*) lasts from the eleventh year to the sixteenth, "usque ad decimum sextum"; St. Thomas Aquinas placed the end of boyhood at the end of the fourteenth year (see the comments of Busnelli and Vandelli in their edition of Dante's *Convivio* [1934], II, p. 303, n. 13; p. 304, n. 5; and V. Branca and P. G. Ricci [1969], pp. 5–7). Indeed, the Church Councils of Toulouse (1229), Béziers (1244), and Albi (1254) had assumed that a boy was responsible for his actions at the age of fourteen, and a girl at the age of twelve. A mosaic of roughly 1476 in the Duomo of Siena declares, "Infans ad VII, pueritia ad XV años," "Infancy to seven, childhood to fifteen years" (see H. Green [1870], p. 407).

We meet with a great difficulty in interpreting cardinal numerals in expressions of age, for often the ordinal was used as a cardinal and vice versa (E. H. Wilkins [1910], p. 369). We are left therefore with a choice of reading St. Albertus' "decimum sextum" as sixteen or fifteen and St. Thomas' "quartum decimum" as thirteen or fourteen! Before being adamant about the length of any one age, we should heed Dante's warning in the *Convivio* (IV, xxiv, 6–7; vol. II, p. 311): "Veramente, sì come di sopra detto è, queste etadi possono essere più lunghe e più corte secondo la complessione nostra e la composizione . . ." ("Truly, as is stated above, these ages can be longer or shorter according to our constitution and our physical make-up . . ."); and before interpreting the passage from the *Corbaccio* too narrowly, we must note that in the context the Spirit himself is merely guessing the age of the protagonist and is leaving ample room for his own deception in the matter: "Se le tempie già bianche e la canuta barba *non m'ingannano* . . ." ("If your temples already white and your grizzled beard *do not deceive me"* [italics added]). With these cautions born in mind, it will be at once recognized that the problem is capable of a far more flexible interpretation.

The beginning of adolescence marks the initiation into sexual relations; the two are always joined in discussions of the ages of man. Hugh of

St. Victor's belief that young men before they are fourteen years old and girls before they are twelve might not, according to the laws, enter into marriage is echoed by Andreas Capellanus in the *De amore* I, 5 (p. 12): "Ante duodecim annos femina, et ante decimum quartum annum masculus non solet in amoris exercitu militare" ("A girl before the age of twelve and a boy before the age of fourteen do not usually take part in love's army"). V. Branca ([1956], p. 140, n. 44) has noted that the age of fifteen is generally chosen as the nubile age in the *Decameron* and in Boccaccio's previous works.

The main problem of the explanations given heretofore has been the critics' tendency to ignore the context of this passage when they use it to date the work. Within the sentence the words "costumi del mondo" clearly refer not, as Padoan believes, to the contemporary mores of society, but to the most worldly of worldly pleasures, the *delicta vana* of *luxuria* or lust. The Spirit is discussing the connection of this vice with the age of human life when it manifests itself most uncontrollably. In the *Esposizioni* (pp. 61–62), after dealing with the gluttony of childhood, Boccaccio was again to ally carnality to adolescence:

> E per ciò che i lacciuoli [compare the "lacciuoli" in the *Corbaccio* fragment above] sono infiniti, li quali la carne, il mondo e'l dimonio tendono alla nostra sensualità, pienamente dire non se ne potrebbe per lingua d'uomo. . . . Sono generalmente i fanciulli vaghi del cibo . . . nella *età più piena procedendo,* quasi come da naturale ordine tirati, nel *vizio della lussuria* discorrono.
>
> Questa, la quale non solamente i giovani, ma i vecchi, fa se medesimi sovente dimenticare, loro con tante e tali lusinghe diletica che, potendo all'appetito la vigorosa età *dell'adolescenzia* sodisfare, con ogni pensiero e con ardentissima affezione quello vituperevole diletto seguendo, tutti si mettono. [Italics added.]

Since the traps which the flesh, the world, and the devil set for our sensuality are numberless, human tongue could not recount them fully. . . . Children are generally fond of food . . . and proceeding to *the next maturer age,* they rush into the *vice of lust* as if drawn by natural order.

This vice, which makes not only the young but even the old forgetful of themselves, tempts them with such flatteries that since the vigorous *age of adolescence* can satisfy the appetite, they all set to it, following that despicable delight with every thought and burning affection.

In the same way in Sonnet LXXXVII of his *Rime* (ed. V. Branca [1958], p. 80), Boccaccio united the word "costumi" to carnal love:

> S'Amor, li cui costumi già molt'anni
> con sospiri 'nfiniti provat'hai,
> t'è or più grave che l'usato assai,

perché, seguendol, te medesmo inganni,
credendo trovar pace tra gli affanni?

If Love, whose ways you have experienced now for many years with
numberless sighs, is now far harsher to you than usual, why in self-
deception do you follow him hoping to find peace amid the
troubles?

In the passage from the *Corbaccio,* the references to lechery ("amorosi
lacciuoli," "fatiche d'amore") are clearly bound in the same way to the
discussion of the various ages of the protagonist's life (*adolescenza,
giovanezza, vecchiezza;* adolescence, youth, old age), and the numbers
in question reflect convention in the divisions of those ages (see also n.
86). Rather than making a mere autobiographical allusion, or a chiliastic
prediction of the end of the world, Boccaccio again followed a literary
tradition. It is difficult to conclude, therefore, that the numbers in question are an indication of the date of composition.

88. *making money:* Boccaccio contrasted the speculative sciences and commerce in a similar manner in the *Genealogie,* XIV, iv (II, 687), insisting
that money-getting is not the end of the former (see C. G. Osgood [1930],
p. 23). Boccaccio shows the same scholarly scorn in other passages; cf.
also, nn. 161, 174, 232, 297.

89. *with heights of genius:* Cf. *Inf.* X, 59: "vai per altezza d'ingegno"
("you go by height of genius"). See *Genealogie* XV, x (II, 775–76),
where Boccaccio declares that his father continually resisted and condemned his early pursuit of letters (see translation in C. G. Osgood
[1930], pp. 131–32).

90. *what love is, what women are:* These topics constitute set topoi in medieval rhetoric and are traceable to the widely disseminated *Life of
Secundus* (last half of second century, A.D.), in which the "silent philosopher" replies to the Emperor Hadrian's questions, "Quid est amor?"
"Quid est mulier?" (see B. E. Perry [1964], pp. 1–10). Such diatribes
against carnal love became commonplace in the Middle Ages. Alain de
Lille has a similar invective in the *De planctu Naturae* (*PL,* CCX, 455;
Anglo-Latin Sat. II, 472); Andreas Capellanus continued the tradition
in Book III of his *De amore* (pp. 330–31) and Guillaume de Lorris in
the *Roman de la Rose,* vv. 4271ff. Boccaccio described "lussuria" (lust
or lechery) in similar terms in the *Esposizioni* (p. 339).

In Rime LXXIV Boccaccio portrayed Love as a "lying, treacherous
and disloyal, fraudulent, deadly, thieving cut-throat, a cruel tyrant, a
perjurer, and a murderer." In the *Filocolo* (ed. A. E. Quaglio [1967],
p. 424) he apostrophized it as being "d'onore privatore, adducitore
d'affanni, destatore di vizii, copioso donatore di vane sollecitudini, in-
degno occupatore dell'altrui libertà, più ch'altra cosa da tenere cara"
("the depriver of honor, the producer of suffering, the arouser of vices,
the abundant giver of vain cares, the unworthy usurper of men's liberty—

liberty which is to be held dearer than anything else"). Later, the author was to vituperate love as the sin of Dante in the *Trattatello* XII (*Opere in versi*, p. 627).

Both G. Padoan ([1959], p. 32, n. 8) and T. Nurmela ([1968], p. 157, n. 193) have suspected "unknown sources" for this passage; see A. K. Cassell (1973) for the derivation.

91. *Love as a young, naked archer:* Compare Brunetto Latini's description of Love [Cupido] in the *Tesoretto*, vv. 2261ff. (ed. G. Contini [1960], II, p. 254):

> io vidi dritto stante
> ignudo un fresco fante,
> ch'avea l'arco e li strali
> e avea penn' ed ali
> ma neente vedea . . .

I saw a young nude boy standing upright, who had a bow and arrows, but who saw nothing . . .

In Boccaccio's *Filocolo* (pp. 306–7), Fileno gives the following diatribe: "Tu, ignudo, non dei poter porgere speranza di rivestire. Le tue ali mostrano la tua mobilità, nè m'è della memoria uscito averti in alcune parti veduto privato della vista: dunque, come di dietro alla guida d'un cieco si può fare diritto cammino?" ("You, o naked one, should not give hope of clothing yourself again. Your wings show your fickleness; nor have I forgotten having seen you in certain places deprived of sight; well, how can one follow a straight path with a blindman for a guide?") Compare also the portrayal of Cupid in the *Genealogie* IX, 4 (II, 453–54):

> Hunc insuper puerum fingunt, ut etatem suscipientium passionem hanc et mores designent. . . . Alatus preterea dicitur, ut passionati instabilitas demonstretur; facile enim credentes cupientesque de passione in passionem evolant. Arcum atque sagittas ideo ferre fingitur, ut insipientum repentina captivitas ostendatur; nam in ictu fere oculi capiuntur. Has aureas esse dicunt et plumbeas, et aureis amorem, plumbeis autem odium inferri, ut amantium ostendatur opinio. . . . Oculos vero illi fascia tegunt, ut advertamus amantes ignorare quo tendant, nulla eorum esse iudicia, nulle rerum distinctiones, sed sola passione duci. Pedes autem gryphis illi ideo apponuntur ut declaretur quoniam tenacissima sit passio, nec facile inerti impressa ocio solvitur.

They depict him [Cupid] as a boy to indicate the age of those who take up this passion and behavior. . . . He is also called 'winged' to show the instability of the impassioned man; for men, readily trusting and desiring, fly from passion to passion. Cupid is depicted carrying a bow and arrows to show the sudden capture of unwary men; for they are, as a rule, captured within the blink of an eye. They say to show the point of view of lovers that his arrows are of gold and of lead and that love is carried by the golden arrows and hatred by the leaden ones. . . . They cover his eyes with a cloth so that we may notice that lovers have no idea where they are going, that their judgment is as nothing and that they have no discrimination, but are led by passion alone. Griffin's feet are attached to him to show that since passion is very tenacious, once it has gained a grip on someone who is sluggish in his idleness, it is not easily shaken off. Boccaccio's iconology was not classically correct; see E. Panofsky (1962), pp. 95–107, esp. pp. 97, 107. For the medieval interpretation of Cupid's attributes, see J. Seznec (1961), pp. 90, 104.

92. *what women are:* The Mannelli MS (Biblioteca Laurenziana, Cod. Pluteo XLII, 1; 179ᵛ, col. 1) bears a rubric at this point declaring "quid sit mulier," and in a fifteenth-century MS the *Corbaccio* (Cod. Pluteo XLII, 32) is followed by a series of antifeminist citations in the scribe's hand. The selections include the story of Secundus (see above, n. 90) and quotations attributed to Seneca, Terence, Lucan, Theophrastus, Solomon, Aristotle, Homer, Demosthenes, and John Chrysostom. The list is similar to that of Antonio Pucci in the *Libro di varie storie,* pp. 208–22. See H. Hauvette (1914), p. 338, n. 1.

For other examples of the "quid est mulier" topos, see A. Wulff (1914), pp. 7–8; C. Brown (1920), pp. 479–82; J. C. Orelli (1819), I, pp. 220–21; A. M. Mazzuchelli (1901), p. 76; St. John Chrysostom, *Homilia XXXII: Mulieris malae descriptio (PG,* LVI, 803); Maximus the Confessor, *Loci communes, PG,* XCI, 911; Fra Salimbene di Adamo, *Cronaca,* I, pp. 192–93; P. Meyer (1886); (1906), p. 576; A. Pucci, *Libro di varie storie,* pp. 214–16; Alain de Lille, *De planctu Naturae (PL,* CCX, 455; *Anglo-Latin Sat.* II, 472); *Strenne nuziali,* ed. Targioni-Tozzetti, pp. 68–69; Cecco d'Ascoli, *L'Acerba,* Lib. IV, 4403–16; and B. E. Perry (1964), p. 96. See also E. Besta (1931), pp. 133–34; A. Viscardi and G. Barni (1966), p. 429.

For a history of the sources and the tradition of this commonplace, see A. K. Cassell (1973).

93. *'ladies':* For a discussion of the uses of "femmina" and "donna" ("woman"; "lady"), see G. Bonfante (1958), pp. 77–109. The *De amore,* II of Andreas Capellanus (p. 178) makes a similar distinction.

Nurmela has indicated that Francesco da Barberino also followed the same usage in his *Del reggimento e de' costumi delle donne,* Part II (p. 32): "Poniamo che sia femmina, ella non è già donna nè vo' che sia tra le donne nominata" ("Let us suppose that she is a woman; she is not at all a lady, nor do I wish her to be named among the ladies"). In Machiavelli's time the word "femmina" had become so pejorative that it meant "prostitute"; see *La Mandragola* Act II, Scene vi (ed. M. Bonfantini [1963], p. 1003): "Perchè io non vo' far la mia donna femmina e me becco" ("Because I do not want to make my wife a whore and myself a cuckold").

94. *woman . . . excited by a thousand foul passions:* A commonplace; see Juvenal, *Satire* VI, 317–18. See also G. Pinelli (1883), pp. 169–92.

95. *a fool who loves them:* Cf. Juvenal, *Satire* VI, 208–10, 222.

96. *the year, soon to begin again:* The Florentine year began on March 25. This passage does not necessarily indicate the date of composition, for Boccaccio is following an important tradition by setting the work at this time of year. Tertullian's opinion that true dreams occurred in early spring (*De anima* XLVIII, 1; 66) was obeyed with few exceptions in the Middle Ages. Such varied works as the *Golias de conjuge non ducenda* ("in verno tempore"; "in springtime"), the *Proverbia quae dicuntur super naturam feminarum* ("el mes de março quando i albri florise"; "the month of March when the trees are in bloom"), the *Apocalypsis Goliae,* the *Roman de la Rose,* the *De planctu Naturae,* Boccaccio's *Am. vis.* and his *Caccia di Diana,* among many others, are all springtime visions.

Spring is coventionally allied both to earthly, carnal love (the theme of the *Corbaccio*) and to the religious idea of rebirth, a new beginning, the time of Christ's conception, death, and resurrection. The *Divina Commedia,* although not technically a dream-vision, took place at Eastertime and also had a clear influence in this regard. See Northrup Frye (1957), p. 57; F. X. Newman (1962), pp. 267–81.

97. *adding to that which nature has lent them:* A topos of antifeminism. Tertullian, in the *De cultu feminarum* I, 2 (*PL,* I, 1417–48), pointed out that according to the Book of Enoch (VII, 1), ornaments and make-up were inventions of the fallen angels and, therefore, of diabolical origin. St. Ambrose (*De virginibus* I, 6; *PL,* XVI, 207) declared that painting the face was equivalent to changing or attempting to excel the work of Nature herself, and consequently the work of God: an admonishment which became commonplace. St. Anselm of Canterbury repeated the rebuke in his *De contemptu mundi* (*PL,* CLV, 696), and he is echoed by Alexander Neckam in the *De vita monachorum* (*Anglo-Latin Sat.* II, p. 190). See A. K. Cassell (1970), p. 87, for other examples of this topos and their importance for the title, "Corbaccio."

The *Decameron* II, 7 (I, 123) referred to the use of cosmetics with the following rebuke: "Voi, graziose donne, sommamente peccate in una [cosa], cioè nel disiderare d'esser belle, in tanto che, *non bastandovi le bellezze che dalla natura concedute vi sono,* ancora con maravigliosa arte quelle cercate d'accrescere . . ." ("You, gracious ladies, sin gravely in one thing: that is, in desiring to be beautiful; since, insofar as you are *not content with the beauty which nature allotted you,* you seek to enhance it with amazing ingenuity . . ." [italics added]).

98. *hook hidden in the bait:* See n. 268 below.

99. *mistresses of a far greater number:* Cf. Juvenal, *Satire* VI, 229.

100. *crowns . . . wealth of clothes:* Criticism of feminine dress was very common in fourteenth-century Florence. Dante himself, in the mouth of

Forese, had railed against feminine immodesty (*Purg.* XXIII, 98–108):

> Tempo futuro m'è già nel cospetto,
> cui non sarà quest'ora molto antica,
> nel qual sarà in pergamo interdetto
> a le sfacciate donne fiorentine
> l'andar mostrando con le poppe il petto.
> Quai barbare fuor mai, quai saracine,
> cui bisognasse, per farle ir coperte,
> o spiritali o altre discipline?
> Ma se le svergognate fosser certe
> di quel che'l ciel veloce loro ammanna,
> già per urlare avrian le bocche aperte....

A future time is already before my eyes for which this hour will not be very old when from the pulpit it shall be forbidden to the brazen women of Florence to go showing the breast with the paps. What barbarous women, what Saracens, ever were there that needed, to make them go covered, spiritual disciplines or any other? But had the shameless creatures knowledge of what the swift heavens prepare for them, they would have their mouths open already for howling ... [adapted from J. D. Sinclair].

At the Council of Lyons in 1274, Gregory X had forbade women to adorn themselves with costly articles. The Council of 1290 discussed whether to issue a declaration limiting feminine fashions; Brunetto Latini was among those consulted. Florence was not alone in promulgating sumptuary laws. Ferrara made an ordinance against finery in 1279; Bologna in 1294; Venice in 1303. Frederick I of Aragon proclaimed a ban at Messina in 1309; Savona in 1325; Modena in 1327; Perugia in 1318 and 1342; Pistoia in 1332; and Milan and Venice again in 1340 (E. Rodocanachi [1907], pp. 123–26, and A. Viscardi and G. Barni [1966], pp. 284–300).

Regulation of women's clothing entered Florentine Diocesan Law in 1310 (R. C. Trexler [1971], pp. 114–17); Dante's "prediction" quoted above was based on hindsight ("in pergamo interdetto"). In his *Cronica* (*Cronisti del Trecento,* pp. 336–37), Giovanni Villani tells us about later civic sumptuary laws in the Arno Republic:

> Nel detto anno [1330] per calen d'aprile essendo le donne di Firenze molto trascorse in soperchi ornamenti di corone e ghirlande d'oro e d'argento, e di perle e pietre preziose, e reti e intrecciatoi di perle, e altri divisati ornamenti di testa di grande costo, e simile di vestiti intagliati di diversi panni e di drappi rilevati di seta e di più maniere, con fregi e di perle e di bottoni d'argento dorato ispessi a quattro e sei fila accoppiati insieme, e fibbiali di perle e di pietre preziose al petto con diversi segni e lettere ... fu sopra ciò provve-

duto, e fatti per certi uficiali certi ordini molto forti, che niuna donna
non potesse portare nulla corona nè ghirlanda nè d'oro nè d'ariento
nè di perle nè di pietre nè di seta nè di niuna similitudine di corona
nè di ghirlanda, eziandio di carta dipinta, nè rete nè trecciere di nulla
spezie se non semplici. . . . I quali divieti fatti, furono molto com-
mendati e lodati da tutti gl'Italiani: e se le donne usavano soperchi
ornamenti, furono recate al convenevole; onde forte si dolsono tutte,
ma per gli forti ordini tutte si rimasono degli oltraggi . . . molto fu
grande vantaggio a tutti i cittadini in non fare le disordinate spese
sulle loro donne, conviti e nozze, come prima faceano . . . .

Since the women of Florence had given themselves over to excess
ornaments of crowns and garlands of gold and silver, of pearls and
precious stones, nets, pearl braids, and other various head adornments of great cost, and, similarly, dresses embroidered with different materials, and cloths appliquéd with silk in different ways, with
embellishments both of pearls and gilded silver buttons thickly
joined together, in four to six rows, and brooches of pearls and
precious stones on their breasts in various designs and letters . . . in
the said year [1330] in the calends of April certain very stringent
ordinances were made against this by certain officials: that no woman
could wear any crown or garland either of gold, silver, pearls, gems,
or silk, or any imitation crown or garland, even of painted paper,
or any nets or plaits except for simple ones. . . . When these prohi-
bitions were made, they were well praised and commended by all
Italians; and if any woman used excess ornaments, she was brought
back to propriety, wherefore all women grieved greatly, but, because
of the stringent ordinances, all refrained from violation. . . . It was a
great advantage to all citizens not to make disordinate expenditures
on their ladies, or on their banquets or weddings as they had previously. . . .

After the expulsion of Gauthier de Brienne, the stern Signoria decreed
in October, 1343, that all women were to register expensive and showy
apparel with the state notary: the courts were told to prosecute those who
violated the ordinance. Wives of some of the leading families—the
Alberti, Bardi, Medici, and Pazzi—were condemned to pay fines up to
one hundred florins. See E. Rodocanachi (1907), pp. 335–47; M. B.
Becker (1967), pp. 105, 228. In 1354 the laws were repealed and jurisdiction over sumptuary affairs was turned over temporarily to the
Bishop's Court; however, the civic laws were reinstated strongly by the
Commune in 1355. See also n. 97 above, n. 249 below, and the translation
of Sumptuary Laws in the Appendix.

An amusing satire on the difficulty of enforcing this legislation can be
read in F. Sacchetti's *Trecentonovelle* CXXXVII (also tale CLXXVIII).
101. *resplendent every day:* Boccaccio's passage owes something to Ovid's
De medicamine faciei liber (*On Painting the Face*), vv. 17–22:

At vestrae matres teneras peperere puellas:
Vultis inaurata corpora veste tegi,
Vultis adoratos positu variare capillos,
Conspicuas gemmis vultis habere manus:
Induitis collo lapides oriente petitos,
Et quantos onus est aure tulisse duos.

But your mothers have borne delicate girls. You wish your bodies to be covered with gold-embroidered gowns, you wish to vary the dressing of your perfumed locks, you wish to have hands that shine with gems: you adorn your necks with stones sought from the East, and so large that that the ear finds two a burden to bear.

The censure is also an echo of the Theophrastus fragment of *De nuptiis* quoted by St. Jerome in his *Adversus Jovinianum* I (*PL*, XXIII, 289): "Multa esse quae matronarum usibus necessaria sint, pretiosae vestes, aurum, gemmae, sumptus, ancillae, supellex varia, lecticae et esseda deaurata" ("Many are the necessities a woman must have at her disposal: expensive clothes, gold, jewelry, household money, servant girls, varied furnishings, litters, and gilded carriages").

John of Salisbury quoted this passage verbatim in the *Polycraticus* (*PL*, CIC, 750), and Boccaccio himself copied it into the *Zibaldone laurenziano* (*Codex Pluteo* XXIX, 8), echoing it again in the *Trattatello* (*Opere in versi,* pp. 583–84) as follows:

Oh fatica inestimabile, avere con così sospettoso animale a vivere, a conversare, e ultimamente ad invecchiare o a morire! Io voglio lasciare stare la sollecitudine nuova e gravissima, la quale si conviene avere a' non usati (e massimamente nella nostra città), cioè onde vengano i vestimenti, gli ornamenti e le camere piene di superflue dilicatezze, le quali le donne si fanno a credere essere al ben vivere opportune; onde vengano li servi, le serve, le nutrici, le cameriere; onde vengano i conviti, i doni, i presenti che fare si convengono a' parenti delle novelle spose. . . .

Oh, the incalculable weariness of having to live and converse, and finally to grow old and die, with so suspicious a creature! I prefer to pass over the strange and heavy cares which those unused to it must bear (especially in our city), namely, the provision of clothes, ornaments, and roomfuls of needless trifles, which women pretend are necessary to proper living; the provision of men-servants, nurses, and chambermaids; the furnishing of banquets, gifts, and presents, which must be made to the brides' relatives. . . [adapted from J. R. Smith].

For a history of the Theophrastus tradition, see P. Toynbee (1892), p. 616.

102. *they can be sure they are the mistress and ruler:*   Compare this passage from the *Trattatello* (*Opere in versi,* p. 585): "Esse imaginano il bene op-

erare ogni menomo servo ritener nella casa, e il contrario fargli cacciare; per che estimano, se ben fanno, non altra sorte esser la lor che d'un servo: per che allora par solamente loro esser donne, quando, male adoperando, non vengono al fine che' fanti fanno" ("They imagine that good conduct on the part of the lowliest servant retains him in the household and that the contrary leads to his dismissal. So they believe that if they themselves do well, their fate is only that of a servant, and they think that they are ladies only so long as, while doing wrong, they yet escape the end to which menials come" [adapted from J. R. Smith]).

103. *for whom they care little:* The preceding passages owe much to Juvenal, *Satire* VI, 208–10, 508–11.

104. *Get over there:* Cf. *Inf.* XXII, 96.

105. *you'll get what's coming to you:* The Italian proverb "a fare a far sia" conveys the notion of *lex talionis.* Cf. *Decam.* II, 9 (I, 159), where the proverb is used in a similar context. See also n. 278 below.

106. *break a leg:* The implication of the sentence is unclear; in the verse adaptation of the *Corbaccio* by Lodovico Bartoli, the *Corbaccino* (p. 257; st. lxxvii), the versifier construed the passage as follows, making the matchmaker of the marriage the recipient of the wished-for broken leg:

> Ben dico fu la mia disaventura
> quando qui venni per cotanta angoscia,
> non fu di riso mai cotal fattura.
> Che ora s'avesse fiaccata la coscia
> chi per me fece mai cotal procura
> ch'i' tua mai fossi o prima o poscia!

Indeed I say it was my bad luck when I came here in such anguish; such a business was never a laughing matter. If only he had broken a leg, he who played the matchmaker for me! That I might never have been yours at any time!

The form of this diatribe belongs to the traditions of antifeminist satire and, in particular, bears many points of resemblance to that of Monna Sismonda's mother in *Decam.* VII, 8 (II, 82): "Alla croce di Dio ... egli non ne fu degno d'avere una figliuola come se' tu ... basterebbe se egli t'avesse ricolta del fango!" ("By the cross of God ... A daughter such as you to be mated with one so unworthy of you.... Why, it is as if he had picked you up from the mud!")

The nightly nagging scene is reminiscent of Juvenal, *Satire* VI, 268–78, and the fragment of Theophrastus' *De nuptiis* in St. Jerome's *Adversus Jovinianum* (*PL,* XXIII, 289); see also the animated elaboration given to the topos in Matheolus' *Lamentations* (pp. 133–34; vv. 1993–2004) and in Jean le Fèvre's French translation. Not realizing the long tradition behind this passage, H. Hauvette ([1914], pp. 17–18) believed it based on Boccaccio's personal reminiscence of the nightly discourses of Margherita di Gian Donato dei Mardoli, his stepmother.

107. *one eye than . . . one man:* The marginal note of the Mannelli MS refers to Juvenal's *Satire* VI, 53–54:

> Unus Hiberinae vir sufficit? ocius illud
> extorquebis, ut haec oculo contenta sit uno.

> But will Hiberina be satisfied with one man? Sooner compel her to be satisfied with one eye!

The passage became a topos of medieval antifeminist satire. Bernard of Morlaix, for example, repeats it in his *De contemptu mundi* (*Anglo-Latin Sat.* II, p. 60):

> Uxor adultera quaerit in infera plus quoque mitti,
> quam comes unius, o furor impius, esse mariti.
> Sufficientior et sibi gratior unus ocellus
> quam comes unicus, o furor ethnicus!

> The adulterous wife would rather be sent to hell than be the companion of only one husband, o impious madness! One little eye [in her head] is more sufficient and pleasing to her than only one male partner. O heathen madness!

A similar charge appears in the *Roman de la Rose* (IV, 13; vv. 13269ff.). In the *Lamentations de Matheolus* (p. 89; vv. 1207–8) the following proverb is quoted.

> Gallinis gallus bis septem sufficit unus
> Sed ter quinque viri non sufficiunt mulieri.

> One cock is sufficient for fourteen chickens, but fifteen men do not satisfy a woman.

See n. 110.

108. *Ethiopian:* Cf. Juvenal, *Satire* VI, 599–600.

109. *provided he is up to it:* Cf. Juvenal, *Satire* VI, 329–34; cf. also the *De amore* III, pp. 353–54:

> Luxuriosa est etiam omnis femina mundi, quia mulier quaelibet, quantumcunque sit dignitatis honore praeclara, si aliquem, licet vilissimum et abiectum, noverit in Veneris opere potentem, illum a suo concubitu non repellit, nec est aliquis in opere Veneris potens, qui etiam cuiusvis mulieris posset quomodolibet mitigare libidinem.

> Every woman in the world is likewise wanton, because no woman, no matter how famous and honored she is, will refuse her embraces to any man, even the most vile and abject, if she knows that he is good at the work of Venus; yet there is no man so good at the work that he can satisfy the desires of any woman you please in any way at all.

110. *tired but unsatisfied:* The Mannelli Codex contains a marginal note referring to Juvenal's *Satire* VI, 116–30. The same charge of prostitution appears in the *De conjuge non ducenda* (*Latin Poems*, p. 81; vv. 97–100):

> Petit licentiam uxor nefaria
> ut vadat peregre per monasteria,

et tecta subiens prostibularia,
plus illa celebrat quam sanctuaria.

The wicked wife begs permission to go on a pilgrimage by way of the monasteries and, stealing into the brothels, frequents them more than the holy places.

Later the Goliard inveighs (p. 83; v. 152), "Una mulier fatigat populum" ("One woman wears out an entire people").

111. *however worthy the cause might be:* The passage is a calque on Juvenal, *Satire* VI, 94–99.

112. *great courage to the shameful things they want to do:* Cf. Juvenal, *Satire* VI, 97: "Fortem animum praestant rebus quas turpiter audent" ("If she be doing a bold bad thing, her courage fails not"). Compare also the *De amore* III (p. 355): "Est quoque ad omne malum femina prona. Quodcunque maius est in hoc saeculo nefas, illud omnis mulier sine timore pro levi occasione committit . . ." ("Woman is also prone to every sort of evil. Whatever evil in this world is greatest, that any woman will commit without fear and for a trivial reason . . ."). In *Decam.* VI, 7, (II, 19), Boccaccio had said of Filippa: "La donna, che di gran cuore era, sì come generalmente esser soglion quelle che innamorate son da dovero . . ." ("Like most ladies that are truly in love, the lady was of great courage . . .").

113. *from their husbands' eyes:* Cf. *Decam.* VII, 5.

114. *hampers:* Cf. *Decam.* V, 10.

115. *chests:* Cf. *Decam.* IV, 10.

116. *across the sea:* Cf. *Decam.* II, 10.

117. *though their husbands are looking:* Cf. *Decam.* VII, 9, and Juvenal, *Satire* VI, 140–41.

118. *other remedies for this:* This is an echo of Juvenal, *Satire* VI, 595–603. The charge of abortion and of poisoning children was common in misogynistic satire; cf. *Les Lamentations de Matheolus* (p. 144), II, vv. 3501–3511 (French version) and vv. 2167–70 (Latin version). See also *Le Roman de la Rose*, vv. 9148–54 (III, pp. 109–10).

From the savin (*Juniperus sabina*) was produced an extract which, according to Tommaseo and Bellini (under "sabina"), who quote *Il libro della cura delle malattie*, "giova alla ritenzione de' mestrui, e giova alla sterilezza" ("aids in the retention of the menses, and aids in sterility"); later medical works give a different explanation. (T. Nurmela, [1968], pp. 160–61, n. 231).

119. *the foundling hospitals:* "Gli spedali"; there were a number of newly founded religious institutions, such as the Spedale di Santa Maria della Scala and the Spedale di Santa Maria da San Gallo in Florence, which gave refuge to foundlings.

120. *woman's least sin is to have followed her lecherous appetite:* A quotation from Juvenal, *Satire* VI, 134–35. Jean de Meung also repeated this in the *Roman de la Rose* (III, 109; vv. 9143–45): "Juvenaus . . . dit . . .

Que c'est li mendres des pechiez . . ." ("Juvenal . . . says . . . it is the least of their sins . . .").

121. *bad-tempered:* A common charge in antifeminist satire. The *Golias de conjuge non ducenda* (*Latin Poems,* p. 82) states: "Nam omnis mulier est irascibilis,/ fallax et invida et nunquam humilis . . ." ("For every woman is bad-tempered, false, and envious and at no time humble . . ."). See also n. 124 below.

122. *working against them:* In *Les Lamentations de Matheolus* (p. 74, n. 1040), there is a passage with the rubric: "Quod mulieres ex natura sua nituntur scire omnia virorum secreta" ("That women by nature strive to know all men's secrets"). Similarly the *De amore* III (p. 347) conveys the same notion of the mistrustfulness of women: "Mulier enim neminem confidit amicum et quemlibet credit penitus deceptorem, et ideo ipsa semper in deceptionis animo perseverat et cuncta, quae loquitur, in duplicitate cordis enarrat et mentis plica fatetur" ("No woman ever trusts any of her men friends, and she thinks every one of them is a downright deceiver; so she always keeps herself in the mood for deception, and everything she says is deceitful and uttered with a mental reservation").

123. *necromancers, witches, and diviners:* This is a classical and medieval topos echoing Juvenal's *Satire* VI, 551–91. The same charge appears in the Theophrastus fragment from Jerome's *Adversus Jovinianum,* I (*PL,* XXIII, 289ff.), which Boccaccio copied into the *Zibaldone laurenziano* (f. 52ᵛ): "Mulier . . . anus, aruspices, et ariolos consulit" ("A woman . . . consults old women, soothsayers, and diviners"), and translated into the *Esposizioni,* Lezione XVI, 36 (p. 694) as follows: "Esse, il più, vanno cercando i consigli delle vecchierelle maliose, degl'indovini" ("They, for the most part, go seeking the advice of old witches, of soothsayers"). See also G. Padoan (1959), p. 32, n. 1. Andreas Capellanus had voiced his disapproval in the *De amore* III (p. 355): "Praeterea nulla vivit in hoc femina mundo, non etiam imperatrix neque regina, quae totam vitam suam more gentilium non consumat auguriis et variis divinationum haruspiciis et, dum vivit, mente credula non insistat, et quae assidue artis mathematicae infinita maleficia non committat" ("Besides, there is not a woman living in this world, not even an empress or queen, who does not waste her whole life on auguries and the various practitioners of divination, as the heathen do, and so long as she lives she persists in this credulousness and sins without measure again and again with the art of astrology").

Matheolus echoed similar sentiments in the *Lamentations* (pp. 99; vv. 1442ff.): "Plus vacat auguriis et deservit mulier quam/ Christi servitiis . . ." ("A woman has more time for diviners and serves them more zealously than the servants of Christ . . ."). And Jean le Fèvre (pp. 99–100; II, 1993–96) rendered it thus:

Femme plus voulentiers devine
Que n'oit la parole divine.

Toutes croient en sorceries
En augurs, en maqueleries.

A woman would rather perform divination than hear the word of God. They all believe in sorceries, auguries and the blandishments of bawds.

124. *snakes have more humanity when enraged than do women:* Cf. Juvenal, *Satire* VI, 646–49. Compare also Boccaccio's statements in the *Trattatello* (*Opere in versi,* p. 585): "Nè alcuna fiera è più nè tanto crudele quanto la femina adirata; nè può viver sicuro di sè chi sè commette ad alcuna alla quale paia con ragione esser crucciata; che pare a tutte" ("Nor is any wild animal crueler than an angry woman, nay, nor so cruel; no man can live in safety who commits himself to one who thinks she has reason to be angry; and they all think that"). The *Decameron* IV, 3 (I, 295), conveys a similar attitude toward woman's ire: the frenzy of wrath "con maggior danni s'è nelle donne veduto, per ciò che più leggermente in quelle s'accende, ed árdevi con fiamma più chiara . . ." ("has been seen with more disastrous consequences in women, since the flame is more readily kindled in them, and burns with a brighter flame . . .").

125. *no friend . . . is spared:* Cf. Juvenal, *Satire* VI, 627–33.

126. *extremely greedy:* A traditional charge of antifeminism; cf. *De amore* III (p. 339): "Nam et mulieres omnes de sexus generali natura tenacitatis et avaritiae vitio maculantur . . ." ("According to the nature of their sex all women are stained with the vice of a grasping and avaricious disposition . . ."). Stealing from lovers was a natural consequence; again *De amore* III (pp. 341–42): "Sed et nulla mulier in tanto cuiquam amoris zelo coniungitur, quae toto mentis ingenio non laboret coamantis substantiam exhaurire" ("Furthermore, no woman is ever so violently in love with a man that she will not devote all her efforts to using up his property"). The "Vieille" in the *Roman de la Rose* (IV, p. 31; vv. 13697–98) has the same idea:

Fole est qui son ami ne plume
Jusqu'a la darreniere plume . . . .

Foolish is she who does not pluck her lover to his last feather . . . . Medieval works augmented Ovid's statements in the *Ars amat.* (I, 420): "Invenit artem/ femina, qua cupidi carpat amantes opes . . ." ("A woman knows the way to fleece an eager lover of his wealth").

127. *no slobbering old man:* Cf. Juvenal, *Satire* VI, 620–23:

Minus ergo nocens erit Agrippinae
boletus, siquidem unius praecordia pressit
ille senis tremulumque caput descendere iussit
in caelum et longa manantia labra saliva . . . .

Less guilty therefore will Agrippina's mushroom be deemed, seeing

that it only stopped the breath of one old man, and sent down his
palsied head and slobbering lips to heaven . . . .

Antifeminist satire commonly attributed the vice of venality to women;
cf. *Golias de conjuge non ducenda* (*Latin Poems,* p. 80):

Ut vestes habeat, quaerit adulterum;
et ut refrigeret ardorem viscerum,
tota succenditur amore munerum,
spernitque misera maritum miserum.

In order to have clothes, she seeks adultery and in order to cool the
ardor of her entrails, she is all kindled by the love of payment and
the wretch scorns her wretched husband.

The *De amore* III declares that it is woman's desire to get rich through
love (p. 338). Contrast the misandrous passages in the *Comedia delle
ninfe fiorentine* (XXXII, 10–12; p. 774) where the young Agapes, married to an old man, laments her situation piteously:

Egli ha ancora, che più mi spiace, gli occhi più rossi che bianchi,
nascosi sotto grottose ciglia, folte di lunghi peli; e continuo son
lagrimosi. Le labbra sue sono come quelle dell' orecchiuto asino pen-
dule e sanza alcuno colore, palide, danti luogo alla vista de' male
compositi e logori e gialli, anzi più tosto rugginosi, e fracidi denti,
de' quali il numero in molte parti si vede scemo; e il sottile collo nè
osso nè vena nasconde, anzi, tremante spesso con tutto il capo, muove
le vizze parti. E così le braccia deboli e il secco petto e le callose
mani. . . .

His eyes also (and this I dislike most) are more red than white,
hidden beneath cavernous brows, thick with long hairs, and always
rheumy. His lips are like those of the long-eared ass, pale, pendulous,
and lacking all color, revealing the sight of his untidy, worn out,
yellow—nay, rather, rusty and rotten teeth—which for the most part
are missing; and his skinny neck conceals neither bones nor veins,
but rather, trembling constantly, together with his head, it shakes his
withered parts. And so too his weak arms, shriveled chest, and
calloused hands. . . .

Later she refers to the way he would embrace her: "E poi che egli ha
molte volte con la fetida bocca non baciata ma scombavata la mia, con le
tremanti mani tasta i vaghi pomi . . ." ("And when he has not merely
kissed, but slobbered over my mouth several times with his stinking
mouth, his trembling hands fondle my lovely apples"). See also *Decam.*
II, 10 (III, 3).

128. *crowns, graceful garlands:* See Appendix for civic regulations limiting
such adornments.

129. *spurious pregnancies:* Supposititious children. Cf. Juvenal, *Satire* VI,
598–603. The poet of the *De conjuge non ducenda,* vv. 105–8 (*Latin
Poems,* p. 81) took up the same charge:

Qui ducit conjugem, rancorem induit;
pascit adulteram qui se prostituit,
partum alterius haeredem statuit,
et nutrit filium quem alter genuit.

He who takes a wife brings rancor on himself;
he who nourishes an adultress, prostitutes himself,
supports an heir given birth to by another,
and nourishes a son whom another has begotten.

The French version of the *Lamentations de Matheolus* (p. 139; II, vv.
3325–27; Latin version, vv. 2090–96) shows a close affinity to the
Corbaccio:

Les maris maintes foys nourissent
Les enfans qui viennent et yssent
D'autruy fait et d'autruy semence . . .

Husbands often nourish children who come from another's deed and
issue from another's seed.

Later the following lines appear (p. 145; II, vv. 3513–18; Latin, vv. 2171–
72):

Et s'il advient par aventure
Qu'en le marris selon nature
Ta femme ne puist concevoir,
Lors te voulra plus decevoir
Par faindre fauls enfantement,
Qu'elle mettra secretement.

If it happens perchance that your wife cannot by nature conceive in
marriage, then she will want to deceive you more by feigning a false
pregnancy which she will deliver in secret.

130. *groping fondlers:* The Italian word is "frugatori" ("rummagers"), a
figurative ribaldry. Cf. Juvenal, *Satire* VI, 421–23.
131. *they are all fickle:* Probably the most famous of misogynistic satire,
this rebuke on the fair sex is echoed ad infinitum.

In the *Évangile aux femmes,* for example (pp. 39, 60, 68, 76, 83, 89),
woman "or velt, or se repent;/ En son propos est ferme/comme est fumée
à vent" ("now wants, now does not; in her decisions she is as firm as
smoke in the wind"). Cf. the *Filostrato* VIII, 30:

Giovane donna, è mobile e vogliosa
è negli amanti molti. . . .

A young woman is both fickle and desirous of many lovers. . . .
132. *presumptuous . . . grudging and disobedient:* Cf. Andreas Capellanus'
De amore III (p. 348): "Inobedientiae quoque vitio mulier quaelibet in-
quinatur . . ." ("Every woman is likewise stained by the sin of disobedience"). The *Lamentations de Matheolus* (p. 79; II, vv. 1287–88)
express the same thought:

La femme d'obeïr n'a cure,
Ains est de contraire nature . . . .

Woman does not care to obey; rather her nature is the opposite . . . .

133. *a rich woman . . . a poor woman:* A topos of medieval antifeminism and clearly a reminiscence of Juvenal's *Satire* VI, 460: "Intolerabilius nihil est quam femina dives" ("Nothing is more intolerable than a wealthy woman"). The Theophrastus fragment quoted by St. Jerome (*PL*, XXIII, 289) contains the same idea: "Pauperem alere, difficile est; divitem ferre, tormentum" ("It is difficult to feed a poor woman; to bear a rich one is torment"). Boccaccio, probably translating from his own autograph copy in the *Zibaldone laurenziano,* rendered the passage as follows in the *Esposizioni* (Canto XVI, 31; p. 694): "Il nudrire quella che è povera è molto difficile cosa, e il sostenere i modi e i costumi della ricca è gravissimo tormento" ("To nourish her who is poor is a very difficult thing; to bear the ways and manners of a rich woman is the gravest torment"). See also John of Salisbury's *Policraticus,* VII (*PL,* CIC, 750–56).

Jean le Fèvre's *Lamentations de Matheolus* (p. 133; II, vv. 3120–21) repeated the same warning:

Ne pren pas femme pour douaire.
On ne peut souffrir riche femme. . . .

Do not take a woman for her dowry. One cannot bear a rich woman. . . .

The original Latin version (v. 1993) had been directly quoted from Juvenal.

134. *black tails in ermine:* According to the Spirit, it is as natural for women to be talkative as it is for this heraldic fur to be powdered with its familiar black tails. Loquacity and pretention to learning were commonplace charges of antifeminism; cf. Juvenal's *Satire* VI, 402–12, 434–45; for the topics discussed, see Virgil, *Georgica* II, 475–82. See also n. 233 below.

135. *the source of the Nile:* In the *De montibus,* Boccaccio dwelled at length on the various theories about the source of this river, a subject which had puzzled men's minds until the nineteenth century. Before that time, no knowledge had been obtained since an expedition sent out by Nero had ended in a huge uncharted swamp. Information obtained by a merchant Diogenes (ca. A.D. 50) passed into the works of Ptolemy and constituted a fairly accurate account proven by the later discoveries. (See also Brunetto Latini, *Trésor,* I, 122.1, 124.3).

136. *crystal . . . from ice:* In antiquity and through the Middle Ages it was believed that crystal and diamond were produced from ice and snow which had been frozen for many years. References appear in Seneca, *Quaestiones naturales* III, xxv, and Pliny the Elder, *Naturalis historia* (which Boccaccio knew in Petrarch's copy); Isidore of Seville (*PL,* LXXXII, 577) followed St. Augustine (*PL,* XXXVII, 1914), who stated:

Traditur ergo crystallum, durata per multos annos et non resoluta nive, ita congelascere, ut resolutio non facilis sit. Nives praeteritae hiemis facile dissolvit aestas adveniens; non enim eis ad confirmandam duritiam accessit annositas. Ubi autem nives multae per annos multos super invicem missae fuerint, et copia sua violentiam aestatis evicerint, non aestatis unius, sed multarum, praesertim in his terrae partibus, id est in aquilonia plaga, ubi nec aestate sol perferventissimus invenitur; ipsa diuturna et annosa duritia reddit hanc speciem quae crystallum dicitur.

The story is told that crystal congeals in such a way from snow that has hardened for many years and has not thawed, so that it is not easily melted. The approaching summer easily melts the snows of the previous winter and no passage of time allows them to harden. But where many layers of snow have fallen over many years, one on top of another, and their abundance has withstood the violent force of summer—not of merely one summer, but of many—especially in the northern regions where the sun is not very hot in the summer, this long-lasting and long-enduring hardness produces the appearance which is called crystal.

Dante refers to the fact that crystal is made from water in his lyrics (Barbi and Maggini [1956], p. 280; Foster and Boyde [1967], II, pp. 195, 245, 270–71); R. Durling ([1971], p. 12) has shown that the tradition was well known to Petrarch.

137. *ounce:* "Dodicina"; the twelfth part of a light pound (libbra sottile). See A. Martini (1883), p. 207.

138. *the maid, the baker's wife . . . or the washerwoman:* Compare Pampinea's speech in the *Decam.* I, 10 (I, 64), in which women's lack of wit is discussed:

> Fannosi a credere che da purità d'animo proceda il non saper tra le donne e co' valenti uomini favellare, ed alla lor milensaggine hanno posto nome onestà, quasi niuna donna onesta sia se non colei che con la fante o con la lavandaia o con la sua fornaia favella; il che se la natura avesse voluto, come elle si fanno a credere, per altro modo loro avrebbe limitato il cinguettare.

> They make believe that their ignorance in conversing with ladies and worthy men proceeds from purity of spirit, so giving stupidity the name of modesty, as if no lady could be modest and converse with anyone but her maid, washerwoman, or bakery woman; if Nature had intended this, as they pretend she did, she would have limited their garrulousness in another way.

Andreas Capellanus also had made a similar rebuke in the *De amore* III (p. 352):

> Est et omnis femina virlingosa. . . . Immo mulier cum aliis commorando nunquam alicui ad loquendum vellet cedere locum, sed

suis semper dictis nititur dicenda committere et in suo diutius ser-
mone durare, nec unquam posset sua lingua vel spiritus fatigari
loquendo.

Every woman is also loud-mouthed. . . . When she is with other
women, no one of them will give the others a chance to speak, but
each always tries to be the one to say whatever is to be said and to
keep on talking longer than the rest; and neither her tongue nor
her spirit ever gets tired out by talking.

139. *how to rob their husbands:* The passage is a calque on Juvenal, *Satire*
VI, 231–38.

140. *a daughter more honest or virtuous:* Cf. Juvenal, *Satire* VI, 239–41:
Scilicet expectas ut tradat mater honestos
atque alios mores quam quos habet? utile porro
filiolam turpi vetulae producere turpem.

Do you really expect the mother to teach her daughter honest ways—
ways different from her own? Nay, the vile old woman finds a profit
in bringing up her daughter to be vile.

Compare the advice of Paolo da Certaldo in the *Libro di buoni costumi,*
pp. 83–84.

141. *a lie:* Cf. *De amore* III (p. 351): "Nam et pro re modica satis mulier
millies iurando mentitur et pro brevissimo lucro infinita mendacia fingit"
("Even for a trifle a woman will swear falsely a thousand times, and for a
tiny gain she will make up innumerable lies").

false tears: Cf. Juvenal, *Satire* VI, 270–75; the *Roman de la Rose* (IV,
17; vv. 13367–74) contains the same theme:
Mais chascune est assez maniere
De bien plourer en quelque place;
Car, ja seit ce qu'en ne leur face
Ne griés ne hontes ne molestes,
Toujourz ont eus les lermes prestes,
Toutes pleurent e plourer seulent
En tel guise come eles veulent.

But every woman is indeed quite used to crying wherever she is, for
even though one does them no offense, shame, or harm, they always
have their tears ready; they all weep and are given to weeping at will.

142. *one of their defects be proven:* Cf. Juvenal, *Satire* VI, 219–24, 279–85.

143. *barbed words of theirs:* The wounding power of woman's words is a
commonplace in antifeminist satire. *De conjuge non ducenda* (*Latin
Poems,* p. 83) warns: "Est lingua gladius in ore feminae . . ." ("The
tongue is a sword in the mouth of a woman"). Jacopone da Todi in his
Laude VIII (vv. 55–58; p. 27) repeats the same:
Non hai potenza, femena, de poter preliare:
ciò che non poi con mano, la lengua lasse fare;

> non hai lengua a centura de saperle iettare
> parole d'addolorare, che passan le corate?

Have you no strength, o woman, for fighting? What you cannot do with your hands you let your tongue do. Do you not have your tongue at the ready, knowing how to hurl from it words which grieve, which pierce hearts?

144. *the stars . . . riches:* These nouns are all of the feminine gender in Italian. The word "planet" ("pianeta," "pianeto"), however, in older Italian could also be masculine (cf. *Inf.* I, 17).

145. *but they don't piss:* A similar device of ribaldry is used in Juvenal's *Satire* VI, 264; after describing ladies who have an exaggeratedly elevated view of themselves, the poet ends with: "Et ride positis scaphium cum sumitur armis" ("Laugh as she lays aside her weapons and squats on the chamber-pot"). Concerning the use of obscenity to teach a moral lesson, see D. W. Robertson, Jr. (1962), pp. 20–22, 206, 361ff.

146. *a Virgin still:* A special place was always accorded the Virgin Mary in antifeminist works. Cf. the *Chastie-musart* (*Oeuvres de Rutebeuf*, III, p. 392):

> Feme est mult haute chose, ce vos di sanz mesprenre,
> Et se vos ne l'savez, si le devez aprendre;
> Bien le vos mostre Diex quant il daigna descendre
> En la vierge Marie et char i daigna prenre.

Woman is a lofty thing make no mistake of it; and if you do not know so, you certainly must learn: God surely showed you it when he deigned to descend unto the Virgin Mary and be incarnate there.

And Cecco d'Ascoli's *L'Acerba*, Lib. *IV, 4394–96*:

> In donna non fu mai virtù perfetta,
> Salvo in Colei che, innanzi il cominciare,
> Creata fu ed in eterno eletta.

There was never perfect virtue in woman except in Her, Who, before the Beginning, was created and chosen for Eternity.

147. *wondrous delight . . . desire:* The description of the Blessed Virgin's beauty and its effect on the souls is reminiscent of *Par.* XXXI, esp. 133–35. Compare the exultation of the Virgin in the *Genealogie, Proemio*, Book IX (II, 435). G. Padoan ([1963a], p. 17) quotes G. Martelotti (1951), p. 16, indicating that the whole encomium there was later replaced by an exaltation of Christ.

148. *phoenixes:* That a good woman was a *rara avis* became a topos of misogynistic satire (see n. 150 below).

The myth of the phoenix appears in Old Sanskrit poetry, in Egyptian literature, and in Greek and Roman writers. According to the legend, there existed only one example of this brilliantly decorated bird from Arabia which lived for 500 or 1,000 years; at its death it burned itself on a pyre of incense and arose again from its own ashes. See Pliny, *Naturalis historia* X, ii, 3–5; Ovid, *Metamorphoses* XV, 392–407; and Lactantius, *De ave phoenice* (*PL,* VII, 278–84). See especially the introduction to Lactantius' *Minor Works* in *The Fathers of the Church* LIV, 207–11, for references in patristic literature. Brunetto Latini also gives a long description of the bird in his *Trésor* I, 162 (p. 147).

149. *leaves the crowd:* "Esce di schiera." Cf. *Inf.* II, 105.

150. *black swans and white crows:* From the Theophrastus fragment of the *De nuptiis* (*PL,* XXIII, 290) came the dictum that a good woman was a *rara avis.* Juvenal declared her rarer than a black swan (*Satire* VI, 165); John of Salisbury quoted him verbatim in the *Policraticus* (*PL,* CIC, 753); and Bernard of Morlaix echoed the figure in the *De contemptu mundi* (*Anglo-Latin Sat.* II, pp. 59–60). Walter Mapes in his *Valerius ad Rufinum* seems to have been the first to unite the theme to a popular proverb by saying she was scarcer than the phoenix (*PL,* XXX, 264), and his invention found favor with Jean de Meung, who also added white crows to his own list of rare birds in the *Roman de la Rose* (III, p. 92; vv. 8693ff.). It is most likely, therefore, that Boccaccio's inspiration for the "white crow" image came from de Meung's poem. The legend of the raven's being turned from white to black because of its garrulousness is found in Ovid, (*Metam.* II, 534ff.); the story there, however, is not allied to antifeminism. In his *Lamentations* Matheolus likened women to birds because of their talkativeness; for the same defect, he recalled, the crow was turned to its opposite color (p. 52; French version, II, vv. 207–17; Latin, vv. 728–31). Boccaccio's use of this long-standing antifeminist topos could be an additional argument indicating derivation of the title "Corbaccio" from "corbo"; that is, "raven" or "crow." See also A. K. Cassell (1970), pp. 83–91.

151. *honor any more of them:* Since Boccaccio completed his work in praise of the ladies, the *De mulieribus claris,* in 1359, this reference could possibly be a reason for dating the *Corbaccio* after that date. For other ideas concerning this problem see G. Padoan (1963a), (1963b).

152. *have . . . lost the path:* "Hanno il cammino smarrito." Compare the wording in *Inf.* I, 1–3.

153. *ears close against his words like those of the asp:* A. Rossi ([1962], p. 388, n. 12) points to the verses from Psalms LVII: 5–6: "Furor illis secundum similitudinem serpentis, sicut aspidis surdae et obturantis aures suas, quae non exaudiet vocem incantantium et venefici incantantis sapienter . . ." ("Their madness is according to the likeness of a serpent: like the deaf asp that stoppeth her ears: Which will not hear the voice of the charmers; nor of the wizard that charmeth wisely").

Compare also the verses from *Il mare amoroso* (*Poeti del Duecento,* I, 496; vv. 250–51; see also I, p. 268, n. 52):

A guisa del dragon c'ha nome iaspis,
che d'udir si disdegna chi lo'ncanta.

Like the dragon which is called the asp which scorns to hear him who charms it.

Boccaccio himself used this comparison also in his letter *Nereus amphytritibus* (*Opere latine minori,* pp. 116, 318): "Sed in effectu contrarius, ritu aspidis surdi, farmaciis monitus aures obturabas . . ." ("But in effect the opposite, in the rite of the deaf asp, you closed up your ears to the admonition of the enchanter . . ."). In Lezione XVII of the *Esposizioni* (Canto IV, p. 275) he gives an allusion which differs from the Vulgate: "E il salmista: Sicut aspides surde, et obturantes aures suas, ut non exaudirent voces" ("And the psalmist: As the deaf asp stopping its ears so as not to heed the voices").

Boccaccio was to employ the image again in connection with lust in the *De mulieribus claris* ("Iole"), p. 102: "Obstandum ergo principiis, frenandi sunt oculi ne videant vanitates, obturande sunt, more aspidis, aures, laboribus assiduis est premenda lascivia" ("First, a man must resist. He must curb his eyes so that they do not see vain things; close his ears like an asp; and tame lust with continual toil").

154. *greedy, reluctant . . . perverse multitude:* This is yet another echo of the "quid est mulier" ("what is woman"), a topos of medieval anti-feminist satire. See A. K. Cassell (1973), p. 359.

155. *blind and dismal prison:* Cf. *Inf.* X, 58–59.

156. *that other abominable sin:* The Spirit of the dead husband is defending himself from the charge of sodomy.

157. *name them:* Cf. Genesis II: 19–23.

158. *the one and only woman in the world:* Eve. See Boccaccio's first entry "De Eva, parente prima" in the *De mulieribus claris* (pp. 28–30).

159. *the good of his intellect:* Cf. *Inf.* III, 18.

160. *a woman:* The traditional prejudice concerning woman's inferiority. The arguments of this passage repeat the words of Ambrogiuolo in the *Decam.* II, 9 (I, 160): "Io ho sempre inteso, l'uomo essere il più nobile animale che tra' mortali fosse creato da Dio, e appresso la femina; ma l'uomo, sì come generalmente si crede e vede per opere, è più perfetto . . ." ("I have always understood that man is the noblest of all mortal creatures created by God, and after him, woman; but man is, as is generally believed, and is seen to be by his works, more perfect than woman . . ."). The story ends with Ginevra, Barnabò Lomellin's wife, showing her superior virtue.

In the *Strenne nuziali* (p. 68), we find the following quote from the contemporary *Disputazione di molti valenti uomini se l'uomo de' tôrre moglie o no:*

Male sta il reame con l'imperio, dove la donna fa et dice et l'uomo sta a vedere. Guai a quella città dove è questo! guai a quello reame! guai a quella casa che la femina parli prima dell'uomo però che tu sai che più vale in senno et in virtù uno uomo che mille femine, però che in mille femine non è altro che lussuria, vanagloria, pompa, et maggioranza. . . .

Ill stands the realm and the empire where woman says and does and man stands and watches. Woe to that city where this is so! Woe to that kingdom! Woe to that house where the woman speaks before her husband: for you know that a man is worth more in intelligence and virtue than a thousand women, for in a thousand women there is nothing but lust, vainglory, pomp, and arrogance. . . .

The tone, vocabulary, and style of this passage have much in common with Boccaccio's *Corbaccio* and *Trattatello*.

161. *the vulgar herd:* "Meccanica turba." Compare Boccaccio's letter to Francesco Nelli (*Opere in versi,* p. 1166): "Io ti dirò un fatto d'un meccanico, e nostro cittadino . . ." ("I will tell you a fact about a workman, our fellow citizen . . ."). T. Nurmela ([1968], p. 168, n. 279) indicates that Boccaccio used the expression in *Decam.* II, 6 (I, 117): "l'oppinion de' meccanici" ("The opinion of the vulgar herd").

In the *Esposizioni* (lez. LVII) the members of the "arti meccaniche" or craftsmen's guilds are set below the station of poets (Canto XV, 87–89; p. 683), and Boccaccio expresses similar sentiments throughout the *De genealogia* XIV, XV. See also C. G. Osgood (1930), pp. 21–32 et passim.

The details of the protagonist's life which the Spirit here reveals to us are reminiscent of those of Rinieri in *Decam.* VIII, 7 (II, 133) who had "lungamente studiato a Parigi, non per vender poi la sua scienza a minuto, come molti fanno, ma per sapere la ragion delle cose e la cagion d'esse, il che ottimamente sta in gentile uomo . . ." ("spent much time studying at Paris, not that he might afterwards sell his knowledge at retail, as many do, but that he might learn the reasons and causes of things, an accomplishment which is well fitting to a gentleman . . .").

162. *solitary places:* This passage clearly reflects the influence of Virgil's *Eclogues,* Petrarch's *De vita solitaria* (1346), and the author's personal acquaintance with the poet of Vaucluse. Boccaccio often repeated the theme of poetic solitude: in the *Genealogie* XIV, xi (II, 712), he declared that poets seek the country, mountains, and woods because "contemplation of divine things is impossible in places like the greedy and mercenary market, in courts, theaters, offices, or public squares, amid crowds of jostling citizens and women of the town" (C. G. Osgood [1930], p. 55).

The idea appears again in the *Trattatello* (*Opere in versi,* p. 583), where Boccaccio states that Dante was "costumato, quante volte la volgar turba gli rincresceva, di ritrarsi in alcuna solitaria parte e, quivi speculando, vedere quale spirito muove il cielo, onde venga la vita agli animali che sono in terra, quali sieno le cagioni delle cose, o premeditare alcune invenzioni peregrine e alcune cose comporre, le quali appo li futuri facessero lui morto vivere per fama . . ." ("accustomed, whenever the vulgar crowd disturbed him, to retire to some solitary place and there speculating, to see what spirit moves the heavens, whence comes life into creatures on earth, what the causes of things are, or to meditate upon some rare discovery, or to compose something which might make him live by his fame among posterity" [adapted from J. R. Smith]). See also *Esposizioni* (Canto I; lez. III; pp. 38ff.).

I find Padoan's suggestion ([1963a], p. 23) that this passage is a clear allusion to Boccaccio's withdrawal from the city of Florence for Certaldo (1361–65) somewhat implausible, given the frequency of the topos of the *locus amoenus* throughout the works of the author. (For the history of this commonplace in medieval literature, see E. R. Curtius [1953], pp. 183–200.)

163. *Castalian nymphs:* The nine Muses. Castalia was a fountain on the lower slopes of Mount Parnassus sacred to the Muses. In the *De montibus,* Boccaccio described how the fountain got its name: "Castalius fons est poetis familiaris plurimum, cum musis sacer sit. Hic in Parnaso monte est, et dicitur Castalius a virgine quadam Castalia, quae cum illi Apollo vim vellet inferre, in fontem se praecipitem dedit et in eo nomen vitamque reliquit" ("The Castalian spring is very familiar to the poets since it is sacred to the Muses. It is on Mount Parnassus and is called Castalian from a certain maid Castalia, who, when Apollo wished to lay violent hands on her, threw herself into the spring and relinquished to it her name and her life"). See also E. R. Curtius (1953), pp. 239–40. Cf. n. 164 below.

164. *that spring:* The Castalian spring (see n. 163), or possibly a reference to the Hippocrene spring whose origin and legend Boccaccio described in the *De montibus* (under "Ippocrene"). In the *Genealogie* XIV, iv (II, 688), Poetry herself is said to visit "antra atque prerupta monitium umbras nemorum, fontes argenteos, secessusque studentium . . ." ("caves on the steep mountainside, or shady groves, or silvery springs, where the retreats of the studious are . . ."). Later (II, 713) the beeches "spread a thick shade . . . the earth is covered with grass and dotted with flowers of a thousand colors"; there are again "clear fountains and silvery brooks" (II, 713; C. G. Osgood [1930], p. 56).

165. *toils of the sun and the moon:* The eclipses of the sun and the moon; cf. note 230 below, "the cymbals of the ancients." Concerning these and various other topics mentioned here, cf. Virgil's *Georgica* II, 475–82.

166. *distinguished ladies:* i.e., the Muses. Theophrastus' *De nuptiis* (*PL,* XXIII, 289), as quoted by St. Jerome, cites the impediment to study as the prime reason for avoiding matrimony: "Primum enim impediri studia philosophiae . . ." ("First, his pursuit of philosophy is hindered . . .").

Contrast the gallant association of the Muses and the ladies in the

Decameron, Introduction to Day IV (I, 273): "Le Muse son donne, e benchè le donne quel che le Muse vagliono non vagliano, pure esse hanno nel primo aspetto simiglianza di quelle . . ." ("The Muses are ladies, and although ladies are not the equals of the Muses, yet they resemble them at first sight . . .").

167. *unbearable yoke:* The association of "coniunx" and "iugum" offered a fertile area for punning in classical and medieval antifeminism: the notion of woman as a yoke was and remained a topos. Juvenal (*Satire* VI, 206–9) had declared:

> Si tibi simplicitas uxoria, deditus uni
> est animus, summitte caput cervice parata
> ferre iugum.

> If you are honestly uxorious, and devoted to one woman, then bow your head and submit your neck ready to bear the yoke.

The medieval *Golias de conjuge non ducenda* (*Latin Poems,* p. 82) reflects the same attitude:

> Vere conjugium est summa servitus
> . . . .
> Qui ducit conjugem ad jugum ducitur. . . .

> Truly marriage is the basest servitude. . . . He who takes a wife is led to the yoke. . . .

Hildebert of Tours (*PL,* CLXXI, 1428) repeated "femina triste jugum" ("woman is a sorry yoke"); and in the *Policraticus* VIII (*PL,* CIC, 751), John of Salisbury contended that a man who takes a second wife is not to be pitied: "Quis enim ei compatietur, qui semel solutus a vinculis, revolat ad catenas. Plane indignus est libertatis honore, et quiete, qui ad excussum servitutis recurrit jugum" ("Who really can have pity on him who, once free of shackles, flies again to his chains? He is plainly unworthy of the honor of liberty and peace who at the shaking off of servitude hastens back to the yoke"). See below, n. 172.

168. *you could not see well for yourself:* Here the Spirit begins the second part of his speech, which treats the peculiar habits and ways of the widow. Cf. n. 85 above.

169. *will and pleasure of my friends and relatives:* Cf. the *De conjuge non ducenda* (*Latin Poems,* p. 77):

> Hinc quidam socii dabant consilium
> ut cito currerem ad matrimonium;
> vitam conjugii laudabant nimium,
> ut in miseriis haberent socium.

> Then certain of my associates used to advise me to hasten swiftly into marriage; they praised married life exceedingly in order to have a companion in their misery.

Boccaccio returned to this idea when dealing with Dante's marriage in the *Trattatello* (*Opere in versi,* p. 581).

170. *wife of another:* Compare the situation in the *Lamentations de Matheo-lus* (p. 4; I, vv. 151–56):

> Las! Las! bigamie me tue
>
> . . . .
>
> Or ay pris vefve en marriage,
> Qui contre moi frondist et grouce
> Et a toute heure me corrouce.

> Alas! Alas! bigamy is killing me! . . . Now I have taken a widow in marriage who criticizes and grumbles at me, and who is always enraged with me.

The second Ecumenical Council of Lyons (1274) had forbidden priests to marry widows and declared such marriages bigamous.

171. *trickery . . . simple dove . . . serpent:* A. Rossi ([1962], p. 386, n. 11) has pointed out the biblical parallels in Matthew XII: 34, and more especially X: 16: "Estote ergo prudentes sicut serpentes et simplices sicut colombae" ("Be ye therefore wise as serpents and simple as doves"), and in the *Proverbia quae dicuntur super natura feminarum* (*Poeti del Due-cento,* I, p. 531, vv. 195–96).

In the *Decam.* VIII, 7 (II, 145), Rinieri uses the same imagery to rebuke the widow Elena: "Per che, quantunque io aquila non sia, te non colomba ma velenosa serpe conoscendo, come antichissimo nemico, con ogni odio e con tutta la forza di perseguire intendo . . ." ("So that, although I am no eagle and since I know you are no dove but a venomous serpent like the ancient enemy [Satan], I intend to persecute you with all my strength and hatred . . .").

172. *I bowed my shoulders:* Cf. Juvenal, *Satire* VI, 206–8. See above, n. 167, "unbearable yoke."

173. *threatening . . . beating:* In the *Roman de la Rose* it is said that men should suffer such treatment meekly (III, pp. 131–35; vv. 9687–9775); for the ill treatment of children, cf. Jean Le Fèvre's *Lamentations* II, vv. 3483–3500; Latin version, vv. 2155–66 (p. 144).

174. *Capalle:* A small village in the Florentine countryside proverbial for the rusticity of its inhabitants ("Podunk"). See n. 232 below for another reference in the works of Boccaccio.

175. *House of Swabia:* "Casa di Soave," the Hohenstaufens, the third dynasty of Holy Roman Emperors, who ruled from 1138 to 1254; they derived their name from a castle on the Hohenstaufenberg in Swabia ("Soave," now "Svevia" in modern Italian; cf. *Par.* III, 119). See n. 229 below.

176. *nobility . . . of her family:* Cf. *De amore* III (pp. 350–51): "Sed et nulla mulier invenitur ex tam infimo genere nata, quae se non asserat egregios habere parentes et a magnatum stipite derivari, et quae se omni iactantia non extollat" ("Furthermore, you cannot find a woman so lowly born that she will not tell you she has famous relatives and is de-

scended from a family of great men and who will not make all sorts of boasts about herself"). Francesco da Barberino's *Reggimento e costumi di donna* (p. 16) contains the following warning: "Ma seria da biasimare dell'altegiar, s'ella il facesse più ch'a suo grado convengna" ("But arrogance is seriously to be censured, if she shows it more than befits her station").

177. *bestial fools:* "Bestiali," that is, "foolish." The Italian pun cannot be rendered into English. See n. 260 below.

178. *a scrap of cloth:* The family banners hung on the walls of churches. Knights had gilded spurs and sword handles; cf. *Par.* XVI, 102.

179. *arrogance:* Cf. *De amore*, III (p. 349): "Superbia quoque muliebrem consuevit maculare sexum" ("The feminine sex is also commonly tainted by arrogance").

180. *tyranny she had assumed:* Cf. Juvenal, *Satire* VI, 30–32.

181. *imposed her own rule on how we lived:* This, and the rest of the paragraph, is reminiscent of Theophrastus' *De nuptiis* fragment quoted by St. Jerome (*PL*, XXIII, 289): "Si totam domum regendam ei commiseris, serviendum est. Si aliquid tuo arbitrio reservaveris, fidem sibi haberi non putabit; sed in odium vertetur ac jurgia, et nisi cito consulueris, parabit venena" ("If you entrust the whole household to her management, you would be a slave. If you reserve anything to your own judgment, she will think you do not have faith in her; but she will turn to hatred and quarrels and unless you take her interests into consideration quickly, she will prepare poisons"). See also Hugh of St. Victor's *De nuptiis* (*PL*, CLXXVI, 1203ff.) and John of Salisbury's *Policraticus*, VIII (*PL*, CIC, 750). Boccaccio copied the fragment into the *Zibaldone laurenziano* (Codex Pluteo XXXIX, 8, f.52^v) and translated it from there into his *Esposizioni* (Canto XVI; p. 694) as follows:

> E se egli avviene, per mostrare che altri abbia in lei piena fede, che alcuno le commetta tutto il reggimento e governo della sua casa, è di necessità che esso divenga servo di lei; e se per avventura il misero marito alcuna cosa riserverà nel suo arbitrio, incontanente essa crederà e dirà che il marito non si fidi di lei, e, dove forse alcuno amor portava al marito, incontanente il convertirà in odio; e se il marito non consentirà tosto a' piacer suoi, di presente ricorre a' veleni o ad altre spezie della morte sua.

> And if it happens, to show that another has complete faith in her, someone entrusts the running and management of his house to her, by necessity he becomes her servant; and if perchance, the wretched husband reserves something to his own judgment, immediately she will believe and will say that he does not trust her, and, whereas she bore him some love, straightaway she will turn it to hatred; and if her husband will not readily agree to her pleasures, at once she hastens to poisons and other methods to kill him.

Compare the lines of the *De conjuge non ducenda* (*Latin Poems*, p. 84):

Voluntas conjugis semper perficitur;
sin autem, litigat, flet, et irascitur:
vir autem patiens clamore vincitur,
et cadens conjugi domum egreditur.

The will of a wife must always be executed; otherwise she quarrels, weeps, and becomes enraged: the suffering husband is vanquished by uproar and, yielding to his wife, he leaves the home.

182. *making dresses just as she pleased:* Although we may find the Spirit-husband's complaint unreasonable in our twentieth-century setting, we must recall that strict Florentine sumptuary laws severely restricted women's clothing and finery. Since the wife was without legal rights and responsibilities, it fell to the husband to pay the heavy fines for infractions. See E. Rodocanachi (1907), pp. 127–28, 349–52; n. 100, above, n. 189, below, and Appendix at the end of the present volume.

183. *Fabricius:* Gaius Fabricius Luscinus, who, although poor in private life, became Roman consul in 282 and 278 B.C. and censor in 275; he was famous for his incorruptible integrity during the invasion of Italy by Pyrrhus, King of Epirus. He is often cited by Cicero as an example of Roman virtue. Cf. Virgil, *Aeneid* VI, 844; Dante, *Conv.* IV, v. 13; *De mon.* II, v, 11 and II, x, 7; *Purg.* XX, 25–27. Compare Boccaccio's *Am. vis.* Canto IX, 67–69:

Seguia Fabrizio che gli eccelse onori
più disiò che posseder ricchezza,
avendo que' per più cari e maggiori.

There followed Fabricius, who desired to possess high honor rather than riches, holding them dearer and greater.

184. *I have told you before:* See n. 45, above.

185. *I . . . the servant and she the mistress:* A common theme (see nn. 102 and 167, "unbearable yoke") in medieval antifeminism. Cf. Juvenal, *Satire* VI, 30–32.

186. *the sweet world:* i.e., Heaven. Cf. *Inf.* VI, 88, where the same words refer to *this* world.

187. *lady, or woman:* Cf. n. 93 above.

188. *Alexandria:* The site of a notorious Egyptian slave market.

189. *I fasted . . . to save:* Cf. n. 182 above. By Florentine law the husband was responsible for his wife's excesses. See Appendix.

190. *pappardelle:* A dish still popular today in the Arno valley; it is made with broad lasagne noodles boiled in broth and served with a meat sauce and Parmesan cheese.

191. *Tower of Famine:* An allusion to the story of Ugolino in *Inf.* XXXIII. The charge of gluttony was a commonplace of antifeminist satire. Cf. *De amore* III, p. 344: "Ventris etiam mulier in tanto manet obsequio" ("Woman is also such a slave to her belly").

192. *partridges:* "Starne." Pre-cooked partridge and other fowl were fried in

NOTES FOR PAGE 41

lard with salt and minced spices, then simmered in water, almond milk, and coriander. For this contemporary recipe see *Il libro della cucina del sec. XIV*, pp. 34–35 ("De le starne").

193. *elderberry fritters:* "frittelle sambucate." Fritters made with a light batter of flour, milk, eggs, ground almonds, and elder flowers, fried in oil and served sprinkled with honey or sugar.

194. *blancmanges:* "Bramangieri." A dish typical of hearty fourteenth-century tastes. It was prepared with sautéed fillet of chicken breast (a contemporary luxury) simmered in a rich velouté of rice flour, white sugar, lard, ginger, (goat's, sheep's or) almond milk, and served with a topping of almonds sautéed in melted fat and sugar. For this and other holiday variations see *Il libro della cucina*, pp. 46–49 ("De' blanmangieri").

195. *aspics:* "Gelatine." Fish poached in wine and a little vinegar, served cold in an aspic made by simmering and reducing the broth to a third, adding to it saffron, bay leaves, spikenard, spices, and wine, straining it and allowing it to cool and set (*Il libro della cucina,* p. 28; "De la gelatina di pesce").

196. *vernaccia da Corniglio:* A wine produced at Vernazza and at Corniglio in the Cinque Terre region of Liguria. This region is still famous for its excellent wines. Dante also mentions "vernaccia" in the context of gluttony in *Purg.* XXIV, 24. See also *Decam.* X, 2 (II, 242).

greco: Many Italian wines have this name (e.g., *Greco di Ghemme, Greco di Sizzano, Greco di Tufo,* etc.); it is also the name of the grapes from which the wine is made (*greca di Vesuvio,* for example). However, the simplest explanation is that Boccaccio means wine imported from Greece; such importation was made at the time (cf. G. Brucker [1969], p. 57). Cf. *Decam.* II, 5 (I, 102): "Ella fece venire greco e confetti" ("She had *greco* and confectionery brought").

A similar list of foods appears in Boccaccio's letter of 1362 to Francesco Nelli (*Opere in versi,* p. 1159); see also *Epistola* XII (*Opere latine minori,* p. 153).

197. *Cinciglione:* A drunkard whose name became generic. Cf. *Decam.* I, 6 (I, 54). The charge of drunkenness was yet another commonplace of misogyny. Cf. Juvenal, *Satire* VI, 300–305; Capellanus makes the rebuke in the *De amore* III, p. 351: "Est etiam omnis mulier ebriosa" ("Every woman is also a drunkard"). The *Lamentations* of Matheolus (p. 119; II, vv. 2718–19), follow suit:

En femme n'a plus grant reprouche
Que de soy par vin enivrer. . . .

There is no greater reproach to woman than that she be drunk with wine. . . .

198. *beauty:* Cf. the description in Juvenal, *Satire* VI, 461–73, and the statements on make-up in the *Decam.* II, 7 (I, 123).

(This paragraph and those following bear a striking resemblance to the fourth-century *Amores* once ascribed to Lucian, although it is impossible to say positively how or if Boccaccio knew the text:

> If at any rate one were to see women when they rise in the morning from last night's bed, one would think a woman uglier than those beasts [monkeys] whose name it is inauspicious to mention early in the day. That's why they closet themselves carefully at home and let no man see them. They're surrounded by old women and a throng of maids as ugly as themselves who doctor their ill-favored faces with an assortment of medicaments. For they do not wash off the torpor of sleep with pure clean water and apply themselves to some serious task. Instead, numerous concoctions of scented powders are used to brighten up their unattractive complexions, and, as though in a public procession, each maid is entrusted with something different, with silver basins, ewers, mirrors, an array of boxes reminiscent of a chemist's shop, and jars full of many a mischief, in which she marshals dentifrices and contrivances for blackening the eyelids.
>
> But most of their efforts are spent on dressing their hair. For some pass unfavorable judgment on their own gifts from nature and, by means of pigments that can redden the hair to match the sun at noon, they dye their hair with a yellow bloom as they do colored wool; those who do feel satisfied with their dark locks spend their husbands' wealth on radiating from their hair almost all the perfumes of Arabia; they use iron instruments warmed in a slow flame to curl their hair perforce into woolly ringlets, and elaborately styled locks brought down to their eyebrows leave the forehead with the narrowest of spaces, while the tresses behind float proudly down to the shoulders.
>
> Next they turn to flower-colored shoes that sink into their flesh and pinch their feet and to thin veils that pass for clothes so as to excuse their apparent nakedness. But everything inside these can be distinguished more clearly than their faces—except for their hideously prominent breasts which they always carry about bound like prisoners. . . . When all their body has been tricked out with the deceptive beauty of a spurious comeliness, they redden their shameless cheeks by smearing on rouge so that its crimson tint may lend color to their pale fat skins [ed. M. D. Macloed, VIII, pp. 210–15].)

199. *sublimated quicksilver:* "Ariento solimato." This white corrosive powder was used in cosmetics to lighten the skin. For the extraordinary risks the widow was running cf. L. Thorndike (1941), V, pp. 458–59:

> Silver sublimate was unknown to the ancients. Albucasis tells how to make it of chalcanthum, quicksilver and vinegar, to which sal armoniacum is now added. The apothecary can buy it at Venice or make it himself. But beware of the fumes, by which some have

been killed, others mutilated, and others afflicted with apoplexy. Brasavola wishes that this poison had never come to light, since it has more disadvantages than benefits. No simple is so poisonous. It kills in less than a half hour, burning the vitals especially those about the heart like fire. Once he touched some with the tip of his tongue to identify its taste. His tongue swelled so that he had to resort to extreme refrigerants. Women employ it to whiten their skin but at great cost, since the teeth decay, the breath takes on a bad odor, the eyes cloud, the skin wrinkles, and they are seized by apoplexy and rush to a sudden death.

See also Thorndike, III, p. 58; IV, pp. 42–43, 230, 346.

Under "solimato" the Tommaseo-Bellini dictionary cites Lorenzo de' Medici's *Canzone a ballo*, "E per far la faccia bella,/Bianca più che ermellino,/Solimato e frassinella,/Biacca ed ariento fino" ("To make the face fair, whiter than ermine, sublimate and dittany, whitewash and refinèd silver"). An Anglo-Norman work, *Ornatus mulierum*, of the thirteenth century (ed. P. Ruelle [1967], pp. 11, 48) warns: "Guardez que vus ne metez vif argent al chef" ("Watch you do not put quicksilver upon your head").

200. *purifying verdigris:* "Verderame." An oxide made by exposing copper or bronze to air in contact with acetic acid (vinegar); it was used as a pigment and as a fixative for dyes.

201. *caught in the glue:* In Juvenal's *Satire* VI, 461–63 we read:

Interea foeda aspectu ridendaque multo
pane tumet facies aut pinguia Poppaeana
spirat, et hinc miseri viscantur labra mariti . . .

Meanwhile she ridiculously puffs out and disfigures her face with lumps of dough; she reeks of rich Poppaean unguents which stick to the lips of her unfortunate husband.

202. *peeling:* "Faccendo gli scorticatoi." There is a pun on the word "scorticatoi" in Italian: it can indicate any action or instrument used in the process of flaying or peeling ("flaying knife"), or it can indicate the process of fleecing a person of his money ("illegal usury"). The old women would be taking money for their services as go-betweens.

Cf. Jacopone da Todi, *Laude* VIII, vv. 43–46; p. 27:

Che farà la misera pro aver polito'l volto?
Porrasece lo scorteco; che'l coio vecchio n'ha tolto,
remette lo coio morvedo; parrà citola molto:
si enganna l'omo stolto con lor falsificate.

What will the wretch do to have her face clean? She will use the skin remover; when it has taken off the old skin, it makes her hide soft again; she will appear very girlish; the foolish man is deceived by their frauds.

Compare this invective with the passage F. Torraca ([1912], p. 208, n. 2) indicated in Boccaccio's *De casibus:* "Exili vitro quas alias carpere nova-cula nequivere pilos e facie tollere cutisque crassitudinem radentes minuere" ("Some women pluck away with a small piece of glass and are unable to remove whiskers from their faces with a knife and to reduce the coarseness of their skin by scraping").

Rinieri, the scholar, in *Decam.* VIII, 7 (II, 151), mocks the practice of decortication while his victim, the widow Elena, languishes peeling after being trapped naked in the scorching summer sun: "Tu, da questo caldo scorticata, non altramenti rimarrai bella che faccia la serpe lasciando il vecchio cuoio" ("Peeled by this heat you will be left as beautiful as a snake sloughing its old skin").

203. *madams:* "Sensali"; here meaning "go-betweens," "pimps," or "bawds"; the use is ironical.

Master Shaft: "Messer Mazzo," i.e., the male member; similar ribaldry concerning the sexual act occurs in Boccaccio's *Il Ninfale fiesolano*, p. 84, st. 245, and *Decam.*, Introduction to Day VI (II, 4).

tears: the *semen virilis*. Passage is to be taken in its ribald sense.

204. *with a vengeance:* "A spada tratta," literally, "with drawn sword."

205. *Acre:* Saint-Jean-d'Acre. This city and seaport of the Holy Land represented the last hold that Christendom had in the area. First taken from the Muslims in 1104, it was lost again in 1187; in 1191 it was recaptured by Richard the Lion-Hearted and Philip Augustus and given to the Knights of St. John (whence its full name). After thriving for exactly one hundred years, it was taken again in 1291 by the Mamelukes under the sultan Khalil in a disastrous battle; 60,000 inhabitants were killed, taken prisoner, or sold as slaves. At this defeat, the Latin kingdom of Jerusalem and the whole of Palestine fell again into Muslim hands.

206. *a certain tangle of silk:* A traditional criticism in antifeminist satire; compare the following passage from Tertullian's *De cultu feminarum* II, vii (*PL*, I, 1438):

Quid enim tanta ornandi capitis operositas ad salutem subministrat? Quid crinibus vestris quiescere non licet, modo substrictis, modo relaxatis, modo suscitatis, modo elisis? Aliae gestiunt in cincinnis coercere, aliae, ut vagi et volucres elabantur, non bona simplicitate. Affigitis praeterea nescio quas enormitates sutilium atque textillum capillamentorum, nunc in galeri modum quasi vaginam capiti et operculum verticis, nunc in cervicem retro suggestum.

What can such excessive care in adorning your hair add to your well-being? Why cannot your hair lie still, now tied back, now spread loose, now piled up, now let down? Some women delight in arranging their hair in curls and others in arranging it in inelegant plainness, so that it hangs down wandering and flying in all directions. Furthermore, you fashion a tangle of false hair tied and woven together which is at one time a helmet-like cap, almost a sheath for the head and covering for the crown, and at another time a lofty headdress piled upon the neck.

207. *peacock's tail:* The image of the peacock is common in antifeminist satire. Women who trick themselves out were often compared to the crow who adorned itself in peacocks' feathers. For the significance this bears to the title "Corbaccio," see A. K. Cassell (1970). Compare Ovid's advice on painting the face (*De medicamine faciei liber,* vv. 32–34): "Virginibus cordi grataque forma sua est/ Laudatus homini volucris Iunonia pennas/ explicat, et forma multa superbit avis" ("Dear to the heart of girls is their own beauty. The bird of Juno [the peacock] spreads out feathers praised by man, and in its own beauty many a bird exults").

Boccaccio used the topos previously in the *Fiammetta* (p. 8):

> E mentre che tutta mi mirava, non altramente che il pavone le sue penne, immaginando di così piacere ad altrui come io a me piacea, non so come, uno fiore della mia corona preso dalla cortina del letto mio o forse da celestiale mano da me non veduta, quella di capo trattami, cadde in terra.

And while I was gazing at myself all over, just as does the peacock her feathers, (thinking to be as attractive to others as I was to myself), I do not know how, but a flower of my chaplet was caught by my bed curtain or perhaps by some unseen celestial hand, and my crown, pulled from my head, fell to the ground.

For the widespread contemporary fashion of wearing peacock's feathers in elaborate hairstyles, see E. Rodocanachi (1907), p. 121.

Boccaccio took the idea of the widow's scolding and mistreating her maids from Juvenal, *Satire* VI, 486–507.

208. *mirror . . . hardly tear herself away:* The evil widow of the *Corbaccio* is a *figura* of lust, both because of her behavior and her accouterments. In medieval art Luxuria (Lust or Lechery) is easily identified by her iconographic attributes: a mirror into which she gazes while tending her hair with a comb. Later these attributes were transferred to the figure of Superbia (Pride) together with the detail of an attendant peacock or peacock's wings and feathers. See the many illustrations in R. Payne (1960), pp. 315ff., and n. 207 above. For a discussion of medieval depictions of Lust see E. Mâle (1913), pp. 117–20, and fig. 59; J. Seznec (1961), pp. 107–8; and D. W. Robertson, Jr. (1962), pp. 92–93, 95, 129, 141, 190, 198, 257.

A marginal illustration in one of the MSS of the *Corbaccio* (Pluteo XLII, 34; f. 41ʳ) shows the widow in déshabillé looking into her glass while pointing to her sex lasciviously with her left hand; see Frontispiece.

The lady in her boudoir was described more sympathetically in *Fiammetta* (p. 14):

> Ma veramente mi fuggì la fidanza, la quale io nella mia bellezza soleva avere, e mai fuori di sè la mia camera non m'avea, senza

prima pigliare del mio specchio il fidato consiglio, e le mie mani, non so da che maestra nuovamente ammaestrate, ciascuno giorno più leggiadra ornatura trovando, aggiunta l'artificiale alla naturale bellezza, tra l'altre splendidissima mi rendeano.

But truly, the confidence which I used to have in my beauty forsook me, and I never went out of my chamber without first taking my mirror's trusted advice; and my hands, newly taught by some strange teacher, by finding lovelier adornment every day and adding artificial beauty to the natural, rendered me radiant among other women.

209. *falcon's hood is removed:* Cf. *Par.* XIX, 34–36, and the *Filostrato*, III, 91: "Si rifaceva grazioso e bello,/come falcon ch'uscisse di cappello" ("He became fair and pleasing again, like a falcon when its hood is removed").

210. *so eager was she to be looked at:* The *Satire on the Ladies* (*Reliquiae antiquae*, I, 162) contains the same idea: "Ke plus est regardée cele porte le prys" ("She who is looked at most carries off the prize").

211. *yielding themselves for any price:* An antifeminist commonplace. In the *De amore* III (pp. 353, 356), Andreas Capellanus wrote:

Luxuriosa est etiam omnis femina mundi, quia mulier quaelibet, quantumque sit dignitatis honore praeclara, si aliquem, licet vilissimum et abiectum, noverit in Veneris opere potentem, illum a suo concubitu non repellit. . . .

Nescit enim mulier aurum vel argentum aut alia sibi oblata munera reiicere neque sui corporis solatia petita denegare.

Every woman in the world is likewise wanton, because no woman, no matter how famous and honored she is, will refuse her embraces to any man, even the most vile and abject, if she knows he is good at the work of Venus. . . .

For a woman cannot refuse gold or silver or any other gifts that are offered her, nor can she deny the solaces of her body when they are asked for.

Les Lamentations de Matheolus (pp. 83–85; II, vv. 1483–1540; Latin text, vv. 1121–45) treat women's alleged avarice in a similar way. See also nn. 126 and 127 above.

212. *Palio:* A footrace run each year in the outskirts of Verona on the first Sunday in Lent; the prize was a green cloth (cf. *Inf.* XV, 122–23). Boccaccio explains it as follows in the *Esposizioni* (p. 686):

Secondo che io ho inteso, i Veronesi per antica usanza fanno in una lor festa correre ad uomini ignudi un drappo verde, al qual corso, per tema di vergogna, non si mette alcuno se velocissimo corridore non si sente.

As I have heard, the Veronese, by ancient custom, have naked men

run a race for a piece of green cloth; out of fear of shame, no man
enters unless he feels himself a very swift runner.

213. *more fuel to their love:* A commonplace. In the *Cronica* of Fra Salimbene di Adamo (I, 192), we find two quotations cited to the same effect:
"Augustinus: 'Oleum enutrit flammam lucerne, et ignem luxurie ac-
cendit collocutio mulierum.' Ysidorus: 'Sicut herba viridis iuxta aquas,
ita concupiscentia in mulierum consideratione' " ("Augustine: 'Oil nourishes the flame of the lamp and talk of women the fire of lust.' Isidore:
'Just as green grass at the side of water, so concupiscence at the contemplation of women' ").

214. *my marriage debt:* "Il mio marital debito." Cf. I Corinthians VII:3.
Chaucer's Wyf of Bath speaks of marital love using the same term in
her Prologue (v. 153) in the *Canterbury Tales.* See n. 215 below.

215. *my rightful love:* "Il mio dovuto amore." Cf. *Inf.* XXVI, 95: "ne'l
debito amore."

216. *the quintain:* This was the figure or object at which knights tilted,
often an upright post or a human effigy (cf. n. 227, "saracen of the
piazza," below), at the top of which was a horizontal bar or pair of arms
turning on a pivot with a sand bag attached to one end, and to the other, a
wide board or shield. It was a game of skill to tilt at the shield with a
lance and pass on before the sand bag could whirl around and strike the
tilter; this is still performed at the Giostra del Saracino at Siena. Here, of
course, Boccaccio uses the reference in a ribald sense. The *Chastie-
Musart* (*Oeuvres de Rutebeuf,* III, 384) employs the image in a similar
context:

> Que valt à chevalier à ferir en quintaine
> Où adès puet ferir et adès remaint seine?
> Ausi fait cil qui aime; il verse en la fontaine
> Où toujours puet verser: ne sera jamais plaine.

> What use is it for a knight to strike at the quintain,
> where he can strike continually without harm?
> The lover does this as well; he pours into the fountain
> where he can keep on pouring: it will never be full.

217. *perform two tasks at once:* "Un viaggio e due servigi farò" ("I will
make one trip and perform two tasks").

218. *the sequence:* see p. 46.

219. *the daring to ask:* Cf. the *De amore* III (p. 356): "Nescit ... sui corporis
solatia petita denegare" ("Nor can she deny the solaces of her body when
they are asked for").

220. *God's love:* "che Dio t'ami." Cf. *Purg.* XIII, 146.

221. *decretals:* Papal decrees forming part of canon law.

222. *Madam Cianghella:* A Florentine lady of infamous repute (d. 1330)
named by her contemporary, Dante (*Par.* XV, 128), in a lament on the
degenerate state of the city. Benvenuto da Imola's *Comentum super*

Dantis Allighierii Comoediam gives a long gloss describing her un-bridled wrath, her irreverent disruption of church services, and the beat-ings she gave to her servants. See Toynbee's *Dante Dictionary* (1968, rev. Singleton) under "Cianghella" and V. Cian (1894), pp. 195–97.

223. *Council of Ladies of Discretion:* The idea of a cabal or school of women plotting their own debauch and the cuckoldry of their husbands is commonly found in classical and medieval antifeminist satire. Cf. Juve-nal's *Satire* VI, 300–351; compare Cianghella's "opinion" to the advice given by the "Vieille" in the *Roman de la Rose,* vv. 13483–84, 13491–98 (IV, 22–23):

> Le fruit d' Amours, se fame est sage,
> Cueille en la fleur de son aage
>
> . . . .
>
> Mais bien sai qu'eles m'en creront,
> Au meins ceus qui sages seront,
> E se tendront aus regles nostres,
> E diront maintes paternostres
> Pour m'ame quant je serai morte,
> Qui les enseigne ore e conforte:
> Car bien sai que cete parole
> Sera leüe en mainte escole.

> If a woman is wise she plucks the fruit of Love in the flower of her years. . . . But well I know that women will believe me, at least those who are wise and that they will follow our rules and will say many a paternoster for my soul when I am dead, since I teach them now and comfort them; for well I know that these words will be read in many a school.

224. *Madam Diana:* Another woman of ill repute whose identity is un-known. Among those charged for contravening the sumptuary laws of 1330 (see Appendix for those promulgated in 1355 and 1356) we read that "Diana Bindi de Medicis de Florentia" was fined five pounds in 1343 or 1344 for having illegal ermine lining and ornamentation on her clothing (*Prammatica delle vesti,* 1343–44, *Liber condemnationum,* fasc. I, ff. 17, 19; published in E. Rodocanachi [1907], p. 345), and that "Dominam Dianam uxorem Francisci Andree populi sancti Laurentii" ("Madam Diana, wife of Francesco Andrea of the quarter of San Lor-enzo") was charged with wearing an unregistered silk cloak of many designs and patterns with a checked lining of rainbow hues (*Prammatica,* 1343–44, fasc. II, f. 15; E. Rodocanachi [1907], p. 346). It is not possible to say whether either of these ladies is to be identified with "Madam Diana."

225. *the refinèd kind:* "Digesto." Compare Statius' description of the process of this refining in *Purg.* XXV, 37–51.

226. *Lancelot:* The hero of the *Livre de Lancelot del lac* (ed. H. O. Sommer

[1910], III), "la flor des chevaliers del monde" ("the flower of the knights of the world"), and most famous of the Knights of the Round Table. He was the son of Ban of Benoic ("Benvich") of Brittany (see n. 309 below); by the intercession of Galehaut, he became the lover of Guinevere. Cf. Dante, *Inf.* V, 128, and *Conv.* IV, xxviii, 8; Boccaccio, *Am. vis.* XI, 10–27. See R. S. Loomis (1959), pp. 176–180, 295–302, 305–8, et passim.

Tristram: Nephew and favorite of King Mark of Cornwall. He fell in love with his uncle's betrothed, Isolde, after drinking a love philter; when their love was discovered, Mark mortally wounded Tristram with a poisoned sword. Dante places the knight among the lustful in *Inf.* V, 67. He is mentioned in *Am. vis.* XI, 38–39. See Chapter XII, "The Origin and Growth of the Tristan Legend," in R. S. Loomis (1959), pp. 122–33 et passim.

Roland: The hero of the *Chanson de Roland* (ed. J. Bédier, 1921), the nephew of Charlemagne and one of the twelve peers of France; he was slain at Roncesvalles by the Saracens after being betrayed by Ganelon. Dante mentions him in *Inf.* XXXI, 18, and in *Par.* XVIII, 43. See also Boccaccio, *Am. vis.* XI, 67–68.

Oliver: Another hero of the *Chanson de Roland,* a model of wisdom and a favorite of Charlemagne. He died at Roncesvalles with Roland. Boccaccio mentions him in *Am. vis.* XI, 69.

227. *saracen of the piazza:* Cf. n. 216 above, "the quintain." The accusation that male ugliness was no hindrance to a woman's libidinous desires appears also in Juvenal, *Satire* VI, 103–12.

228. *Morold of Ireland:* Morholt, Morhout, Amoroldo, or Morold was a character in the Tristram legend; the brother of Blancheflor, Queen of Ireland, and uncle of Isolde, he was slain by Tristram after he had demanded from King Mark a tribute of Cornish youths. Boccaccio had mentioned him in *Am. vis.* XI, 34. See R. S. Loomis (1959), pp. 56, 123 et passim.

229. *those of Bavaria:* "Quelli di Baviera." The Hohenstaufens. See n. 175 above.

royal house of France: "Reali di Francia." T. Nurmela ([1968], p. 176, n. 376) points to *Decam.* VI, 8 (II, 22): "Se stata fosse de' reali di Francia, sarebbe stata di soperchio" ("Were she of the royal house of France it would have been an exaggeration").

230. *cymbals of the ancients:* Ancient superstition ascribed eclipses of the moon to witches who would summon down the moon and obtain a magical scum or foam from it; their spell could be aided by the *iynx* or bird-wheel which would torture and dim the moon. Striking cymbals drowned out the magical incantations and allowed the moon to come out of eclipse. Cf. Tacitus, *Annales,* I, 28; Titus Livy, *Ab urbe condita*

XXVI, 5, and Ovid, *Metamorphoses* IV, 331–33; Virgil, *Eclogue* VIII, 69; Pliny, *Historia naturalis,* II, viii, 54. See esp. Juvenal, *Satire* VI, 442–43: "Iam nemo tubas, nemo aere fatiget:/ Una [femina] laboranti poterit succurrere Lunae" ("Let no one blow a trumpet or clash a cymbal again: one woman will be able to bring succor to the laboring moon!").

231. *whether Queen Giovanna slept last night with the King:*   Queen Giovanna I ruled Naples 1343 to 1382 and had four husbands: Andrew of Hungary until 1345, when he was murdered; Louis of Taranto from 1347 to 1362; James III of Aragon and Majorca from 1362 until 1375; and, last, Otto of Brunswick. In the *De mulieribus claris* Boccaccio alluded to the "coniugum austeros mores"—"austere customs of the married couple" (in Ch. CIV, added in 1362 before his ill-fated journey to Naples; cf. P. G. Ricci [1962], pp. 17–18). G. Padoan believes that the reference in the *Corbaccio* is to the third, James of Majorca, who left the Queen promptly after marrying her and seldom returned to Naples; for the importance of these facts for the dating of the treatise at 1365–66, see his articles (1963a), pp. 23, and (1963b), pp. 199–202, esp. p. 200, n. 6.

However, the reference (small and vague) could as easily refer to Louis of Taranto (d. 1362), whom, E.-G. Léonard ([1944], p. 45) says, "Giovanna had certainly wanted as a lover, and even as her husband—provided he did not limit her sentimental liberty too much." Boccaccio's allusion could well be to cuckoldry and to the bitter strife which arose between the couple.

Boccaccio put Queen Giovanna in the Triumph of Beauty in *Am. vis.* XLII, 10–21; in *Buccolicum carmen* III, IV, V, VI; and in *De mulieribus claris,* pp. 443–49.

232. *those in power:*   The Priors ("reggenti"). Boccaccio intends satire on the immigrants who at the time (after 1343 and especially after 1348, the year of the Black Death) had become rich and influential enough to run for government. Compare Boccaccio's statements about these "new men" in his letter to Pino de' Rossi (*Opere in versi,* p. 1118):

> Senza che, se alcuno luogo a spirito punto schivo fu noioso a vedere o ad abitarvi, la nostra città mi pare uno di quelli, se a coloro riguarderemo e a' loro costumi, nelle mani dei quali, per la sciocchezza o malvagità di coloro che avuto l'hanno a fare, le redine del governo della nostra repubblica date sono. Io non biasimerò l'essere a ciò venuti chi da Capalle e quale da Cilicciuale e quale da Sugame o da Viminiccio, tolti dallo aratro e dalla cazzuola e sublimati al nostro maestrato maggiore, per ciò che Serano, dal seminare menato al consolato di Roma, ottimamente, colle mani use a rompere le dure zolle della terra, sostenne la verga eburnea ed esercitò il magnifico ufficio.

> Moreover, if any place were tiresome to see and live in for a spirit which is the least bit shy, our city seems to be one of them, if we

consider the people and the customs of those into whose hands are given the reins of our city government through the stupidity and wickedness of those concerned in it. I do not censure their having come, some from Capalle, some from Ciliciuale and others from Sugame or from Viminiccio, taken from the plough and the trowel and exalted to our highest magistrature, since Seranus brought from his sowing to the consulate of Rome, excellently held the ivory staff and exercised the magnificent office with hands used to breaking hard clods of earth.

In the *Corbaccio* all estates of society come under Boccaccio's vitriol, including these *nouveaux riches* who had entered Florence to fill the population vacuum left by the various plagues. (M. Meiss [1951], p. 70, n. 48, suggests that the reference to the "reggenti" of Florence is a criticism of these *novi cives*. However, curiously led astray by F. Macrì-Leone [1890], p. 109, he bases his statement upon a nonexistent quotation from the *Corbaccio:* "In the *Corbaccio,* written in 1354–55, Boccaccio compared the rulers of the city to a person lacking liberal studies ... 'Zoppa del piè diritto come quella cui mancavano liberi studi.'")

See also G. Brucker (1962), p. 52; and n. 174 above.

233. *where she gets all that breath:* Compare the charge of loquacity and presumption of knowledge in Juvenal's *Satire* VI, 398–456.

234. *Galehaut of the Distant Isles:* "Galeotto di lontane isole." Galehaut or Galeotto, though Lord of the Lointaines Isles and King of Sorelois, nevertheless, in admiration of Lancelot's deeds, swore allegiance to King Arthur. Later, as go-between, he arranged the interview between Guinevere and Lancelot (an episode rendered yet more famous by Dante's *Inf.* V, 137). (See R. S. Loomis [1959], p. 299 et passim; *Lancelot del lac,* ed. H. O. Sommer, III, 269ff.)

Boccaccio (echoing Dante's "Galeotto fu il libro e chi lo scrisse"), with waggish intent, subtitled his *Decameron* "Prencipe Galeotto." Galeotto also appears in *Am. vis.* XI, 28–30.

235. *Febus:* A reference to Fébus le Fort, or Febus-el-Forte, a personage in the Arthurian cycle. R. S. Loomis (1927), p. 306; (1959), pp. 350, 426; *Febusso e Breusso* (ed. Lord Vernon [1847]); E. Melli (1960), pp. 129–68; and ed. A. Limentani (1962).

236. *Marco Bello ... Bel Gherardino:* Two main characters of the *Cantare del Bel Gherardino,* St. 15–17; see ed. F. Zambrini (1867).

237. *a shrewd doctor:* The metaphor of the doctor and harsh medicine may have been suggested by Walter Mapes' *Valerius ad Rufinum* (PL, XXX, 269), which Boccaccio copied into the *Zibaldone laurenziano:* "Dura est manus chirurgici, sed sanans. Durus est hic sermo, sed sanus. Sed utinam tam utilis quam devotus" ("Hard is the hand of the surgeon but healing. Hard too is this discourse, but wholesome, and I wish it may be as profitable to you as it is well meant").

238. *the hard chains:* Cf. Petrarch's *Secretum* III (p. 612): "Duabus adhuc

adamantinis dextra levaque premeris cathenis, que nec de morte neque de vita sinunt cogitare" ("You are still weighed down on the right and the left by two adamantine chains [love and glory] and they do not let you meditate either on death or life").

239. *the reaping hooks and the hatchets:* Compare the *De planctu Naturae* (*Anglo-Latin Sat.,* II, pp. 474-75; *PL,* CCX, 456):

> Sed si eius scintilla in flammam evaserit, vel ipsius fonticulus in torrentem excreverit, excrementi luxuries amputationis falcem expostulat, exuberationis tumor solatium medicamenti desiderat; quoniam omnis excessus temperatae mediocritatis incessum disturbat, et abundantiae morbidantis inflatio quasi in quaedam apostemata vitiorum exuberat.

> But if its spark shoots into a flame, or its little spring rises to a torrent, the rankness of the growth demands the pruning knife, and the swelling and excess requires an assuaging medicine; for all excess disturbs the progress of well-regulated temperance, and the pride of unhealthy extravagance fattens, so to speak, into imposthumes of vices.

240. *hue of swamp-fumes:* Cf. *Inf.* VIII, 12: "Se 'l fummo del pantan nol ti nasconde" ("If the fumes of the swamp do not hide it from you").

241. *knotted like molting birds:* "Broccuta quali sono gli uccelli che mudano." For the importance of this passage in revealing the meaning of the title, see A. K. Cassell (1970), pp. 89-90.

242. *when whitewash is applied . . . unnatural wonder:* See above, nn. 97, 100, 198, 206, 207, 208; cf. Juvenal, *Satire* VI, 461-73, and Jacopone da Todi, *Laude* VIII, vv. 27-28 and 31-34 (p. 26).

243. *Pisans rode with red on their lances:* A ribald metaphorical allusion to the menstrual period and a contemporary mockery of Pisa, always rival to the Florentines.

244. *a load of dung, or a mountain of manure:* Such scatalogical similes are legion in antifeminist literature. St. Anselm of Canterbury, for example, warned his brother monks in the *Carmen de contemptu mundi* (*PL,* CLV, 697):

> Viscera si pateant, pateant et caetera carnis,
> Cernes quas sordes contegat alba cutis.
> Si fimum vilum praefulgens purpura velet,
> Ecquis ob hoc fimum vel male sanus amet?

> If her innards lay exposed, and if the rest of her flesh were revealed, you would see what filth her white skin conceals. If a gleaming purple cloth were to cover loathsome dung, who, except a mad man, would love the dung because of this?

Alexander Neckam quotes St. Anselm verbatim (*De vita monachorum; Anglo-Latin Sat.* II, p. 188). In the *Lamentations de Matheolus* (p. 132; vv. 1973-74), the querulous defrocked priest sinks to the same comparison: "Vestibus ornata mulier nive stercus copertum est" ("A woman adorned in clothes is dung covered with snow"). Jean le Fèvre translated his complaint preserving the original metaphor (p. 132).

245. *the beatitude which I await:* i.e., the bliss of Heaven which is the sight of God.

246. *white wimple:* "Bianche bende." See n. 70 above.

as experts: "Sì come experti." The whole sentence is a comic perversion of the *Vita Nuova,* XXVI, 2, where Dante describes the grace and virtue of Beatrice. Such inversions of Dante's language are common in the *Corbaccio.*

247. *blighted plums:* "Bozzacchioni." C. Muscetta, in N. Sapegno and E. Cecchi, eds., *Trecento* ([1965], p. 345, n. 6), glosses the word as it appears in the *Comedia delle ninfe fiorentine* (p. 688): *"bozzacchioni:* fragole e susine rese più grosse dalla puntura degl'insetti" ("strawberries and plums swollen by the blight of insects").

248. *unripe apples, delightful to both the touch and sight:* This passage marks a contradiction in the Spirit's otherwise seemingly implacable enmity toward his widow. The delight in her past youthful beauty bleeds through the tiresome insistence of her ugliness.

249. *hoods . . . à la française:* Boccaccio's point is, of course, that such long pointed caps *were* worn in Florence at the time. Compare the following ironical *ballata* from *Il Pecorone* (see C. Muscetta [1965], pp. 539–41), by Boccaccio's contemporary, Giovanni Fiorentino:

> Quante leggiadre foggie truovan quelle,
>   che voglion sopra l'altre esser più belle!
> Fan di lor teste belle tante chiese,
>   per esser ben da gli amanti guardate,
>   e fan ne i vistir tante devise,
>   per parer più che l'altre innamorate.
> Queste son quelle che son vagheggiate,
>   perchè ne gli atti lor son tanto snelle.
> Veston villani e cioppe alla francesca,
>   cinte nel mezzo all'uso mascolino,
>   le punte grandi alla foggia tedesca,
>   polite e bianche quanto un ermellino.
> Queste son quelle donne d'amor fino,
>   ch'hanno i lor visi più chiari che stelle.
> Portano a lor cappucci le visiere,
>   e mantelline a la cavaleresca,
>   e capezzali, e strette alle ventriere,
>   co i petti vaghi alla guisa inghilesca.
> Qualunque donna è più gaia o più fresca,
>   più tosto il fa per esser fra le belle.
> Vanne, ballata, alla Città del fiore,
>   là dove son le donne innamorate;

di' dove io ti criai, e per cui amore,
a vedove e donzelle e a maritate;
di' che le foggie ch'elle hanno trovate
fanno parer più ch'elle non son belle.

How many lovely fashions these ladies find, who desire to be more beautiful than the others! They make their fair heads like so many churches to make their lovers look upon them, and use so many styles of dress in order to appear more enamored than the others! These are the ladies who are cherished because they are so nimble in their movements. They put on peasant's dress and hooded gowns *à la française* belted in the middle as men wear them, long peaks of the German type, clean and white as ermine. These are the ladies of refinèd love whose faces shine more than stars. They wear visors on their hoods, short riding mantles, and capes cinched at the waist, with their lovely breasts adorned in the English manner. The merrier and more blooming the lady, the more inclined she is to follow, so as to be counted among the beautiful. Go, O Ballad, to the City of the Flower, where ladies in love are found; tell widows, maids, and matrons where I created you and for whose love; tell them that the fashions they have found make them appear more beautiful than they are.

On the novelty and extravagance of French fashions adopted by Florentine women, see E. Rodocanachi (1907), pp. 120–23. In his *Cronica,* Giovanni Villani accused Gauthier de Brienne of corrupting the Republic by importing French extravagance in dress. C. Piton (Paris, n.d., p. 52), publishes an illustration of a "bourgeoise du XIVe siècle" wearing such a hood. In Florence this garment ("cappuccio") was worn by both sexes and by all classes of society (C. Merkel [1898], pp. 73–81). See nn. 97, 100, above and Appendix.

250. *like an empty bag:* Such satire on misshapen breasts is common in medieval antifeminism; in *Les Lamentations de Matheolus* (p. 21; vv. 296–97) we find an almost identical image:

Concava, nigra foris pendet laxata mamilla,
Instar pastoris burse rugosa fit illa.

Her breasts hang down empty, black, stretched, and wrinkled like a shepherd's bag.

See Frontispiece.

251. *put the devil in the oven:* "Infornare il malaguida," a ribaldry referring to the sexual act. Cf. *Decam.* III, 10 (I, 260–62).

252. *Gulf of Setalia:* A ribaldry based on an actual geographic location. Setalia was an important commercial port on the coast of Asia Minor; the gulf, being large, was considered exposed to all winds. T. Nurmela ([1968], p. 179, n. 410) cites a passage in the work *Luzerner Pilgerreisen zum heiligen Grab in Jerusalem vom 15. bis 17. Jahrhundert* (ed. J.

Schmid [Lucerne, 1957], p. 133), which states the following: ". . . die truog uns hindersich in den arm oder gollfo de Satalia genant in Caramania, wöllichs das gefärlichiste ort ist uff disem Mör" ("It carried us behind it into the arm or gulf called 'Satalia' in Caramania, which is the most dangerous place on this sea"). He also quotes D. Comparetti's *Virgilio nel medio evo* ([1941], II, p. 195), where there is a citation of an unpublished French poem which states "de Sathanie est li goufre apellés" ("it is called the Gulf of Satania"). J. Bourciez (1958), p. 332, notes that a line of the *Renart* (vv. 629–30) refers to "li gorz de Satenie" ("the gorge of Satania").

253. *King Robert's armada:* An allusion to the powerful fleet created by the King of Naples in the spring of 1338 in order to reconquer Sicily, then occupied by the Aragonese.

254. *Scylla and Charybdis:* Two rocks opposite each other at the Strait of Messina; the treacherous currents formed in the strait were portrayed as mythological monsters under these names in antiquity. Any ship passing through, in avoiding one, became prey to the other. See Ovid, *Metam.* XIII, 730–31, and more especially Marbodus of Rennes, *De meretrice* (*PL,* CLXXI, 1699): "Femineam speciem gerit irrequieta Charybdis, / Quae trahit in mortem sorbens sibi proxima quaeque" ("Tireless Charybdis, who drew to its death everything near to her by sucking it in, wears the appearance of a woman"). Note also Secundus' definition of woman as the "naufragium hominis" ("the shipwreck of man"), common in the "quid est mulier" topos; see n. 90 above.

255. *Evilhole:* "Malpertugio"; another ribaldry reflecting a geographic location. In Bologna it was the name of a gate of the city through which criminals passed to be hanged (P. G. Ricci, *Opere in versi,* p. 534, n. 14). In Naples it was the name of an unsavory part of the city around the port; Boccaccio used the site as a setting for the story of Andreuccio da Perugia (*Decam.* II, 5). See B. Croce (1911), pp. 24–28, for a map and discussion.

256. *Mongibello:* Mount Etna. Boccaccio gives a description in the *De montibus:*

> Aetna mons in medio siciliae orbi toto celeberrimus fama: et cum sublimis plurimum sit: solitusque culmine caelso globos ignis emittere hodie deficiente iam subterraneo sulphure solum fumos emittit. Cuius in summitate duos esse crateres: e quibus olim eructabat flamma dicunt indigenae . . . terremotibus agitatur regio.

> Mount Etna is in the middle of Sicily and is the most famous mountain in the entire world. It is very high, and it used to emit balls of fire from its lofty summit; but today because the underground supply of sulfur is fading out, it emits only smoke. On its summit are two craters from which, the natives say, flames once belched forth . . . the region is often shaken by earthquakes.

257. *smell like a lion's den:* One of the frequent animal comparisons of antifeminist satire; cf. *De conjuge non ducenda* (*Latin Poems,* p. 84; vv. 183–84).

> Nam cum leonibus morarer potius
> quam nequam conjugi fuissem socius.

> For it is better to stay with lions than ever to have been a companion to a wife.

258. *Val di Chiana:* The Chiana was a small, swampy affluent of the Tiber stretching from the Arno near Arezzo to Chiusi; once infamous for its malaria in summer, the river has now been deepened and the area drained. Cf. *Inf.* XXIX, 47.

259. *pigs in a poke:* "Le gatte in sacco," literally buying "cats in sacks." The idea of marriage as a process of buying uninspected merchandise was first voiced by Theophrastus in his *De nuptiis* and quoted by St. Jerome in the *Adversus Jovinianum* (*PL,* XXIII, 289); Boccaccio copied this fragment into the *Zibaldone laurenziano* and translated it thus in the *Esposizioni,* Canto XVI, 33 (p. 694): "Il cavallo, l'asino, il bue, il cane e vilissimi servi e ancora i vestimenti e vasi e le sedie e gli orciuoli si pruovan prima e, provati, si comperano; sola la moglie non è mostrata, acciò che ella non dispiaccia, prima che ella sia menata" ("Horses, asses, oxen, dogs, vile servants, and even clothes, vases, chairs, and jugs are tested beforehand, and only when tested are they purchased; only a wife is not displayed before marriage in order that she will not be found displeasing"). The theme is also repeated in the *Trattatello* (*Opere in versi,* p. 585). See. P. Toynbee (1892), p. 616; and T. Nurmela (1968), p. 180, n. 418.

260. *foolish beast:* There is a pun in the Italian which is difficult to render into English. "Bestia" means "fool" as well as signifying a "beast" devoid of intellect. See n. 177 above.

261. *blood around it abscessed:* Seneca in the *De ira,* IV, xx, alludes to the Stoic belief that anger was excited by the boiling of blood around the heart, the seat assigned to anger because it was thought that the breast was the warmest part of the body. Cf. Aristotle, *De anima,* 403ª 2–23: "accensio sanguinis circa cor" (the inflammation of the blood around the heart").

262. *released from my mortal body:* Cf. *Purg.* II, 88–89.

263. *widow:* One of Boccaccio's favorite subjects. In the *Filocolo* (pp. 433–37) he discussed the relative merits of loving a maid, a married woman, and a widow, and reached a conclusion which followed Andreas Capellanus: "Amisi più tosto la vedova che la pulcella" ("The widow is rather to be loved than the maid"). The same opinion is voiced in the letters of Petrarch (*Familiares* XXII, 1; *Seniles* IV, 5), and in Boccaccio's *Rime* LXXXI and LXXXII. Widows too were Criseida of the *Filostrato* (II, 69, vv. 1–3): "giovane, bella vaga e lieta, / vedova, ricca, nobile ed amata . . ." ("young, beautiful, charming and gay, a widow, rich, noble,

and beloved . . .") and Elena (among other merry ladies) of the *Decam.*
(VIII, 7). See V. Branca (1956), p. 181, n. 86. In the *De mulieribus claris,*
XL (Dido), Boccaccio condemns the marriage of widows; the Council of
Lyons of 1274 had declared such a marriage bigamy, and forbade it to
the clergy. It was as a result of this decision that the *Lamentations de
Matheolus* were written; see A.-G. Van Hamel, (1892–1905), I, pp. cvii–
cxiv.

264. *these lies:* "Questo suo infinto parlare." T. Nurmela's edition ([1968],
p. 117) reads "infinito" ("endless") at this point, which is a misprint;
the editor gives no variants here but all six MSS used by him, the editions
of Moutier, Sorrento, Bruscoli, and Ricci, read "infinto."

265. *the friars' church in which you first met her:* The Franciscan church
of Santa Croce? Meeting and falling in love in a church is a traditional
theme used by Cavalcanti, Dante, and Petrarch. Boccaccio himself used it
many times before, in the *Filocolo,* the *Comedia delle ninfe fiorentine,* the
Amorosa visione, and the *Fiammetta;* for a discussion of this convention,
see V. Branca (1956), p. 141, and B. König (1960).

266. *consolers of widows:* Anticlerical satire. The *Lamentations* of Matheolus in Jean le Fèvre's translation (pp. 71–73; II, vv. 947–1022) express
the same thought strikingly; compare the following lines:

> Les freres des religions
> Venans de pluseurs regions
> De l'ordre noire, blanche et bise,
>
> . . . .
>
> Font a nos dames grans soulas. (vv. 973–75, 998)

The friars of religious orders coming from many regions, those
black, white and grey . . . give great consolation to our ladies.

Andreas Capellanus had winked at the dalliance of the clergy "since
hardly any one ever lives without sin" (*De amore* I, 7; pp. 219–21).

267. *enters the church . . . not . . . to worship:* Cf. *Roman de la Rose* (IV,
24; vv. 13522–28):

> Souvent aille a la maistre iglise
> E face visitacions,
> A noces, a processions,
> A jeus, a festes, a queroles,
> Car en teus leus tient ses escoles
> E chante a ses deciples messe
> Li deus d'Amours e la deesse.

Let her often go and pay visits to the main church, attend weddings,
processions, plays, festivals, and carol singing, for the god and
goddess of love keep school everywhere and sing mass for their
disciples.

In the *Lamentations* (Latin, v. 997; French, II, vv. 965–66; p. 72),
Matheolus charges that a woman "prostibulum facit ipsa domum Dom-

ini"; "fait de la Dieu maison/ Bordel contre droit e raison" ("makes of God's very house a brothel, against law and reason").

268. *lay her nets . . . a baited trap such as birdcatchers make to snare doves:* Cf. Psalms XC: 3, and Eccles. VII: 27 ("And I have found a woman more bitter than death, who is the hunter's snare, and her heart is a net, and her hands are bands"). The snare became synonymous with *luxuria,* carnal love or lechery. Images of fowling and hunting are commonplace in antifeminist satire: "mulier laqueus est inevasibilis" ("woman is an inescapable snare") ran the refrain (see A. Wulff [1914], p. 78); woman was the net, trap, or birdlime of Satan the Fowler (B. G. Koonce [1959], pp. 176–84). Marbodus of Rennes began his *De meretrice* (*PL,* CLXXI, 1698) as follows:

> Innumeros inter laqueos callidus hostis,
> Omnes per mundi colles camposque tendit,
> Maximus est, et quem vix quisquam fallere possit.
> Femina, triste caput, mala stirps vitiosa propago,
> Plurima quae totum per mundum scandala gignit.

> The enemy is skilled in innumerable snares. He has bent his course throughout the hills and plains of the world. Very powerful is he, for scarcely anyone can escape his notice. Woman, the wretched head and evil child of vice, produces many temptations throughout the entire world.

In the *Roman de la Rose* (IV, 27; vv. 13589–90) we find: "Ausinc deit fame partout tendre/ Ses reiz pur touz les omes prendre . . ." ("A woman must also set her nets everywhere to catch all men . . ."). In the same vein is Leonardo del Galluacco di Pisa's poem *Sicome il pescie a nasso* (*Antiche rime volgari* II, 63–66).

269. *changing her food:* Cf. *Decam.* VII, 6 (II, 67): "E come spesso avviene che sempre non può l'uomo usare un cibo, ma talvolta disidera di variare, non sodisfaccendo a questa donna molto il suo marito, s'innamorò d'un giovane . . ." ("And as it often happens that one cannot always eat the same food but at times desires to vary it, so this lady, finding her husband unsatisfying, fell in love with a youth . . .").

270. *looking carefully around:* In *Decam.* VIII, 7, (II, 133), the widow Elena behaves in the same manner: "La giovane donna, la quale non teneva gli occhi fitti in inferno, ma quello e più tenendosi che ella era, artificiosamente movendogli, si guardava dintorno e prestamente conosceva chi con diletto la riguardava . . ." ("The young lady was not used to keeping her eyes cast down toward the infernal regions; but, rating herself at no less, if not more, than she merited, she artfully moved them as she looked around and quickly discerned who was gazing at her with pleasure . . .").

271. *pappardelle:* See n. 190 above.

272. *Lancelot and Guinevere, Tristram and Isolde:* See n. 226 above. The

heroine of the *Fiammetta* also delighted in "li franceschi romanzi" ("French romances," p. 155). Boccaccio's own first productions were greatly influenced by *Floire et Blancheflor,* the *Roman de Troie,* and the *Roman de Thèbes.*

273. *Song of the Riddle:* "Canzone dello indovinello." An allusion to the *Novella dell'Indovinello.* See V. Cian (1889), p. 448, n. 1.

274. *Florio and Blanchefleur:* A well-known French poem (see n. 272 above), and one of the sources of Boccaccio's *Filocolo.* See ed. V. Crescini (1889–99). *Il Cantare di Fiorio e Biancofiore* (ed. Giovanni Crocioni [1903]) is dependent on Boccaccio's work.

275. *certain little animals:* In medieval art the lady in love was commonly depicted carrying a furry creature, a patent symbol of her sex. For this motif see D. W. Robertson, Jr. (1962), pp. 191–94, 203, and his end illustrations nos. 8, 65.

276. *second Absalom:* Cf. n. 80 above.

277. *Joseph:* The lines are clearly an echo of Dante's *Rime* 74 (Foster and Boyde [1967], I, 154–55; II, 262):

> E tal giace per lui nel letto tristo,
> per tema non sia preso a lo 'mbolare,
> che gli appartien quanto Giosepp'a Cristo.

> And there's one who lies in bed distraught for fear that he'll be caught red-handed, who has as much to do with him as Joseph with Christ.

Far from sharing the sublime adoration shown to the Virgin Mary, St. Joseph, though venerated, came to be considered as "Joseph le rassoté" ("Joseph the fool"), a ridiculous clown in the Middle Ages; that Joseph is used in this passage as the *figura* or type of the cuckold reveals that the union of Joseph and Mary was the subject of some speculation in the popular mind. See J. Huizinga (1954), pp. 169–71; A. K. Moore (1943), p. 27.

278. *as doth the ass unto the wall:* "Quale asino dà in parete tal riceve." This popular and widespread proverb conveying the idea of *lex talionis* appears also in *Decam.* II, 9; V, 10; VIII, 8 (I, 159 and 408; II, 154). We are to understand from this that the Spirit of the dead husband is the true father of "Absalom's" child. See n. 105 above.

279. *to such a good and saintly life:* Perhaps an ironical allusion to *Par.* XV, 130–31.

280. *to come here:* "Here" ("di qua") apparently refers to Purgatory, and "there" ("di là") to the world of the living. However, in the clause following ("it is granted to us by God to come here"), the "here" apparently refers to this world and to the "Pigsty of Venus."

281. *mocked with amazing guffaws:* Cf. the tale of Rinieri and Elena in *Decam.* VIII, 7 (II, 135–36): "Con l'amante suo, che già in parte era contento, se n'andò a letto e grandissima pezza stettero in festa ed in

piacere, del misero scolare ridendosi e faccendosi beffe" ("She went to bed with her lover, who was now partly reassured, and they remained reveling in pleasure for a long time mocking and guffawing over the wretched scholar").

282. *Sir Lout:* "Ser Mestola." Cf. *Decam.* IV, 2 (I, 288).

283. *they embraced and kissed:* Cf. *Decam.* VIII, 7 (II, 136): "Adunque—diceva la donna—or mi bascia ben mille volte, a veder se tu di' vero.—Per la qual cosa l'amante, abbracciandola stretta, non che mille, ma più di centomilia la basciava . . ." (" 'Well,' said the lady, 'now kiss me a good thousand times to show if you are telling the truth.' Therefore the lover, embracing her tightly, gave her not merely one thousand kisses, but more than one hundred thousand . . .").

The vivacity and humor of this episode are striking; one can hardly believe that Boccaccio would so revel in this scene if it were autobiographical.

284. *has a long shaft:* A ribaldry.

285. *the wrong end of the stick:* "Questi la cavalca." Nurmela suggests that the expression means the same as "cavalcar la capra" ("ride the goat"), i.e. "to argue unreasonably," and points to its use in *Decam.* II, 10 (I, 176).

286. *weed your onions:*. . The emblem of Certaldo was an onion on a white field. G. Padoan (1963a), p. 24, has suggested that this is an allusion to Boccaccio's retirement to Certaldo in 1361 and, thus, evidence for the later dating of the *Corbaccio* (1365–66). But as he admits, it could as easily be a reference to the poet's family origin.

Introducing Frate Cipolla in *Decam.* VI, 10 (II, 25), Boccaccio wrote: "Certaldo, come voi forse avete potuto udire, è un castel di Valdelsa posto nel nostro contado . . . nel quale . . . usò . . . d'andare, ogni anno una volta a ricoglier le limosine fatte loro dagli sciocchi un de' frati di santo Antonio il cui nome era frate Cipolla, forse non meno per lo nome che per altra devozione vedutovi volentieri, con ciò sia cosa che quel terreno produca cipolle famose per tutta Toscana" ("Certaldo, as you may have heard, is a town of Val d'Elsa in our region . . . to this place, in order to gather the alms the fools gave them, would come one of the friars of St. Anthony whose name was Friar Onion; he was welcomed warmly there, perhaps no less because of his name than for any other reason, since that land produces onions famous throughout Tuscany").

Concerning onions mentioned by Pliny in the *Natural History,* a comical annotation in Boccaccio's own hand (Bibliothèque Nationale, Par. Lat. 6802, c. 153ᵛ) reads, "Nondum certaldenses erant" ("There were not any from Certaldo yet")! See M. Pastore Stocchi (1963), p. 66.

287. *ripped you to shreds:* "Come t'erano . . . graffiati gli usatti," literally, "how your boots were scratched up."

288. *Slops tipped out after nine:* "Acqua versata dopo le tre." In spite of strict laws forbidding noxious or foul waters being tipped into Florentine streets, it was permitted to throw slops out after "le tre" or nine in the

evening, after curfew (Archivio di Stato di Firenze, *Statuti della Podestà, 1355,* Codex 19, ff. 121ᵛ and 130ᵛ: "Della pena di colui che gitterà acqua o spazzatura in via publica anzi il terzo suono della campana"). Any householder violating the statute was fined ten *fiorini piccioli* and was obliged to pay ten more to the person denouncing him.

289. *rams from Maremma:* "Montoni maremmani." An expression of contempt. The Tuscan Maremma was formerly a wild place to be shunned, an infamous, swampy hotbed of malaria—a disease, of course, not contagious to sheep, though they would be prone to liver flukes and diseases which would make them unfit for consumption. Boccaccio used the place name here merely as a comical intensifier as he had done, for example, in the *Decam.* VI, 6 (II, 18), "nel mondo o in maremma" ("in the whole world and the Maremma"). "Montone" was a common pejorative epithet, the ram being considered the touchstone of stupidity; cf. *Decam.* V, 1 (I, 347), "che amor l'avesse di *montone* fatto tornare uno uomo" ("love had turned him from a *fool* back into a man"); and *Decam.* III, 3 (I, 203), "alla fine il *frate montone* diede la borsa e la cintura all'amico suo" ("finally the *stupid friar* gave the purse and the belt to his friend").

290. *much of the night:* Cf. *Decam.* VIII, 7 (II, 137). "L'amante, che tutto udiva ed aveva sommo piacere, con lei nel letto tornatosi, poco quella notte domirono, anzi quasi tutta in lor diletto ed in farsi beffe dello scolar consumarono" ("The lover who heard everything to his great delight, returned to bed with her; they slept little that night but rather spent almost all of it in their pleasure and in making jokes about the scholar").

291. *suspicious of her vanity and fickleness:* Cf. *Decam.* VIII, 7 (II, 134): "Ultimamente, avendo ella al suo amante ogni cosa scoperta ed egli essendosene con lei alcuna volta turbato ed alcuna gelosia presane, per mostrargli che a torto di ciò di lei suspicasse, sollecitandola lo scolar molto, la sua fante gli mandò . . ." ("At last, when she had revealed everything to her lover, who at times became disturbed at her and became jealous, she, to show him that his suspicions were groundless and since the scholar urged her warmly, sent her maidservant to him . . .").

292. *if your mind and intellect had been as healthy:* Cf. *Inf.* IX, 61: "O voi ch'avete li'ntelletti sani" ("O you who have healthy intellects").

293. *about the second:* See n. 85 above, and trans. p. 21: "the causes that brought you to so much grief." It is actually the third topic to be treated.

294. *pointed you out:* There is a rudundancy in the text: "te a dito mostrava," "ti dimostrava."

295. *none can act wisely:* Matheolus had the same complaint; see the *Lamentations,* p. 121; for the French, II, vv. 2765–70; the Latin, vv. 1760–68.

296. *lessened those of others:* Of her two dead husbands.

297. *senators:* The eight Priors of the Signoria, the city executive. By the Ordinances of Justice of 1293 and 1295 the magnates were excluded from elected positions, and the government was entrusted to the *priori delle arti,* who were chosen from the twenty-one great guilds, one for each

ward of the city, and were changed every two months. The popular commune which replaced the oligarchical patrician regime after 1343 continued to hold the nobility and the rich and powerful in low esteem and did not permit its members to hold office. The political punishment of ennoblement, i.e., of declaring a citizen a magnate, became an effective tool of curtailing the political activity of these and the troublesome. See G. Brucker (1962), pp. 64–67, 105; (1969), pp. 133–34; M. Meiss (1951), pp. 62–64; M. Becker (1960), pp. 421–34; H. Baron (1960), pp. 440–51. The Spirit, having once denied the widow's nobility, here seems to support it (one of the many contradictions present in the work).

298. *the scrutiny:* "Lo squittino," the complicated civic electory system by which citizens were chosen as one of the eight Priors, who together with the Gonfaloniere or Standard Bearer, made up the Signoria. To gain eligibility for this supreme executive, the citizen had to gain a two-thirds majority vote on an electoral commission made up of groups from within and without the city government. Every three years new lists of candidates were presented to this assembly for review, and every two months a new group of priors was drawn by lot from a leather bag (*borsa*) containing the names of successful nominees. The entire electoral procedure was extremely elaborate, and each stage was surrounded by complex safeguards. Only citizens over thirty years of age who were enrolled in one of the twenty-one great guilds (*arti maggiori*) and were neither magnates, bankrupts, nor delinquent in their taxes were fit for selection. For a detailed explanation see F. Schevill (1936), pp. 209–10, 339, 355; G. Brucker (1962), p. 66; (1969), pp. 133–34.

299. *those who can advance you:* For those continuing to accept a close autobiographical interpretation of the treatise, this reference to protectors could be of concern for the dating of the *Corbaccio.* By the note of obvious fond nostalgia and optimistic possibility in this passage, it seems apparent that it is not a reference to Boccaccio's own ill-starred trip to Naples in 1362 to seek Niccolò Acciaiuoli's patronage, an episode about which the writer felt so bitter (cf. *Epistola a Francesco Nelli,* in *Opere in versi,* pp. 1150–93); however, see G. Padoan (1963a), p. 22. E. G. Léonard (1944) makes an interesting examination of this Neapolitan sojourn.

Petrarch speaks similarly of fleeing protection and patronage in his *Letter to Posterity* (*Posteritati,* in *Opere,* p. 974):

> Principum atque regum familiaritatibus ac nobilium amicitiis usque ad invidiam fortunatus fui. Multos tamen eorum, quos valde amabam, effugi: tantum fuit michi insitus amor libertatis. . . .

> Because of my familiarity with princes, monarchs, and the great, I was fortunate enough to arouse envy. All the same, I shunned many of those whom I loved best, so strong in me was the love of my liberty. . . .

300. *watch the cinders:*   Cf. *Decam.* V, 10 (I, 403): "E da che diavol siam noi poi, da che noi siam vecchie, se non da guardar la cenere intorno al focolare?" ("And what the devil are we good for then, when we are old, except to watch the cinders around the fire?")

301. *in the nets:*   See n. 268 above.

302. *shown . . . before:*   See nn. 92, 148, and 160 above.

303. *well-proportioned in her limbs:*   Cf. the description of Criseida in the *Filostrato,* Pt. I, 27:

> Ella era grande, ed alla sua grandezza
> rispondeano li membri tutti quanti,
> e'l viso avea adorno di bellezza
> celestiale. . . .

> She was tall and all her limbs were in good proportion to her height, her face was adorned with celestial beauty. . . .

304. *wash . . . rarely . . . improper for men:*   The passage echoes a traditional topos stemming from classical and medieval sources. Ovid, in *Ars. amat.* I, 509, had declared: "Forma viros neglecta decet" ("An uncared-for beauty is becoming to men"). Tertullian's *De cultu feminarum* II, 8 (*PL*, I, 1439), had indicated that his criticism of excessive care in women was also applicable to men; St. Ambrose (*De virginibus* I, 9, 54; *PL,* XIV, 215) repeats the idea: "In vobis rejecta decoris cura plus decet; et hoc ipsum quod vos non ornatis, ornatus est" ("Your refusing to care about adornment is more seemly and by the very fact you do not adorn yourself, you are adorned"). The *De amore* I, 7 of Andreas Capellanus quotes Ovid's *Heroides* IV, 75–76, to the same effect, and declares that women should avoid men who anoint themselves all over like women. A similar criticism of men's adornment appears in the *Roman de la Rose* (III, vv. 9063ff.).

305. *not . . . to such good use:*   Compare the scolding Rinieri gives to Elena in the *Decam.* VIII, 7 (II, 145): "Dove per te non rimase di far morire un valente uomo, come tu poco avanti mi chiamasti, la cui vita ancora potrà più in un dì essere utile al mondo che centomila tue pari non potranno mentre il mondo durar dee" ("Whereas you did not hesitate to try to put to death a worthy man, as you called me a short time ago, whose life will still be more useful to the world in one day than one hundred thousand of your ilk until the end of time").

306. *first . . . last . . . central:*   The first, that he is a man and she a "mere" woman; the last, that nature has granted her the boon of being older than the distressed protagonist (!); and the central, their respective good looks and stature, which are, apparently, equal. The Spirit seems to have forgotten how ugly he had made the widow appear.

307. *you still fix the eyes of your mind:*   Cf. *Purg.* XV, 64–65, and nn. 11, 27 above.

308. *opinion of the vulgar crowd . . . true nobility:* The wording here closely parallels Ghismonda's defense of Guiscardo's nobility in *Decam.* IV, 1 (I, 281), and reflects a notion common in medieval literature: that true nobility first arose from virtue. The *De amore* of Andreas Capellanus had stressed the idea:

> Nam quam omnes homines uno sumus ab initio stipite derivati unamque secundum naturam originem traximus omnes, non forma, non corporis cultus, non etiam opulentia rerum, sed sola fuit morum probitas, quae primitus nobilitate distinxit homines ac generis induxit differentiam (pp. 17–18).
>
> Probitas sola quemque dignum facit amore (p. 311).

> For since all of us human beings are derived originally from the same stock and all naturally claim the same ancestor, it was not beauty or care of the body or even abundance of possessions, but excellence of character alone which first made a distinction of nobility among men and led to the difference of class.
>
> Good character alone makes any man worthy of love.

Jean de Meung in the *Roman de la Rose* had repeated the same thought (cf. III, 128–31; vv. 9603–78, and IV, 236–37; vv. 18607–46).

The most important inspiration for the passages, however, appears to have been Dante, who treated the question in *Conv.* IV, i, 7 (ed. G. Busnelli and G. Vandelli [1934], II, esp. pp. 10, 25–27, 373), and who concludes that nobility is virtue, "l'umana bontade in quanto in noi è da la natura seminata e che 'nobilitade' chiamare si dee" ("the human goodness which is sowed in us by nature, and which should be called 'nobility' ").

309. *Ban of Benwick:* "Bando di Benvich," Ban de Benoic, the father of Lancelot. Cf. n. 226 above; R. S. Loomis (1959), pp. 297, 324; and *Lancelot del lac,* ed. H. O. Sommer (1910), p. 3.

The *De amore* III (pp. 333–34) contains a similar warning.

310. *the lady of my mind:* An echo of the *Vita nuova* II: "La gloriosa donna de la mia mente" ("the glorious lady of my mind"). Boccaccio used it also in the *Comedia delle ninfe fiorentine* (p. 798): "E da quella ora innanzi, sì come ricordare vi dovete, sempre come singulare donna della mia mente vi riguardai . . ." ("And from that hour forth, as you must recall, I regarded you always as the special lady of my mind").

311. *you have sinned naturally:* De amore I, Dialogue VIII (p. 162), expressed a similar thought: "Credo tamen, in amore Deum graviter offendi non posse; nam quod natura cogente perficitur, facili potest expiatione mundari" ("I believe, however, that God cannot be seriously offended by love, for what is done under the compulsion of nature can be made clean by an easy expiation"). Boccaccio gave a similar definition in *Decam.* III, 7 (I, 231–32): "L'usare la dimestichezza d'uno uomo una

donna è peccato naturale . . ." ("A woman who has intimate relations with a man commits a natural sin . . ."). For the concept of "natural sin" see the remarks by D. W. Robertson, Jr. (1962), pp. 22–28, 44.

312. *so remorseful:* "Così compunto." Cf. *Inf.* I, 15: "quella valle / che m'avea di paura il cor compunto" ("that valley which had pierced my heart with fear"). See n. 58 above.

313. *abyss:* Hell.

314. *the first . . . the second:* The sacrament of penance consists of three parts: contrition of the heart, confession of the mouth, and atonement or satisfaction in deed. Cf. p. 12: "From this knowledge, such great contrition and repentance for my evil deeds came to me. . . ."

315. *hatred:* Cf. Rinieri in *Decam.* VIII, 7 (II, 137): "Il lungo e fervente amor portatole subitamente in crudo et acerbo odio trasmutò . . ." ("The long and fervent love he had borne for her changed immediately into harsh and bitter hatred . . ."). What for Rinieri was a natural and spontaneous change from love to hatred is here—oddly—a divine ordinance imposed through a relay of Divine Grace.

316. *her beauty:* The Spirit has already told us that this beauty is nonexistent, that the widow's face has the "color of swamp fumes" when she arises in the morning, that her figure sags, and that one would rather remain in a malarial marsh than suffer her body odor; he contradicts himself strangely here. Does Boccaccio intend to show us, perhaps, that the antithetical feelings of earthly love are still present in this unpurged soul from Purgatory?

317. *something which you do so excellently:* As will be made clear, the Spirit is referring to the writing of literature.

318. *even by fiction:* "Mentendo." Traditional in medieval literary exegesis was the division made between the literal level and the meanings and truths that the literal level contained and concealed. Cf. Dante's "una veritate ascosa sotto bella menzogna" ("a truth hidden beneath a beautiful lie") of *Conv.* II, i, 3 (ed. G. Busnelli and G. Vandelli [1934], I, 97).
  Boccaccio absolved the poet of the charge of "lying" in the sinful sense in *Genealogie* XIV, 13 (II, pp. 717–23), explaining that the fiction of poets is "very like truth" and is more like history than falsehood. ("Poetas non esse mendaces," "That poets are not liars"; see also C. G. Osgood [1956], pp. 62–69. Osgood's Introduction is also useful in this regard.)
  Consult the Introduction to this translation.

319. *draft my prose:* Compare the protagonist's promise to that of Rinieri in *Decam.* VIII, 7 (II, 147): "E dove tutti mancati mi fossero, non mi fuggiva la penna, con la quale tante e sì fatte cose di te scritte avrei ed in sì fatta maniera, che, avendole tu risapute, che l'avresti, avresti il dì mille volte disiderato di mai non esser nata" ("And even if all other means had failed me, the pen did not forsake me; with it I would have written such and so many things about you and in such a way that when you

learned of them, as you would have done, you would have wished a thousand times that day that you had never been born").

320. *with the sword:* Compare Rinieri's attitude in *Decam.* VIII, 7 (II, 145): "La fine della penitenza nelle selvatiche fiere come tu se', e similmente della vendetta, vuole essere la morte" ("The outcome of penitence and, likewise, of revenge in savage beasts such as you, should be death"). Later he rails: "Io ucciderei una vile e cattiva e rea feminetta" ("I would slay a base, evil, and wicked woman").

321. *not . . . in the same way:* "Non . . . ad un modo." T. Nurmela ([1968], p. 138) punctuates the phrase to read "ad un modo che" and treats the expression as a subordinating conjunction meaning the same as "di modo che" ("so that"). But it seems to me more likely that it is an adverb ("not . . . in the same way"), for the protagonist has taken to heart the Spirit's teaching that he has *separated himself from,* and is worth more than, other men, insofar as he is a scholar and thus should not be treated as others are. Compare *Decam.* VIII, 7 (II, 145), as the scholar Rinieri takes revenge on the widow Elena: "Insegnerotti adunque con questa noia che tu sostieni che cosa sia lo schernir gli uomini che hanno alcun sentimento e che cosa sia lo schernir gli scolari . . ." ("I shall therefore teach you by this affliction which you are suffering what it means to scorn men who have some intelligence, and what it means to scorn scholars . . .").

322. *testimony . . . in more lasting verse:* No verse form by Boccaccio has come down to us. There exists, however, a rendering into *ottava rima* by a Florentine notary, Ser Lodovico Bartoli, entitled *"Corbaccino perchè disceso egli è del gran Corbaccio"* ("The *Lesser Corbaccio* because it is descended from the great *Corbaccio*"), and published by G. Mazzoni (1888), pp. 240-301. At the end of his adaptation, Bartoli advised that Boccaccio had despised his work after it was written ("da llui . . . non pregiato lo valer d'un fico," "not considered worth a fig by him")—a comment which may explain the unpolished quality of the work and provide a reason why a poetic version may never have been written.

323. *that which is to come:* The heavenly allegorical light. Cf. nn. 30 and 59 above, and n. 327 below.

324. *burn with charity:* Cf. *Purg.* XV, 55-57:

> che, per quanti si dice più lì 'nostro,'
> tanto possiede più di ben ciascuno,
> e più di caritate arde in quel chiostro.

> The more they are who say "ours" there, the more good each one possesses and the more charity burns in that cloister.

The Spirit forgets his charity later as he exhorts the protagonist to hate the Widow; the incongruity is striking.

325. *than I:* "Di me . . . che non son io." There is a repetition in the text.

326. *the peace which you await:* The bliss of heaven. Cf. *Purg. III,* 74-76:

"per quella pace/ ch'i' credo che per voi s'aspetti" ("by that peace which, I believe, you are awaiting").

327. *raised my head ... and saw a light:* Cf. *Inf.* I, 16–18. P. G. Ricci (*Opere in versi,* p. 558, n. 4) comments: "Trasparente simbolo della verità che sta per illuminare l'ottenebrata mente del Boccaccio" ("A transparent symbol of the truth which is about to enlighten Boccaccio's clouded mind").

328. *weight:* A conventional reference to the "weight of sin" and perhaps a reminiscence of Dante's concept of Purgatory, where, at each *cornice,* a "P" ("peccato," "sin") is removed from the Wayfarer's forehead as he climbs upwards more freely and lightly.

329. *my breast, afflicted ... by its past distress:* Reminiscent perhaps of *Purg.* I, 13–18.

330. *I turned back to look at the place:* Cf. *Inf.* I, 26: "l'animo mio .../ si volse a retro a rimirar lo passo" ("my mind ... turned back to gaze upon the pass").

331. *free ... act according to my own judgment:* A reminiscence of *Purg.* XXVII, 140–42.

332. *he and my sleep disappeared at the same time:* Perhaps reminiscent of *Purg.* IX, 32–33, or XXX, 49–51, but Boccaccio's conception is closer to Cicero's *Somnium Scipionis* (*De re publica,* VI, xxvi, 29): "Ille discessit; ego somno solutus sum" ("He departed, and I awoke from my sleep"). The author had used the same technique in his *Comedia delle ninfe fiorentine* (p. 147): "A un'ora esse e'l sonno si dipartirono" ("They and sleep departed at the same time").

333. *praise be to Him Who brought it about:* Compare the Goliard's gratitude in the *De conjuge non ducenda* (*Latin Poems,* p. 77; vv. 1–4):

Sit Deo gloria, laus, benedictio!
Johanni pariter, Petro, Laurentio,
quos misit Trinitas in hoc naufragio,
ne me permitterent uti conjugio.

Glory be to God, praise and benediction, to John the same, to Peter and to Lawrence, whom the Trinity placed in this shipwreck in order to prevent my getting married!

Compare also Rinieri's joy and praise of God for being able to take revenge on the unfortunate widow, Elena, in *Decam.* VIII, 7 (II, 139).

334. *presumes to mock others:* Cf. *Decam.* VIII, 7 (II, 145). Cf. n. 321 above.

335. *hand its rest:* The motif of rest after hard toil expressed at the end of the work is a rhetorical topos. See M. Pastore Stocchi (1963), pp. 20–21.

336. *the young ... trusting too much in themselves:* Cf. *Filostrato* VIII, 29, and Marbodus of Rennes in his *De meretrice* (*PL,* CLXXI, 1699):

Si formosa vocat mulier te fallere quaerens,
Tuque tibi fidens properas certamen inire

150

Pectore robusto spernens hostilia tela
Faleris ignarus. . . .

If a beautiful woman calls out seeking to deceive you, and you hurry
to enter the contest overtrusting your own abilities and spurning
the weapons of the enemy with hardy courage, being inexperienced,
you will surely fall. . . .

337. *the sharpest goad:* Cf. Eccles. XII:11. Petrarch noted the traditional
moral effect of sharp words in the *De sui ipsius et multorum ignorantia*
(*Prose*, p. 746):

Nostri [scil. auctores latini] autem—quod nemo nescit expertus—
acutissimos atque ardentissimos orationis aculeos precordiis ad-
movent infliguntque . . . ita ut terrena iam sordeant et conspecta vitia
ingens sui odium [pariant]. . . .

Everyone who has become thoroughly familiar with our Latin
authors knows that they stamp and drive deep into the heart the
sharpest and most burning stings of speech . . . then earthly things
become vile; the aspect of vice arouses great hatred for itself. . . .

However, Boccaccio here echoes the curious *congedo* from Dante's
most sado-masochistic poem of the *Rime petrose,* in which the convention
was reversed and applied to petty revenge for unrequited love:

Canzon, vattene dritto a quella donna
che m'ha ferito il core e che m'invola
quello ond'io ho più gola,
e dàlle per lo cor d'una saetta:
ché bell'onor s'acquista in far vendetta.

Song, go straight to that woman who has wounded my heart and
robs me of what I most hunger for, and drive an arrow through her
heart: for great honor is gained through taking revenge (Foster and
Boyde [1967], I, 174–75).

It is clear that the narrator is still enmeshed in his passion for the
widow: the ending reveals an extraordinary twist in the normal moral
outcome of a dream-vision. (See the Introduction.)

Appendix: Sumptuary Statutes of 1355 and 1356

Ordinances against Women Who Wear Forbidden Articles of Clothing [1355][1]

First that no woman of any class, rank, or station whatever, single or married, may wear, be permitted to wear, or wear as her clothing in her home or without, any dress or outer garment woven with gold, silver, or silk on the outside such as are described as embroidered, or any garment adorned with pearls or any precious stones or with anything else of any worth, or any trimmings or ornaments which are worth more than ten gold florins, under pain of a fifty-*lire* fine in Florentine *denari piccioli*[2] which is to be levied upon each woman for each violation.[3]

Furthermore, that no woman of any class, age, rank, or of whatever high station may wear, or be permitted to wear, any mantle, cloak, or any

1. *Statuti del Capitano del Popolo del Comune di Firenze del 1355,* Archivio di Stato, Florence; the Italian text of Codex 13, folios 214ʳ–217ᵛ, is published in E. Rodocanachi (1907 and 1922), pp. 349–52.

2. The *denaro picciolo* (penny), the smallest Florentine coin, was minted in copper and had originally been equal to 1/12 of a *soldo* (shilling) minted in silver. The gold *lira* or florin first issued in 1252 was supposed to be equivalent to 20 *soldi*. However, as the worth of the various metals fluctuated, merchants began a new system using the copper *denaro* and its multiples of 12 and 240 for everyday usage. Since gold had increased in value, the 240 copper *lira* (the *lira di piccioli, fiorentinello,* or *fiorino piccolo,* never minted and purely "money of account") was worth far less than the gold florin. In 1337 the gold florin equaled 744 copper *denari;* by 1380 it equaled 840. See A. Evans (1931), pp. 481–96.

3. For the various articles of clothing worn in contemporary Florence, see esp. C. Merkel (1898) and A. Viscardi and G. Barni (1966), pp. 287–310.

other article of clothing lined or adorned in any way with vair,[4] miniver, ermine, rabbit, or any fur trim at the hem or at the gussets so that it shows outside, under any pretext, warrant, or cause, under pain of a ten-*lire* fine in Florentine *denari piccioli* which is to be levied on each woman for each offense. However, the wives of knights are to be exempted from this regulation and command.

Furthermore, that no maid, adult woman, or lady beyond her tenth year may wear, be permitted to wear, or wear as clothing on her head or upon her person, in her home or without, materials smocked in any way, much or little. Nor may any married woman go abroad with an outer girdle, that is, belted outside her cloak, cape, or any other outer clothing, under pain of twenty-five-*lire* fine in Florentine *denari piccioli* which is to be levied on each of them for each offense. But this latter order is intended for those women joined each to her husband.

Furthermore, that no woman, of whatever class or rank she may be or of whatever reputation she may be judged, may wear or be permitted to wear any leather girdle, strap, or belt which exceeds fifteen gold florins in value, nor any crown, garland, circlet, or any other adornment for the head which exceeds ten gold florins in value and appraisal. In addition, she may neither have on nor wear at the same time anything beyond a single girdle, or leather belt, or garland, or circlet of this value, under pain of one-hundred-*lire* fine in Florentine *denari piccioli* to be levied on each woman for each violation.

Furthermore, that no man or woman of whatever class or rank whatsoever of the City of Florence is permitted or may dare, under any pretext, warrant, or cause, by himself or herself, or by others, to send any strongbox, or receive same, in which there are jewels which exceed the value of sixty gold florins [nor dare to] present, concealed in or about the strongbox in any way, or under whatever pretext, as when making wedding gifts, and [as if] sending the said sum in the strongbox, any jewel which exceeds the aforesaid amount, counting those things aforementioned. And furthermore, that no one may give to him or to those or to anyone or to several who carry or bear the strongbox, more than one gold florin in money or gifts under whatever pretext, or warrant, under pain of one-hundred-*lire* fine in *denari piccioli* to be levied on each person for each violation.

4. Grey or white squirrel fur used for trimming and lining.

Furthermore, no woman or man of any rank or high station whatsoever may make or be permitted to make or have made for his or her children, either boys or girls, his or her brother, nephews or grandchildren, or any relative by blood or marriage alike, or even friends of more than seven years of age, any smock, or any other garment or mantle which exceeds the value of five gold florins under pain of twenty-five-*lire* fine in Florentine *denari piccioli* which is to be levied upon each man and woman for each violation.

Furthermore, no person or persons, man or woman, alone, in pairs, or severally, of any class or station whatsoever, or however rich, or whether in holy orders, or any ecclesiastical person subject to the authority of the said Commune in any way, may or be permitted to spend or cause to have spent, under any pretext or warrant, more than one gold florin on the baptism of children and on godparents who shall assemble by reason of the said baptism, or on confectionery, or on candles, or on any additional presents or things for all the godfathers and godmothers, or for themselves alone or for himself; nor may there be at the same baptism, in all, more than three sponsors, counting men as well as women, under pain of twenty-five-*lire* fine in Florentine *denari piccioli* to be levied on each man and woman for each violation.

Furthermore, that no woman may at one time wear upon her finger or fingers more than two rings under pain of twenty-five-*lire* fine in Florentine *denari piccioli* to be levied upon her for each violation.

In each and all the penalties, each and every person and those collectively who are found by the officials or retainers of the Executor of the Ordinances of Justice of the People and the Commune of Florence, or any of these, are liable to and must be punished and be condemned by this Executor and be constrained by this condemnation to pay [the fine] in fact, forthwith, and summarily.

Furthermore, the father for his son or [un]married daughter, the brother who is next-of-kin for his sister who has no father and is unmarried and for his brother who has no father, the husband for the wife he has taken in marriage, and uncles for their nephews and for their unmarried nieces who have no father or brother who is of legal age [all aforesaid responsible adults] may be constrained as aforesaid by such condemnation or to pay [the fine].

That each Executor of the Ordinances of Justice of the People and of the Commune may and must have, and must be held responsible for

having, at least on every Sunday, holiday, and feast day, under pain of
five-hundred-*lire* fine in Florentine *denari piccioli* which must be with-
held from his salary, a solemn search made for those who violate the
aforestated commands or any of the aforestated commands in any way,
and he must condemn those found guilty, and, in addition, the above-
mentioned people and punish them as is provided for above.

Of every amount of money which the said Executor shall cause to come
into the aforesaid Commune for the aforesaid causes or for any of them,
by this authority he may and must have two *soldi* of Florentine *denari
piccioli* for each pound of that amount of money; and by this authority
the Chamberlains of the Commune of Florence, who will be in office
for the term, may and must give and pay, and be held responsible for
paying without fail to this Executor the said quantity of two *soldi* in
Florentine *denari piccioli* per *lira* without the necessity of his having any
voucher or any license of any kind for this, and out of whatever money
of the said Commune which is not conceded or assigned to others.

It is expressly declared that all condemnations for the aforesaid causes,
or for any of them which are paid by the husband of any woman for any
wrong committed by this woman, be understood to be paid [in fact]
and to be paid out of her dowry and out of the amount of the dowry of
this same woman, and henceforth, by that sum and quantity of money of
the said dowry as will be so paid, it shall be understood that the husband
of the said woman, and his heirs, and any other person who might be
obligated in the restitution of the said dowry, are to be freed and totally
absolved.

*Ordinances against Ladies' Excessive Ornaments and against Excessive
Expenses for Weddings and Funerals* [*1356*][5]

Written below are the ordinances and provisions made by Schiatta
Ridolfi[6] and by the honorable fellow citizens appointed by this Commune

5. *Ordinamenti e riforme del 1355 (con aggiunti del 1357), Codex* 33, folios
17[r]–21[r], Archivio di Stato, Florence. This Appendix contains only the laws pertaining to women's attire. A published version is found in P. Fanfani (1851), pp. 366–
82, 429–37. See also A. Gherardi (1886), p. 175.
6. Schiatta Ridolfi belonged to one of the most prominent families in the government of Florence; he, with other great families such as the Alberti, Ricci, Medici,
Acciaiuoli and Covoni, allied himself to the *gente nuova* and artisans against the
oligarchical group led by the Albizzi family.

to make provisions and ordinances for the repression and punishment of those who henceforth commit murder or assault in the City of Florence or its district, and for the repression and regulation of excessive expenditures by citizens for clothes and ornaments for their ladies, girls, and women, and for their weddings, marriages, banquets, and burials and other things such as are contained below, in this Year of Our Lord 1356, by vigor of their office, jurisdiction, authority, and power granted to them by the appropriate councils of the people and Commune of Florence, enscribed by Ser Piero di Ser Grifo[7] notary and scribe of the said Reforms. They begin:

First, that no married woman or girl of whatever rank she may be is permitted, or may dare or presume to wear in the City of Florence, in her home or without, any dress of samite[8] that is interwoven with gold or silk, or any dress of silken cloth except of simple silk. And similarly, none of the aforesaid women is permitted or may dare to wear in her home or without in the City of Florence any dress, hood, or hat in which or upon which there may be any gold, silver, precious stone, pearl, mother of pearl, or any embroidery, or any animal figure, or vair, ermine, rabbit, or any fur trim. Nor may any of the aforesaid women or girls dare to wear any hood that is fringed or bears cutwork. Nor any garment or dress with ribbons or trim or upon which or in which there may be gold, silver, pearls, precious stones, or any other enameled design or design with enamel, mother of pearl, or anything else. With the exception that each of them is permitted to wear with impunity a simple trim or decoration of gold or silver without any enamel or anything else placed over it. The decorations of the said trim cannot be wider than half of one-eighth of a *braccio*.[9] This trim is permitted and may be around the collar and at the sleeves of the cloak and only at their edges; and on the sleeves of the gown at the side of the buttons up to the elbow and no further; and on the *cottardita*[10] at the collar and on the right side of the sleeves only, and not otherwise, or in any other way, provided the said trim is not worn in or on garments that are particolored, that is, of simple samite or several

7. Ser Piero was a famous and perennial member of the Florentine chancellery; see D. Marzi (1910), pp. 88–91; G. Brucker (1962), p. 60.

8. Samite (*sciamito*), a heavy fabric women with threads of six filaments and often interwoven with gold and silk threads.

9. A *braccio,* literally "an arm's length"; 0.5836 meters or about 2 feet.

10. The *cottardita* (Old French: *cottehardie*), a long, flowing outer garment worn by both sexes.

kinds of samite, or that are of samite and wool, or of samite and silken cloth or camlet.[11] And furthermore, on the said garments or dresses or any of them, there may not be, nor may there be worn, any facing of silken cloth or of camlet or of sendal,[12] vair, ermine, rabbit, or any other type of lining whatsoever, with the exception that upon the mantle a turned-up facing of silken cloth may be worn with impunity. And whosoever of the aforesaid persons violate any of the aforesaid things shall be sentenced to give two hundred *fiorentinelli piccioli* to the Commune of Florence for each offense.

No lady, woman, or girl may dare to wear in the City of Florence in her home or without, any row of enameled buttons or any enameled buttons on any dress or any dress upon which there is enameling, pearls, precious stones, or mother of pearl; and no row of buttons on any dress of the aforesaid ladies, women, or girls may pass the elbow of their sleeves. And no buttons may be worn on any of their dresses where there are no eyelets to fasten these buttons. And no lady, woman, or girl may dare or presume to wear in the City of Florence, in her home or without, any fur trim, ermine, vair, rabbit, or indisia,[13] or possess any that are turned up at the sleeves, or on the side or at the openings of the cloak, the *cottardita,* or the mantle. And the lining of the said garments or any of them may not pass beyond the cloth or the openings in any way. Anyone violating the aforesaid provisions is to be sentenced to [a fine of] fifty *lire di piccioli* for each offense. However, the wives of knights are to be immune and exempted from the things that are contained in this present section, and from each of those things.

Item: None of the aforesaid women is permitted or may dare to wear on her head in the City of Florence, in her home or without, any crown of gold, silver, pearls, precious stones, mother of pearl, or anything else, even though it be imitation, under pain of two hundred *lire di piccioli* for each offense. With the exception that ladies and girls each may wear with impunity for the adornment of her head a garland or circlet, except that it be made or formed in the shape of a crown. This garland or circlet may be of gold, silver or pearls, gilded, silver plated or imitation, with enamels, but [it may] not [have] precious stones or mother of pearl and [must] not

11. Camlet (*ciambellotto*), a light, costly Eastern cloth of camel's hair or angora wool used for outer garments; or a satiny fabric of silk and wool or goat's hair.

12. Sendal (*zendado*), a light silken fabric used for dresses and banners.

13. Indisia, a kind of silk cloth used for lining.

be valued at over ten gold florins. These garlands and circlets permitted above must be appraised first by the chief officer of the Assay for Gold Florins of the Commune of Florence, who for the term will perform the said duty. This official, having first sworn an oath to appraise well, and truly, and in good faith, must appraise the said garlands and circlets; and for every garland and circlet that he shall appraise, he may receive in salary twelve *denari piccioli,* and no more, under pain of a fine of ten *lire di piccioli* for each time he takes more. And henceforth [these adornments] must be recorded by one of the friars who are chamberlains of the Chamber of Arms of the Palazzo del Popolo of Florence,[14] who, for the term, will perform [this task], or [it shall be performed] in his presence. And such garlands and circlets as shall be appraised and recorded in such manner may and must be written down and registered in a ledger by Ser Agnolo di Ser Andrea di Messer Rinaldo, notary and Florentine citizen (or by his aide whom Ser Agnolo will nominate once and several times), placing and writing in the said book the name of the lady, her husband, and her quarter [of the city] and the true appraisal of such garland or circlet. And otherwise these things may not be worn, under pain of [a fine of] fifty *lire di piccioli* to be levied on anyone in violation of the aforesaid provisions. The aforesaid Ser Agnolo, or his aide for the recording of any of the aforesaid garlands and circlets, may take two *soldi* in *denari piccioli* for his trouble, and no more, under pain of a fine of twenty-five *lire di piccioli* if he takes more. With the exception that any garland or circlet that is appraised at less than two gold florins does not require recording or appraisal in the aforesaid manner.

No woman or girl is permitted to wear in her home or without in the City of Florence, any garment or clothing of samite completely or partly fringed, or with fringes. And, similarly, no woman or girl may wear fringes on any of her dresses which has a lining showing outside, or which is turned up with a lined facing, or anything else, under pain of [a fine of] fifty *lire di piccioli* for each offense. And no fringe may be larger than one-half a *braccio.*

Item: No maiden or young girl who is over the age of ten years is permitted to wear on her head or on her person, at home or without, clothes or dresses which are smocked, lapped, or pleated in any way, either much or little, nor [may she wear] any dress in which there are

14. The Palazzo della Podestà, or Bargello.

more than eight insets,[15] large or small. And no married woman is permitted to go about at home at the time of her wedding or nuptials wearing her belt over all of her clothing, or outside her home at any time, [wearing a belt] over a cloak or *cottardita* lined with vair, sendal, or any other lining, under pain of [a fine of] twenty-five *lire di piccioli* [to be levied] on each woman for each offense.

Item: No woman of whatever station or rank she may be, or by whatever name she may be called, may wear or be permitted to wear any girdle, strap, or belt that exceeds fifteen gold florins in value, or any girdles, straps, or belts in which there are precious stones, pearls, mother of pearl, or any of these things. Nor is she permitted to carry a purse on which there is a pearl or are pearls, mother of pearl, or precious stones, under pain of [a fine of] one hundred *lire di piccioli* for each woman in violation and for each offense.

Item: That no woman is permitted to wear at the same time on her finger or fingers more than two rings; [these may contain] only one pearl or precious stone each, under pain [of a fine] of twenty-five *fiorini piccioli* to be levied on each woman in violation for each offense.

No married woman or widow is permitted to go outside her home through the streets of the City of Florence in her stocking feet wearing hose or stockings whether with soles or without; nor [may she] wear stamped shoes or shoes of any colored fabric, silken cloth, or samite; nor [may she] wear tongues and buckles on her shoes, or on golden or silver or gilded slippers, under pain of [a fine of] twenty-five *fiorini piccioli* to be levied on each woman in violation for each offense. With the exception that the wives of knights are permitted to wear the said tongues and buckles with impunity.

Item: That no woman or man of any station or rank whatsoever is permitted to make or have made for his daughters or sons, brothers, grandsons or nephews, relatives, kinsmen or friends under the age of seven years, any gown, dress, or mantle that exceeds the value of five gold florins, under pain [of a fine] of twenty-five *lire di piccioli* for anyone in violation and for each offense.

No woman of the City of Florence of any station or rank whatever is permitted to wear outside her home in the City of Florence any mantle

15. Insets (*gheroni*), triangular-shaped pieces inserted base-down in seams to give a flare to skirts and dresses.

lined with vair or ermine, or with any heads, ruffs, or paws of vair or ermine, under pain [of a fine] of one hundred *lire di piccioli* to be levied on each offender for each violation.

Item: That no lady, woman, or girl of whatever rank she may be, is permitted or may dare or presume to wear or clothe herself in any woolen garment or dress striped, patterned, or checked with silk, or worked with silk, or woven or appliquéd in silk, under pain [of a fine] of one hundred *lire di piccioli,* to be levied on anyone who violates any of the aforesaid things, and of confiscation of the said forbidden garment and dress; the latter shall become the property of the Comune of Florence by complete right of law.

No man or woman of any station or rank whatsoever of the City of Florence or its district under any pretext, warrant, or cause, is permitted or may dare, by himself or herself, or by others, to send or receive any strongbox in which there are jewels exceeding the value or worth of fifty gold florins in all, including the value and worth of the said strongbox. This latter may not be of greater price than three gold florins and must be of wood or of simple leather bound with iron, and not gilded, silver-plated, enameled, or decorated with ultramarine. However, the arms of the husband and wife may be painted on it. Among the jewels of the aforesaid value which are sent in this strongbox, there can be no attire or anything forbidden by order of the present ordinances. And together with the said strongbox none of the aforesaid persons are allowed secretly or openly, in any way or under any pretext, to present or receive any jewel that surpasses the aforesaid amount of the said value of all those things totaled together which, as is said above, are sent in this strongbox under the said amount. And no one may give more than one gold florin in money or gifts under any pretext whatsoever to the person or persons, one or several, who bears or bear the strongbox, under pain [of a fine] of two hundred *lire di piccioli* to be levied on each offender for violating any of the aforesaid provisions.[16]

. . . .

No housemaid or other woman, no nurse, maidservant, or servant girl of any citizen or resident of the City of Florence is permitted or may dare to wear in the home or without in the City or through the City of Flor-

16. In *Codex* 33, folios 18ᵛ, 19ʳᵛ, and 20ʳ deal with weddings; they are not translated here.

ence, any hat or hood of samite or any manner of silken cloth or camlet. Nor [may she wear] any hat or hood lined with cloth, samite, camlet, any silken cloth or sendal; nor possess any which are black or white; nor wear slippers outside the house. Nor are any of the aforesaid persons permitted to wear inside the home or without, any hat or hood in which or upon which there is any embroidery or any other ornament forbidden by order of any of the aforesaid ordinances. And that none of the aforesaid persons is permitted to wear any dress slashed at any part, or with netting or mesh, or any silver or gilded buttons or any row of buttons that goes beyond her elbow, under pain [of a fine] of fifty *lire di piccioli;* each of those women who violate any of the aforesaid provisions shall be sentenced to give this amount to the Commune of Florence for each time [she commits the offense]. Any woman who does not pay this fine within fifteen days from the day upon which the sentence is read is to be whipped naked through the City of Florence from the Stinche [Prison] to the Mercato Nuovo, and around and around the said Mercato Nuovo. When this whipping is completed she must be allowed to go free. But none or any of the aforesaid things apply to the public prostitutes who yield their bodies to lechery for money.

Item: That for each and every ordinance or provision written immediately above, and for their observance, execution, and effect, and for the payment of fines and penalties (which by vigor of these ordinances and provisions or by any of them, shall be made henceforth through the foreign official[17] appointed for the term by the Commune of Florence over the execution and observance of the said ordinances and provisions) each and every man and person who is sentenced, his guarantors, and each of them may and must be constrained and held liable in person, property, and even by destruction of his goods: the husband for his wife; the father and mother for their son and daughter, should she be married to a foreigner; a brother who is next-of-kin for his sister, should she be unmarried and have no father; and in the case of minors who commit an offense and are sentenced by vigor of the above-written ordinances to pay the penalties decreed in the aforesaid manner, the father and mother are to be held liable and constrained, and may be held liable and constrained by the said official; [and] guardians, male and female, for the boys and

17. It was the practice to hire officials from other parts of Italy for certain offices to insure impartiality.

girls for whom they are guardian. With the exception that should any person be condemned by vigor of the present ordinances who is in the prison of the Commune, no other person can be held liable or be constrained or molested in any way concerning his person or his goods.

Item: That each and every sum of money that shall be paid henceforth to the Commune of Florence or to any person in conformity with these ordinances by the husband for the penalty incurred by his wife (this penalty is to be exacted by the foreign official of the Commune of Florence, appointed, as is stated above, over the execution of the present ordinances by vigor of these same ordinances, or by any of them) [this sum] is to be appropriated, and is henceforth to be understood to be and to have been appropriated by vigor of the present provision, from the sum of the dowry of the said wife who may be sentenced, as has been stated, so that thus, when the case may arise to ask for the return or restitution of the dowry, the aforesaid sum and sums paid by the husband for the penalty of the said wife who has been sentenced, as has been said, are to be and must be made up for and recompensed out of the payment or restitution of the said dowry. And, further, for the sum of money thus paid in the case of restitution of the dowry, neither the husband, his heirs, nor any other person shall be held responsible or liable. Nor must any woman or anyone speaking for her be heard to the contrary by any rector, judge, or official of the Commune of Florence [. . . .]

Item: That whatsoever husband fails to pay the penalty incurred by his wife by vigor of the present ordinances to the chamberlains of the Commune of Florence, who receive for this Commune, within fifteen days from the day on which penalty is imposed, may not be elected or accepted into any office of the said Commune until he has paid the said penalty and one-quarter more, if the one-quarter more be incurred. And if his name be drawn, or if he be elected or elevated to an office, such election and drawing by this reason alone is to be null and void, and the token with his name must immediately be torn up by the Notary of the Reforms. And anyone who accepts any office of the Commune of Florence in violation of the said procedure is to be fined five *lire di piccioli*. With the exception and reservation that any husband who shall present his wife who is sentenced, in the manner aforesaid, to the power of the Commune of Florence, may not be held liable in any way for paying the said penalty, nor may any of the aforesaid liabilities be charged to him.

And by the duty of his office and by his oath, it is the responsibility and duty of the foreign official of the Commune of Florence, who for the term shall be appointed for the execution of these ordinances, to report in writing to at least two of the chamberlains of the Chamber of the Commune of Florence who shall be [in office] for the term, every woman, lady, girl, housemaid, nurse, servant, or serving wench whom he or his retinue find wearing or possessing anything forbidden by order of the present ordinances. [He must make a written report] immediately on the day that he finds her, with her name and surname and the name of her husband, if she has one, or of her master or mistress with whom she lives, mentioning the forbidden article with which she was found, under pain of [a fine of] one hundred *lire di piccioli* to be levied on the said official for each time he fails to report any of the aforementioned things.

And with this section this official must be expressly charged: It is expressly declared that the discoveries of violations that shall thus be made by the aforesaid official or by his retinue on holidays and feast days, whose observance is customarily proclaimed by the Cathedral Church[18] of the City of Florence, require only that the said written report be made to one of the chamberlains of the aforementioned Chamber.

18. The Cathedral Church of Santa Reparata (popularly "Santa Liberata") was demolished in 1375, after being enclosed within the gigantic structure of the new *duomo*, Santa Maria del Fiore. Santa Reparata has now been excavated and is once again a functioning church beneath the Cathedral.

Bibliography of Works Consulted

Abbondanza, Roberto. "Una lettera autografa del Boccaccio nell'Archivio di Stato di Perugia." *Studi sul Boccaccio,* 1 (1963), 5–13.

[Alain de Lille] Alanus de Insulis. *De planctu Naturae. PL,* CCX, 431–82; and *Anglo-Latin Satirical Poets and Epigrammists of the Twelfth Century.* Ed. Thomas Wright. London, 1872. II, 429–522.

———. *The Complaint of Nature by Alain de Lille.* Trans. Douglas M. Moffatt. Yale Studies in English. New York, 1908.

[Albertus Magnus]. *De aetatibus sive de iuventute et senectute,* in *B. Alberti Magni, Opera Omnia.* Ed. August Borgnet. Paris, 1891. Vol. 9.

Ambrose, Saint. *Opera omnia. PL,* XIV–XVII.

———. *De virginibus. PL,* XVI.

Andreas Capellanus. *De amore libri tres.* Ed. E. Trojel. Munich, 1964.

———. *Trattato d'amore: Testo latino del sec. XII con due traduzioni toscane inedite del sec. XIV.* Ed. Salvatore Battaglia. Rome, 1947.

———. *The Art of Courtly Love.* Trans. John Jay Parry. *Records of Civilization.* New York, 1941; reprint, New York, 1959, 1969.

The Anglo-Latin Satirical Poets and Epigrammists of the Twelfth Century. Ed. Thomas Wright. Rolls series, 59. 2 vols. London, 1872.

Anselm of Canterbury. *De contemptu mundi. PL,* CLV, 696ff.

Antiche rime volgari secondo la lezione del Codice Vaticano 3793. Ed. Alessandro d'Ancona and Domenico Comparetti. Collezione di opere inedite o rare. 5 vols. Bologna, 1875–88.

Apocalypsis Goliae. See *The Latin Poems Commonly Attributed to Walter Mapes.*

Aquinas, Saint Thomas. *Basic Writings of Saint Thomas Aquinas.* Ed. Anton C. Pegis. 2 vols. New York, 1945.

Aristotle. *De anima*. Trans. Kenelm Foster and Silvester Humphries. New Haven, 1954.

Augustine, Saint. *Ad Marcellinum de civitate Dei contra paganos. PL,* XLI.

———. *De genesi ad litteram.* Ed. Iosephus Zycha. *Corpus scriptorum ecclesiasticorum latinorum,* 28 (1), 1–456. Vienna, 1895.

———. *St. Augustine's Confessions.* Trans. William Watts (1631), preface by W. H. D. Rouse. 2 vols. Loeb Classical Library. London and Cambridge, Mass., 1912.

[Babrius]. *Babrius and Phaedrus.* Ed. and trans. Ben Edwin Perry. Loeb Classical Library. London and Cambridge, Mass., 1965.

Barberino, Francesco da. *Del Reggimento e de' costumi delle donne.* Ed. G. E. Sansone. Turin, 1957.

Baron, Hans. *The Crisis of the Early Italian Renaissance: Civic Humanism and Republican Liberty.* 2 vols. Princeton, 1955; rev. in one vol., 1966.

———. *From Petrarch to Leonardo Bruni: Studies in Humanistic and Political Literature.* Chicago, 1968.

———. "The Social Background of Political Liberty in the Early Italian Renaissance." *Comparative Studies in Society and History,* 2 (1960), 440–51.

Bartoli, Lodovico. "Il Corbaccino di ser Lodovico Bartoli." Ed. Guido Mazzoni. *Il Propugnatore,* n.s. 1 (1888), 240–301.

Battaglia, Salvatore. "Elementi autobiografici nell'arte del Boccaccio." *La Cultura,* 9 (1930), 241–54.

Becker, E. J. *A Contribution to the Comparative Study of Medieval Visions of Heaven and Hell.* Baltimore, 1899.

Becker, Marvin B. *Florence in Transition.* 2 vols. Baltimore, 1967, 1968.

———. "Florentine Politics and the Diffusion of Heresy in the Trecento: A Socioeconomic Inquiry." *Speculum,* 34 (1959), 60–75.

———. "Some Aspects of Oligarchical, Dictatorial and Popular *Signorie* in Florence, 1282–1382." *Comparative Studies in Society and History,* 2 (1960), 421–39.

Bernard of Morlaix. *De contemptu mundi* in *The Anglo-Latin Satirical Poets and Epigrammists of the Twelfth Century.* London, 1872. II, 3–102.

Bernardo, Aldo S. *Petrarch, Scipio and the Africa: The Birth of Humanism's Dream.* Baltimore, 1962.

Besta, E. *Le persone nella storia del diritto italiano*. Padua, 1931.

Billanovich, Giuseppe. *Restauri boccacceschi*. Rome, 1947.

Bishop, Morris, ed. and trans. *Letters from Petrarch*. Bloomington, Ind., 1966.

Boccaccio, Giovanni. *L'Amorosa visione*. Ed. Vittore Branca. Autori classici e documenti di lingua pubblicati dall'Accademia della Crusca. Florence, 1944.

——. *La Caccia di Diana*. Ed. Vittore Branca. *Tutte le opere di Giovanni Boccaccio*, 1. Milan, 1967.

——. *Comedia delle ninfe fiorentine (L'Ameto)*. Ed. Antonio Enzo Quaglio. *Tutte le opere di Giovanni Boccaccio*, 2. Milan, 1964.

——. *Il Corbaccio secondo la lezione del testo Mannelli*. Ed. Ignazio Moutier. *Opere volgari di Giovanni Boccaccio*. Florence, 1828, V, 155–255.

——. *L'Ameto, Lettere, Il Corbaccio*. Ed. Nicola Bruscoli. Scrittori d'Italia. Bari, 1940.

——. *Il Corbaccio*. Ed. Tauno Nurmela. *Suomalaisen Tiedakatemian Toimituksia: Annales Academiae Scientiarum Fennicae*, ser. B,146. Helsinki, 1968.

——. *Il Corbaccio*. Ed. Luigi Sorrento. Bibliotheca romanica. Strassbourg, [1910].

——. *De casibus illustrium virorum. A Facsimile Reproduction of the Paris Edition of 1520*. Ed. Lewis Brewer Hall. Gainesville, Fla., 1962.

——. [*De casibus*]. *The Fates of Illustrious Men*. Ed. and trans. Lewis Brewer Hall. New York, 1965.

——. *Il Decameron*. Ed. Charles S. Singleton. 2 vols. Scrittori d'Italia. Bari, 1955.

Boccaccio, Giovanni. *Decameron: Edizione diplomatico-interpretiva dell'autografo Hamilton 90*. Ed. Charles S. Singleton. Baltimore and London, 1974.

——. *L'Elegia di Madonna Fiammetta*. Ed. Vincenzo Pernicone. Scrittori d'Italia. Bari, 1939.

——. *Esposizioni sopra la Comedia di Dante*. Ed. Giorgio Padoan. *Tutte le opere di Giovanni Boccaccio*, 6. Milan, 1965.

——. *Il Filocolo*. Ed. Antonio Enzo Quaglio. *Tutte le opere di Giovanni Boccaccio*, 1. Milan, 1967.

——. *Il Filostrato*. Ed. Vittore Branca. *Tutte le opere di Giovanni Boccaccio*, 1. Milan, 1967.

———. *Genealogie deorum gentilium libri.* Ed. Vincenzo Romano. 2 vols. Scrittori d'Italia. Bari, 1951.

———. *Le Lettere edite e inedite di Messer Giovanni Boccaccio.* Ed. and trans. Francesco Corazzini. Florence, 1877.

———. [*De montibus*]. *Genealogiae Joannis Boccatii: cum demōstrationibus in formis arborū designatis. Eiusdē de mōtibus & sylvis. de fontibus: lacubus: & fluminibus.* . . . Venetiis: per Augustinum de Zannis, 1511.

———. *De mulieribus claris.* Ed. Vittorio Zaccaria. *Tutte le opere di Giovanni Boccaccio,* 10. Milan, 1967.

———. [*De mulieribus claris*]. *Concerning Famous Women.* Trans. Guido A. Guarino. New Brunswick, N.J., 1963.

———. *Il Ninfale fiesolano.* See *Opere in versi,* etc. Ed. Pier Giorgio Ricci.

———. *Opere in versi, Corbaccio, Trattatello in laude di Dante, Prose latine, Epistole.* Ed. Pier Giorgio Ricci. La letteratura italiana: Storia e Testi, 9. Milan-Naples, 1965.

———. *Opere latine minori (Buccolicum carmen, carminum et epistolarum quae supersunt, scripta breviora).* Ed. Aldo Francesco Masséra. Scrittori d'Italia. Bari, 1928.

———. *Rime, Caccia di Diana.* Ed Vittore Branca. Padua, 1958.

———. *Trattatello.* See *Opere in versi,* etc. Ed. Pier Giorgio Ricci.

———. *The Earliest Lives of Dante Translated from the Italian of Giovanni Boccaccio and Leonardo Bruni.* Trans. James Robinson Smith. New York, 1901; republished with an introduction by Francesco Basetti-Sani, New York, 1963.

———. *Zibaldone boccaccesco mediceo-laurenziano, Pluteo XXIX–8.* A cura della Biblioteca Medicea-Laurenziana. Ed. with an introduction by G. Biagi. Florence, 1915 (facsimile).

Boethius. [*De consolatione*]. *Boethii Philosophiae consolationis libri quinque.* Ed. Wilhelm Weinberger. *Corpus scriptorum ecclesiasticorum latinorum,* 67. Leipzig, 1934.

———. *The Consolation of Philosophy.* Trans. Richard Green. Library of Liberal Arts. Indianapolis and New York, 1962.

———. *The Theological Tractates and the Consolation of Philosophy.* Eds. H. F. Stewart and E. K. Rand. Loeb Classical Library. Cambridge, Mass., and London, 1908.

Bonfante, G. "Femmina e donna." *Studia philologica et litteraria in honorem Leo Spitzer.* Ed. Anna Granville Hatcher and Karl Selig. Berne, 1958.

Bourciez, Jean. "Sur l'énigme du Corbaccio." *Revue des langues romanes,* 72 (1958), 303–37.

Bourland, Caroline Brown. *Boccaccio and the Decameron in Castilian and Catalan Literature.* New York, 1905.

Bowsky, William M., ed. *The Black Death: A Turning Point in History.* European Problem Studies. New York, 1971.

Branca, Vittore. *"L'Amorosa visione* (tradizione, significati, fortuna)," *Studi di filologia italiana,* 7 (1950), 20–47.

———. *Boccaccio medievale.* Florence, 1956; revised, 1970.

———. "Non sconfessato il *Decameron,*" *La Fiera Letteraria,* XL, no. 49; December 19, 1965.

———. "Notizie di manoscritti. Codici di opere del Boccaccio." *Lettere italiane,* 10 (1958); 12 (1960).

———. "Profilo biografico." *Tutte le opere di Giovanni Boccaccio.* Milan, 1967. I, 3–203.

———. *Tradizione delle opere di Giovanni Boccaccio.* Rome, 1958.

———, and Pier Giorgio Ricci. *Un autografo del Decameron (Codice Hamiltoniano 90).* Opuscoli Accademici dell'Università di Padova, 9. Padua, 1962.

———, and Pier Giorgio Ricci. "Notizie e Documenti per la biografia del Boccaccio." *Studi sul Boccaccio,* 5 (1969), 1–18.

Brown, Carleton. "Mulier est hominis confusio." *Modern Language Notes,* 35 (1920), 479–82.

Brown, Margery L. "The 'Hous of Fame' and the 'Corbaccio.'" *Modern Language Notes,* 22 (1917), 411–15.

Brucker, Gene A. *Florentine Politics and Society, 1348–1378.* Princeton Studies in History, 12. Princeton, 1962.

———. *Renaissance Florence.* New York, 1969.

Bullough, Vern L. "Medieval Medical and Scientific Views of Women." *Viator,* 4 (1973), 485–501.

———, and Bonnie Bullough. *The Subordinate Sex: A History of Attitudes toward Women.* Urbana, Ill., 1973.

Burkhardt, Jacob. *The Civilization of the Renaissance in Italy.* Trans. S. G. C. Middlemore. London, 1960.

Caggese, R., ed. *Statuti della Repubblica Fiorentina.* 2 vols. Firenze, 1921.

The Cambridge Economic History of Europe. Ed. M. M. Postan et al. 6 vols. Cambridge, 1941–65; 2nd ed., 1966.

Il Cantare del bel Gherardino. Ed. Francesco Zambrini. Scelta di curiosità letterarie, 79. Bologna, 1897.

Il Cantare di Fiorio e Biancifiore. Ed. Vincenzo Crescini. Scelta di curiosità letterarie, 233 and 249. Bologna, 1889–99.

Il Cantare di Fiorio e Biancofiore. Ed. Giovanni Crocioni. Rome, 1903.

Carpentier, Élisabeth. "Autour de la peste noire: famines et épidémies dans l'histoire du XIVe siècle." *Annales: Économies, Sociétés, Civilisations,* 17 (1962), 1062–92.

Casagrande, Gino. "Dio e fortuna nel *Decameron.*" *Proceedings, Pacific Northwest Conference on Foreign Languages Eighteenth Annual Meeting, March 17–18, 1967.* University of Victoria. XVIII, 115–21.

Cassell, Anthony K. "An Abandoned Canvas: Structural and Moral Conflict in the *Corbaccio.*" *Modern Language Notes,* 89 (1974), 60–70.

———. "*Il Corbaccio* and the Secundus Tradition." *Comparative Literature,* 25 (1973), 252–360.

———. "The Crow of the Fable and the *Corbaccio:* A Suggestion for the Title." *Modern Language Notes,* 85 (1970), 83–91.

Cassirer, Ernst. *The Individual and the Cosmos in Renaissance Philosophy.* Trans. Mario Domandi. New York, 1963.

[Cecco d'Ascoli]. Francesco Stabili. *L'Acerba.* Ed. Achille Crespi. Ascoli Piceno, 1927.

Chanson de Roland. Ed. J. Bédier. Paris, 1921.

Chaucer, Geoffrey. *The Canterbury Tales.* Ed. F. N. Robinson. Oxford, 1933.

Chrysostom, Saint John (formerly attributed). *In Evangelium Matthaei. PG,* LVI, 611–946.

Cian, Vittorio. "Briciole dantesche." *Rassegna bibliografica della letteratura italiana,* 2 (1894), 195–97.

———. "Pei 'Motti' di M. Pietro Bembo." *Giornale storico della letteratura italiana,* 13 (1889), 448.

Cicero, Marcus Tullius. *De re publica, De legibus.* Ed. and trans. Clinton Walker Keyes. Loeb Classical Library. London and Cambridge, Mass., 1948.

———. *De inventione: De optimo genere oratorum, Topica.* Ed. and trans. H. M. Hubbell. Loeb Classical Library. London and Cambridge, Mass., 1960.

———. *Ad C. Herennium de ratione dicendi*. Ed. and trans. Harry Caplan. Loeb Classical Library. London and Cambridge, Mass., 1964.

Cioffari, Vincenzo. *Fortune in Dante's Fourteenth-Century Commentators*. Cambridge, Mass., 1944.

———. "The Conception of Fortune in the *Decameron*." *Italica,* 17 (1940a), 129–37.

———. *The Conception of Fortune and Fate in the Works of Dante*. Dante Society of Cambridge, Mass., 1940b.

———. "The Function of Fortune in Dante, Boccaccio and Machiavelli." *Italica,* 24 (1947), 1–13.

Ciotti, Andrea. "Il concetto della 'figura' e la poetica della 'visione' nei commentatori trecenteschi della *Commedia*." *Convivium,* n.s. 3 (1962), 264–92.

The Comedy of Eros: Medieval French Guides to the Art of Love. Trans. Norman R. Shapiro; notes and commentary by James B. Wadsworth. Urbana, Ill., 1971.

Comparetti, Domenico. *Virgilio nel medio evo*. Ed. G. Pasquali. Florence, 1941.

[Contini, Gianfranco, ed.] *Poeti del Duecento*. La Letteratura italiana: Storia e Testi, 2. 2 vols. Milan and Naples, 1960.

Cipolla, C. M. *Studi di storia della moneta: i movimenti dei cambi in Italia dal secolo XIII al XV*. Pavia, 1948.

[Corazzini, Francesco, ed.] *La Visione di Tugdalo. Volgarizzata nel secolo XIV ed ora per la prima volta posta in luce*. Bologna, 1872.

Cottino-Jones, Marga. "The *Corbaccio*: Notes for a Mythical Perspective of Moral Alternatives." *Forum Italicum,* 4 (1970), 490–509.

Crescini, Vincenzo, ed. *Il cantare di Fiorio e Biancifiore*. Scelta di curiosità letterarie, 233 and 249. Bologna, 1889–99.

———. *Contributo agli studi sul Boccaccio*. Turin, 1887.

Croce, Benedetto. *La Novella di Andrea da Perugia*. Bari, 1911.

Cronisti del Trecento. Ed. Roberto Palmarocchi. Milan, 1935.

Curtius, Ernst Robert. *European Literature in the Latin Middle Ages*. Trans. Willard R. Trask. New York, 1953; reprint, 1963.

Dante Alighieri. *La Commedia secondo l'antica vulgata*. Ed. Giorgio Petrocchi. 4 vols. Milan, 1966–67.

———. *Il Convivio*. Eds. G. Busnelli and G. Vandelli. 2 vols. *Opere di Dante*, 5. Florence, 1934; reprint. 1964.

———. *La Divina Commedia*. Ed. C. H. Grandgent. Boston, 1933; rev. Charles S. Singleton, Cambridge, Mass., 1972.

———. *The Divine Comedy of Dante Alighieri*. Ed. and trans. John D. Sinclair. 3 vols. Oxford, 1939; reprint, New York, 1961.

———. *The Divine Comedy*. Ed. and trans. Charles S. Singleton. Bollingen Series, 80. Princeton, 1970–75.

[Dante] Dantis Alagherii. *Epistolae: The Letters of Dante*. Ed. Paget Toynbee. Oxford, 1920; reprint, 1966.

Dante Alighieri. *Dante's Lyric Poetry*. Ed. Kenelm Foster and Patrick Boyde. 2 vols. Oxford, 1967.

———. [*De monarchia*]. *On World Government*. Trans. Herbert W. Schneider. Library of Liberal Arts. Indianapolis, 1949; reprint, 1957.

———. *Opere di Dante Alighieri*. Ed. Fredi Chiappelli. Milan, 1965.

———. *Le rime della "Vita nuova" e della giovinezza*. Ed. Michele Barbi and Francesco Maggini. Florence, 1956.

———. *Vita Nuova*. See *Opere di Dante Alighieri*.

De conjuge non ducenda. See *The Latin Poems Commonly Attributed to Walter Mapes*. Ed. Thomas Wright.

Della Torre, Arnaldo. *La Giovinezza di Giovanni Boccaccio*. Città di Castello, 1905.

De Lubac, H. *Exégèse médiévale*. Seconde Partie, II. Paris, 1964.

Deschamps, Eustache. *Oeuvres Complètes de Eustache Deschamps*. Ed. Le Marquis de Queux de Saint-Hilaire and G. Raynaud. 11 vols. Société des Anciens Textes Français, 24–34. Paris, 1878–1903.

Doren, Alfred. "Fortuna im Mittelalter und in der Renaissance." *Vorträge der Bibliothek Warburg*, 1 (1922–23), 71–144.

Douie, Decima L. *The Nature and the Effect of the Heresy of the Fraticelli*. Manchester, 1932.

Durling, Robert M. "Petrarch's 'Giovene donna sotto un verde lauro.'" *Modern Language Notes*, 86 (1971), 1–20.

Évangile aux femmes. Ed. George C. Keidel. *Romance and Other Studies*, 1. Baltimore, 1895.

Evans, Allan. "Some Coinage Systems of the Fourteenth Century." *Journal of Economic and Business History*, 3 (1931), 481–496.

Fanfani, P. "Legge suntuaria fatta dal comune di Firenze l'anno 1355 e volgarizzata nel 1356 da Andrea Lancia." *Etruria,* I (1851), 366–82, 429–37.

Faral, Edmond. *Les arts poétiques du XIIe et du XIIIe siècle; recherches et documents sur la technique littéraire du moyen âge.* Paris, 1924.

Farinelli, Arturo. "Note sulla fortuna del *Corbaccio* nella Spagna medievale." *Bausteine zur Romanischen Philologie: Festgabe A. Mussafia.* Halle a. S., 1905.

[*Il Cantare di Febus-el-Forte*]. *Febusso e Breusso.* Ed. Lord Vernon. Florence, 1847.

Fèvre de Resson, Jehan le. *See* Jehan le Fèvre de Resson.

Frye, Northrop. *An Anatomy of Criticism.* Princeton, 1957.

Garin, Eugenio. "La cultura fiorentina nella seconda metà del '300, e i 'barbari britanni.'" *La rassegna della letteratura italiana,* 64 (1960), 181–95.

Getto, Giovanni. *Vita di forme e forme di vita nel Decameron.* Turin, 1966.

Gherardi, Alessandro. "Gli Ordinamenti contro alli soperchi ornamenti delle donne e soperchie spese de' mogliazzi e de' morti." *Miscellanea fiorentina di erudizione e di storia,* I, 11 (November, 1886), 175.

Gilson, Étienne. "Poésie et Vérité dans la *Genealogia* de Boccace." *Studi sul Boccaccio,* 2 (1964), 253–82.

Goldschmidt, E. Philip. *Medieval Texts and Their First Appearance in Print.* London, 1943.

Golias de conjuge non ducenda. See *The Latin Poems Commonly Attributed to Walter Mapes.* Ed. Thomas Wright.

Green, Henry. *Shakespeare and the Emblem Writers.* London, 1870.

Green, Richard Hamilton. "Alan of Lille's *De planctu Naturae*." *Speculum,* 31 (1956), 649–74.

Guillaume de Lorris and Jean de Meung. *Le Roman de la Rose.* Ed. Ernest Langlois. 5 vols. Société des Anciens Textes Français. Paris, 1914–24.

Hauvette, Henri. *Boccace, étude biographique et littéraire.* Paris, 1914.

———. "Une confession de Boccace 'Il Corbaccio.'" *Bulletin Italien,* I (1901), 3–21.

———. *Una confessione del Boccaccio.* Trans. Giuseppe Gigli. Florence, 1905.

Hays, H. R. *The Dangerous Sex: The Myth of Feminine Evil.* New York, 1964.

Hentsch, Alice A. *De la littérature didactique du moyen âge s'adressant spécialement aux femmes*. Halle a. S., 1903.

Highet, Gilbert. *Juvenal the Satirist: A Study*. New York, 1954; reprint, 1961.

Hildebert of Tours. *Venerabilis Hildeberti Primo Cenomanensis Episcopi deinde Turonensis Archiepiscopi Opera Omnia. PL,* CLXXI.

Hugh of St. Victor. *De nuptiis. PL,* CLXXVI.

Huizinga, Johan. *The Waning of the Middle Ages*. New York, 1954.

Jacopone da Todi. *Laudi, Trattato e detti*. Ed. Franca Ageno. Florence, 1953.

Jean de Meung. *See* Guillaume de Lorris.

Jeffery, Violet M. "Boccaccio's Titles and the Meaning of the *Corbaccio*." *Modern Language Review,* 28 (1933), 194–204.

Jehan le Fèvre de Resson. *Les Lamentations de Matheolus et le Livre de Leesce (Poèmes français du XVIe siècle)*. Ed. A.-G. Van Hamel. 2 vols. Paris, 1892–1905.

Jerome, Saint [Hieronymus]. *Opera Omnia. PL,* XXII–XXX; *Adversus Jovinianum libri duo. PL,* XXIII; 222–354.

John of Salisbury. *Policraticus. PL,* CIC.

———. [*Policraticus*]. *Frivolities of Courtiers and Footprints of Philosophers being a translation . . . of the Policraticus of John of Salisbury*. Trans. Joseph B. Pike. London, 1938.

———. [*Policraticus*]. *The Statesman's Book of John of Salisbury*. Trans. John Dickinson. New York, 1927.

Jones, John Winter. "Observations on the Origin of the Division of Man's Life into Stages." *Archaeologia,* 35 (1853), 167–89.

Jordan, Robert M. *Chaucer and the Shape of Creation: The Aesthetic Possibilities of Inorganic Structure*. Cambridge, Mass., 1967.

[Juvenal, *Satire VI*]. *Juvenal and Persius*. Ed. and trans. G. G. Ramsay. Loeb Classical Library. Cambridge, Mass., 1965.

Klibansky, Raymond; Erwin Panofsky; and Fritz Saxl. *Saturn and Melancholy: Studies in the History of Natural Philosophy, Religion and Art*. New York, 1964.

Koerting, Gustav. *Boccaccios Leben und Werke*. Leipzig, 1880.

König, Bernhard. *Die Begegnung im Tempel, Abwandlungen eines literarischen Motivs in den Werken Boccaccios*. Hamburger romanistische Studien, Reihe A, Band 45. Hamburg, 1960.

Koonce, B. G. "Satan the Fowler." *Medieval Studies,* 21 (1959), 176–84.

Lactantius [attributed]. "Carmen de ave Phoenice." Ed. Emil Baehrens in *Poetae latini minores*. Leipzig, 1881. III, 247–62.

———. *De ave Phoenice. PL*, VII, 278–84.

———. *De ira Dei. PL*, VII, 79–148.

———. *The Minor Works*. Trans. Sister Mary Francis McDonald. *The Fathers of the Church*, 54. Washington, D.C., 1965.

Landau, Marcus. *Giovanni Boccaccio, sein Leben und seine Werke*. Stuttgart, 1877.

The Latin Poems Commonly Attributed to Walter Mapes. Ed. Thomas Wright. Camden Society, 16. London, 1841.

Latini, Brunetto. *Livres dou Tresor*. Ed. Francis J. Carmody. University of California Publications in Modern Philology, 22. Berkeley, 1948.

———. *Il Tesoretto*. See *Poeti del Duecento, 2*. Ed. G. Contini.

Léonard, E.-G. *Boccace et Naples: Un poète à la recherche d'une place et d'un ami*. Paris, 1944.

Leone, Michael. "Autobiografismo reale e ideale in *Decameron* VIII, 7." *Italica* 50 (1973), 242–65.

Levi, Attilio. *Il Corbaccio e la Divina Commedia*. Turin, 1889.

Il Libro della cucina del secolo XIV. Ed. Francesco Zambrini. Scelta di curiosità letterarie, 40.

Limentani, Alberto, ed. *Dal Roman de Palamedès ai Cantari di Febus-el-forte, testi francesi e italiani del Due- e Trecento*. Collezione di opere inedite o rare, 124. Bologna, 1962.

[Livy]. Livius, Titus. [*Ab urbe condita*] *Livy*. Eds. and trans. B. G. Foster et al. Loeb Classical Library. 14 vols. London, New York, and Cambridge, Mass., 1919–59.

Loomis, Roger Sherman, ed. *Arthurian Literature in the Middle Ages*. Oxford, 1959.

———. *Celtic Myth and Arthurian Romance*. New York, 1927; reprint, 1967.

Lopriore, Giuseppe. "Osservazioni sul *Corbaccio*." *Rassegna della letteratura italiana*, 60 (1956), 483–89.

Luchaire, Julien. *Boccace*. Paris, 1951.

[Lucian]. *Lucian*. Eds. and trans. A. M. Harmon, K. Kilburn, M. D. Macloed et al. 8 vols. Loeb Classical Library. London, 1913–67.

MacCulloch, J. A. *Early Christian Visions of the Other World*. Edinburgh, 1912.

Machiavelli, Niccolò. *La Mandragola, in Opere.* Ed. Mario Bonfantini. Milan, 1963.

Macrì-Leone, Francesco. "La Politica di Giovanni Boccaccio." *Giornale storico della letteratura italiana,* 15 (1890), 79–110.

[Macrobius]. *Commentariorum in somnium Scipionis,* in *Macrobius.* Ed. Franz Eyssenhardt. Leipzig, 1868; reprinted, 1893.

Macrobius. *Commentary on the Dream of Scipio.* Trans. William Harris Stahl. Records of Civilization, Sources and Studies, 48. New York, 1952.

Mâle, Émile. *The Gothic Image: Religious Art in France of the Thirteenth Century.* Trans. Dora Nussey. London, 1913; reprint, New York, 1958.

Map[es], Walter. *Ad Valerium de conjuge non ducenda. PL, XXX,* 254.

———. *De nugis curialium.* Ed. M. R. James. Oxford, 1914.

Marbodus of Rennes. *De meretrice. PL,* CLXXI, 1698–99.

Martellotti, G. *Le due redazioni delle Genealogie del Boccaccio.* Rome, 1951.

Martines, Lauro. *The Social World of the Florentine Humanists.* Princeton, 1963.

Martini, Angelo. *Manuale di metrologia ossia misure, pesi e monete.* Turin, 1883.

[Matheolus]. *Les Lamentations de Matheolus et le livre de Leesce (Poèmes français du XIVe siècle).* Ed. A.-G. Van Hamel. 2 vols. Paris, 1892–1905.

[Maximus the Confessor]. *S. Maximi Confessoris. Loci communes. PG,* XCI, 721–1018.

Mazza, A. "*La Divina Commedia* e alcuni aspetti della poetica del Boccaccio," *Annali dell'Istituto di Studi Danteschi dell'Università di Milano,* 1 (1968).

Mazzoni, Guido, ed. "*Il Corbaccino* di Ser Lodovico Bartoli." *Il Propugnatore,* n.s. 1 (1888), 240–301.

Mazzuchelli, Alice Vizmara. "Come si venne formando l'antifemminismo nella letteratura italiana." *Rassegna pugliese,* 17 (febbraio-marzo, 1901), 69–82.

Meiss, Millard. *Painting in Florence and Siena after the Black Death.* Princeton, 1951; reprint, New York, 1964.

Melli, Elio. "Le fonti del *Febus el Forte,* Cantare del sec. XIV." *Filologia romanza,* 7 (1960), 129–68.

Merkel, Carlo. *Come vestivano gli uomini del "Decameron."* Rome, 1898.

Meyer, Paul. "Les manuscrits français de Cambridge." *Romania*, 15 (1886), 336–39.

———. "Notice du MS. Bodley 57." *Romania*, 35 (1906), 576.

Migne, Jacques-Paul, ed. *Patrologiae cursus completus, series graeca.* 161 vols. Paris, 1866–89.

———. *Patrologiae cursus completus, series latina.* 221 vols. Paris, 1844–64.

Mommsen, Theodor E. "Petrarch and the Story of the Choice of Hercules." *Journal of the Warburg and Courtauld Institutes*, 16 (1953), 178–92.

———. *Medieval and Renaissance Studies.* Ithaca, N.Y., 1959.

Montgomery, R. L., Jr. "Allegory and the Incredible Fable. The Italian View from Dante to Tasso." *PMLA*, 81 (1966), 45–55.

Moore, Arthur Keister. "Studies in a Medieval Prejudice: Antifeminism." Ph.D. dissertation, Vanderbilt University, 1943.

———. *Studies in a Medieval Prejudice: Antifeminism (Abstract of Dissertation).* Joint University Libraries. Nashville, 1945.

Muscetta, Carlo. "Giovanni Boccaccio e i novellieri." *Il Trecento. Storia della Letteratura Italiana.* Eds. Emilio Cecchi and Natalino Sapegno. Milan, 1965. II, 316–558.

Mussafia, Adolfo. "Sulla visione di Tundalo." *Sitzungsberichte der philos.-historischen Classe der kaiserlichen Akademie der Wissenschaften*, 67 (Vienna, 1871), 157–206.

Nardi, Bruno. "Osservazioni sul medievale 'accessus ad auctores.'" *Studi e problemi di critica testuale.* Convegno di studi di filologia italiana (7–9 April, 1960). Bologna, 1961.

Neckam, Alexander. *De vita monachorum. The Anglo-Latin Satirical Poets and Epigrammists of the Twelfth Century.* London, 1872. II, 175–200.

Neff, Theodore Lee. *La Satire des femmes dans la poésie lyrique française du Moyen Âge.* Romance Monographs, 53. Paris, 1900.

Newman, Francis Xavier. "Somnium: Medieval Theories of Dreaming and the Form of Vision Poetry." Ph.D. dissertation, Princeton, 1962.

Novati, Francesco. "Nuovi studi su Albertino Mussato." *Giornale storico della letteratura italiana*, 7 (1886), 1–47.

Nurmela, T. (1968). See Giovanni Boccaccio, *Il Corbaccio.*

―――. "Études critiques sur le texte du *Corbaccio* de Boccace." *Mémoires de la Société Néophilologique de Helsinki,* 25 (1963), 5–53.

―――. "Manuscrits et éditions du *Corbaccio* de Boccace." *Neuphilologische Mitteilungen,* 54 (1953), 102–34.

―――. "Il testo del *Corbaccio* e il codice di Mannelli." *Primo Congresso degli Italianisti Scandinavi: Atti. S. 1.* (Stockholm, May 20–22, 1963.) Eds. S. Ponzanello and D. Ghio [1965].

Orelli, Johann Caspar. *Opuscula graecorum veterum sententiosa et moralia.* Vol. 1. Leipzig, 1819.

L'Ornement des Dames (Ornatus mulierum), texte anglo-normand du XIIIe siècle. Ed. Pierre Ruelle. Travaux de la Faculté de Philosophie et Lettres, 36. Brussels, 1967.

Osgood, Charles G., ed. and trans. *Boccaccio on Poetry: Being the Preface and the Fourteenth and Fifteenth Books of Boccaccio's Genealogia Deorum Gentilium.* Princeton, 1930; reprint, New York, 1956.

Ovid. [Ovidius Naso, Publius]. *The Art of Love and Other Poems.* Ed. and trans. J. H. Mozley. Loeb Classical Library. Cambridge, Mass., 1962.

―――. *Heroides and Amores.* Ed. and trans. Grant Showerman. Loeb Classical Library. Cambridge, Mass., 1947.

―――. *De medicamine faciei liber.* See *The Art of Love and Other Poems.*

―――. *Metamorphoses.* Ed. and trans. Frank Justus Miller. 2 vols. Loeb Classical Library. Cambridge, Mass., 1966–67.

―――. *Remedia amoris.* See *The Art of Love and Other Poems.*

Padoan, Giorgio. *L'Ultima opera di Giovanni Boccaccio.* Publicazioni della Facoltà di Lettere e Filosofia dell'Università di Padova, 34. Padua, 1959.

―――. "Sulla datazione del *Corbaccio.*" *Lettere italiane,* 15 (1963a), 1–27.

―――. "Ancora sulla datazione e sul titolo del *Corbaccio.*" *Lettere italiane,* 15 (1963b), 199–201.

Panofsky, Erwin. *Hercules am Scheidewege und andere antike Bildstoffe in der neueren Kunst.* Studien der Bibliothek Warburg, 18. Leipzig and Berlin, 1930.

―――. *Studies in Iconology.* New York, 1939; reprint, 1962.

Paolo da Certaldo. *Libro di buoni costumi.* Ed. Alfredo Schiaffini. Florence, 1945.

Paparelli, Gioacchino. "Fictio. La definizione dantesca della poesia." *Filologia romanza,* 7 (1960), 1–83.

Paré, Gérard Marie. *Les idées et les lettres au XIIIe siècle: le Roman de la Rose.* Montréal: Université de Montréal, 1947.

Pascal, Carlo. "Antifemminismo medievale." *Poesia latina medievale, saggi e note critiche.* Catania, 1907.

———. "Misoginia medievale." *Studi medievali,* 2 (1906–7), 242–48.

Pastore Stocchi, Manlio. *Tradizione medievale e gusto umanistico nel "De montibus" del Boccaccio.* Padua, 1963.

Patch, Howard Rollin. "The Goddess Fortuna in the *Divine Comedy.*" *Dante Society of Cambridge Massachusetts, 33rd Annual Report* (1913–14), 13–28.

———. "Chaucer's Desert." *Modern Language Notes,* 34 (1919), 321–28.

———. *The Tradition of the Goddess Fortuna in Medieval Philosophy and Literature.* Smith College Studies in Modern Languages, 3. Northhampton, Mass., 1922.

———. *Fortuna in Old French Literature.* Northhampton, Mass., 1923.

———. *The Goddess Fortuna in Medieval Literature.* Cambridge, Mass., 1927; reprint, New York, 1967.

———. *The Other World According to Descriptions in Medieval Literature.* Cambridge, Mass., 1950.

Paton, Lucy Allen. *Studies in the Fairy Mythology of Arthurian Romance.* Radcliffe College Monographs. Boston, 1903.

Payne, Robert. *Hubris: A Study of Pride.* London, 1951; reprint, New York, 1960.

[Perry, Ben Edwin, ed.] *Babrius and Phaedrus.* Loeb Classical Library. London and Cambridge, Mass., 1965.

———. *Secundus the Silent Philosopher.* Ithaca, N.Y., 1964.

Petrarca, Francesco. *Invective contra medicum.* Ed. Pier Giorgio Ricci. Rome, 1950.

———. *Lettere familiari di Francesco Petrarca.* Ed. Giuseppe Fracassetti. 5 vols. Florence, 1863–67.

———. *Lettere senili di Francesco Petrarca.* Ed. Giuseppe Fracassetti. 2 vols. Florence, 1869–70.

———. *Opere.* Ed. Emilio Bigi. Milan, 1964.

———. [Francisci Petrarchae]. *Operum.* 3 vols. Basel, 1554; reprint, New York, 1965.

———. *Petrarch's Testament*. Ed. and trans. Theodore E. Mommsen. Ithaca, N.Y., 1957.

———. *Prose*. Eds. G. Martellotti, P. G. Ricci, E. Carrara, and E. Bianchi. La Letteratura italiana: Storia e Testi, 7. Milan and Naples, 1955.

———. [*Secretum*]. *De secreto conflictu curarum mearum* in *Opere*. Ed. Emilio Bigi. Milan, 1964.

———. *De vita solitaria (secondo lo pseudo-autografo vaticano 3357)*. Ed. Antonio Altamura. Naples, 1943.

———. *The Life of Solitude by Francis Petrarch*. Trans. Jacob Zeitlin. Urbana, Ill., 1924.

Pinelli, Giovanni. "Appunti sul 'Corbaccio.' " *Il Propugnatore,* 16 (1883), 169–92.

Pirenne, Henri. *A History of Europe*. Trans. Bernard Miall. 2 vols. New York, 1958.

Piton, Camille. *Le costume civil en France du XIIIe au XIXe siècle*. Paris, n.d.

Pliny [Plinius Secundus, C]. *Natural History*. Ed. and trans. H. Rackham. 10 vols. Loeb Classical Library. Cambridge, Mass., and London, 1938–67.

Poeti del Duecento. Ed. Gianfranco Contini. La Letteratura italiana: Storia e Testi, 2. 2 vols. Milan and Naples, 1960.

Pucci, Antonio. *Libro di varie storie*. Ed. Alberto Varvaro. Atti della Accademia di Scienze, Lettere e Arti di Palermo, serie quarta, XVI, parte seconda: lettere, 2. Palermo, 1957.

Rajna, Pio. *"Il Corbaccio* ridotto in ottava rima da Lodovico Bartoli." *Studi su Giovanni Boccaccio*. Società Storica della Valdelsa. Castelfiorentino, 1913.

———. "Il libro di Andrea Capellano in Italia nei secoli XIII e XIV." *Studi di filologia romanza,* 13 (1890).

Reliquiae antiquae. Eds. Thomas Wright and James Orchard Halliwell. 2 vols. London, 1841; reprint, New York, 1966.

Ricci, Pier Giorgio (1965). See Giovanni Boccaccio, *Opere in versi* etc.

———. "Notizie e documenti per la biografia del Boccaccio." *Studi sul Boccaccio,* 6 (1971), 1–10.

———. "Studi sulle opere latine e volgari del Boccaccio." *Rinascimento,* 10 (1959), 3–32; 13 (1962), 17–18.

Robertson, D. W., Jr. *A Preface to Chaucer: Studies in Medieval Perspectives*. Princeton, 1962; reprint, 1970.

————. "Some Medieval Literary Terminology, with Special Reference to Chrétien de Troyes." *Studies in Philology*, 48 (1951), 669–92.

Robinson, James Harvey, and Henry Winchester Rolfe. *Petrarch: The First Modern Scholar and Man of Letters*. New York, 1914.

Rodocanachi, Emmanuel. *La Femme italienne à l'époque de la Renaissance: sa vie privée et mondaine, son influence social*. Paris, 1907; reprint, 1922, with the title *La Femme italienne avant, pendant et après la Renaissance*.

————. *Boccace, poète, conteur, moraliste, homme politique*. Paris, 1908.

Rogers, Katharine M. *The Troublesome Helpmate*. Seattle and London, 1966.

Rossi, Aldo. "Proposta per un titolo del Boccaccio: *Il Corbaccio.*" *Studi di filologia italiana*, 20 (1962), 383–90.

Rüegg, August. *Die jenseits Vorstellungen vor Dante und die übrigen literarischen Voraussetzungen der "Divina Commedia."* Cologne, 1945.

Rutebeuf. *Oeuvres complètes de Rutebeuf, trouvère du XIIIᵉ siècle*. Ed. Achille Jubinal. 3 vols. Paris, 1839.

Sacchetti, Franco. *Il Trecentonovelle*, in *Opere*. Ed Aldo Borlenghi. Milan, 1957.

[Fra] Salimbene di Adamo. *Cronaca*. Ed. Giuseppe Scalia. 2 vols. Scrittori d'Italia. Bari, 1966.

Sapegno, Natalino. *Il Trecento. Storia letteraria d'Italia*, 4. Milan, 1934.

Scaglione, Aldo D. *Nature and Love in the Late Middle Ages: An Essay on the Cultural Context of the Decameron*. Berkeley and Los Angeles, 1963.

Schevill, Ferdinand. *History of Florence*. New York, 1936; reprint, 2 vols., 1963.

Seneca, Lucius Annaeus. *De ira*. See *Moral Essays*, below.

————. *Ad Lucilium epistulae morales*. Ed. and trans. Richard M. Gummere. 3 vols. Loeb Classical Library. London and New York, 1925.

————. [*Dialogi*]. *Moral Essays*. Ed. and trans. John W. Basore. 3 vols. Loeb Classical Library. London and New York, 1928.

————. *Naturales Quaestiones*, in *Seneca in Ten Volumes*. Ed. and trans. Thomas H. Corcoran. Loeb Classical Library. London and Cambridge, Mass., 1971.

Seznec, Jean. *The Survival of the Pagan Gods*. New York, 1961.

Singleton, Charles S. *Dante Studies I: Elements of Structure*. Cambridge, Mass., 1957.

Solerti, Angelo, ed. *Le Vite di Dante, Petrarca e Boccaccio*. Milan, 1905.

Sommer, H. O., ed. *Le Livre de Lancelot del Lac. The Vulgate Version of the Arthurian Romances*, 3. Washington, D.C., 1910.

Spitzer, Leo. "A Note on the Poetic and Empirical 'I' in Medieval Authors." *Traditio*, 4 (1946), 414–22.

Strenne nuziali del secolo XIV. Ed. Ottaviano Targioni-Tozzetti. Leghorn, 1873.

Symonds, John Addington. *Giovanni Boccaccio as Man and Author*. New York, 1895. Reprint, Sandoval, N.M., 1961, and New York, 1968.

Tacitus, Cornelius. *The Annals*. Ed. and trans. John Jackson, in *Tacitus*. 4 vols. Loeb Classical Library. London and Cambridge, Mass., 1937.

Tertullian. *De anima*. Ed. J. H. Waszink. Amsterdam, 1947.

———. *De cultu feminarum*, in *Opere Omnia. PL*, I, 1418–48.

Theophrastus. *De nuptiis* (fragment), in St. Jerome. *Adversus Jovinianum. PL*, XXIII, 289.

[Thomas Aquinas, Saint]. S. Thomas Aquinatis. *In decem libros Ethicorum Aristotelis Expositio*. Ed. R. M. Spiazzi. Turin and Rome, 1949.

———. *Commentary on the Nicomachean Ethics*. Trans. C. I. Litzinger. 2 vols. Library of Living Catholic Thought, 1. Chicago, 1964.

———. *Opera omnia*. 16 vols. Rome, 1882–1948.

Thorndike, Lynn. *A History of Magic and Experimental Science*. 8 vols. New York, 1923–58 [esp. vol. 5, 1941]; reprint, 1964–66.

Tietze-Conrat, E. "Notes on Hercules at the Crossroads." *Journal of the Warburg and Courtauld Institutes*, 14 (1951), 305–9.

Tommaseo, Niccolò, and Bellini, Bernardo. *Dizionario della lingua italiana*. 7 vols. Turin, 1916.

Torraca, Francesco. *Per la biografia di Giovanni Boccaccio*. Rome, 1912.

Toynbee, Paget. *Dictionary of Proper Names and Notable Matters in the Works of Dante*. Rev. Charles S. Singleton. Oxford, 1968.

———. "The 'Liber de nuptiis' of Theophrastus in Medieval Literature. *Academy*, 41 (June 25, 1892), 616.

Il Trecento. Ed. Emilio Cecchi and Natalino Sapegno. *Storia della letteratura italiana*, 2. Milan, 1965.

Trexler, Richard C. *Synodal Law in Florence and Fiesole, 1306–1518*. Studi e testi, 268. *Città del Vaticano*, 1971.

Ulrich, J. "Recueils d'exemples italiens." *Romania*, 13 (1884), 46.

Utley, Francis Lee. *The Crooked Rib*. Columbus, Ohio, 1944.

Villani, Giovanni. *Cronica*. Selections in *Cronisti del Trecento*. Ed. Roberto Palmarocchi. Milan, 1935.

[Virgil]. *Virgil*. Ed. and trans. H. Rushton Fairclough. 2 vols. Loeb Classical Library. London, 1916–18; reprint, 1969.

Viscardi, Antonio, and Barni, Gianluigi. *L'Italia nell'età comunale*. Società e costume, panorama di storia sociale e tecnologica, 4. Turin, 1966.

Waddell, Helen. *The Wandering Scholars*. New York, 1961.

Wilkins, Ernest Hatch. "The Date of Birth of Boccaccio." *Romanic Review,* 4 (1910), 369.

Wulff, August. *Die frauenfeindlichen Dichtungen in den romanischen Literaturen des Mittelalters bis zum Ende des XIII^{en} Jahrhunderts*. Halle a. S., 1914.

Welther, J.-T. *L'Exemplum dans la littérature religieuse et didactique du moyen âge*. Paris and Toulouse, 1927.

Zaccaria, Vittorio. "G. Boccaccio, *Il Corbaccio*. Introduzione, testo critico e note a cura di T. Nurmela." *Studi sul Boccaccio,* 5 (1969), 331–40.

Bibliographies of Manuscripts
and Editions of *The Corbaccio*

Boccaccio, Giovanni. *Il Corbaccio*. Ed. Tauno Nurmela. *Annales Academiae Scientiarum Fennicae,* ser. B,146. Helsinki, 1968. Contains full
list of extant MSS, pp. 23–27.

Branca, Vittore. "Notizie di manoscritti. Codici di opere del Boccaccio."
Lettere italiane, 10 (1958); 12 (1960).

———. "Un nuovo elenco di codici." *Studi sul Boccaccio,* 1 (1963), 15–26.
See esp. pp. 17–18.

———. "Un terzo elenco di codici." *Studi sul Boccaccio,* 4 (1967), 1–8. See
esp. p. 2.

———. *Tradizione delle opere di G. Boccaccio.* Rome, 1958. See esp. pp.
24–39.

Grayson, Cecil. "Two Recent Books on Boccaccio." *Romance Philology,*
13 (1960), 283–86.

Nurmela, Tauno. "Études critiques sur le texte du *Corbaccio* de Boccace."
Mémoires de la Société Néophilologique de Helsinki, 25 (1963), 5–53.

———. "Manuscrits et éditions du *Corbaccio* de Boccace." *Neuphilologische Mitteilungen,* 54 (1953), 102–34.

———. "Il testo del *Corbaccio* e il codice di Mannelli." *Primo Congresso
degli Italianisti Scandinavi: Atti. S. 1.* (Stockholm, May 20–22, 1963.)
Eds. S. Ponzanello and D. Ghio [1965].

Some Modern English Translations of Boccaccio's Works

[*De casibus virorum illustrium*]. *The Fates of Illustrious Men*. Trans. Lewis Brewer Hall. New York, 1965.

[*Il Decameron*]. *The Decameron*. Trans. G. H. McWilliam. Baltimore, 1972.

The Decameron. Trans. J. M. Rigg, with an introduction by Edward Hutton. 2 vols. London and New York, 1930; reprint, 1955.

[*Eclogue XIV*]. *Boccaccio's Olympia*. Ed. and trans. I. Gollancz. London, 1913; republished in *Pearl: An English Poem of the XIVth Century*. London, 1921.

[*L'Elegia di Madonna Fiammetta*]. *Amorous Fiammetta*. Ed. Edward Hutton. New York, 1931. A republishing of Bartholomew Young's 1587 translation. Reprint, Westport, Conn., 1970.

[*Il Filocolo*]. *The Most Pleasant and Delectable Questions of Love*. Illustr. A. King. New York, 1950.

Thirteene most pleasant and delectable questions, entituled A desport of diverse noble personages in his boke named "Philocopo." Intro. Edward Hutton. London, 1927. Reprint of translation by H. Grantham (London, 1567) of "Questions of Love" of *Filocolo*.

[*Il Filostrato*]. *The Filostrato of Giovanni Boccaccio*. Trans. with parallel text by Nathaniel Edward Griffin and Arthur Beckwith Myrick. Philadelphia and London, 1929; reprint, New York, 1967.

[*Genealogie deorum gentilium libri*]. *Boccaccio on Poetry, Being the Preface and the Fourteenth and Fifteenth Books of Boccaccio's Gene-*

alogia Deorum Gentilium. Ed. and trans. Charles G. Osgood. Princeton, 1930; republished, New York, 1956.

[*De mulieribus claris*]. *Concerning Famous Women*. Trans. Guido A. Guarino. New Brunswick, N.J., 1963.

[*Il Ninfale fiesolano*]. *The Nymph of Fiesole*. Trans. Daniel J. Donno. New York, 1959; reprint, 1960.

Nymphs of Fiesole. Trans. Joseph Tusiani. Rutherford, N.J., 1971.

[*Teseida*]. *The Book of Theseus*. Trans. Bernadette Marie McCoy. Medieval Text Association. Sea Cliff, N.Y., 1974.

[*Trattatello in laude di Dante*]. *The Earliest Lives of Dante*. Trans. from the Italian of Giovanni Boccaccio and Leonardo Bruni by James Robinson Smith. Yale Studies in English, 10. New York, 1901; reprint, New York, 1968.

Some General Studies on Boccaccio in English

Branca, Vittore. *Boccaccio: The Man and His Works*. Trans. Richard Monges. Washington Square, N.Y., postponed. A selection of Branca's many important writings.

Chubb, Thomas Caldecot. *The Life of Giovanni Boccaccio*. Port Washington, N.Y., 1969; facsimile reprint of 1930 London ed. Useful if used with care.

Cottino-Jones, Marga. *An Anatomy of Boccaccio's Style*. Naples, 1968. Essays on the *Decameron,* some chapters in Italian.

Cummings, Hubertis Maurice. *The Indebtedness of Chaucer's Works to the Italian Works of Boccaccio: A Review and Summary*. University of Cincinnati Studies, 10, pt. 2. Menasha, Wis., 1916; reprint, New York, 1967.

Hutton, Edward. *Giovanni Boccaccio: A Biographical Study*. London and New York, 1910. Outdated, but useful on certain points if used with care.

Lepschy, Anna Laura. "Boccaccio Studies in English 1945–1969." *Studi sul Boccaccio,* 6 (1971), 211–229.

MacManus, Francis. *Boccaccio*. New York, 1947. A superficial, romantic treatment of Boccaccio's life and works.

Scaglione, Aldo D. *Nature and Love in the Late Middle Ages: An Essay on the Cultural Context of the Decameron*. Berkeley and Los Angeles, 1963.

Symonds, John Addingon. *Giovanni Boccaccio as Man and Author*. New

York and London, 1895; reprint, Sandoval, N.M., 1961, and New York, 1968. A delightful example of Victorian criticism.

Wright, Herbert Gladstone. *Boccaccio in England from Chaucer to Tennyson*. London, 1957.

Index